WASHOE COUNTY LIB
3 1235 29029 2775
P9-DWE-423

Jackie Disaster

ALSO BY ERIC DEZENHALL

Money Wanders

Eric Dezenhall

Jackie Disaster

THOMAS DUNNE BOOKS
ST. MARTIN'S MINOTAUR
NEW YORK

THOMAS DUNNE BOOKS.
An imprint of St. Martin's Press.

www.minotaurbooks.com

Design by Kathryn Parise

LIBRARY OF CONGRESS CATALOGING-IN-PUBLICATION DATA

Dezenhall, Eric.
Jackie Disaster / Eric Dezenhall.—1st ed.
p. cm.
ISBN 0-312-30769-1
1. Atlantic City (N.J.)—Fiction. 2. Crisis management—Fiction.
I. Title.
PS3604.E94J33 2003
813'.6—dc21

2002037136

First Edition: June 2003

10 9 8 7 6 5 4 3 2 1

For Stuart and Eliza

Author's Note

Novelists have been known to make things up, and I'm no exception. While some of the personalities and places in *Jackie Disaster* may seem familiar, none of them is based on anything other than the mischievous fantasies of a fiction writer who likes people to think his life has been more exciting than it's really been.

To be honest, I was ready to let God into my life, but there's absolutely no room. I've already got six sleeping on my front-room floor.

—London mobster Dodgy Dave Courtney

A party is never given for someone. It is given against someone.

—Guest at Truman Capote's Black and White Ball, 1966

BOOK I

Is This Class?

Success, *n.* The one unpardonable sin against one's fellows.

—Ambrose Bierce, *The Devil's Dictionary*

Allegation Sciences, Atlantic City, New Jersey

"My job was to make bad news go away."

"Is *this* class?"

This was more of a commandment than it was a question that Sally Naturale wielded to smite her customers. She signed off all of her television advertisements this way. From Cricket Crest, her baronial estate in South Jersey's Pine Barrens, Sally hawked promises ranging from organic food that would nurture a prize-winning fetus, to home furnishings, such as Naturale's Classware, that could be emblazoned with a customized family coat-of-arms "betraying your clan's noble lineage," which Sally pronounced in two syllables, *LIN-yidge*. This was the Philadelphia-South Jersey accent known as Phlersey. Class was pronounced *klee*-es; water was *wudder*. I spoke Phlersey myself and had not been aware that there was something odd about my speech until I made the mistake of "branching out" during college by leaving my local Glassboro State to become an exchange student at Notre Dame. A girl there, with whom I wrongly suspected I had been making progress, introduced me to another Fighting Irishwoman with the addendum, "Jackie De Sesto grew up in a place where they speak less than one language."

"Yes, Sally, it's *klee*-es," I answered with a touch of self-loathing, freezing the videotaped image of Sally gesturing toward the hemorrhaging vastness of Cricket Crest. In that frozen still, I made out swanlike people floating about in the background at a party that made one of Gatsby's affairs look like a tractor pull. Sally herself had sent me the reel of her ads via courier, as if it would explain why a Salem County woman, Murrin Connolly, was suing her. Murrin was claiming that Naturale's Real® Soy Milk had made her so sick that she lost her unborn baby. This was not an allegation she made frivolously. During the past few weeks, the most dangerous place to be in the Delaware Valley was midway between Murrin Connolly and a news camera. As a result of Murrin's media crusade, shares in Naturale's Real Living were plummeting.

Every news presentation of the controversy featured a wailing Murrin, her finger pointing somewhere unspecific, crucifix-a-swayin' (Murrin was a strict Catholic), juxtaposed with a stock photograph of Sally with her hands raised triumphantly toward the oak buttresses of Cricket Crest.

In a brief note, Sally asked me to call her as soon as I was done reviewing the tape. She wanted "a consultation," a term I associated more with interior design than my racket. She scribbled her private telephone number to underscore the sensitivity of the matter, and signed off with the observation, "A unique situation!" as if I didn't get the point. Unique situations, of course, were the kind that my firm, Allegation Sciences, Inc., was often called upon to, well, make a little less unique.

The truth was that, in my ghoulish specialty of damage control, all of my "complex" cases could be summarized in a moronic narrative that could be twisted into a vivid headline by a Pulitzer-horny reporter. I kept the headlines from my favorite cases on the corkboard beside my desk: ARTIFICIAL TESTICLE EXPLODES . . . ANTI-DEPRESSANT ISN'T . . . WASHING MACHINE LOSES QUARTER (GAINS ARM) . . . CONCIERGE TRIPS PARAPLEGIC . . . FAKE SWEETENER SOURS GENUINE COLON . . . PILOT: *"WHAT RUNWAY?"* . . . HAMBURGER GROWS TAIL . . . SKANK SUES DEEJAY FOR CALLING HER "HOSEBAG" . . . HUNGER STRIKER STARVES.

My job was to make bad news go away, which, in the age of the fabled spin doctor, was thought to be eminently doable with the right trick. To pull off disappearing acts, I needed to prove that the allegations against my corporate clients were false and that something other than justice motivated the charge. I then had to translate this intelligence into some form of communication for mass consumption—after all, my clients hired me because of the public relations implications of their problems. I accomplished these things with the help of a merry band of middle-aged adolescents who had prudently decided to work for me instead of going to prison after I nailed them in mid-con. Not that my clients appreciated what I did for them. People hate it when you save them, because it reminds them that they couldn't do it themselves.

Allegations Sciences is anchored in a very simple principle: Not every attack on a successful business or public figure is noble, and not every defense of society's "Haves" is sleazy. This philosophy conflicts with everything that modern journalism and Naderite activism stands for, namely that the merchandising of grievance and, accordingly, the destruction of any target is

God's work. Fact is, when facing a lynch mob, the businessman has nowhere to turn. The media hound him, the government extorts him, and the courts rob him. In my experience, while my clients are often flawed (and occasionally guilty), their critics are invariably worse, something that rarely gets out because, after all, they're each the virtuous "little guy" who always cries foul when I go after him. Myself a child of the Jersey-Shore working class, I learned long ago that it's possible to be both financially and morally bankrupt at the same time. Sometimes the little guy is just another grifter. I plead guilty to suffering from compassion fatigue, having a hair-trigger alarm for emotional sleight-of-hand, and smelling a Boardwalk hustle whenever I hear the word "empowerment." Anyhow, when my clients' enemies call me unethical, it just means I caught them.

Not only do I come up against blatantly awful corporate stalkers and extortionists, I was increasingly encountering an even more insidious predator among America's chronically violated, folks who wrapped up their dirty agendas in the mantle of the sanctified whistleblower. My clients are the biggest companies in the world, and they live in mortal terror of a nun with a guitar showing up at a shareholders meeting. There were, of course, the SNEGs (Subversive Nuns with Electric Guitars), who could give a CEO a stroke with one strum of a chord; ASPs (Armageddon Science Projects) done by precocious little shits who wanted to get into Princeton by leveling a hideous safety allegation against a conglomerate; the dreaded BLUCS (Bored, Loud Utopian Chicks from Suburbia), who never had a divorce that wasn't caused by a food additive; and occasionally a Rebel Without Applause, a twenty-something activist who didn't care what he railed against as long as it drew a crowd and got him laid. Most Rebels were rich kids, which I had used against them on more than one occasion. A few years ago, I disrupted a particularly worrisome protest by seeing to it that the lead Rebel—a young heir to a real estate fortune whose parents had set him up in a townhouse near Philadelphia's Rittenhouse Square—didn't get his mail for a month. No trust fund check, no revolution. In addition to receiving two grand, the mailman got a bang out of it.

Sometimes my client work was improvised. A few years ago, a big pharmaceutical company called me in because somebody broke into their North Jersey plant where they made a drug to enhance sexual performance. They wanted me to help keep the break-in quiet, and discreetly investigate whether or not a competitor had been behind it. They were thinking about pursuing legal action. I had a different approach. Rather than engage in a long and fruitless investigation and lawsuit, I suggested that my client embrace the break-in and leak it to the press and online chat rooms. The endgame: Create a buzz that the drug was so hot that people were breaking in to steal it. The drug became a blockbuster. The company's ad agency got all the credit, but I didn't care; I got a bonus.

Allegation Sciences' offices were in Atlantic City's Golden Prospect Hotel & Casino. It may seem strange that a corporate consultant like me would rent offices in a casino, but it actually makes a lot of sense. Legalized gambling is far and away the fastest growing business in the U.S. Casinos are habitual targets of scams and shakedowns, everything from blackjack dealers with unfettered fingers to vacationers who conveniently slip on tiles by the swimming pool shortly after losing their mortgages at the baccarat table. All of these hustlers were convinced that their scams were original, and were stunned to discover that guys like me existed for the express purpose of stopping them. In the days when the gangster Mickey Price and his boys ran the Golden Prospect, accidents didn't happen. Nobody fell down. Nobody cheated. People must have been nicer then.

Everything changed when Mickey died a couple of years ago, and ownership passed from his gang to Ivy League MBAs who think skim is what you pour on your All-Bran. This includes Angela Vanni, who runs the place now. Angela was my original client. Even though her dad, Mario, was a stone-cold racketeer, Angela is all software and "focused marketing," a term I nodded at knowingly when she said it. In truth, I was distracted by that little dimple in her cheek that appeared and disappeared when she spoke. While the New Jersey Gaming Commission respected Angela's moral hygiene, the creepy crawlies that teemed beneath the boardwalk did not, and the Golden Prospect became a target for veteran scam artists.

This lurch in larceny had actually begun when Mickey Price's health declined in his final years, so he hired me to spread hideous stories about what was *still* happening to cheats under his rule. Given that my conventional media contacts were off-limits to gangster work, I used a gossip chain of degenerates that I had cultivated over the years. In return, Mickey shared a tip or two about how he had dissuaded cheats. Hint: The graphic leveraging of mob lore on the Internet and in the gambling community had more utility than actually killing people, something I didn't do because, as Richard Nixon once said, "That would be wrong."

After setting the Golden Prospect straight, word got around in the broader business community that I didn't screw around. My skills at stopping casino maggots turned out to be transferable to squelching a growing mob of anti-corporate hustlers. Make fun of New Jersey all you want, but just off those turnpike exit ramps lie the most powerful corporations in the world: After decades of legalized shakedowns by trial lawyers, activists and labor unions, the boys and girls of Business Casual had stopped screwing around, too, thus my opportunistic formation of Allegation Sciences. As I once told my priest, Father Ignacio, I spend my life in search of a lower truth.

Sure, I had gotten offers over the years to work directly for a big corporate client, but during the few all-day "business meetings" I had attended during my career, all I kept thinking as I looked around the conference table was, *It's twelve forty-five in the afternoon, where's the fucking food?* Corporate people didn't eat, they didn't have human needs. I'm Italian. I did.

Among other criteria, I specialized in companies that were close to home, companies like Naturale's Real Living, which was a short drive away. In addition to my general opposition to new experiences, I would not fly to meet clients, and for good reason: I didn't think I'd ever get there. Friends always told me that my fear of flying was irrational, that driving was more dangerous. Bullshit—what are the chances that I was going to plummet thirty thousand feet into the side of a mountain while driving my Cadillac on the Atlantic City Expressway? Besides, working for industry as I did, I knew that companies—say, airlines—offset their investments in safety against the low probability that bad things would happen. In other words, they played the odds, which was very different from guaranteeing that flying was safe. Given the horrors that had already befallen me in my life, I calculated that the odds of being pulverized into rose-hued pus were pretty damned good.

The thing I liked best about my job—in addition to the fact that when clients needed me, they needed me so badly that they didn't quibble about invoices—was my office. From my vantage point behind a curved glass cockpit of a desk, a huge window was on my right overlooking the boardwalk where the May morning sunlight, greasy illusions and the scent of roasted peanuts indistinguishably mingled. I had never been comfortable with Atlantic City by day. I always preferred it in the night, when neon made the town look like a giant dessert counter, all sparkling toppings—jimmies, Gummi Bears and M&Ms. Maybe Atlantic City by day made me so anxious because the place didn't look so great beneath sunlight. In the evening, even homelessness had the patina of mystery, *a man with a past.* There was nothing romantic about a bum pissing on a mailbox as he squinted into the morning sun.

Sometimes I would stare out at the ocean for a long time. I had always been fascinated with pirates. Ever since I was a little kid cutting catechism and fearing Hell, I would sneak books on pirates out of the library and then stare at the waves rolling in, thinking that if I hung around long enough I'd see Blackbeard's galleon wash ashore. It's embarrassing to admit, but I actually thought about stuff like this. My dad did, too, in a way, but he liked shipwrecks in particular, and memorized the big ones that sunk off of New Jersey. There had been many.

Beyond my guest chairs was an interior window—a one-way mirror, really, that offered a panoramic view of the winking casino floor. I didn't really spy out the casino or the boardwalk from my office, but the design conveyed a certain omniscience, and I played it to my advantage. Consulting was three quarters optics: Any consultant who wasn't on amphetamines knew damned well that the key to marketing was implying that you had some influence in things that would have happened anyway. For moral support, I kept a quotation from the Bible (Book of Samuel) above my office's exit: "Thou art the man."

Behind my desk, there was a solid beige wall centered by a giant photo of my brother, Tommy, who was pumping a fist moments after winning the welterweight title that qualified him for the U.S. Olympic Boxing Team in 1992. He was shooting that DeSesto snarl that we shared. The Death Snarl, as *The Philadelphia Bulletin* had once called it. Not long before he was set to fly out to become an Olympian, he died in the ring during a routine sparring session. Tommy's wife responded by jumping off the Ben Franklin Bridge (on the Jersey side), leaving me to raise their infant daughter, Emma, who was now ten. I had done this without the benefit of a wife or kids of my own. I framed every painting and drawing that Emma had ever made for me, and displayed them inside a cabinet that I kept closed when I had guests. I didn't like people to know I cared about anything.

I had been a decent boxer, but the highest official title I ever held was Golden Gloves Welterweight Champion of South Jersey. There had been some buzz about my eligibility for the 1980 Olympic trials, but I was disqualified after I got into an unscheduled fight with a guy on the boardwalk over something stupid. Boxers aren't supposed to beat the crap out of random mopes, so the Boxing Commission slapped a conduct sanction on me. I honestly don't think I would have made it into the Olympics anyway, but my brother—they used to play the theme music to the rock opera *Tommy* when he climbed into the ring . . . well, I turned my back on Tommy.

I promised Sally Naturale via voice mail that I could be at her headquarters in Medford Lakes by noon. If I left by eleven, it would be a straight shot down the Atlantic City Expressway, barring no breakdowns by big-assed casino bus convoys. Right now, it was about ten-thirty, and two of the shore's remaining mafiosi spread like fleshy plagues across my squat guest chairs.

A Couple-a Guys in My Guest Chairs

"You weren't no cop, Jackie."

My leg bounced at hyperspeed as I waited for the first Nobel laureate before me to state his case. He was known as Frankie Shrugs because of his habit of shrugging his mountainous shoulders after he had managed to squeeze out a cogent point. Officially, he was a union quality-control consultant. Unofficially, he was a wise guy trolling for scraps, which, contrary to popular lore, was all these boys could get in Atlantic City these days.

Frankie Shrugs made me sick. The illness manifested itself as a gastric cramp. It was caused by revulsion, not fear. Frankie Shrugs was the scourge of prosperous Italians—guys like me—that strove to make respectable lives for ourselves, even if we couldn't always pull it off. He was the cringing reason why non-Italians winked when they heard a last name ending in a vowel. As a veteran ethnic cringer myself, I saw Frankie Shrugs as a hulking, felonious wop who did his business in America's gaudy shadows, emerging only to hold up his middle finger, and smirk, "Who me?" Friends of mine of different ethnicities had their own cringe-worthy characters: blacks had the slick pimp; Jews had the gold-bedecked sharpie who acted as if being Chosen meant a guaranteed spot at the head of the movie line; and the Irish had the gregarious but alcoholic uncle who inspired communal laughter, but not much else. As much as these vile cartoons mortified their respective ethnic constituencies, I couldn't imagine finding them as shameful as Frankie Shrugs' portrayal of the Italian man, but then we're most prickly about our own.

Frankie Shrugs' partner, who was quieter, was Petey Breath Mints. This was not the gangland name this veteran crack dealer had hoped for. Petey Breath Mints got his name because the smell from his throat could knock a fly off a shit wagon. For a brief time, he had been called Petey Ass Teeth, but he must have appealed to the *capo* of Mafia name dispensing for a new moniker. Petey who was more ferret than human, liked to squint and smirk sagaciously, presumably either to convey smoldering intelligence or as an excuse to keep his mouth shut. Petey Breath Mints ended up just looking constipated, which he may have been, from chomping so many Certs.

Frankie Shrugs commenced, his gray meaty tongue emoting with flattery: "I need Jackie Disaster." As he waved his hands mystically, the scent of Paco Rabanne or a similar remnant of Reagan-era gangland chic wafted my way. He slowly dragged his eyes across me. Maybe he liked my suit. It was a nice one, an Armani I got in Philly. Most guys my age, with their softening bellies, couldn't carry off a suit like this. At forty, I could, so I did.

Jackie Disaster was not, of course, my given name. Legally, I was Giovanni De Sesto, but when I boxed in my stupider days (the *Rocky* movies had once been to the Delaware Valley what the Koran is to Islam), my dad, who managed me, jumbled our surname, and I became, in the ring, Jackie Disaster. Tommy, predictably, had fought as Tommy Disaster, and had actually earned the moniker. For me, it had more ironic bark than bite, and I always felt its application to me was somewhat of a joke when compared to Tommy.

"I'm honored, Frankie," I said. "And what can Jackie Disaster do for you?"

Frankie leaned forward and held his hands together prayerfully, while Petey maintained his intestinal jumble.

"You, Jackie, you know how things work."

Translation: You know that we kill people.

"Sure, Frankie, that's true."

"People, ah, you know how people are, am I right? They steal, they fake you out. The world's a fuckin' mess."

"It sure is, Frankie."

"Things here aren't how they were with the old management."

The mob can't skim the casinos like we did for decades.

"I know how the old guys were. They did what they did."

"See, it all happened so fast," Frankie said sadly.

The mob can't skim the casinos like we did for decades.

"Not really, Frankie, it took years."

"Right, years. But here with this place, it was like *voom* and we're out. That's when the lowlifes started with their scams and all." Frankie Shrugs' short pedestal of a neck revealed itself slightly, and then retracted into his potato sack body.

"We've cleaned that up though," I said.

"Not all of it."

Give us a little skim, and the rest of it will go away.

"Enough, though."

"Maybe. But it ain't right the way Mario's kids—may he rest in peace a course—walk in with their Ivory League briefcases and, what, we're out on our asses?"

"I'm not an executive of the casino, Frankie. I'm a consultant. I don't have the power you think I do."

Frankie Shrugs slapped constipated Petey Breath Mints on his knee, which caused Petey to jump up and click to a new expression. It was half-laugh, half-snarl. Petey Breath Mints thought the expression conveyed "I get the joke," but the tightness of his jaw transmitted "I hope I don't have to go all the way downstairs to the crapper."

"We're here, Jackie, because of your power," Frankie Shrugs said with a far-off glance that he had ripped off from James Gandolfini.

If we shook down Angela Vanni directly, the cameras would pick it up and there would be a record of this visit. You're an outsider who just happens to have keys to the place, so play ball, numbnuts.

"Look, Frankie, I'll be direct with you because I don't want to insult you. I just can't put a skim operation in place. I'm the guy they brought in to keep things straight, remember? Even if I wanted to do it, I wouldn't know how to do it. It's not Vegas 1952. I know things are tough, guys, but it's not going to happen here. Hell, I was once with the Atlantic City Police Department, c'mon."

"Ah, you weren't no cop, Jackie," Frankie Shrugs fired back.

I flinched because this was technically true. I had been the spokesman for the A.C.P.D. Detective's Unit, a job I got after serving as the press secretary for Atlantic City's mayor—a gig that went south after the mayor was convicted for bribery about ten years ago. I had always taken pride in the fact that my boss was acquitted on the homicide charge. Everybody, I suppose, has a benign delusion and this was mine: I always hoped that people would assume that I had been a cop because of my flack job with the A.C.P.D. I never lied; I just gambled that my reputation could take refuge under the ill-defined aegis of law enforcement.

I had hung out with the cops, and even trained with firearms. I was actually a pretty good shot, and took to carrying a little Beretta shortly after the Commissioner informed me that I couldn't actually have a badge. In a fit of childlike desire for legitimacy, I had asked for one, my rationale being that I needed to identify myself at crime scenes so that I could comment accurately on the status of investigations. Nice try, lame-o. The truth was that I was a great damage control consultant because I had found my niche as a grown-up, not because I had been a *former* badass police detective. Anyway, even as a middle-aged man with a few shekels saved, I was stung when somebody had the audacity to point out the core truth, that I had been a local political operative who had a non-badge job with the fuzz.

As I nodded a sincere "of course" to Frankie Shrugs, Petey Breath Mints scratched both of his eyebrows. Somehow, they managed to itch evenly. "Somethin' could be in it for you, Jackie. Didja think about that?" Petey said. The Kaopectate grin again from the Pete-ster. He winked. Petey Breath Mints actually thought he had introduced a variable that I hadn't considered.

"Guys," I said, "I can't do it. I know who you are and I respect what you're capable of, but this isn't going anywhere good for anybody." I thought about adding "I'm sorry," but decided against it. With these guys there could be no vulnerability or signs of leeway. Besides, I had already stumbled with my little cop pose.

Frankie Shrugs frowned and shot me a hurt look, as if he was my big brother trying to protect me from getting my heart stomped by the homecoming queen. The air was pregnant with unfinished business. Frankie Shrugs' eyebrows suddenly came together as if he had just registered my rejection.

"You know, Jackie, I seen you walking around sometimes in that leather jacket you got. You don't know if you wanna be a cop or be with us, do you?"

Petey Breath Mints dug the insult. He snickered, so comfortable to be on the inside of Frankie Shrugs' malice, rather than on the outside as he was accustomed to.

The worst damage-control strategy on earth is to engage your attacker on his terms. His comments said more about his agenda than they did about you. Go with the insult. Play it. Love it. Cuddle it like a kitty cat, but don't fight it.

"You know, Frankie, I was gonna ask you if I could swing by and pick up an application for the *borgata*. You guys have summer internships for a *cugine* like me to peddle crack to black toddlers or anything?"

Frankie Shrugs hesitated. He had expected a meltdown, a defense. "Aw, Jackie, you couldn't cut it with us. We're the real deal. Like your brother, Tommy, was the real deal. A shame what happened to him," Frankie Shrugs said, as if he knew a secret.

"That's the point," I said. "I wanna be the real deal, too. I dunno guys, I feel like I've been living a lie."

Frankie Shrugs and Petey Breath Mints exchanged glances. I had been accused of being a fraud and had essentially copped to it, disarming them. I held my gaze.

"Don't worry about it," Frankie Shrugs finally said.

"I am worried, though, Frankie. I mean, think about it. Say a bunch of guys come into a place with guns, knives and baseball bats and they beat the shit out of some poor guy. You gotta be tough to do that. I used to climb into a boxing ring, little candy-ass me and these girl fists."

"Don't worry about it, Jackie," Frankie Shrugs said again, uncomfortable.

"Hey, you know Saul's Deli down the boardwalk? What do you say the three of us beat up old Saul. How old would you say he is, ninety? I'd love to roll that bald head-a his. Look, is there something else you guys want?" I asked, as the boys rose and glanced across my desk.

"You working' on anything good?" Frankie asked.

"Never," I said.

"Ah, Jackie, you're a good egg. Lemme see that snarl, heh-heh. Don't go lookin' over your shoulder, now. We're all right, but a guy's gotta ask, don't he?"

"Sure, Frankie."

"I was polite, too. Remember that, Jackie D."

"I will."

"You got anything good goin' otherwise?"

"Not really, no."

As the scraps of the mob left, the Lord oozed into my office, a toothpick dangling from his lips: "You want me to slap a homer on his ass?"

The Imps

"The purpose of the Hellevator's drop was to instill rapid loss of bowel control."

This Lord was no Messiah or member of Parliament. He was Artie Lord, who, according to my friends at the A.C.P.D., was a thief who had never been caught, despite his penchant for taking obscene risks. He had never been caught at burgling, that is.

Unlike the other guys who worked for me, the Lord had never attempted an honest day's work in his life. I had caught him in his capacity as a lookout in a pick-pocketing scam. His function had been to watch for undercover hotel security, then give the go-ahead for his partner to make his move. Over a period of several months, I had noticed that one particular guy, who turned out to be the Lord, often showed up in video footage the same day as pick-pocketing reports spiked. He was always standing by the boardwalk entrance to the casino, checking out what we assumed to be a sporting event on a mini-TV. Nope.

During the course of a long winter, the Lord had managed to insert small homing devices into the pockets of the casino's security staff. As proud as I was of the progress we had made in the Golden Prospect's security department, our crew was still only one step up the food chain from the big-assed nitwits at airports who might as well wear signs reading WELCOME, BIN LADEN.

During his pick-pocketing scam days, the Lord had been monitoring the whereabouts of security personnel on the mini-TV. To do this, he had to stand near an exit, because a real portable TV wouldn't have gotten good reception deep within the casino. While his homing device didn't actually need antenna reception, the Lord knew that we would realize that portable TVs didn't work well inside, so he played up the sports junkie ruse by sticking close to the outermost doors.

The next time the Lord showed up (crooks truly believe that the rest of us are morons, and they always get cocky), we dragged his ass into my office. We had his partner, the actual pick-pocket, arrested, but I decided to bank the Lord, and keep him as an asset for Allegation Sciences, if he so chose.

He so chose.

On this late spring day, now safely in my employ, the Lord was listening in on my conversation with Frankie Shrugs and Petey, and wanted to monitor them by attaching a homing device to their vehicles. That the two men were killers only made the Lord's interest stronger.

Befitting his career choice, the Lord was neither handsome nor ugly. He had thick, shaggy brown hair that gave him a retro-1970s look. He was of average height and in decent physical condition for a man entering middle age. He reminded me of a guy who would play the neighborly handyman in a TV sitcom. His natural facial expression was one of wonderment, which could have either been due to the way his face was constructed or because he really never knew what the hell anybody was talking about. The Lord favored pocket T-shirts and jeans.

"No need for a homer yet, Lordo."

"You think they'll try something?"

"This isn't the first time they've made noises, but I doubt it. It's not like it used to be."

"Why wasn't I invited to Marty Scorcese's surprise party?" inquired a mellifluous voice from the outer office. "Isn't that what you've got going?"

The fey voice belonged to Teapot Freddy, who was wearing a one-piece orange pleather jumpsuit. A former hairdresser, he had also been the shore's greatest shill until I nailed him. He'd sit at a blackjack table with his moist doe eyes and he'd win and he'd win and he'd win, clapping his hands together as a come-on to the ladies with the aqua helmet-hair who inevitably gravitated to him. I never understood why women assumed that a flamboyantly gay man wouldn't cheat them, but they did. It wasn't just the women, either. Gruff men concluded that Teapot Freddy's dealer must have been a weak mark if a "guy" like him could keep winning the way he did.

I had grown up with Teapot Freddy in Margate. He had gotten his nickname in fourth grade when he sung "I'm a Little Teapot" with a little too much exuberance for everybody's comfort. He really got into the whole "Here is my spout" part, which was when we choirboys realized there was something very different about the Fred-man. We were too young to understand precisely what that difference was, but we tagged the guy for close observation. As different as we all were, my brother and I always felt protective toward Teapot Freddy and looked out for him whenever we could, even though he was a *finook*. Teapot Freddy leaned his tiny hips against my desk.

Next, Nate the Great sprinted into my office wearing his workout gear. A former Philadelphia plastic surgeon, Nate did everything fast. This had become a problem for Nate, who performed a nose job on a woman who had already had one a few years earlier. Not being one to ask probing questions about how much of a nose one could pulverize, Nate did the job, which left the vivacious Mrs. Sylvia Liebowitz looking like an electrical outlet. Furthermore, her facial features, having nothing to do with Nate the Great's work, had already been stretched back so far that she wore a freakish expression of perpetual alarm, as if to say, "Don't plug a VCR into my nostrils!!!"

Nate was sued, lost his practice, not to mention the billboards where he advertised his practice and dubbed himself "Nate the Great." I'm convinced he missed the billboards more than the money. He tried to gamble his fortune back, and, finding that he lacked the talent, began to cheat. Nate the Great cheated pretty well—until I had the heat turned up full-blast at his table, and caught him card-counting.

I had known Nate the Great the longest. He had been one of my roommates in the summer of 1980 when we rented a basement apartment, a dive on Baton Rouge Avenue. Nate had had a job working in the emergency room at Atlantic City General Hospital; I had worked as a cook in the White House—not 1600 Pennsylvania Avenue—the sub shop on Arctic Avenue in Atlantic City.

Nate now stood next to Teapot Freddy, checking out his own biceps, which were actually pretty impressive for a guy his age. Nate may have been muscular, but he was also short, which gave him the aura of either a former varsity wrestler or a little dude spoiling for a fight, lest anybody mistook short for weak.

Together, the Lord, Teapot Freddy and Nate the Great made up my full–time staff. We used to have a secretary, Marcia, but she had this proclivity for baby talk *(wike a wittle girl),* and I decided that if I didn't fire her, I'd end up splitting her head open like a pomegranate with a hammer the next time she came in at ten o'clock and said, "Marcia wate for work 'cause Marcia fall down and go boom . . ."

I referred to Teapot Freddy, the Lord, and Nate the Great as "the Imps," because, no matter how I liked to package our trade, we were really just a bunch of kids ringing doorbells and running away. Despite our ages, we remained obsessed with the cop shows of the 1970s and, sometimes on capers, we'd even call each other by some of the characters' names. Teapot Freddy was especially big on this. My employment of the Imps was more than stone-cold banking; I felt responsible for these guys because I saw myself in them, a weakness which, despite my hard-ass pose, had probably caused them to exploit my sentimentality on more than one occasion. To hedge my bets, I maintained a small army of Imp-like resources beyond my core crew that I could tap into when special skills were called for.

Nate the Great, preternaturally jumpy, seemed particularly antic this morning. He was pulling at his goatee, as if to make it grow faster.

"What is it, Nate?" I asked.

"Got some canned heat down by the Hellevator," Nate said, his eyes darting around and blinking like an insect. "I registered." "Register" was code for getting rid of a casino cheat and scaring the hell out of the person sufficiently that he or she wouldn't come back.

"So?"

"She's not talking."

"Then you didn't communicate properly," I said.

"Right. That's why I'm asking you to do it."

I turned on a television monitor by my desk. A camera in the basement of the Golden Prospect was trained on a cruelly beautiful woman, late twenties, sleek as a thoroughbred. Whenever I encountered a woman like this, I was torn between wondering what I was missing and being relieved that I was missing it. She was being detained in a questioning room adjacent to the "Hellevator." The Hellevator was a small mirrored elevator that was engineered to drop at great speed from the casino level to a secret basement questioning room. The purpose of the Hellevator's drop was to instill rapid loss of bowel control. The mirrors forced the perpetrators to look at themselves long and hard until we opened the Hellevator's doors.

On the screen, the detainee reminded me of the actress Gina Gershon. You know, that mouth. She had an ace bandage around her left wrist, about which Teapot Freddy sniped, "Must have been a freak lap-dancing accident." Andy, one of the uniformed casino security guards stood with his arms folded, leaning against the table where the terrified Gina rested her palms.

Teapot Freddy and the Lord rolled their eyes at Nate. Nate the Great couldn't handle Gina Gershon, no way, which was what the other Imps' skepticism was about. Nate had never made the transition from high-end service provider to professional dissuader, not that any normal person could make such a transition. I had always harbored seeds of doubt that a woman could be as thoroughly corrupt as a man. Beauty, having great authority, only made it harder to get a woman to confess.

The boys popped in the video of Gina Gershon's cheating technique. Not surprisingly, there was something admirable about her hustle. She was what we called a card replacer. In blackjack, the first card the dealer deals you is face down. When our lady friend didn't like her face-down card, she replaced it using sleight-of-hand with one that improved her odds. That card was usually brought from outside the casino and hidden in her sleeve.

"You have a printout on her, I take it," I said.

"Yeah, I printed one out before," Nate said, just standing there.

"Can I have it?" I asked, snappish, a tone I fell into more and more. Jesus. Nate appeared hurt. *Why tell me you printed one out before and just stand there? Why not give it to me?* Nate rifled through a few papers then handed me a one-page dossier, which I scanned. I took another peek at Gina Gershon and passed the printout onto Teapot Freddy.

"Frederick," I said, "Why don't you talk to her. See if she's worth banking."

"Can I be Ponch?" Teapot Freddy asked, rising.

"Yeah, Freddy, you can be Ponch," I said.

"I just love Ponch," he mouthed.

We trailed "Ponch" through the casino, a walk that I never ceased to enjoy. The fun part was profiling the patrons, a little mind game I played with the boys to keep my synapses firing during down time. I nodded respectfully to a sharply dressed man (in a 1970s, cologned kind of way) with a pencil-thin moustache and deep, confident dimples, who stood at a baccarat table beside two women who had the look of dental hygienists on their day off. The man personified a casino species that I had tagged "Trumplets." These were the little men—dentists from Secaucus, advertising executives from San Juan—who mistook the worship of those whose paychecks they signed with geopolitical significance, not unlike how a certain Mr. Trump saw himself. To Trumplets, there could be no higher state of existence than being Donald Trump. I distinctly recall an optometrist from Reading who brought his mistress along with him, waxing loudly on the boardwalk about the opening of his second "optical gallery," as if he owned half of Manhattan. The greatest of the Trumplets were the ones who had bodyguards, not because they were afraid somebody was going to kill or rob them, but because they wanted their girlfriends to think they were men worth killing or robbing.

One time, I walked Angela Vanni through the casino pegging all of her patrons—the Trumplets, the Basic Instincts, the Falsettos—and she was horrified. The Basic Instincts ("BIs") were aging *femmes fatales* who acted aloof and complex around squat high-rollers secretly hoping to land one. My favorites were the Falsettos, non-Italians, who wanted desperately to be seen as *Sopranos*-style mafiosi, but who fell a few octaves short. Angela thought I was being mean, but I actually liked the very same people that I pigeonholed. Grandiosity was what America was all about. Self-delusion built the country. It was both constructive and tragic, depending upon how your individual case turned out. There was nothing wrong with, say, being a Falsetto, provided that you didn't actually whack somebody. While it was hard for me to give my own breed a name, I always suspected I was full of shit, but in a way that ultimately made me better than I would have been without the pose.

After Teapot Freddy whispered "another Trumplet" in my ear as we passed him, I felt a tap on my shoulder.

"Hey Jackie." The voice and the tap belonged to Angela Vanni's chief operating officer, Dirk Romella.

Dork You-*smell*-a, I thought, as the Imps stepped aside to let me deal with the classier-than-thou Dirk.

I turned around, and upon meeting Dirk's eyes, I said, "Hi, Dirkles!" knowing he hated me. "*Wop*, bop-a-loo-bop, a *wop* bam-boom!" I rapped.

Dirk rolled his eyes. "You mind stopping up to my office at some point, Jackie? I've got a few questions about your invoice."

"Questions? Is this like a Wharton exam about balance sheets?" I asked.

"No, Jackie, I'm sure you can handle these questions," Dirk said. "I just need to know what we got for the services rendered."

I did not like Dirk Romella, because he was an asshole. I knew that he disapproved of my career, and I always suspected he poisoned Angela's thoughts with invective about me. Whenever I saw the two of them together, which was often, I felt my ass spasm. On top of whatever political friction that existed between us, there was a matter of blood identity that pulsed beneath our skin. Dirk may have been an Italian American, but I was more of an American Italian, or so I felt. Dirk's ethnicity was a footnote; mine was the frigging book cover. I imagined in my more paranoid moments that Angela saw Dirk as the future of Italians in America—the WASP; and I was the past, the Wop. I suspected that Dirk saw me the way mocha-skinned blacks saw their charcoal-skinned cousins. It wasn't that our appearances were all that different, it was how we saw ourselves.

I went back and forth on whether or not I should be threatened by Dirk

Romella. The *strunz* grew up on the Main Line, in Wynnewood. He had gone to college at Haverford (Blow me, why don't ya?) where he played polo, and earned his law and business degrees from Penn. His parents were professors. He was a good-looking guy, I guess, in an I-have-a-squash-racket-up-my-ass kind of way. He was a little bit taller than me, thin, with very sharp features that were somehow fragile, pretty even. He used gel in his hair to affect a carefully-studied casual look. I never got that. I took care of myself, but I wanted to look like a guy who took care of himself. In Dirk's world, the goal was to make it seem as if you didn't care how you looked when, in fact, there's no way you can get his windblown look when you're out in the real wind. I thought about whether Dirk and Angela had ever comped themselves a hotel room in the Golden Prospect after a hard day's work, and hoped that it wasn't something Angela had even considered. But c'mon, everybody that works together evaluates their colleagues naked.

Now, I was getting pissed.

"You know, Dirkles," I said, "I'm in the middle of what may be a scam bust. As soon as I'm done, I'll come up and we can talk about how much I'm skimming from the Prospect."

"I didn't say that, Jackie," Dirk qualified.

"You like my new watch?" I asked Dirk.

"It's fine, Jackie. Stop up when you can. Just looking to avoid a, ah, disaster."

Clever.

"You got it," I said, having no intention of paying Dirk a visit. As the Imps moved back toward me, I felt the need to remind Dirk that he hadn't come as far from Naples or Palermo as he wanted to believe, so I began singing softly in my best Harry Belafonte, "*Da*-go! *Day*-ay-ay-go. Da-go come and he wanna play polo."

Teapot Freddy pushed the button for a normal elevator and we rode it down to our little Hell.

A Talk With Teapot Freddy

"If I had legs like that, I'd give 'em names."

Gina Gershon's clone had a heart-shaped face, and raven hair that fell across her cheeks. Her eyes were grand gray ovals and her bow-shaped mouth held the smirk of a woman who had probably known only victory in a series of short-term conquests. She wore a hounds tooth jacket and a short black skirt. Her legs were bare, save the dagger heels. I was thinking, wolf. Or one of those Patrick Nagel lithographs of sleek, fanged women that were in every hair salon and restaurant in the 1980s.

"Woooweeee, look at you, sugar cube!" Teapot Freddy/Ponch said, plopping down and spinning around in a chair in the stark interrogation room. Sugar cube. He habitually fired off word combinations and endearing names that I couldn't have conjured up given a year.

Gina the Wolf winked at Teapot Freddy, coy. "This is quite an inquisition you've got here," she said, looking around at the rest of us, who were lined up like lemmings on the side wall. She liked our little teapot. Hated the rest of us.

"Oh, don't I know it, Sister Love, the big oafs," Teapot Freddy said, brushing us away with his hands. He wasn't totally wrong. The line-up of the Lord, Nate the Great, Andy the security guard and me did seem gratuitous. But I wanted to stay. I thought gratuitous was good here. So we stayed. Quiet.

"I'm Ponch," Teapot Freddy began. "They're trying to intimidate you, love bug, you know that, don't you?"

"That was my sense," Gina the Wolf said.

"So look at you with the legs. Why did they bring you down here?"

"The oaf in the uniform said I was replacing."

"Did he actually *say* that?"

"No, the pit boss did. Before he grabbed my ass."

"God, they're all pigs that think with their Mr. Clintons. Oinkity-oink-oink. What's your name, peaches 'n cream?"

"Marty Collins," she said, chortling. Actually, we all laughed. You couldn't *not* laugh watching Teapot Freddy in action. He was all burlesque.

"Marty, huh?" C'mon, string bean, that's not your real name."

"No, it's Martina, legally."

"Martina. Like the tennis wenches. Love 'em. Just love 'em! Such courage the older one had to come out and tell it like it is. That day when Billie Jean King beat that oinker, Bobby Riggs, in tennis—it's like I was born again, even though I was only ten or something. Billie Jean was a little mannish for my taste, but what are you gonna do, huh? Do you play tennis?"

"No. I mean, I have, but I do aerobics mostly."

"And don't we all know it, honeysuckle! Look at those calves! I'm serious, Marty. Just look at them." Marty looked down at her own calves. So did we. "That muscle tone. I would *kill* for muscle tone like that. If I had legs like that, I'd give 'em names. Quisp and Quake, like those sugary cereals—hey, stop looking at her that way!" Teapot Freddy scolded us. "What did I tell you about the oinkers, cupcake? Did I tell you? Turn up the heat in here and we've got ourselves some bacon."

Marty Collins laughed aloud. "It's genetic, I think. The legs."

"You better believe it's genetic. I've tried to get calves like that for years. A big fat goose egg is all I get. Get the genes, that's my philosophy, because nothing you do can give you legs like that. Andy, did you search Ms. Collins pocketbook?" Ponch said this in a bored way, running his aggressive request right against the flattery. Andy nodded *no* like Baby Huey.

"Oh, you're such a shmuck-a-saurus. Well, do it already. Go. Go. Go."

"He can't search me," Marty Collins said, disarmed.

"Sure he can, you silly goose." Ponch grabbed her Desmo pocketbook from the table and tossed it to Andy. Marty Collins stood, her mouth falling open. She topped it off with a squint. I couldn't decide whether her mouth was vulcanizing into a smile or her face was frozen in a mask of contempt. Andy began rifling through it.

"Would you empty your pockets please?" Ponch requested.

"Do you have a warrant or some kind of, I dunno, right?" She looked as if she was going to cry.

"You are on private property, willow," Ponch said. "You are not under arrest, but when you are under this roof, which is a property at high-risk for crime, you forfeit some of your freedoms. It just sucks, don't I know it."

"This is bullshit."

"Yes, right, kinda like that incident at the Sandals facility in the Turks & Caicos? Kinda like that? Oh, you're such a naughty little minx, Martina. We understand from our friends in Reno that you were once a magician's assistant, Miss Tricky Fingers."

"What are you talking about?"

"They settled that case with you, remember? Remember, back in ninety-eight. You alleged a roulette wheel was rigged. Turned out that some slicky-boy you were with rigged it, but you threatened to go to the media saying that the place was cheating customers, so they paid you off. Remember that? And we hear that the Philly police are keeping an eye on you for something they haven't been able to nail you on yet."

Andy the guard put her purse back down on Nate's desk, satisfied, I suppose, that there was nothing interesting in there.

"Empty your pockets, Marty, and no little church girl talk from you." Ponch added a gesture of holding his nose. The Lord walked out of the room, afraid he was going to burst out laughing.

She emptied her pockets. A lipstick container, a pillbox. Ponch was disappointed, and frowned in an obvious way. Marty Collins flared her nostrils at him, betrayed, and crossed her whippet arms. Twenty years younger and she would have said "nanny-nanny-foo-foo." Too cocky.

"Inside pockets, too, please. I smell something. Do you smell it?" Ponch asked.

"I don't have anything in my inside pockets," Marty Collins snarled. Her lip curl now made her look more like Elvis than Gina Gershon. *Grrrrshon.*

"Humor me, cuddlebug."

She opened the right side of her jacket and reached inside. "Ooh," she said.

"What?" Ponch asked.

"I forgot." She grinned, girlish, for a change, as she struggled with the pocket. I heard something click and, slowly, she withdrew a sleek recording device. "I make reminders to myself with this."

I grabbed the device from her and examined it. It had been playing for several minutes. Then I handed it to Ponch pointing out that it had been playing.

"Why was it important to record our time together?" Ponch asked with a big old frown.

"Sometimes it just goes on."

"Siddown, Marty Collins. I knew I smelled something."

"I prefer to stand."

"Fine. Then stand." Ponch moved within six inches of her face. "You want my theory?"

"Not really." She sat back down in her chair, slouchy, and gazed off in the direction of the smitten Nate the Great. Her eyes begged, "Save me, Nate." His face registered a what-are-you-gonna-do expression.

"Let me tell you my theory, Marty Collins," Ponch began. She was shaking. "You came to play blackjack. You came to win. You got pinched, so you registered a complaint against a dealer. He grabbed your ass or something. Oh piggy-pig-pig. When the pit boss came, you argued with him. The argument didn't go your way. You still lost twenty-five-hundred dollars. You made an allegation to the floor boss that the pit boss grabbed your ass. Hell, sweetheart, I'd grab your ass and I don't even like your species. There's a young lady upstairs who claims she witnessed the incident.

"While you were waiting in here, we checked the cameras in our parking garages and out on the boardwalk. Martina Collins, naughty-naughty, you came here with your witness and planned this out, as you did a few months ago, according to our friends at Harrah's. As you did twice last year up in Connecticut with the Pequots, and as you did in upstate New York at the Turning Stone Casino. You communicate with your little buddy—who got away by the way—after we pinched you with whatever you've got in that little bandage there. You had a slightly different deal going down in the islands, but you slimed your way out of it with a fifteen-thousand-dollar settlement, so it was worth the trip.

"As for today, you had a plan in case you got pinched. You'd provoke abuse, you'd record it, and, with that mouth of yours, yessireebob, maybe you'd even get a slaparooski, a cost of doing business that I bet you rather fancy."

The color fell from Marty Collins' face and all but made a thud as it hit the floor. She looked cadaverous now, like a fourteen-year-old girl who had been caught smoking pot in her attic while wearing her mother's misapplied makeup. She huffed, and the same lips that had struck me as being sexy moments ago now appeared comically large.

"What can you give us, Martypants? What can you give us to avoid a trip to the Pine Barrens or prison? I have news for you, neither of these places will provide a peak experience to talk about with your Cosmo friends. Think about it for a tad, would you?" With that, Ponch brushed his hands together, got up, patted Marty Collins on the head and walked out. Nate the Great, the Lord and I followed, awestruck, allowing Andy the hulking security guard to shut the door behind her.

The thing about crooks is that they are usually crooks to their core. Occasionally, Allegation Sciences would run across a fundamentally decent soul who had a lapse of judgment, but, by and large, the folks we nailed are into all kinds of bad stuff. Marty Collins struck me as the fuse reaching out for the fire. Teapot Freddy had captured it perfectly with his reference to peak experiences. There was a certain breed of woman, often cursed with the kind of acute physical beauty that had spoiled her so badly among mortals, that all she could do after a while was tweak the gods to see just how much of the universe she could make hers. This tended to piss off the gods who, sooner or later, trip her up with a lightning bolt to the knees.

Today, the Teapot threw that lightning bolt. After her little ride back up in the Hellevator, Marty Collins would be held for a while by Andy The Oaf, and then accompanied by the Imps to her Society Hill, Philadelphia apartment where we would search out an annuity of greater potential value to Allegation Sciences than a run-of-the-mill bunko conviction.

Teapot Freddy sat on my office couch as I fetched my suit jacket from the closet in my office.

"That Marty Collins was really something," I said.

"Jackie," Teapot Freddy said, singsong, "She doesn't want the panda."

Teapot Freddy invoked the panda incident whenever he felt I was out of my depth with a woman. It was a never-ending source of humiliation for me, but I always felt that Freddy was just trying to protect me from predators the way I had protected him growing up.

The panda incident had happened about fifteen years ago when we were all still in our twenties. I had fallen hard for this woman from Philly, a lawyer with a blue-chip firm. Things had been going really well between us.

One Saturday night before taking her to dinner, I stopped into a toy store in Society Hill near where she lived and bought her a little stuffed panda bear. When I gave it to her in her apartment—pleased with my own tender sensibility—she held the little thing away from her body as if I had just placed a poodle turd in her hand. She studied it, her lip curling like it stunk. We went out for an interminable dinner, spoke very little, and when I called her the next morning, she said she couldn't see me. Despite follow-up calls, I never even spoke to her again, let alone saw her. I was pretty upset about it, although I tried to play it cool with my friends.

When he finished interrogating me, Teapot Freddy brutally deconstructed what had happened between Ms. Iron Tits, as he dubbed her, and ruled conclusively: "She didn't want the panda." He added: "*You* wanted the panda."

I didn't talk to Teapot Freddy for the remainder of the summer after he did this to me. I had been emasculated first by a Tea Leoni-lookalike attorney and then by a *finook* hairdresser. I was Jackie Disaster! The panda buyer.

I never formally apologized to Teapot Freddy for freezing him out of my life that summer. I just invited him to a Labor Day barbecue or something. He never rubbed my face in my narcissistic injury; he just reminded me of the panda on occasions when he felt I was chasing danger with two X chromosomes.

I debriefed with the Imps as we walked to my car, and Teapot Freddy lectured us about why none of us could handle Marty Collins.

"You boydogs can't do it because you think you have a shot."

"Nate wasn't hitting on her, Freddy," I said.

"Not in actuality, no, but somewhere inside you guys think there's a way to play it. You've got a happily ever after fantasy, despite the pick up lines you come up with. What was that one I heard you use once, Lordo—'There's a party in my pants and you're invited'? Smooth."

"Somebody's got to end up with a woman like that though," I said.

"You are wrong, Jackie," Freddy said, pounding his fist on an imaginary desk like a judge's mallet. "You are wrong, wrong, wrong. A woman like Marty Collins ends up alone. We boys are the romantics. No matter what the Harlequin novels say, we boys are the ones who dream of growing old with someone, not the girls. But boys of your persuasion can't admit that this is the way you think. You think if you admit it, it makes you, you know, like me."

"Then what happens to Marty Collins?" I asked, curious.

"Oh, my precious Jackie, you're with your guns and brass knuckles, worried about Martypants. She'll be fine. She'll pout for a while, get lost in a romance novel, and it's rush-rush-rush, she'll go to her shrink, who will convince her that she's the victim in all of this, and she'll turn up in Reno in six months. She didn't bewitch *me.* No, Jackie Disaster, Marty will be just fine. It's you I'm worried about, Danger Boy. You want to make a move with you-know-who, but, for some reason you think pursuing sex is rude."

"Don't start with this now, Freddy."

Teapot Freddy made a zipping motion across his lips as we approached my car in the parking lot.

Before I got into my car, I broke up laughing, looking at Teapot Freddy standing there in his orange jumpsuit. "You know, Fred, you look like a fucking carrot."

He checked himself out proudly and brushed his arms off. "Vitamin A is *awesome* for your eyes."

"Great. In the meantime, check our database. See what we can find out about Sally Naturale."

"Are we working with her?" the Lord asked, a little surprised.

"It looks like it, yeah."

"I always wanted to knock that broad square on her ass. I don't know why," the Lord said reflectively.

"Seems somebody shares your view. Check the database."

The Dome in the Woods

"I think I hear crickets."

As I pulled out of the Golden Prospect's parking lot, two Atlantic City broads of the trailer park genus, with big cabooses, were walking across the driveway. Spandex is a privilege, not a right ladies. When they saw the smiling grille of my 1974 Cadillac El Dorado, they slooooowed down. *Uh-uh, baby.* The ladies' eyes narrowed into their fleshy faces, which were burned a little too pink from the sun. They probably thought their "tans" looked good, though. Theirs was the same look my father gave me when he first saw my car. His very expression was an attack. Somehow, my buying a car was an assault on him, a validation of my neglect. As for those two urban hillbillies before me, they didn't have the power to buy my car, but they had the power to slow it down. *Uh-uh, baby.* Jackie Disaster's fast car was laughing at their molasses asses. *Where's your narrow ass goin' Jackie D? Slow down, ya hear?*

Even though these little class wars occurred every day, I had less and less patience with them. My fuse was shortening in step with the passage of time, and it was starting to scare me. It drove me nuts when I would ask the Imps a question where a one-word answer would suffice, and instead they spat forth a lot of prose. I was sick of lengthy E-mails. If they were longer than two lines, I deleted them. Then there were eternal telephone answering machine messages that began with drawn-out preambles: "You've reached the answering machine of Bonnie and Clyde. We're not available at the moment, but your call is very important to us. . . ." Bite me—if my call was that important to you, you would have answered the damned phone. Then there are the sighs that chronically accompany the messages my father leaves on my answering machine. Sigh this. The minute I hear his messages I hang up. I didn't know what my rage signified, but throughout my fifty-minute drive to Medford Lakes, my mind became a panorama of ultimatums—*If I encountered one more slow-ass driver in the passing lane I'll . . .*

I flicked on my Elvis Costello CD, hoping it would be an audio tonic. I had to have the sound system installed by a classic car expert, because there weren't CDs when the '74 El Dorado was manufactured. I bought the car—black exterior, red interior—from an old bookmaker, because it looked and behaved like a car: big, muscular, and mean (kind of like a pirate ship, I thought). The contemporary Caddies, like every other car these days, look like toasters, and I don't drive lightweight household appliances. I love one particular Costello song, *Beyond Belief,* and skipped to it. *I'm just the oily slick in the windup world of the nervous tick . . . I hang around dying to be tortured. You'll never be alone in the bone orchard . . .* I played the song over and over, like an anthem, until my free-floating rage dissipated when I saw Sally Naturale's geodesic dome rising like a glowing cocoon above the pines of Medford Lakes.

Medford Lakes was a South Jersey suburb in the Pine Barrens, the vast woodlands that comprised one-fourth of the state. The Pines had spawned cannon fodder for the American Revolution and the legend of the Jersey Devil. The dome was Naturale's Earth, the stadium-size corporate headquarters and utopian shopping mail. The roof of the dome was white, technically, but the sunlight caused it to reflect back a brilliant golden shade. A statue of a woman, also gold—she appeared to be a goddess wearing a toga or something—stood dramatically at the top of the dome.

Directing shoppers in the parking lot was a poor, sweaty soul in a Beefeater-style uniform, puffy hat and all. The entrance to the dome itself was covered with granite and supported by a circle of ionic columns. Greeting shoppers above the golden archway into the shopping area was a huge black and white photograph of Jack and Jackie Kennedy walking along the Cape Cod surf. I felt strange even thinking of them as Jack and Jackie, because it presumes that I had known them, which I sure hadn't. They were the patron saints of this church, yet there was something falsely familiar about the way the President's tan offset his square white teeth, and for a brief moment I smiled moronically as if I had just bumped into old friends from summer camp. As I walked beneath the photo, I swallowed hard, realizing that I was roughly the same age that Jack had been when it was taken.

There was a whirl of activity beneath the expansive dome, and my head swiveled like a compass trying not to miss anything. In the organic food section, I passed a bakery distributing free samples of Naturale's Upper Crust Pizza or Royce Rolls and Annen-Burgers which could be washed down with a glass of Iced High Socie-Tea or Crème de la Creamer Gourmet Coffee. There were Carnegie Melons in the produce aisle and Rocke-Flowers and David Geffences in the gardening section. In the travel section, Sally was hawking an Old Money Belt, Inheri-Tents for camping and Cabot-Lodgewear, which looked like pajamas to me. In the clothing section, scrubbed models walked the aisles in HyanniSportswear and Onassis Sunglasses. Swimmers could lug Billion Air Inner Tubes to the beach, blow their noses with Naturale's Tischues, and the urchins of summer could keep their heads covered with Manor-Born Baby Wear. Business people could stock up on Anglo-File office products and, for entertaining, clearly a Naturale obsession, the oddity of Wee Butler Uniforms, in which one could dress their presumably cooperative children in servant's gear. In one corner, a display was set up for the products of Sally's younger brother, Bebe, which included mostly Italian gourmet items such as Bebe Naturale's Olive Oil, Tomato Paste and Mozzarella.

When I picked up a courtesy phone, an operator put me through to Sally's office. I was instructed to meet Sally's aide-de-camp, one Milton Smartfarkle in Naturale's Bistreau, which was basically a restaurant with an "e-a-u" at the end of it. It took me about ten minutes to find the Bistre-a-u. One of Naturale's floor people, Baroness Margo Schafer of Maple Shade, showed me the way. All of the workers wore nametags that identified them by royal rank. Salespeople had names like Contessa Jennifer Garvey of West Deptford or Viscount Steve Owens of Cherry Hill. Sections managers were Duke Jim Capello of Almonesson and Lady Fern Goldman of Pennsauken.

I must have appeared confused, because the Bistreau hostess, a teenage summer jobber, Duchess Julie Schwartz of Haddonfield, asked if she could help me. I told her that I was looking for a Milton Smartfarkle.

"Who should I tell Count Smartfarkle is waiting?" Duchess Schwartz asked.

"Earl of De Sesto," I said.

"You got it, Earl babe," Duchess Schwartz answered with a snap of bubble gum, "I'll get him." I was escorted to a table overlooking a vast, muddy lake where I was to meet Count Smartfarkle. As I wondered what sin I had committed against the Heavenly Father who had condemned me to this hell, I spotted a dock floating at the water's edge next to a small sign that read: "Ferry to Cottage." Across the lake rested what was presumably the punch line, the money shot: Cricket Crest, Sally Naturale's forty-thousand-square-foot "cottage" set high on a bluff. Predictably, diners at the Bistre-a-u were seated at tables that were angled in the direction of Cricket Crest, most of them gazing longingly—and upward—across the water like Lilliputians whose cars had broken down on Exit Four of the New Jersey Turnpike. A group of rowers on the lake slowed down to gawk at the smoke rising from a massive, altar-style barbecue on the veranda of Cricket Crest. I wondered what was being sacrificed.

I sat at the table and aped my neighbors, staring at the gargantuan flagstone erection before me. I cannot explain why I felt what I felt next. It was a deep and acute sadness that situated itself right behind my eyes, near where I suppose my sinuses were. The whole scene made me feel lost and terribly far from home. I began missing my niece, Emma, and wondered how pathetic I would seem if I picked her up early from school to take her out for ice cream. I rotated my head all the way around to shake any loose any kinks that may have been causing this madness and thought of Teapot Freddy's effeminate admonition that it had been I, Jackie Disaster, who had wanted the panda. I felt lightheaded, took a deep breath as a low cloud slid across Cricket Crest like a crown, and decided that I wanted to smash Sally Naturale into one of her stone cutting boards because she was responsible for creating this cold, meretricious world where people did not have real homes with real parents.

My pager went off. I recognized the number as belonging to Timmy, the plant manager for one of the South Jersey oil refineries, EnJersey, I had done some work for. I tapped a terse message back to him, telling him I'd call as soon as I could. This was going to be a bear of a day. As I reattached my pager, a cunning, cadaverous, and bald little man who looked like a human wiener said, "You must be Earl De Sesto,"

"I'm sorry," I said. I was in a fog, transfixed by Cricket Crest.

"Earl De Sesto?"

"*Jackie* De Sesto."

"That's what I thought. You're Jackie Disaster. Duchess Schwartz had said Earl."

"Yeah, well, I'm the Earl of Asswipe."

"Azwyche?" the man strained, prune-faced.

"Right."

"I'm Count Smartfarkle," he said, holding out his hand as if a scepter balanced in his palms.

I was exhausted and had only been here seven minutes. "Look, I was told you'd take me over to see Sally. She wanted to talk."

"Yes, yes, of course," the little fussbudget said, and motioned me to follow him. "Sally receives all of her visitors at the cottage."

"Hmm," I said.

"Pardon me?"

"Most people in Sally's position would rather people not see where they live."

"Oh, but Mr. De Sesto, seeing is believing. Those who work with the House of Naturale must believe. We'll show you around."

"Uh huh," I said following him past the Warren Buffet tables for outdoor entertaining. "You guys ever thought of selling Pew toilet paper?"

"Excuse me?" Count Smartfarkle said.

"Pew, the Sun Oil family. From Philly. Pew toilet paper and bathroom stuff. Ya know, like P.U."

"No, we don't sell that," the Count said straight-faced.

That's because you're an enormous tool.

We climbed aboard a covered ferry, which puttered across the nameless lake. I could have sworn that I heard a faint chirping echoing from the hills. I must have squinched up my face in an odd way, because Count Smartfarkle asked if there was something wrong.

"I'm fine. I think I hear crickets."

"You do yes."

"Okay."

Count Smartfarkle didn't appear to be interested in commenting any further and focused straight ahead on the awaiting dock. Maybe he didn't like my Pew idea, which I thought was brilliant.

The ferry docked and was tied to the moorings by a muscular-looking woman, Lady Shelly Randall of Westmont. At the base of a long stone staircase, there was a glass-enclosed holding room that faced the great dome across the lake. In golden letters above the receptionist, it read: "*Things don't happen—they are made to happen.*—Rose Kennedy." There was an operating fireplace in the center of the stark lobby. A roaring fire in late May in South-Freaking-Jersey. Immense black and white photos of Sally with famous people adorned the otherwise sparse walls. The photos were touched up to look old. *Olde.* Sally with Gorbachev. Sally with Leonard Bernstein holding a conductor's baton. (*I never got* conductors, I thought to myself. *What do they actually do, and how could anybody tell which ones were geniuses?*) There was Sally, orgasm-faced, with Princess Diana. She was wearing a tiara—Sally, I mean. Sally raising a fist with a woman who was presumably an African queen. Sally hugging Streisand. My teeth were beginning to itch.

Scattered throughout the boxily furnished lobby (I had the sense that it might have been some kind of high-fashion design that I was too classless to know about) were neatly coiffured consultants. For the most part, the men wore Jos. A. Bank-ish suits with the occasional see-me-be-casual polo shirt underneath. The women were less experimental with their casualness, and their lapels were razor sharp—like my buddy Marty Collins, but with any hint of sex smothered by Ann Taylor. The room smelled of hygienic hope mixed with, well, raw capital. Mild cologne and cash. Underarm deodorant and the ink from freshly printed contracts. When we approached the registration desk, fully suited, the consultants' eyes widened with promise, as if to ask me, "Are you someone who can give me money?" Under the processed scents and crisp white collars were basically upper-middle-class urchins who hoped to perform some task for Sally in exchange for a buck.

I nodded politely at a cluster of hopefuls, who ignored me immediately after my nod. Gum. I was chewing gum. This, combined with the boxing scar beneath my right eye, must have sent a Darwinian signal that I was not a man with a checkbook. I signed into the guest book at the Count's direction, put on a corporate badge and threw my gum away in a trashcan, the sticky flick from my fingers taking a few tries, to the delight of the manicured vendors of the lobby. *Sure, we're peddling something, but YOU, Jackie Disaster, you're so . . . Jersey.*

I followed Count Smartfarkle down a never-ending cobblestone hallway featuring photographs of Sally standing beside glowing people that I did not recognize. These photographs were smaller than the ones in the lobby of Sally with the big celebrities. All of the people in the photos wore desperate, camera-ready smiles. I slowed down and looked more closely at the photos. Count Smartfarkle crept up behind me. "That one there," he pointed, "Is Ingrid Casares."

I shrugged my shoulders, oblivious.

"She's a friend of Madonna's," he reminded me. "A nightclub impresario."

"Okay," I said, still oblivious.

"And those right there," Count Smartfarkle spoke to me like I was a mongoloid, and pointed to two silvery wisps of calcium flanking Sally, "Are the Hilton Sisters."

In addition to middle-age making me impatient, it was making me stupid. Not only did I not know who these people were, but this man seemed surprised that I didn't know who they were, and they appeared to be nothing more than friends of famous people. A nightclub impresario? What was that exactly, someone who went to nightclubs? Did this make me a urinal impresario? I glanced again at the photos. Something in the smiles of these friends of the gods conveyed more than desperation. Maybe it was even enthusiasm, or an acceptance of their roles as lubricants in the vast and temperamental engine of celebrity. Sally's eyes flashed more brightly than the others, however, as if she believed there was room to maneuver past the glossy protoplasm of the others to somewhere higher.

After a brief elevator ride, we ended up in a square sanctuary of a living room, which terminated with a colossal window overlooking the lake and the dome. Immediately before the window, there was a singular, puffy white chair on an elevated riser. Everything in the room was insane-asylum white. Similarly styled, but less puffy, sofa chairs were in listening positions at the foot of the higher chair.

"Let me go fetch Sally. She just got done with her workout," Count Smartfarkle whispered conspiratorially. While Oscar Meyer did his fetching, I took the liberty of walking down a nearby hall.

There was a narrow golden table in the hallway with the new edition of *Vanity Fair* pressed open to a page with a montage of party photos. I caught a shot of a young, slick-haired Hollywood talent agent whispering something confidentially to a boy-band singer who had pencil thin lines of facial hair striping his face. The agent wore the archly confident expression of a man shrewd enough to have oozed into this shot, but not wise enough to know that every other toddler in Armani at the party had a mother who had hinted to him at his confirmation that someone other than God had really created the heavens. And this talent agent knew who that someone special was.

I stopped to read the photo caption, which read, "Only five people on the planet have Mike Merolla's cell phone number, and two of them are named Tom." So this was his shtick, the guinea fixer like the Chicago mob's Johnny Roselli, the Man of Mystery pulling strings so invisibly silky that only he could see them. What kind of world had I entered where a page like this was flagged? So many older Italians were offended by the mob stigma, yet young guys like my buddy Mike Merolla went out of his way to affect Mafia chic—the larcenous whispering, the winking eyes, the Gotti come-and-get-me crooked smile.

My bitter little reverie came to an end when I heard music echoing from one of the rooms down the hall. I followed it. The music pulsed from behind a set of double doors, which I opened. Inside, an athletic Adonis tidied up sets of little weights and sit-up cushions as the *Fiddler on the Roof song* "If I Were a Rich Man" played. He set down a pair of thick, hand-held pads, the kind that trainers held while kick-boxers did target practice.

"Can I help you?" Adonis asked with a self-satisfying flex of his pectorals. It wasn't hard for a boxer to take down a guy like this. Sooner or later, every bodybuilder fell sufficiently in love with his body that he lost use of his brain. That's when they tried to box, and sooner or later they'd end up in the ring with a smaller guy like me who was conditioned to avenge playground torments. There were three steps to such a slaughter. First, the nose. A nose shot was painful, bloody and psychologically traumatizing. Adonises were caught between two impulses once you nailed them in the nose: Did they avenge the insult and restore their masculinity, or leave the ring and primp? That was the key to understanding Adonis: He didn't want to fight, he wanted to be *known* as a fighter.

After I got the nose, I'd dance to the side and crack Adonis in the side, where the ribs are thinnest. If I was lucky, I'd break one, and this hurt like a bear, not to mention the psychic trauma of hearing the snap of bone. If Adonis survived these two attacks, which he seldom did, then I'd just dance around and let him get tired. As he tired, he'd also reached the conclusion that you—not him, *you*—sucked as a fighter because you really hadn't hit him that many times. That's when a flurry of jabs to his head ended things.

Adonis smiled, scout-like, so I felt guilty about having just rolled him in my fantasy.

"No. I was waiting for Sally. We're meeting," I said.

"She's showering up. She'll be out soon."

"Okay," I said admiring the workout facility. "Does Sally kick-box?"

"Yes. She's pretty good, too."

I had the childish urge to tell Adonis that I had been a champion boxer, but decided that it would make me seem insecure, so I didn't.

"Are you all right?" he asked.

"Yeah. Yeah, I'm fine," I faked a sincere smile. "I always liked this song."

"What can I tell you? Some women work out to disco, Sally likes show tunes. She always winds down with *If I Were A Rich Man.*"

"It's a good one," I said, backing away. I quietly sung along with the song. *When you're rich they think you really know.* Great verse. True, too.

"Can I ask you a question?"

"Sure," Adonis said.

"Do you hear crickets outside, or am I nuts?"

Adonis approached me. He glanced around to make sure no one was coming. He appeared to be nervous. " 'Cricket Crest,' get it? Crickets."

"Not totally, no."

Adonis looked around again. Then he made that circling motion with his fingers around his ears signifying that somebody close by was fucking nuts. I returned to the sanctuary and focused on the raised puffy chair.

Sally Floats In

"Nowadays, the world sees the predator as the victim."

Jackie Disaster. Such a name," Sally Naturale said, gliding into the room like a leaf on a lake. Sally was a tiny thing with black hair that highlighted henna when the sunlight from the great window fell on her. She had an angular face and a perfectly straight nose. In the commercials, I always thought she was a hot number for a woman old enough to be my mother, but up close, I wasn't so sure. Each feature was flawless, but there was a low-grade tremor just under the surface that made me wonder if her entire head might not explode, after which her taut little body would unravel like a million brittle plastic springs. She looked like a blurry video dub of an older Jacqueline Kennedy. She appeared to be about sixty, and somewhat fragile, and her eyes were very red.

"It's been with me a while. The name," I said.

"You don't *look* like a disaster."

"Oh, but I am."

"But you're John by birth, right, son?"

"My given name is actually Giovanni."

Sally approached me and stood inappropriately close. She studied my eyes.

"Your eyes," she said. "One is green, the other is brown."

"I'm a mutant, I guess. They've always been that way."

"Perhaps it's a good mutation, a gift."

"I've never thought of my eyes that way. More of a novelty than a gift."

"I see. Please sit then, Mr. De Sesto. May I ask you something?" she asked, bringing her hands together in prayer.

I sat and she continued.

"Do I seem like the kind of person who makes people sick?" Sally asked me.

Well, yeah.

She sat on the elevated chair. I sat on one of the lower ones. Count Smartfarkle bowed officiously and left the two of us alone.

I studied Sally before answering her. I felt torrentially sad again. Just looking at her made me sad. Perhaps it was the whole desperate Jackie Kennedy thing she was angling for. She now held out her arms as if she were going to receive her royal manicure, and then clapped her hands together as if I, her attendant, had not moved quickly enough.

"No, Ms. Naturale, you don't look like that kind of person, no."

"You can call me Sally, son. I am not a witch. I would never do anything to make people sick. You see, this business of mine, it's not all dollars and cents. Business may be business, but to me it's personal. I never had a child. This business is my child. That's what no one understands about businesspeople. The media think we live to do harm. To many of us, our businesses are our children. Why would anyone think we would do anything to bring shame on our children?"

"You may be thinking that what people say is what they mean."

"Why would they lie?" Sally asked, suddenly childlike, as if she had forgotten her perch atop the Most Serene House of Naturale.

"Your attackers want something, Sally. Money, fame, revenge. They hide the thing they're really after in something that sounds like a cause."

"But, Jackie, this Murrin is a . . . victim."

"Nowadays, the world sees the predator as the victim. The victim package is everything. Maybe we can create our own victim."

"When I see that picture of Murrin in the newspaper with her finger pointing, I could scream."

"I understand that. Whoever points the finger owns the camera."

"So what do *you* do?"

"I snap fingers off."

Sally clapped her hands together. "I knew I would find you. I knew I needed you and I knew I would find you."

"How did you find me?"

"I remembered reading about you in an article about that singer who was extorted a few years ago."

"Oh, sure. In *Philly* magazine."

"Besides, I'm very spiritual." *Sprichull.* "I'm always on the lookout for highly developed souls, people who understand what I'm trying to do. I need to redeem myself with my consumers."

"Hmm. I'm not trying to turn you off or anything, but I'm not sure I'm that, uh, developed or spiritual. I just have a specialty."

"You're very successful, Jackie. That impresses me." I felt like I was being worked. "I read that article about you and have talked to other people. Businesspeople like me. I'm not ashamed of my biases." "Everyone . . . everyone like me knows that he or she will need someone to help them fight off devils."

"When you say 'everyone like you' . . ."

"People who have missions, things they are trying to do. The devil is always out there, Jackie. Jersey has a devil. Right out here in these woods, too. But other wildernesses have devils. Now I've got this sad, sad young Murrin woman who says I sold her soy milk that killed her baby. Can you imagine such a thing? Somebody's sending out E-mails saying that I used cloned chemicals or some such nonsense."

"I have to ask you a hard question, Sally."

"I know your question, son. 'Did I sell soy milk that isn't real soy milk, but is some chemical concoction?' Is that your question?"

"Yes, it is."

"The answer is no. Soy milk is soy milk. This criticism of me is unholy. If Murrin lost her baby, something else took it. Murrin's sorry she lost her baby. *I'm* sorry she lost her baby, but I'm no baby killer. Now she's trying to kill my baby, this business. I'm a saleswoman, a marketer, not a scientist. However the law says to make soy milk is how we make it."

"Can I have my people check out the plant where it's made?"

"Of course. Count Smartfarkle can arrange it. Have you seen what they're saying about me on that Internet?"

"I've seen a few things."

"They say I'm really a man. They say I have a child chained up in my basement. Maybe I'm just too thin-skinned." Sally fanned herself with her hands, and then held the back of one hand to her forehead, Scarlett O'Hara style.

"Sally, in my whole career, I've never met one person, not one, with thick skin. They don't exist."

"Interesting."

"Do you have security people, public relations people on staff?"

"You will work with me. They'll know the bare minimum."

"Good. They shouldn't know anything."

"What do I do with them?"

"Do a PR campaign to distract them."

"Do PR to distract my PR people?"

"Yeah. Make them think they're handling things. Have them do web sites and fact sheets on the safety of your products. Let them blow up balloons. Don't mention me. Don't tell them anything important."

"But they'll look like idiots to the press."

"We want the press to think they're idiots."

"Why?"

"If they're idiots, nobody'll think *they're* capable of what *we're* really doing. I also sense that you don't trust them."

"You have to understand something, Jackie. When success comes to someone—and comes outrageously—people can't deal with the . . . inequality of it all. They can't see why God gave so much to one, but so little to them. So they begin to think they created you."

"It's good to be wary. In a crisis like what you've got, "PR" stands for *prepare resume.* Flacks are thinking about their personal survival. They don't care about you, and they won't want a guy like me around."

"Why is that?"

"Flacks dodge and appease. I confront. Appeasement is the best way to avoid being associated with a screw up, which is how flacks survive." This was utterly true. What was worse was that flacks viscerally opt for trying to make things pretty even when they're not. They tend to assure audiences that all's well when it's not. It's an ingrained comfort with lying that is made acceptable through the invocation of soft, New-Age rhetoric. Empowerment. Inclusiveness. Diversity. Empathy. How about *kiss my ass*? How about that?

"Tell me your fantasy, Sally. If I could do anything, work miracles, what would that be?"

"You would find out why Murrin thinks I did this to her. You would find out why she is suing me."

"How about money? That's usually why people sue people."

I studied Sally's face as she considered my question. I wondered what she knew, or really suspected.

"Who knows?" she said.

"I feel a little uncertain about something, I guess," I said.

"What's on your mind, that when you came in here, you thought I might be a few wicks short of a candelabra?"

"Maybe that."

"What else, son? We need to be open with each other. Let me have it."

"When I was back in the dome, I couldn't believe all of that status stuff. I wasn't planning on liking you, if you want to know the truth."

"Do you like me now?"

"Yeah, but, you're not apologetic or subtle about any of this stuff, the way you attach to rich people . . . David Geffences? I mean, Jesus."

"My market isn't subtle. My market is Americans." Sally said this utterly without guile or self-awareness, any more than a toddler felt shame dropping a load in a diaper.

"No regrets, huh, Sally?"

With this question, Sally rose and walked to the great window. "I regret some of the things I had to do, I don't regret what I've achieved. You think a lot, Jackie, for a mercenary."

"Maybe I'm not a mercenary."

"Ah, a crusader. I knew it!"

"A crusader with a business to run."

"There's no shame in that. Spend time with me, son, I'll show you around Cricket Crest, and you'll see why apologizing isn't even an impulse." She leaned forward and slapped her hand on the table before her to make sure I got the point.

"Okay."

"Will you find out what's happening and will you stop them?"

Normally, when I agree to work with someone, I equivocate on my capacity to work miracles. There was something about Sally's vulnerability that made me want to give her a stronger assurance. "Yeah, I'll find them and I'll stop them."

"Good. It will be affirming for you."

For me? Another billionaire client who thought that working for her was payment in and of itself.

"Okay."

"Now, let me show you around the house."

I wasn't getting it. Was there something about me that made me look like a guy who needed a tour?

As we rose, a gruff voice shouted from somewhere in the vast Cricket Crest echo chamber. I couldn't make out exactly what the man was saying. It sounded like a long, drawn out, *"Sell!"* as if he were trading bonds.

Sally's face immediately became pained. The voice continued bellowing. I felt like an idiot when I figured out the man was shouting, "Sal!"

Sally mouthed "shit" and whispered, "My little brother. He doesn't need to know our business."

A squat, thuggish-looking gnome waddled in, visibly confusing his girth with toughness. He wore a Ron Jeremy-style porno moustache, Sam Giancana sunglasses and a wise guy track suit, which I'm certain he never ran in. Guys like this were especially easy to drop. Gut shot. Chest punch. Jaw.

I rose and surrendered an obsequious smile. "Bebe Naturale," the brother barked, extending his hand.

"Jackie De Sesto."

"My sister treating you good?" Bebe asked, jolly.

"Working me over a little."

"She does that." Bebe winked at his sister. As I moved my eyes back and forth between the two of them, it was hard to fathom that they were in any way related. Slim-wristed Sally and her finger bowls and her *animale* brother, an extra from *The Sopranos.* The only connection I could conjure up was their ingrained Phlersey accents, which Sally was able to occasionally suppress.

Bebe stood, his legs apart, his face a snarling mask, demanding an explanation for my presence with his eyes. All the while, he smiled like Dom DeLouise. "What do you do, Jackie?" he asked.

"Public relations," I said.

"Yes, public relations," Sally echoed.

"Yeah? What's he working on?" *Whutziwurkinnun.* "Did you fire that Cherry Hill agency?"

"No, Bebe, he is a specialist. He specializes in damage control."

"We got damage?" he chuckled, his belly jiggling. On second thought, there was something more comic about him than menacing.

"That crazy woman with the soy milk," Sally explained.

I nodded at Bebe, feeling like an idiot. I wasn't sure what I was allowed to say.

"Ah, that mess," Bebe growled. "Nobody sues you when you're poor."

"Do you think it's all about money, Mr. Naturale?" I asked.

"Yes, I do, Jackie. Yes, I do. Do you advise us to do a recall or something?"

Sally cut in. "He's just getting the facts right now, Bebe. Then he'll come back with strategies and messages."

"That's what we need," Bebe said. "Strategies and messages. Finally we're gonna do something about this mess."

Bebe began shuffling away and then he stopped suddenly. "What other clients you got, can I ask?" *Kennayaast.*

"Well, I've got security agreements with my clients, but I do a lot of casino work, some pharmaceuticals."

"Pharmaceuticals? What kind of damage do they need to control? All that beefing about high costs?"

"That kind of thing, sure."

"I checked out Jackie's credentials," Sally said with false patience. "He's the best in the business."

"You two are the PR whizzes," Bebe said, again jolly. "Me they keep back in operations."

"The core of our business," Sally reassured, clapping her hands together in the manner Elizabeth Taylor did when she played Cleopatra.

"The core," Bebe echoed with a jolly wave, and disappeared. *Duhkor.* "Jackie, seriously, once you get some traction, let me know. I may have some ideas. I'm worried about this thing."

"I will," I said, feeling a bit guilty about having judged the man so thoroughly by his appearance.

What I Do

"Every way of life has its enforcers."

Sally really wanted to give me a frigging tour of her house. I hate smiling and nodding at art and other crap, but did my best to fake it. There was something antiseptic about Cricket Crest. The ceilings were high, the walls were white, the sculptures looked like shit-on-a-stick, but I managed to squeeze out a few "humms," as if I might actually be in the market for bronzed feces. By the way Sally flicked her fingers at the pieces as she explained them, I sensed she didn't care much for art either, but felt compelled to demonstrate that art was important to her. I actually felt kind of sorry for her and had an impulse to say, "Hey, sweetheart, outside of a couple of poems my niece wrote, I don't think about art either!"

Sally asked me if I minded working in the summer, as if playing on center court at Wimbledon were an alternative. I assured her that I didn't mind.

"Do you vacation much, Jackie?"

"Not really, no. I took my niece and my dad to Maine last summer."

"Ah, Maine. I summered there as a wee girl."

Wee.

"Where in Maine?"

"Oh. Something harbor. One of those harbors."

"Uh-huh."

I followed Sally into a guest bathroom. I couldn't imagine what she felt I needed to see in there. It was a rather standard, but very large bathroom. She sat down on the edge of the bathtub and rested her head in her hands. The room's only odd feature was a photograph of Frank Sinatra and Mia Farrow dressed formally and wearing glittery masks.

"No one can hear us in here," she said. So this was the purpose of our "tour."

She gestured toward the closed toilet, which I sat on reluctantly.

"Jackie, what would you do first? To redeem me. I'm just not sure how all of this works."

I explained that my first move would be to look into Murrin Connolly to determine if there were reasons to believe she was corrupt in some way—lying, in a financial pickle that might motivate an attack like this, fronting for a competitor.

"Do you know Murrin, Sally?"

"I wouldn't know Murrin if she fell into my lake."

"Well, I want to check out some batches of this soy milk, have one of my guys look at the plant, and dig around on Murrin. I don't know much yet. She's twenty-nine. Her husband is in the military, overseas now. Religious people."

"Yes, he referred to the baby a few times in an interview as 'the fetus'."

"Right. I saw that. Murrin went to Salem County Community College for a year. She was a receptionist at a law firm. Last week she bought one of those moonsuits, the kind you wear to sweat weight off, on her Visa card."

"Oh, those things don't work," Sally said, ducking how impressed she was with the little I knew.

"No, but they sell, especially for people who don't want to work out or diet."

"Is there some . . . softer way, maybe educating people on how we make our milk?"

"I don't think this is about milk, Sally. If it were, I'd say that an ad campaign would be fine. This is an attack, not a conventional marketing problem. We may be up against a guerilla here, not a competitor saying they make a better product."

"I believe you have to reach out to customers in a way that feels quite personal," Sally said.

"There needs to be a simple explanation for what's going on," I said. "If you don't feed the public a plausible story, they'll gravitate to the worst possibility, which is that you make a dangerous product."

"You think in conspiracies."

"So does the public. They see greed and malice behind everything. They do not accept Acts of God. They don't accept that soldiers get killed. They enjoy seeing big companies falter and rich white people getting a pie in the face. It's an entertainment story, and right now there's only one story line: You make a bad product. Unless we offer up another, you've got a real problem."

"What do you propose, that I accuse Murrin of killing her child?"

"You? No. You're a corporation. In a fight between you and a grieving mom, the mom wins. Moms make bad villains, great victims. But if we can demonstrate that something else happened, we may have something."

"I just think that if people know all of the facts . . ."

"Don't believe that if we all just learn more things will work out, Sally."

"You're against learning, Jackie?"

"There's a limit to learning. Sometimes things are what they are."

"This all sounds very rough to me. Spies and spooks and creepy crawlies."*

"Sally, whoever alleges wins. Whoever apologizes loses. Every way of life has its enforcers."

"See, that's exactly what I mean. Scary talk."

"George Washington and FDR were our country's greatest spymasters. People think that we, you, anybody, can have all of these goodies of freedom without getting our hands dirty."

Sally nodded, impressed, I think, that I had a sense of history. What I did not feel compelled to disclose is where I had plagiarized the quip about enforcers. Hint: It wasn't Kissinger, but another Jewish immigrant of lesser renown. After the 1993 bombing of the World Trade Center, Mickey Price had sat in the Golden Prospect's casino-observation room lamenting the collapse of America's spy network, the kind of network he felt was necessary to protect against such atrocities. When I observed that contemporary Americans would not tolerate such hardball, Mickey barked something about Americans living in a fantasy world and punctuated his rant with: "Every way of life has its enforcers."

"See, kid," Mickey had said, "We've had it so good for so damned long that we can't believe anybody really wants to hurt us. So when we get hit, we figure we must have done something wrong."

Sally got down on one knee, as if she were preparing to propose to her toilet-bound bound damage control consultant.

"Jackie, find out the author of my misfortune and stop it. Help me repent with people." I think Sally was misusing the word *repent,* but I didn't know her well enough to know exactly what she had in mind. "Show me how crisis management works."

*Most clients plead virginity before they realize what must be done, suppressing any memory of how they originally got where they did. The trick is to show them evidence of their attacker's amorality, which reminds them of the techniques they had been comfortable with the first time they got attacked in the marketplace.

"I'll do my best. A crisis, Sally, isn't a science. It's Dodge City. There are two people you can be in Dodge City. You can be the store owner who just keeps her head low and hopes she won't be hurt."

"Or?"

"You can be the new sheriff."

"And what does she do?"

"She throws a brick through a glass window where the bad guys are playing cards, she cocks her shotgun, and she says, 'Come out and play.'"

Pest Control

"No bat, no cameras."

On the way out of Naturale's parking lot, I pushed the little button on the side of my pager and it spit a phone number at the EnJersey refinery back at me. I attached my wire earpiece to my cell phone, nearly running over a Girl Scout Troop in the process, and called Timmy, my contact there.

"Hey, it's me, I'm in Medford," I said.

"We've got a problem here," Timmy said in his Southern drawl (even though he was from Swedesboro, in South Jersey).

"We've got a giant bat outside our plant."

"What am I, pest control?"

"No, it's a balloon bat, like in those parades. It's fifty feet high and seventy feet wide. Black. It's these protestors from the union. Every time they put up this goddamned bat, the news crews show up. They're going with a whole bloodsucker theme, like the bat's a vampire, you know."

"Union, huh?"

"Yeah, same crowd. This fuckin' bat is scaring the workers, scaring kids in school buses that drive by. I've got camera crews, I can't reason with these people."

"Well, stop trying to reason with them."

"What are we supposed to do?"

"Let's make this real simple," I said, pulling onto 295. "You've got a big bat. You want it gone. Right?"

"Right."

I looked at my watch. One thirty. "I'm about fifteen minutes out. Here's what I want you to do. Pull a bunch of cars up to the gate near where the bat is flying. At two o'clock, turn the radio to WFIL and blast it like a son of a bitch. When the song that plays at the top of the hour is over, turn the radios off and pull the cars back to where they normally go."

"What are you going to do?" Timmy asked.

"Do you want a damage control lesson or do you want to get rid of the damned bat?"

"The bat. We want it out."

"Then drive up at two and blast that station."

I called my cousin Ronnie, who worked at WFIL. He was a studio technician. Occasionally, when he wasn't completely ripped, they let him do a show. A heavy metal freak since he was thirteen, Ronnie had had his share of troubles, which I had helped him with from time to time. Let's say Ronnie owed me.

"Ronzo, it's your cousin," I said, after directory assistance hooked me to the station.

"Whoa, Jackie!"

"I need a favor."

"You got it, boss."

"You don't even know what it is yet."

"Oh, yeah, like, right."

"Do you have any AC/DC?"

"Tons of it."

"Good. At two, play something fierce. Just one song. Something with a lot of thumping."

"Do I wanna know why?"

"Yeah, because otherwise I'll lock you up in a room and play the Bee Gees till your ears bleed."

"No way, man."

"So you'll do it?"

"I'll do anything to dodge the disco bullet."

"Thanks, Ronzo."

I pulled off the Runnemede exit and whizzed by Timmy's plant, where there was indeed a great inflatable bat hovering above the entry gate. There were about twenty protestors gathered around the ropes that held the bat. Some of them were waving placards reading "EnJersey = Death."

Subtle. Some of the protestors appeared to be high-school age. I understood the syndrome: You can't cut school just for yucks; you've got to be protesting something. Why not roll a few joints, wave a few placards, and then drive down the shore in a smoke-filled Volvo feeling like Ché Guevara? I counted two camera crews filming the proceedings.

I drove about a quarter mile past the EnJersey gate and looped back around, pulling my El Dorado in between two trees on the opposite side of the road to the plant. The woods weren't thick, but thick enough. I retrieved a duffel bag from the trunk of my car and removed my dirty-work clothes and an old, clean revolver, a .22. I changed from my suit into jeans and stripped to my undershirt.

I dodged trees on my run toward the plant, which took about two minutes. I slowed down as I spotted the great bat. I was surprised at how fast my heart was beating. Was this normal? Should I have been this winded? I always prided myself in looking and feeling better than other men my age, but my medical sensitivity was disconcerting. I placed the .22 in my rear pocket reasoning that it was better to shoot off part of my ass than to detach Mr. Clinton himself, and began climbing a tree. The roughness of the pine bothered me and I actually said "Ow" out loud like a wuss. I wouldn't have done that ten years ago. I would have thought the scrapes were cool. When I got about twenty feet up, I moved out on one of the stronger limbs and drew a bead with my revolver on the bat, which loomed in its frightening doofdom about two hundred yards away.

It was an awkward shot. Although I knew that the leaves wouldn't stop a bullet, it was disconcerting to see them drift to and fro in the breeze. I began to get angry when I realized how dumb it was to be pissed off at the breeze. It was as if I expected God himself to peel back the branches so I'd have a clear shot.

The cars on the plant grounds began to pull up on the inside of the property. There were about twenty of them in all with their grilles against the fence. This was a more confrontational look than I had been going for, but whatever. The protestors squinted and cocked their heads. They were tittering amongst themselves trying to figure out what was going on. Having visible opposition, they began pumping their fists in the air, but recoiled when the thumping intensity of AC/DC's *Dirty-Deeds* split the late spring air. A few of them plugged their ears with their fingers. Others just pumped their fists even harder, envisioning themselves on Max Yasgur's Woodstock farm, an experience they claimed to have recalled fondly, despite its having occurred decades before most of them were born. From my distance, I felt the ground vibrate. With the lyrics *done-dirt-cheap,* an utterance I detected more from the beat than the words, I squeezed the trigger three times. *Crack. Crack. Crack.* None of the protestors heard, the music having overwhelmed the sound of gunfire.

I shimmied down the tree and walked quickly back toward my car, craning my neck to make see how the bat was faring. For a few moments, nothing. I began to worry. Had the branches flicked the bullets off course? Then, gradually, the bat began to frown when the weight of the sagging plastic overwhelmed it as helium began to escape.

I got back in my car and did one swing-by. The cars were all gone. The bat's wings had folded and it appeared to be hunched over like a sick and skeletal Dracula. It's face was now against its chest and the protestors were frantically trying to keep it afloat; either that or they were trying to pull it back over the fence to their side. They were scrambling. As I took the exit back onto 295, I saw the bat's head swing back up once, as if he were looking at me. I caught a glimpse of his betrayed eyes in my rearview mirror when my cell phone rang. I popped in the earpiece. It was Timmy.

"What's up?" I asked.

"Question is, what's down?"

"So, what's down?"

"The big bat."

"No shit. Any news crews?"

"No, they've left."

"You know why?"

"Why?"

"No bat, no cameras."

"Nothing to shoot, I guess. The damned thing fell on our property."

"That's litter! That's vandalism!" I said. "Those bastards trashed your property. You've got an incinerator, right?"

"Right."

"Dispose of it. If anybody gives you shit later, say they trashed your property."

"Do you just think of this stuff?"

"Yeah, why?"

Classic Blueblood Package

"Sally Naturale didn't exist before The Bicentennial."

I was back at the shore by mid-afternoon and met the Imps at Macko's Subs on Ventnor Avenue. Macko's had been there forever. I always envisioned that even the Lenape Indians had hung out at Macko's, the way my crew did in the summers. After we had a boxing match, my brother Tommy and I would come here all banged up—even the pain felt good back then—and move from table to table in our tank tops posing in front of the mirrored walls. All the guys did the same thing—pretending we were being social when all we were really doing was checking out our triceps. Honest to God, the same orange booths were there, the same photos of summertime gatherings in cheap-ass frames, the same smell of sauteed onions, and even the same guys hanging out—just a little fatter, balder, and more disappointed.

I ordered a diet cola, even though I hated all diet drinks. I was at that point in my life where I couldn't just exercise weight off the way I used to; I had to reduce intake, which wasn't easy for me. When I drank regular soft drinks, I grew handles. If I grew handles, I reasoned, I *was* Frankie Shrugs.

"I thought you hated that diet swill," the Lord spoke.

"Tastes like acid," I said.

"Then why do you drink it?" Nate the Great asked.

"To stay thin and suffer," Teapot Freddy explained for me. "God forbid he should have a regular Coke, he might turn into Raymond Burr."

"Ironside," the Lord nodded. "His ass is dead, ain't he?"

"Yes, Lord," Teapot Freddy said. "The poor thing purchased some rural property a few years ago."

"Huh?" the Lord asked.

"Bought the farm," I clarified. "Freddy has to make things more complicated. He can't say 'kicked the bucket', he has to say 'stumbled upon a pail' or something like that."

"Look who can't even have a Coke without thinking he's going to Hell," Freddy said.

I could see that we were on the Concorde to nowhere, so I got to work.

"Fred, what did you find out about Sally in our database?"

"Only the bullshit they put in her official bio, boydog."

"Well, that's something. What does it say?"

"Let me read it to you Jack-attack, and get ready to engage in some world-class projectile vomiting. 'Sally Naturale was raised all over the world by her industrialist father, San Benedict "Nonie" Naturale and her mother, Lillianne Naturale, a sculptress descended from the Belgian House of Duodenum-und-Polyp. Young Sally—or Salvita, as she was known—got her start by making gourmet dishes and crafts for her parents guests at the family's summer cottages in places ranging from Monte Carlo to Cape May, New Jersey. During all of her world travels, however, Sally's heart belonged to southern New Jersey, which she has turned into a beacon of American style with, of course, the European flare of her youth.' Are you ready to heave yet, boys?"

"Jeez, Teapot. What does that really tell us about Sally?" I asked.

"Nada. Sally Naturale didn't exist before the Bicentennial, when she started getting noticed."

"How can that be?" I asked.

"It be, brotha," Teapot Freddy said.

"Keep digging."

"I'm your little coal miner, Jackie," Teapot Freddy said. "Tell us about your meeting with Miss Fancyass."

"Wacky little broad. Up close, it looks like her face has been done."

"You needed a sit-down to see that?" Nate the Great said, "Classic—what I used to call the BP—a blueblood package. Straight nose, squared jawline." Nate explained this while performing an isometric exercise that made his arms and pecs ripple beneath his tank top.

"Yeah, she looks fragile," I said.

"Most of 'em are," Nate explained. "See, a slight job of some kind is no biggie. We all have something we want to change, which doesn't make you a wackadoo or anything. The blueblood package . . . these broads were touched. Guys, too."

"Guys had that kind of surgery?"

"Sometimes. Usually guys from Teapotville, if you catch my drift."

Teapot Freddy rolled his eyes. "We love those skinny Christy Turlington noses, we do, we do."

"What about the women?" I asked.

"Women who get BPs? Hmm," Nate pondered. "Usually they're ethnic. Italians, black chicks who want to be white, Jewish broads who want to be Episcopalian, small-town girls with rounded features who want to be angled-up models in New York, or marry some polo-playing pantload." Like Dirk Romella, I thought.

"Sally's looked like this for years," I said.

"What's your point?" Nate the Great asked.

"Say she got the blueblood package. Say she got it around here, I don't know, twenty years ago, maybe more. Where would she have gotten it in those days?"

"There weren't many places around here to go for that in the sixties and seventies, if that's what you mean," Nate explained. "A doc in Bryn Mawr named Yale Pennington was the guru, he used to do these jobs where you went in with a celebrity's picture and he'd replicate the features."

"Can you talk to him, Nate? I asked.

"He's been dead for a while now. He's not an option. His assistants are probably long dispersed, too, impossible to find." Nate pulled out a tiny comb and began brushing his goatee.

I rubbed my temples. "Sally's brother, Bebe is a masterpiece. Wears a porno mustache, Sam Giancana sunglasses."

"I like him already," Teapot Freddy said.

"Lordo, get a stringer to see about Bebe," I said. "He's one of those guys who talks gruff, but may be a sweetheart underneath. I can't tell yet. Sally seemed nervous about him."

"Who do you think is right for that?" the Lord asked, lifting up his pocket T, rubbing his hairless stomach, and running his hands through the kind of thick hair that we all admired when *The Partridge Family* was still producing new episodes.

"Who do we have in Camden, Burlington counties who won't lose his mark?"

"Remember Swervin' Mervin?" the Lord offered.

"Yeah."

"Him."

"Okay, tell Merv nothing risky, we just want basic patterns on Bebe."

"Got it."

I moved my head around hoping for either a liberating crack of cartilage or a suggestion on how to proceed from the boys. Neither came. This was one of the things that always disappointed me about the Imps. They always waited for me to suggest a path forward. It wasn't that they were dumb guys, they were actually pretty creative. The problem was that their talents only came through after I shoved them a little.

"Guys, my gut tells me two things," I said. "Sally was pretty ripped up about the idea that she would peddle bad stuff. It may be an act, but maybe not. Nate, you understand all that science stuff, so call her guy, Smartfarkle, and test the milk out. Maybe it's bad, maybe it's not. Maybe it's bad and she doesn't know it, or maybe it's good and Murrin is the trouble. Do you have an address on her yet?"

"Yeah," said the Lord, "Little crib in Salem County."

"Good. I want to get a look at her close up. Let me know if you get anything on where she goes, what she does."

"Okay. Do you know if she has a history with Sally?" the Lord asked.

"Sally says she doesn't know Murrin. That's what I need you and Freddy to do. Let's find out about old Murrin. What's she all about? We know she's Catholic because she shoves it down everybody's throat. Does she have some other thing going on medically that would kill her baby? Was there even a baby? We don't know anything now. Lordo, you can slap a homer on her car if you want, tail her. See about her medical background. Freddy, check our database, look for criminal stuff, maybe use your way with women to get close to her."

"Way with women? What the hell?" the Lord said.

"C'mon, Lordo, you know how Freddy is with women," I said. "Hell, my theory is that the guy's straight and this whole gay thing is his . . . hook or something."

"No-no-no, my dear boydogs, I is what I is, and I keep all my girlyparts to myself, I don't have to go trolling for the fair gender. I'm like the Saudi Arabia of estrogen reserves, baby. It's how God made me."

"That's foul," Nate the Great said. "I can't take it when you start talking like that." Nate pinched his smallish lips together and neatened his goatee, which made him look a bit prissy himself.

"Then go do some plastic surgery, Nate" Teapot Freddy said. "Oh, wait, you can't, you lost your license because you gambled your . . ."

"Enough, guys," I said. "Look, Nate, I'm still weird about Sally. Give some thought to how you can look at her surgery."

"She could have had that done anywhere in the world," Nate said.

"Just start thinking about it, okay? Lordo, I want to go back to Naturale's with you one night soon. Something's bothering me."

"What?"

"Crickets. I heard crickets."

"So?" the Lord said. He ran his fingers through his Grand Funk Railroad hair and left it tousled.

"They're night creatures. They don't make noise in the day. I asked a few people there about the sounds, and they wouldn't say anything. Even this muscleman clammed up."

"So?" the Lord repeated. "What does that tell you?"

"Fear, boydog." Teapot Freddy interjected.

"What about the slick chick from this morning. Marty Collins?" I asked.

Nate the Great said, "She knows we are banking her con." At the moment, I had only a glimmer of an idea of how she might be used, but nothing more.

I must have been wearing a mask of discontent, because Teapot Freddy piped up with: "Now, now! Tend to your *bashert,* Jackie Boy, and don't let Dirky Lips muck you up with his hair gel." *Bashert* was a Yiddish word referring to one's destiny. The Teapot was alluding to Angela Vanni, who he had been razzing me about for years. He had probably overheard the word being used by his clientele from his salon days. Teapot Freddy himself was Irish.

Angela Vanni managed to be a low- and high-maintenance client at the same time. She never asked for much, and seemed to be content with every progress report and invoice I had ever sent her. While the notoriously provincial and snobbish Philadelphia-area business community sneered at her ascent, no one denied that she was a very competent businesswoman.

But Angela's confidence in conventional management obscured what I found to be an astonishing naïveté about the sharp edges of her business. She talked M.B.A. talk, which was probably why she had that robot, Dirk Romella, around. Despite her clean record, it was widely assumed that Angela and her younger brother Chris had learned a larcenous thing or two from their Mafioso father, Mario. I wasn't so sure. Popular culture took its gangland instruction from *The Godfather,* where, despite perfunctory nods to legitimacy, the family business always stayed crooked, as if this were a moral strike of protest against a corrupt establishment. My experience had been that the smartest wiseguys—and Mario Vanni had been one of them—desperately strove for their children's legitimacy.

Then there was Angela Vanni, who didn't want to know how her security people dealt with grifters. She had me around to deal with that. Her only instruction was "no Pine Barrens stuff." The Pine Barrens were, legend had it, where generations of foolish and unlucky punks had met their ends. My personal belief, based upon talks with Mickey Price, was that there had indeed been some violence in those haunted woods going back to Prohibition, but the quantity of murders had been grossly exaggerated for effect. I had enjoyed trafficking in piney lore, winking and implying first-hand insight of deadly deeds all the way. It was good marketing.

Even though I knew the darkest aspects of my own legend were embellished, I walked through life fearing that someday I would be fingered for something awful that I didn't do. Angela had a similar dual nature—a hard and shadowy mystique surrounded her, but there was a punishment in her eyes that a sociopath wouldn't have carried so visibly. Angela was tough like finished mahogany—very solid, but you could scuff her up. Mario Vanni and Mickey Price had been tough like raw steel, and softened only on the subject of their children.

I couldn't deny being protective of Angela. She had been a good client and I had always felt an intangible sense that we knew each other's secrets, but I never thought to ask her out. Teapot Freddy wasn't totally wrong. Maybe I thought it would be rude somehow to pursue her. The emergence last year of that human power-tool, Dirk Romella, only threw another obstacle to whatever stop-and-go impulses I was having.

In the wake of my visit from Frankie Shrugs and his constipated killer ferret, Petey, I carried a free-floating worry about Angela. To compensate, I made my rounds of the Golden Prospect security force to make sure that nobody had been engaging in any Pine Barrens stuff. As I watched a hard-looking woman slam quarters into a slot machine and curse its impotence, it occurred to me that Sally Naturale couldn't have gotten where she did by being patient, and my pacing around the casino floor wasn't making a dent in her problem.

Hi There!

"These chairs are the worst."

I always liked to face down my targets. Perhaps it was lethal thrill seeking on my part—the kind usually associated with murderers that liked to attend the funerals of their victims—but I always felt I learned something from the encounter, however intangible. It could be the false empathy of a sociopath, the lip-quiver of an honest soul with a legitimate complaint against my client, or a hint of my subject's pedigree gleaned from a crooked tooth that would have never gone uncorrected in Cherry Hill but may have been overlooked in Deptford. I played a game with myself: After my intercept, I'd write down the one word that came to mind after encountering my subject. As my project wound down, I'd look at the word I had used to describe my first impression to see whether or not I was right.

The Lord tailed Murrin from her house to her mother's place a few miles away. Murrin honked for her mother, who climbed into the passenger seat of Murrin's Jeep. They proceeded to a nearby shopping center where the Lord said they had entered a Starbucks. I had been no further than two miles away from the Lord, and never within Murrin's range of view.

"What does she look like?" I asked. "I only saw the one photo in my clips pile."

"Sooo-eeey!" the Lord, hollered unkindly.

"A dainty broad, huh?"

"Mama Cass. Or maybe, Mama Ass."

"Point conveyed."

I lingered outside of the Starbucks holding my cell phone to my head, and pretended to be talking. I looked inside and watched Murrin—who perfectly matched the Lord's description—and her mother standing in line. When the two women took a seat, I went in and hoped to catch Murrin's eye. I did. I smiled at her broadly, outgoing people-person that I was. Murrin shot me a confused expression from behind a criminally bad perm. Her hair was blonde, but without the glamour associated with that color. You'd never call Murrin a "blonde." Sharon Stone was a blonde. Michelle Pfeiffer was a blonde. Even though Murrin's hair was essentially the same color, she was not a blonde. She wore a loose-fitting sleeveless shirt over her immense chest. That her bra size was probably a seventy-two triple-F was no asset. When a man described a woman as being buxom, it was usually done with the raising of an eyebrow or two, implication being he'd like to get lost somewhere in there. Not so, Murrin. Her breasts were humongous because she was obese. Sex was nowhere to be found. Her shorts—which she should not have been wearing—were a lime green spandex. Her eyes were small and jaundiced, darting around in search of an insult. Her skin was the white of a grade-school nurse's office, circa 1966. Murrin's mother was an older, smaller and more fossilized version of her, but with the creased face of a bulldog, miserable but resilient.

I kept my asinine grin going for longer than was appropriate as I passed her table. When she eventually suspected me of being someone she knew (my objective), she smiled back. After I passed her, I heard the suction sound that the roll of fat from her thigh made when she shifted in her chair. *Thupp.*

"These chairs are the worst," Murrin said to her mother. So it was the chair's fault that they didn't hold aircraft carriers.

"They're all right," her mother said.

I hated coffee, so I bought a bottle of water.

"It's hot out there," I said to the girl with the unfortunate overbite and forty-seven nose rings behind the counter.

"Uh-huh," the girl said, unimpressed with my attempt to justify my purchase.

On the way out, I graced Murrin's mother with my sincere face. "Hi there!" I said, all perky, a trait that no one that knew me would ever use to describe me.

"Oh, hello," Murrin's mother said.

"I think I know you from someplace," I said to Murrin.

The two women smiled, revealing little corn-like teeth. "Really?" Murrin said.

"Are you a TV person?" I asked.

Murrin's pale eyes brightened and her small, flat nose spread wider beneath them. "I've been on TV," Murrin acknowledged.

"I thought so," I said, as if this were a good thing. "Well, good luck."

"Are you on TV?" Murrin asked me, giving my Armani the once-over.

I chuckled, attempting to convey that I got the joke, even though there was no joke. "Nah," I said. "I just dress like this when I want to impress pretty ladies.

Murrin and her mother exchanged vague-yet-friendly expressions and waved goodbye to me.

When I got into my car, I pulled out an index card from my pocket and jotted down the word *possessed.*

Hollow Points

"Jackie, they're out there."

Look at this one," my niece, Emma, said, holding a painting she made in art class.

"Whoa, cool," I said. "Who is it?"

"It's you, Jackie." The painting featured a man with a suit and tie getting into a car. He appeared to be in a hurry—whooshing lines were shooting out from his body.

Emma was pleased with her drawing, judging from her ear-to-ear grin, which was a rarity. Emma was tall for her age, rail thin, with shoulder-length light-brown hair. Her small blue eyes were serious and knowing, and she had her mother's tiny, rounded nose, as opposed to the aquiline De Sesto model. She also had a perpetual pout that was going to cause me more than a little terror in years to come. Emma did not look remotely Italian; in fact, she reminded me of a girl you'd see at a prep school in Connecticut, not that I had ever seen one.

We were sitting in our living room watching *The Simpsons.* Emma always climbed up next to me during this time of night, which was sandwiched in between dinner and bedtime. We both tended to be quiet during dinner, I suppose, because we were decompressing from the day. Afterward, when it was time for homework or a few idiotic news shows, Emma unleashed her day on me.

"Why am I in such a hurry?" I asked, pointing to her picture.

"You always are," she said, very businesslike.

"Nah."

"Yes, you always have to be somewhere very important."

"Do I look in a hurry now?"

"No, not with me."

"Why do you think that is?"

"Because I'm your favorite thing in the world."

"Ooh, pretty cocky, aren't you?" I smothered her face in a sofa pillow.

"That's a bad word."

"What is?"

"The one you said about me."

"Cocky? It's not a bad word. It just means you think a lot of yourself."

"Don't say it."

"I won't, but why do you think it's a bad word, Emmalina?"

"I looked it up once and there were some bad words around there in the dictionary."

"Well, look closer next time."

Emma was big on looking up words. She kept a little diary, which she wrote in habitually. Sometimes she would write in it immediately after doing something with me. I know she wrote about me in there, and I very much wanted to see what she was thinking, but I never peeked in the diary, which struck me as being a sacrilege.

I held up the painting of me again. "So, Emmalina, do you think I have a beak nose like this?"

"It's not a beak, it's a little 'L'."

"Do I have an 'L' nose?"

"No, but it's better than how the other kids make noses."

"How do they make noses?"

"Two dots."

"Like a pig nose?" I pulled up my nose, piggy style. She mirrored this, but when I saw the bridge of her nose change color I pulled her hands down. "Don't do that to your nose. It's a beautiful nose."

"*You* did it."

"I broke mine in a fight years ago. Yours is too pretty to break."

"Maybe I'll be a girl boxer."

"Maybe you won't!"

"There are girl boxers now."

"There are, but they're stupid. Not like you."

"Why isn't it stupid when boys box, but it is stupid when girl's box?"

I didn't know whether the pouty mouth or what came out of it would kill me, but my future did not bode well. Not only would Emma have the kind of looks that would make boys gaze at the ocean in a perpetual ache, but she had the purple soul and wit that would lead every one of them to believe that she came from a period in time that they were too dim to access.

"It's stupid when anybody boxes, smartass."

"Another bad word."

"Sorry."

Emma put her arms around me and we watched Homer Simpson vascillate wildly between idiocy and genius until it was her bedtime.

I counted two of them—three, if I included the midget in the El Camino. My mother warned me that they were out there, an exceptional feat, given that she had been gone for twenty-five years.

Our Margate house was on the beach block that ran perpendicular to the main thoroughfare, Atlantic Avenue, which ran from Atlantic City in the north to the mansions of Longport in the south. Margate was a well-kept, but not super-rich town next to Longport. The lawns here were small, the back yards non-existent. Our neighbors' houses were about fifteen feet away on either side. There were also houses across the street, probably eighteen per block in all. It wasn't unusual for shoebees—out-of-towners—to pull onto side streets and change, even at odd hours.

I had been asleep, and felt the mattress tilt down near my feet. When I opened my eyes, I saw my mother—she looked just like she did before she got sick. "Jackie, they're out there," she said. Her straight black hair was hanging down around her shoulders the way it was when she went to sleep.

My heart galloped until it hurt, and I sat up. My mother had vanished from the bed. I rose in my jockeys and held my breath, as if doing so would muffle the twanging of the mattress. The last thing I wanted to do was wake up Emma while I was going insane. Everything in this house was old and creaky; every step across the floor groaned hellishly, no matter how softly I walked. The house creaked less in the summer months, but even in late spring it was chilly at night down the shore.

I opened the blinds at the front window of my bedroom and saw them: Two figures moving across the cool May grass toward the rear of the house and, freakily, a midget standing watch from the flatbed portion of a Chevrolet El Camino, the most hideous vehicle ever manufactured.

I walked into Emma's room and woke her up.

"Get up lovebug. There's somebody outside."

"Who?" she asked, springing up.

Like I knew midgets who drove devil-cars.

"I don't know. Go to the slip-out room. If I tell you to go, climb out the window onto the roof." Emma was insanely brave and just went. Her gazelle legs needed only a few strides to the slip-out room, which was a large upstairs hallway closet I had converted into an escape hatch.

It occurred to me fleetingly that I was in my underwear, and Emma was getting to an age where I should cover up around the house. But it was dark, strange men were outside, and her dead grandmother had been the one who jolted me out of bed.

Security was more than an element of my job, it was a disease with me. I couldn't call it a psychosis because, given what I do for a living, I had made enemies and had reason to take precautions. The hall itself was lined with shelves with books on pirates. One of the shelves was on hidden rollers that could be pushed back, allowing us to walk through a corridor and climb out a window onto the roof of the kitchen.

I removed the lock box from a dresser drawer in my bedroom. I set the box down on the floor, punched the code and withdrew my Beretta. I crept into the hallway listening for footsteps downstairs but heard none. I quickly peeked down the steps and saw nothing move. I turned to go back to the slip-out room when I heard what sounded like a door handle jiggling at the rear of the house. I reached up against the hallway wall and pressed the panic button of the alarm system. Immediately, a piercing horn began to wail, and I could see that the outside lights had begun to flood the small yard. The light added depth and shape to what I could see indoors which, at three in the morning, wasn't much.

Between the screeching bursts of the alarm, I heard someone—he did not sound American—say "Shit!" A shot was fired into what I thought was the rear door of the house. I flinched and almost dropped my gun. Emma shouted "Jackie!" from the slip-out room. "Emma," I said in a soft-but-panicked voice to my gun.

Where do I go now? Christ! I turned toward the slip-out room, but then I heard the door downstairs swing open and smash against the wall. A mechanized voice from the alarm repeated *"Intrusion! Intrusion!"* This was real. This was real. "This is real," I said aloud, hoping my mother could hear me. "Of course it's real, what are you going to do about it?" she'd demand.

Now I heard the footsteps.

"Intrusion! Intrusion!"

From my perch in the hallway I pushed another button on the alarm control panel, which activated a stadium-strength light at the top of the stairs, aimed downward. The light, along with a few other security goodies, had been installed by a former Secret Service psychological-operations guy.

I pointed my gun down the stairs and glanced quickly down the barrel of my gun.

A dark form emerged at the foot of the steps and then pulled back when he was blinded by the power of the stadium light—the purpose of the apparatus. I jerked my gun back beside my ear and stayed behind the corner.

"Intrusion! Intrusion!"

"Go," a voice raged from somewhere below me, and I heard a footstep on the stairs.

I grabbed the railing where it curved around from the stairs for support, swung around, and fired twice down the narrow stairwell.

Thup. The sound below. *"Ugh,"* a voice gurgled with it.

"Intrusion! Intrusion!"

"Jackie!" Emma shouted.

"Go now, dammit!" I ordered.

An audibly masculine voice groaned from downstairs.

I turned off the stadium light. The hallway turned black, black like I imagined Emma's mouth to look, wide open in terror, like one of those Peanuts kids when they cry. All blackness.

I flipped on the stadium light and reached around the stairs again. I fired, the bullet not landing anywhere that I could determine. I saw one man on the floor gasping as he looked down at his chest. Another man stood over him, appearing bewildered.

"Fucker!" the second man shrieked. *Fah-ker.*

As I caught my breath I thought, *Why the hell are you pissed off at me? You're pissed that I shot back?*

A shot came back up as I hid behind the staircase wall. The returned shot had gone through the wall at the side of the stairs and emerged, gaping, out the other end of the upstairs wall beside me. Gaping? The hole was softball size. They were using hollow point bullets. *Hollow points!* These boys had come to kill, not rob or frighten. It's real. It's real.

I turned and saw that the bullet had passed into the opposite hallway wall—the one outside of slip-out room. Where Emma was. I couldn't tell if it had gone through. No sound was coming from the room.

Something snapped. The newspapers always used that term about "normal guys" who shoot up churches. Now I felt it within myself. I actually heard a clicking sound, a shifting of some gear in my brain.

I banged the stadium light switch off, reached around the stairs and fired three times, screaming a madman's gibberish: *"Goddamned farce!"* Two pops and an absorbed *thup.*

"Intrusion! Intrusion!"

"Aaa!" the second voice screamed. Then I heard furious footsteps going through the dining room toward the back of the house. I heard the slip-out room window yawn open somewhere behind me. I knew at least one of them was down.

I ran down the hall and pushed the bookcase open.

"Jackie!" Emma said when she saw me. She was outside on the roof.

"Are you okay?"

"Uh-huh!"

Like an air-raid horn, the alarm wailed into the night.

I edged the bookshelf/wall closed behind me and climbed out the window. A backup surge of adrenaline was released into my bloodstream: Emma moved toward me.

"Down! Stay down!" I pushed her down hard. I saw lights go on in several nearby houses, but no human beings.

I crouched on the edge of the roof and looked down. The back door was open, but no one stood there. I crawled on my knees around the perimeter of the roof, the shingles cutting up my legs. Nobody. Nothing down there.

She began hugging the roof against the house. Her legs were pointed back as if she were on the wing of a jet during takeoff. Her back was rising and falling with her labored breathing. Emma's bare legs were sticking out of her flannel nightgown and into a puddle of water.

"I'm cold," Emma said.

When I got around to the third wall atop the roof, I heard wheezing. I rose and saw him beside the carport where there was a lone bulb illuminating the space around my truck. The prick was hyperventilating and half-crying as he jerked his head from side to side. I couldn't tell if he had been hit. It never dawns on killers that their targets might shoot back, clothed or not. This guy was young, late twenties, and he wore all black with a knit cap. He had a scruffy beard and long blond hair dangling at his shoulders.

"What the hell's going on out there?" a male voice shouted in the night. It came from one of my neighbor's houses behind me.

I could see out of my peripheral vision that the filth below me had heard Emma's voice and glanced upward. He titled his head to the side momentarily puzzled by my near-nakedness. He raised his gun toward me. I fired three times down into him. I did not feel the kick of the gun. It was as if the bullets had come straight from my fingertips. As he fell, he fired once, shattering glass from a window above where Emma clung to the shingles. I studied the man and thought he might be moving, however slightly. With a two-handed grip, I aimed my Beretta at his head and fired until it rolled onto its side. I saw the red circle form on his cheekbone.

"I'm calling the cops!" I heard my neighbor yell.

The El Camino at the front of the house peeled away.

I turned toward Emma. Gone. On the far side of the roof, I saw eight worms wiggling on the edge. I made it over in two leaps, bent over to grab Emma's wrists below the wiggling worms, her fingers.

"I got you," I said.

Emma's blue lips were tightening against her chattering teeth, and graduated into an eerily peaceful grin, as if her dangling off the edge of the earth had been a destiny she had accepted. At that moment, I reached a medical understanding of the word heartbreak because that's what I was feeling, my heart ripping apart like a loaf of sourdough.

"I know you do, Jackie," she said.

I pulled Emma up from a fall she did not deserve. A brave neighbor, Bill Dalton, ran toward our house holding a shotgun and wearing a bathrobe.

As a police siren grew louder, Emma was now comforting me as I nearly castrated myself on a gutter spout. I caught my breath and scanned the backyard for my mother, teeth chattering, my Beretta rattling against the house.

We Need You to Get Better

"I'm not the one called Disaster."

They had me flat on my back in a large, cavernous hospital room that smelled like ammonia. Emma sat on an orange chair writing something in her diary. She hadn't been injured at all, and was disturbingly serene, as if men with guns tried to kill us every night after *The Simpsons.*

My injuries were minimal—cuts on my palms, bruises and a little glass embedded in my shoulder, which was not hard to remove with tweezers. The mercurochrome the nurse sprayed on hurt more than the prod of the tweezers. Once I was bandaged, the nurse propped me up on a pillow so I could face Emma.

"What are you writing there, Emmalina?"

"About what happened."

"Why would you write about something sad like that?"

"Because it happened. Not everything can be happy."

"No, it can't. I just hate to see you go over such bad stuff."

"Why did those men hate us?"

"I don't think they hated us."

"Then why would they do that?"

"It may have had something to do with my business."

"I think you are wrong. They must hate us."

"No, Emma, I don't think that's it."

"I saw the man on the ground outside. Is he dead?"

"Yes."

"Is he dead from your gun?"

"Yes."

"Were there dead men inside the house?"

"Just one."

"Are you glad that you killed them?"

"No, Emma, of course not."

"You won't kill all of the bad people, will you Jackie?"

"What do you mean?"

"The other bad people who sent them."

"How do you know someone sent them?"

"I heard a car drive away."

"No, I won't kill all the bad people."

"You did it to save us."

"That's a brave way to look at it. I don't think most people your age would see it that way."

"Most kids would only be sad. I'm sad and glad."

"That makes sense, Emmalina."

"Are you sad and glad?"

"I guess."

"But you're sadder than glad?"

"Right now I am, yes."

"I knew you would be."

"You know me well. Do you know I love you?"

"Of course."

"You know, kiddo, I'm going to ask Papa Blinky if you can stay with him for a while." Emma called my father Papa Blinky.

"How long?"

"I don't know. Not too long."

"Can I bring my books?"

"Sure."

Emma thought about this, scrunching up her face.

My heart began thumping the way it had back in the house. I put my head back because I was getting dizzy. I thought I might be in for a quarrel about her staying with my father, but that's not what she had on her mind.

"What's God for anyway?" Emma asked.

I inched up on the bed. "God's the swivel," I said.

"The swivel?"

"Yeah, you know how there's a swivel on my heavy bag under the porch?"

"Yes."

"That's kind of what God is. When you hit the bag, it flies around wild. That's what happens in the world sometimes. Punches and kicks and things happen that make the bag go crazy. But the swivel up there always brings the bag back."

"I thought God was supposed to boss everybody around."

"I did, too, once. I don't think that anymore. Things fly around crazy and God can't stop all of it, and that's real bad. I fly around, you fly around, people do bad things, and that's not going to stop, Em. But that swivel's up there to bring the bag back to the middle, and that's all you can expect God to do."

"You don't think God's all that tough, do you Jackie?"

"Yeah, he's tough, just not about everything all the time."

"Isn't the swivel with the heavy bag nailed to the ceiling?"

"Pretty much, yeah."

"What if it gets too heavy?"

What if it gets too heavy?

And there you had it. Here I was, shirtless on the hospital bed, having just survived a massacre and thinking I was a philosophical genius with my swivel theory, and the Em tosses me out of the pantheon. I had no answer for her. I was back to being an aging hooligan. I smiled knowingly at Emma, but of course I knew nothing, and I think she knew it. I began poking at my shoulder injury as a distraction when Angela Vanni and Dirk Romella appeared beneath a sign reading "No Visitors." She had to bring Dirk Romella?

Angela's face was a mask of panic. There was a vague sunset of redness surrounding her coffee-brown pupils. Her wavy brown hair fell wildly across her shoulders. Normally, she had it pulled back in a more severe manner. Today, I thought, she looked more Greek than Italian, but I couldn't pinpoint why I thought this. Was there a formal difference? When she moved closer, and I got a better look at her Chanel suit, her professional sleekness momentarily registered, then melted away when she saw the red on the bandages around my shoulder. I remembered the photographs of her father, Mario, lying on the ground, bleeding to death outside of Olga's Diner, and her distress made more sense. Perhaps it was her father she was re-mourning for the most part, not Danger Boy, not Jackie Disaster.

"Hi, sweetheart," Angela said to Emma, booping her on the nose with her finger. "What did your uncle do to himself?" A tear fell onto Emma's shirt. Angela's tear. Whereas up to now, I had felt only rage, suddenly I felt depressed. What I did to *myself*?

Dirk hovered in the background, like the giant bat I blew away at the EnJersey plant.

"Angela, I'm fine."

Angela leaned over and kissed my forehead, which made me suddenly conscious of being shirtless.

"Buon giorno," Angela said.

"Buon giorno," I answered.

I made that face that people do when they strain their necks forward to check themselves out below the neck. It sent a sharp pain to somewhere unspecific. Here I was, having just escaped slaughter and I was worried about whether or not my pecs were toned.

As Angela stood beside me, it occurred to me that we didn't have this kind of . . . kissing relationship. Just because a client was a woman, you didn't run around kissing them. It just wasn't right.

Dirk stepped forward. "Was it a bullet that hit you, Jackie?"

"No, some glass shattered. Sorry, Dirk. The bullets missed."

"Jackie!" Angela admonished.

Dirk chuckled through his nose. "I didn't wish this on you, Jackie."

"I know," I said, for the sole purpose of not wanting to act like too much of a tool in front of Angela.

"Dirk, can you give me a second with Jackie?" Angela asked.

"Sure," he said. "You want to come with me kiddo?" Dirk asked Emma. It made me feel a little guilty about wanting to stuff the guy into a wood chipper.

"Not right now, thank you," Emma said.

Dirk left.

"So that's from glass," Angela said, pointing to my injuries.

"Yeah, it was just glass, uh, glass from the window," I said brilliantly. As opposed to glass from, say, a rhinoceros.

"You got them," she said.

"One got away. I think he was your boyfriend, Smirk."

"Smirk?"

"Smirk Oh-*HELL*-a. Oh, I mean Dirk Romella."

"What are you, in high school, Jackie?"

"Well, Angie, I have to pull stunts like this, you know, to get you to pay attention to me."

"I pay attention to you."

"Is that why you've been stalking me? It's like you're obsessed with me," I winked. "It's a lot of pressure to be the object of your fantasies. Em, get out of here for a minute, would you?"

Emma sighed, and left.

"Don't flatter yourself, Disaster," Angela said. "I'm only here out of sympathy. You know me, I like to help the wretched."

"So that's why you spend so much time with Dirkweed. Anyhow, one of the shooters really did get away. I think he was a midget."

"That rules out Dirk." Angela bit her lip.

"Maybe not. I saw Dirk once in the Golden Prospect's locker room. He's got some pretty small accessories."

"I'll tell him you said that."

"Tell him I said worse."

Angela glanced out the window. She was silent and appeared to be collecting a businesslike face. She pulled her hair back as if she was going to pin it up, or whatever the hell you did with hair, but she let it drop again.

"Don't worry that this is about the casino," I said.

"Do you think it is?" Angela asked urgently.

I wanted to say no in an absolute way.

"I don't know, Angela. Frankie Shrugs and Petey Breath Mints visited me yesterday morning."

"They did?"

"They were hinting around about . . . working together."

A burst of sunlight angled into the room through the window and brightened Angela's face. Mild crow's feet were beginning around her eyes. Nothing deep or dramatic, but she was a thirty-ish businesswoman now. When I met her, she had just graduated from law school and had a coltish demeanor. I was the grownup who knew how the world worked. Back then, Angela had walked around as if in a minefield, never knowing where one of her father's enemies had planted doom. This had not been an irrational fear—there had been mines out there, and one of them got the old man. Still, I thought, Angela looked stronger now, in a taut, athletic way. She didn't look hard and cynical like Marty Collins who, beneath that it's-hard-to-be-a-woman jive, had provoked her own detonations. Angela hadn't.

"When do you think you'll be back in the office, Jackie?"

"Right after Memorial Day Weekend."

"That's this weekend."

"Sure, what else am I going to do? I have these ruthless clients that make me jump through all kinds of fire hoops. Horrible people," I shuddered, aiming my eyes right at her.

"Don't come in on my account."

"You're the one I worry about most. Face it, you need me."

"You think *I need you?*" Angela asked. "I'm not the one called Disaster."

"I bet you keep a picture of me in a heart-shaped frame on your desk."

"You've been in my office, Caped Crusader. Have you ever seen a picture of yourself?"

"You hide it when I come in."

"You're all talk," she said.

Angela backed away slowly and left.

A few minutes after she was gone, the Lord walked in, looked over his shoulder, and sidled up to me. "I heard there's a midget," he said.

"There was," I answered.

"Not many of those."

"You know any?"

"Nah, but may have heard-a one."

Happiness is Relief

"Death brings out an interest in small clinical facts."

You alive there, Mr. Disaster?" the lean black man in the poplin suit asked. He took up the height of the doorframe to my hospital room where I was sitting in my underwear. This was Trouble Hartwell, former U.S. Secret Service agent, Camden-born champion middle-distance runner, and currently Atlantic City Chief of Police.

He got the job after I left the A.C.P.D., but we had known each other years ago when we were rising stars in local athletics. He had left the Secret Service to make more money after his baby daughter was diagnosed with cystic fibrosis. She was in her teens now and doing all right as far as I knew. Trouble did private-eye work for a while, and traded on his Secret Service background to become the youngest Atlantic City police chief in years. We were about the same age and often came into contact, given what we both did for a living. He always asked about Emma, impressed, I think, that I raised her. The Imps had taken Emma out for breakfast, then home. She was so strong, and it frightened me to think about how everything she had inside might explode some day.

"I'm alive," I said.

"You've shot before," Trouble said, businesslike, but I could tell he was concerned. When a guy from a similar background nearly gets iced in his prime, you put yourself in the morgue mentally. The nurse was applying dressing to my knees. I winced as the ointment stung where the roof shingles had torn back my skin.

"I'm not a marksman, but those guys weren't that far away," I said.

"Dead as roadkill. Both of 'em hippies or something. You did good, Jackie."

"I sit up nights thinking about stuff like that. Paranoid, I guess."

"It ain't paranoia if they're really out there. How's the girl? Emma?"

"Ten times tougher than I am."

Trouble grinned. "Sometimes the little ones are, the ones who have seen so much so young. You think this could be tied to your casino work?"

"Could be. I've got a million thoughts. Hell, why would a midget want to kill me?"

"A midget?"

"Yeah, the one who got away."

"Oh, right, my guy said something about that. We're dealing with a special kind of vermin, Jackie. Vermin who don't care about hurting children. Whether they intended to do away with everybody, we don't know, but even those racket boys wouldn't kill a man in front of his family."

I thought again about the hollow point bullets. "Like that Manson gang or something, Trouble."

"I can put a patrol car around your house, but, my God, this is some deal we've got here. We don't even know who those guys were. Did you get a look at 'em up close?"

"It was so dark."

"They didn't have any i.d. Can I ask you to have a peek at 'em now?"

"Sure," I said, as if I looked at shot-up corpses all day long.

When the nurse finished dressing my injuries, I put some clothes on and followed Trouble through a narrow hallway and into a mammoth elevator. When the doors closed, I became claustrophobic in anticipation of facing, for the first time in my life, men that I had killed. I breathed slowly hoping that he wouldn't see how anxious I was. After an impossibly long ride down one floor, the Hades Express bounced to a stop and, after about ten interminable seconds that convinced me we were trapped, opened up.

When Trouble led me through the double doors to the morgue, I was overcome by a powerful smell—pickled cerebellums or something. I braced myself against the puke green tile on the wall, held my nose, and then inhaled deeply.

"You all right?" Trouble asked.

"*Whoo.* Yeah. Not good at this. *Whoo.*" Yeah, Jackie, you're tough.

"I beg to differ, Jackie. I've never seen a civilian do what you did back there at your house. Never."

"It's hospitals, I think." I remember feeling similarly weak when I visited my dying mother.

I followed Trouble into a large square room with blinding florescent lights and colorless tile. A gaunt attendant with pockmarked skin stood in waiting. He reminded me of Lurch from *The Addams Family*. How in God's name did someone end up with a job like this? Did he want to be here? Maybe he did. A row of steel doors stood beyond a set of tan file cabinets, a veritable Stiff-O-Rama. Both men lay naked on steel gurneys in front of the vault, where presumably corpses bunked. They were both young, in their twenties. One guy was stocky and dark-haired with pasty pale skin that had probably preceded his death, or, put more bluntly, preceded when I killed him. He had two neat bullet holes in him. One was just north of his belly button. The other was in his chest, where his hair had been matted down with some kind of ointment. His teeth were bad. One gray eye was open.

"Would you mind closing his eye?" I asked. Lurch complied. "I don't know him," I said. "I got him on the staircase," I added helpfully. The eye flicked back open, and I flinched. Lurch covered the face with a towel.

"I know, Jackie," said Trouble. "We found him at the bottom."

"Young, huh?"

"Uh-huh. But that's not your fault."

"No. Guess not."

"How'd you know they were out there anyhow?"

"It's the weirdest thing. I woke up from a dream I was having. My mother was sitting on my bed."

"I thought she was deceased."

"No. I mean, yeah. She's been gone since I was sixteen. It was a dream. I got up, kind of wigged out, and I looked outside and saw them." I couldn't tell Trouble that my mother had actually warned me.

"You probably heard something that shook you."

"Must have."

Trouble looked at me like I was a mental patient.

I looked down at the gurney on my right. This was the hyperventilating carport dude. He reminded me of a surfer with his blond hair. He had two shots below his neck and one in his cheekbone.

"I don't know him either," I said, looking away. "It's hard to believe that a few little shots could put these guys down." I don't know why I said this. Death brings out an interest in small clinical facts.

"You didn't see the other side of 'em," Lurch said, borderline excited.

Lurch rolled the surfer over. The back of his neck was gone. "Looks like you got hollow points," he said.

I peeked then jerked my head away. I did not need to see my ballistic craftsmanship close up.

"When you care enough to send the very best," Trouble concluded.

"They were using hollow points," I added, defensively.

"I know."

"You know, Trouble, when they came into the house, one of them said 'shit' when the alarm went off. It sounded strange, foreign maybe. *Zhee-att!* Like that."

"Good to know, Jackie."

"Can we leave here now?"

"Sure."

I thought of Emma and how she was alive. I thought of something else Mickey Price had once told me that made no sense until now: Happiness is relief.

The Jersey Devil

"He's always out there."

The next morning, I had just gotten Emma off to school when the phone rang. I picked it up after the first half ring.

"Earl De Sesto?" the voice asked.

Jesus. *Him.*

"Yeah."

"It's Count Smartfarkle."

"Yeah, Count."

"We heard about what happened. Sally's quite crestfallen. Are you all right?"

"A little banged up, but I'm okay." I wondered how the hell the Naturale crowd knew about what had happened to me. It hadn't made the papers.

"Thank goodness. Oh, thank goodness. Sally wants to drive down to see you."

"That's all right. No need."

"No, she insists. Will you be at your home?"

"Yeah."

"We'll be there. What's the address?"

I gave him the address of Villa Disaster.

After disembarking from the tanker-sized Lincoln Navigator, Sally and Count Smartfarkle climbed up the front stairs where I was sitting on the porch. Both the Count and Sally were carrying a basket of food from Naturale's Earth.

After saying my obligatory but sincere you-shouldn't-haves, and setting down the baskets, the Count admired my shirt, which was a short-sleeved sweater Emma got me last Father's Day. Some of my dressings and medical wraps were visible.

"That's a wonderful shirt," Count Smartfarke said. "Is that cashmere?" He felt the sleeve around my bicep with his dry little hot dog fingers.

"It's a rare cashmere, actually, imported from Douchebagistan." I said this quickly and with great pride.

"Really? And where is that?"

"About an hour's flight out of Ufarta. I had business a few years ago with the Douchey government."

"I see."

Sally covered her mouth and asked Count Smartfarkle if he minded if the two of us spoke on the beach. He sat down in one of our porch chairs and fiddled with some of his papers he had in his breast pocket.

Sally and I walked outside onto the seawall. She wasn't wearing any makeup and her face looked like a tabletop puzzle still in progress.

"Count Smartfarkle doesn't know how to take you," Sally said. "He thinks you're serious."

"I'm a very serious man."

"You want people to think so. You're like a gremlin or something."

"You didn't have to come down here, Sally."

"I must be honest with you, Jackie, I'm very worried."

"About me?"

"Well, sure, but . . . about getting involved with this whole thing."

"About getting involved with me?"

"It's not that. It's that, I don't know, it all seems so dangerous. Things that we do could backfire."

"This is no time to dance around your concerns, Sally. You're afraid to work with me."

"I am concerned, yes."

"Do you think I'm a bad guy?"

"You're bad, but not *bad* bad."

"Oh, no, Sally, I'm very bad."

Sally laughed. "I thought you'd try to convince me that you weren't bad."

"I want to work with you Sally, but there's something you have to understand."

"What is that?"

"You may be up against some *really* bad people, the kind of people who do things like what just happened to me. It's not a risk-free proposition."

Suddenly, Sally started to cry. I didn't know what to do. I had known this woman all of forty-eight hours. She was a client. Did I hug a new client? Angela had just kissed me on the forehead. What, were we in Hollywood all of a sudden? I couldn't ignore Sally. I put my hands on her shoulders. It was a stiff gesture, but it was the only one I could summon. She took this cue and hugged me, hard and bawling.

"Oh, Jackie!" she cried, "He's always out there."

"Who's always out there?"

"In the woods. You know," she whispered.

"No, Sally, I don't know."

She took out a tissue and dabbed her eyes beneath her Onassis Sunglasses. "You'll laugh, son. You'll just laugh."

"I believe in evil, Sally. I know it's out there. I'm already sold."

"That's what I mean, then. The Jersey Devil," she cackled falsely.

"Call him whatever you'd like. I'm okay with it."

Sally cupped my face in her tiny hands. "Then you'll protect me?"

"I'll find who is behind all of this. What happened to me, to you, whether it's connected or not. Unless you want to pull the plug right now. I'll send you a bill and we'll part ways, honest."

"And you'll protect me, right, Jackie?" she demanded, not hearing my withdraw proposal.

Thou art the man, I thought.

"Yes, Sally."

She hugged me with phenomenal strength. It was more than the clinging of a frightened client; it was the embrace of someone who also felt guilty, someone who suspected that hiring me may have been interpreted by someone heinous as an act of war.

"Okay, then. We'll keep going," Sally said.

As soon as Sally left, I did something that I haven't done in many years: I took a nap at home on a weekday. The sheets were cold and I liked the feeling because I could measure my comfort by how warm they became the longer I rested. Sleep came quickly, but so did the same dream I had been having for a long time.

Habit and sex were not two concepts that had coupled particularly well in my actual life, but ever since I took on Angela Vanni as a client, the fantasy arrived reliably as the sheets warmed. It always begins with Angela and me talking on the sofa in her office. She confesses her longstanding preoccupation with me and makes a tender remark about the boxing scar near my eye. Somehow, we end up in a shower adjacent to her office. I think of a line from my favorite Elvis Costello song—"*her body moves with malice*—because she is both toned from exercise, and soft, the way women were in the James Bond films made in the 1960s. The water against Angela's lips gives them a swollen look, like a Tahitian goddess beneath a waterfall. I had expected her to be more passive, and begin kissing her harder than she is kissing me. After the shower, we end up in a room that looks a lot like the bedroom I had as a kid, and we're doing stuff in there that may not technically be legal in some counties in the South. Things are going well.

A few times during one repeat of the dream, Angela's dead father, the gangster, walks in on us. Mario Vanni is unfazed, which convinces me that we are all going to Hell together, so I might as well not stop. See, if he had beaten me to death, I wouldn't have gone to Hell because I would have been punished. Then, I wake up, hugging my pillow pretending that it's Angela, and fall back to sleep wondering if anybody is aware of how warped I am.

Every other time I had this dream, I woke up accepting it, the way I would an eccentric neighbor who lived next door for twenty years. Dreams were dreams, they were mind garbage. Today, though, my Angela dream took on urgency, a call to action. Perhaps it was because in this iteration of the dream, we were interrupted by the midget in the El Camino. It may have been the unusual time when I had the dream. Or it may have been because somebody had just tried to kill me. I had always had the dream during the night, which is infinite, tiptoeing slowly into morning. But having the dream during the day was a different thing. Night didn't tiptoe, it *fell.* Falling was bad. Falling was loud and final.

I had to stop suppressing this thing with Angela, Dirk Romella or no Dirk Romella. I couldn't continue allowing this mummy with an M.B.A. to remain an excuse for inaction. If I turned out to be another guinea suitor, then now was as good a time as any to take the hit. I never got anywhere in the ring by just dancing around the ropes like a hunk of *mortadella.* Teapot Freddy, the gonzo god of inner selves, was right. But what was I supposed to do, call Angela up and explain the dream? I couldn't. Not yet, anyway.

Greasy Lake

"I never knew there were railroads in the Pine Barrens."

Everybody at Naturale's was big on giving frigging tours, which, given my tendency to see everything as a red herring, gnawed at me. Why the great desire to show off all that was Naturale, but when I asked about the cricket sounds, everybody shut up? I was determined to figure out what was up with the crickets.

The crickets, however, were a symptom of a deeper concern. Clients that hire me always portray themselves as victims of a sinister outside force. Clients tend to self-censor, and the first thing that gets censored is their own complicity in whatever problem they're having. While they'd have to tell the whole truth under oath, clients reason, they are under no legal obligation to tell it to their damage control consultant. What that meant, in short, was that from time to time I had to take a hard look at my own client. Under cover of darkness.

Case in point: A few years ago, I had an industrial client that had denied that a controversial volatile chemical was used in the manufacture of a household cleanser. The company had publicly pledged that it had discontinued the formulation. Nevertheless, a reporter I trusted insisted that the company was lying, and that I was looking like a scumbag for publicly claiming that they had cleaned up their act. I became suspicious when the company beefed up security at its plant. Most of the guards were armed. That kind of security either means you're manufacturing sensitive stuff or you're hiding something. Concerned—and unable to get into the plant—the Lord and I staged a car accident with one of the company's delivery trucks, and ripped off a container that had indeed turned out to hold the volatile chemical. The company hadn't stopped using it; they had started to disguise their use of it. I walked away.

I had parallel worries about Sally. I figured that even if she wasn't making lethal soy milk, it was always possible that she was up to something else rotten. One way to figure out how naughty she was was to evaluate her security, the primary objective of tonight's little visit.

On the Friday after Memorial Day weekend, when the Delaware Valley was slowly migrating down the shore, the Lord and I crept quietly west to Medford Lakes. The parking lot beside the great Naturale dome was empty, save a few ancient cars with flashy hubcaps that probably belonged to the cleaning people. The whole crappy car-slick hubcap phenomenon fascinated me to an unhealthy degree. I suppose the logic was, "Look, we'll never have a BMW, so let's just slap some expensive stolen hubcaps on this 1984 Pontiac Grand Prix, and maybe everybody'll think we invented the Pentium chip." I was never sure whether I condemned these people out of genuine disapproval or because I harbored a latent fear that I was capable of such classlessness.

The Lord parked his rented Geo Prism in a space closest to the woods. There was no barrier to entering the parking lot. No security guards were visible. We were dressed in a full-Liddy—break-in gear we named after the Watergate burglar, including black jeans, black sweatshirt, black sneakers and socks, dark knit O.J Simpson decapitation cap, nylon gloves, night-vision goggles, a knife and aluminum knuckles.* I never carried a firearm on spook jobs. I used flashlights only as a last resort, because they were so easily spotted. Exploring the Pine Barrens isn't easy because the trees are so thick, moonlight does not survive through the leaves. While there were lights around Naturale's Earth, there were too few of them to be of much use. We stepped out of the car into the thick darkness like a couple of commandos ready to, I don't know, beat up a few campers.

"Hey, Jackie, I'm up for the caper, but you know, there are *supposed* to be crickets in the woods at night," the Lord said.

"But not in the day. Keep your eyes open, Lordo. I'll look for crickets. You check out the security."

Night vision goggles were great for seeing distances at night, the problem was that you couldn't see immediately around you. In other words, you could spot a guy with a rifle a mile away, but if somebody wanted to come up beside you and slit your throat you were hosed.

*Aluminum is much lighter than brass and equally as effective. When I was younger, the main benefit of knuckledusters was the damage they inflicted. At my age, what I really like about metal knucks is the way they protect my hand and wrist, which my doctor says are becoming arthritic from injury.

We walked close to the building. As we made our way toward the lake along a flat dirt path, I stubbed my foot on something protruding from the ground and fell forward into a clump of bushes. "Son of a bitch," I said under my breath. This kind of thing really pissed me off, especially since I scraped up my already tender hands through my gloves. My goggles were the only thing saving me from getting a stick right through the eye.

"You all right?" the Lord asked.

I hated that question so I didn't answer it. The strap for my goggles came loose so I took them off. I tried for a second to put them back on but it just loosened the strap even more. Screw it, I just wore them around my neck.

I crouched down and closely scanned the earth. I saw something glinting up at me. It was a metal rod. "What the hell is this?" I whispered to the Lord as I felt around the ground.

The Lord knelt beside me and shone his flashlight onto the same spot.

"Careful," I said.

We traced our flashlights along a metal strip and quickly noticed something odd: There was another metal strip running parallel beside it, and they were connected by a series of flat wooden slats.

"I never knew there were railroads in the Pine Barrens," the Lord said.

"There aren't, I don't think."

"Then what the hell is this?"

"Railroad tracks."

"Where do they go?"

"Up my ass. How the hell do I know where they go?"

"Should we follow them?"

"If they're railroad tracks, they probably go pretty far, or else they'd just move stuff by truck. We can go up a little ways."

"Wait a minute. A railroad goes into Atlantic City."

"I know," I said, "but it's much further south. Tomorrow, why don't you check out some maps and records and see what kind of rail action is on record."

"That makes more sense than looking for crickets."

"Either Naturale's is protected by the Mossad or they don't give much thought to security."

"Uh-huh," the Lord agreed.

We moved along the railroad tracks, the Lord still wearing his goggles. I was holding mine onto my head because the piece-a-shit strap still didn't work. We heard grunts in the distance and the sound of liquid being poured. The Lord and I held our breath. I could hear the thrumming of my heartbeat as I slowly exhaled. I turned my head trying to follow the footsteps while making sure no one saw me. I motioned to the Lord to crouch down the way I was. As I eased lower, my knees cracked, and the sound ricocheted through my skull. The Lord and I froze. I crossed myself hoping that no one else heard the cracking. We waited until the grunting stopped and the footsteps of the men to whom the grunts belonged disappeared into the woods.

"We can't get over to where they were," the Lord whispered.

He was right. There was a clearing in between where we stood and where the grunting men poured something out. There was too much risk. Besides, we didn't even know what we were looking for. All we could do was watch the greasy water roll away in the night toward Cricket Crest.

The Thing With the Milk

"It's only radioactive because the press makes it that way."

If given the choice between being dragged naked across hot coals or debriefed on a technical issue by a science guy, I'd go for the bag of Kingsford briquettes. I'm not saying that I'm stupid, just that the cord through which I receive information is very narrow. I respond to conclusive bursts of information and could care less about the process that produced that information. This is my way of saying that I was about to murder Nate the Great, who was here to debrief the Imps and me on his tests of Sally's soy milk. Nate couldn't differentiate between what he found stimulating and what was vital. The thing I had to train myself to do was to not pistol whip him.

Case in point: A few years ago, Nate the Great thought he could help me analyze why a roulette player at the Golden Prospect won so often. We sensed that the cheat had figured out a way to time the machine, we just didn't know how. Using a medical audio device, Nate decided to monitor the sounds made by each of the spinning roulette wheels in the Golden Prospect. At first, I thought this had been one of his academic exercises, until he reported that the machine the cheat favored had a higher-pitched clicking noise than the others. Nate the Great made his euphoric presentation, which was filled with graphic printouts of decibel this and nanoseconds that. He was really happy with himself, but there was one problem: I didn't know what the hell he was talking about.

"Nate!" I shouted, practically weeping, "Let me say this tactfully: *Who gives a shit?*"

As he gathered up his things, dejected, I started feeling like a shitheel. "Nate," I said gently, "I'm sorry. I just don't get it."

He rolled up his graph paper and frowned. "Well, if you don't want the guy . . ."

The moment I heard Nate say this, I sat him next to me on the sofa in my office and proceeded to ask him a series of questions. I used small words, rarely more than a syllable—for me, not for him. When he described a certain mechanism, I would gently ask him things like, "What does that mean?" or "is that a good thing?"

Nate the Great had buried his lead, as they say in journalism. He had been so focused on the gee-wizardry of the cheating scam that he overlooked the main point, which was that the wheel had been rigged with a governor, thus the higher pitched sound when it spun, and that the casino employee would have had to be in on the scam. Ultimately, Nate had been right, and we busted the cheats.

I was lounging with the Imps on the sofa and chairs in my office. We looked like a bunch of frat boys, our feet on tables, and our legs bent over the sides of the chairs.

"So, you want to know about the thing with the milk," Nate the Great said, after I explained that I wanted to know about the thing with the milk.

"Okay, Mr. Science, what kind of milk is coming out of Sally's udders?"

"Murrin says she drank Sally's soy milk and lost her baby. Soy. Okay, soy. Almost all of it is processed in the U.S. Almost half of that has some sort of genetic modification."

"Ew, gross," Teapot Freddy said helpfully.

"What does that actually mean, modification?" I asked.

"It means they add bacteria, other plants and shit to the bean," Nate said.

"They add shit to the bean?" the Lord asked.

"No, nimrod, they add stuff to the bean," Nate the Great answered. "They mix the bean with genes from other plants that'll hold up better to pesticides. They basically make a super bean."

"But we're not talking just Sally's soy beans."

"Right," Nate explained, "Almost half of the soybeans grown in the U.S. have some genetically-altered component. That doesn't mean what you think it means, though."

"What *does* it mean, Nate?" I asked.

"Broccoli and cauliflower are genetic mixtures. Stuff we eat every day is altered, so it's not a big deal."

"Do you mean to tell me that Murrin is saying Sally's cloned milk is unique when everybody's doing this genetic stuff?" I asked.

"Jackie," Nate the Great said, as if I were a total moron, "I'm trying to tell you, genetically-altered food has been a way of life for centuries. It doesn't mean anything. It's only radioactive because the press makes it that way."

"Okay," I said, getting hot. "Is there any disease that could be caused by genetic soy?"

"I found some studies about increased estrogen, stuff like that, but Jackie," Nate argued, "this stuff is everywhere. It's in infant formula. They wouldn't put it in infant formula if it kills kids!"

"But it killed Murrin's kid," I huffed, "or so she claims. If this is bullshit, why is everybody scared of cloned food? Is it people going batshit or is there something behind it?"

"Yeah," Nate said, "There's something behind it."

"What?"

"The food processors who don't use the genetic soy want the genetically-modified people to tank. They're in bed with the trial lawyers funding these scares."

"Any chance they're funding Murrin?" Teapot Freddy asked.

"Don't know," Nate said. "All I know is the chances that she lost her kid due to cloned milk are improbable."

"Improbable isn't helpful, Nate. Be clear."

"Okay, Jackie, I'll be clear, okay?"

"Okay."

"There's nothing wrong with Sally's milk."

Jackie Confesses

"You spent some time in catechism, didn't you?"

I paced through the offices of Allegation Sciences the following morning singing lines from Springsteen's *Blinded by the Light.* I mimicked that pained face Bruce gets when he sings, the corners of his mouth retreating back toward his neck. *With a boulder on my shoulder feelin' kinda older, I tripped the merry-go-round . . .*

I took the elevator up to Angela's office, walked right in, shut the door behind me and tried not to look at the door on the other side of her office, because that might be where the bathroom with the shower was, and if I looked over there, I figure that she'd know the whole dream.

Angela sat at her conference table, dressed casually, going over the floor plans for a new pool house for the Golden Prospect. She wore quirky, reddish wire-rimmed glasses that made her look like a Bohemian artist.

"Hey, Jackie," she drawled, her voice a little raspy. She brushed her hair over her shoulder. My chest began to ache and I wondered if I might be having a heart attack. I had read that, with heart attacks, one's left arm was supposed to hurt. I moved my left arm in a few different directions to see if it hurt.

"What's wrong?" Angela asked.

"Oh, I, uh, slept funny."

"Is it the injury from. . . ."

"No. I don't think so. That was my right side." I held up my right arm in the event Angela didn't know which one my right side was.

"Uh-huh."

I pretended to be interested in Angela's floor plans. "How's that coming along?"

"Okay."

"Oh, good."

"Are you okay, Jackie?" she asked.

"No," I said like a fourth-grade schoolboy who just had his lunch money ripped off.

"Would you like to talk?" Angela took off her glasses. Her eyes reminded me of Greek islands. I had never been to Greek islands. What the hell was I thinking about? Where was Jackie Disaster?

"I guess I have to." I sat down at her business table.

"Is something happening at the casino? More trouble?" she asked, concerned.

"No. Things are okay."

"Is this a personal thing?"

"It's both. A little personal. A little business."

She was looking at me like the sexy teacher every guy has at some point when he's young, but he doesn't understand why he loses thirty I.Q. points when he catches her reflection in those narrow classroom door windows. I think Angela was feeling sorry for me, in a quizzical you're-such-a-goofball way. This was not good for business.

"Okay, Jackie, I'm not going to bite you."

But what if I want *you to bite me?*

"Look, you may end up hating me for this, but you've been a great client and all, so I'll just tell you what this is about."

"Okay."

"I'm not working for you anymore. I can't. It's too hard to work for you."

Angela sat up drill-sergeant straight.

"Is it because of what happened? The attack?"

"No."

"Did I do something?"

"Yes. And it's a real problem."

"What did I do?"

Showtime. Get the boulder off your shoulder, Jackie, 'cause you're feeling kinda older.

"You've been sneaking into my room a lot and getting into bed with me. It's pretty damned pushy if you ask me."

Angela's head fell to the side. "I have?" She emitted an involuntary laugh.

I stood up quickly and walked away from her. I surveyed the boardwalk and the beach below us from her windows.

"I've been having these dreams, all right? They're always about you and we're . . . doing all this stuff, and it's been going on for a while. Teapot Freddy says you're *bashert,* and I have to take showers in the middle of the night because I'm breathing so hard, and midgets are chasing me, and you showed up . . ."

I love you.

"What's *bashert?*" Angela asked.

"It's this goddamned Jewish word for somebody's destiny, the person they're supposed to end up with. But I'm not Jewish, and Teapot Freddy's Irish, so how the hell could he know what's *bashert* and what's not, you're driving me nuts, and you think I'm a psycho and couldn't possibly have any respect for me anymore, so I'll totally understand if you fire me because I can't even look at you anymore without feeling guilty."

I love you.

"Jackie?"

"What?"

"You spent some time in catechism, didn't you?"

"Yes."

"In all the time I've known you, I don't think I've heard you talk as much as you did in the last sixty seconds."

"But what can I do about this? I'm not happy about this, I gotta tell you, I feel like I'm screwing everything up with the sex dreams, sorry for saying 'screw,' then there's the midget . . ."

I love you.

Angela's face fell into her hands and she broke up laughing. Between cathartic convulsions, the word "midget" escaped from her lips while I stood there, a disaster, feeling around my left arm to see if the heart attack was still there. Finally, in desperation, I knelt at Angela's feet and said, "I'm really sorry about this."

Her hands dropped from her face. I could see that her eyes were red and that her makeup had been smeared from her laugh-cry. "You spend a lot of time feeling sorry, don't you?" she asked. Then, Angela fell to the floor right on top of me. I winced when my injured hand rubbed against the carpet. Angela kissed my hand, and I felt like the coolest guy in the whole school.

Nobody Gives You Nothing

"You try to cure what you can't live with,
and, if you can't, you try to live with
what you can't cure."

I could have been wrong, but it occurred to me that Angela might want to spend time with me doing something other than getting carpet burns from rolling around on the floor of her office. After a half hour of making out under her table, I asked her to dinner. I had a vague recollection that normal people did these things in the reverse order—the dinner and the making out—but better late than never. Angela countered with an offer to make me dinner at her apartment in the Golden Prospect. "Up in the penthouse," she said.

My heart raced at the mention of "penthouse," because it made me think of the magazine that my late mother found behind one of my books on shipwrecks. There was a pictorial entitled, "Have a Little Faith." The chick in the layout's name was Faith. Get it? To make matters worse, I discretely, uh, "borrowed" the *Penthouse* while closing up shop at a newsstand where I once worked nights to raise money to buy new boxing gloves. When my mom became ill and died a year later, I was convinced that my depravity and her loss were connected. When I was old enough to drive, I even drove over to Brigantine and confessed to a priest at a strange parish, who did not disabuse me of my theory. It's a quarter century later, and I still suspect a link.

I accepted Angela's invitation. I called my dad, who lived inland in Pleasantville, to see if he was willing to spend the night with Emma at my place. He had called me shortly after the shooting attempt, and reamed me for putting myself in the position of getting shot. I apologized, not because I genuinely felt remorse, but because it was the quickest way to get him off the phone.

That Blinky Dom De Sesto lived in a town called Pleasantville was one of the greater ironies of my life. My dad had earned his nickname after attempting to box without his glasses in the mid-1950s. This led to him failing to see his opponent (a disadvantage in boxing), which caused him to get knocked out of the ring during a match in Camden before I was born. As he was being pummeled, Dom didn't hit back, he just blinked a lot, as if to advertise to the audience that it wasn't his fault he was losing, it was the fault of some witchcraft beyond his control. Blinky Dom had spent his long career, which, technically, was still underway, in the boxing world. He trained fighters, managed them, and ran a small boxing club in Atlantic City. In his spare time he listened to Coast Guard radio frequencies for updates on boating accidents. To my knowledge, Blinky Dom had never been on a boat.

Oh, and despite his residence in Pleasantville, my father was not pleasant. He was a despondent but harmless elf to the outside world, but a flesh-eating troll to the few that had had the misfortune to live under his roof. Only I had survived. Every encounter with the man was like a biopsy: I was a mess knowing a visit approached, and when we parted, I felt like the tests had come back negative and I was reborn.

He knocked on the door and announced, "I could bring peace to the goddamned Middle East before I could find a parking space on Atlantic Avenue!" He pressed his thick glasses up on his nose and inspected the family room for evidence of a conspiracy against him. He had a paperback on the exploration of the Titanic wreck under his arm.

"Well, you know," I said, making sure that the collar of my shirt wasn't tackily overlapping my lapel.

"Nobody gives you nothing," Blinky Dom said swatting away a patch of air that appeared to vex him. "Not God neither." Rarely does a singular statement summarize so universally not only one man's philosophy, but the core difference between that man and his son. My father viewed God as a failed dispenser of goodies, and was in a perpetual state of rage when one of his lunatic bets—on a boxer, on a horse, or on an investment—didn't pay off big. He tended to attribute a bet gone south to God, as if our Maker was primarily focused on rigging carnival games against degenerate gamblers. (God: "Screw Heaven and Earth, angels, see where Dom threw the dice and make sure somebody else wins.") While I believed in God, it never occurred to me that He had given me a moment's thought, as opposed to the devil, who, I was convinced, was stalking me. I assumed that if I ever succeeded in making something of myself, I'd meet God at the end of my life and He'd politely say, "Good for you," and move on to somebody else.

"So, you leave me here with the baby, is that it?" Blinky Dom said, wincing and massaging one of his temples as if he had a blood clot.

You killed your mother.

"I'm almost eleven," Emma said, overhearing.

"That makes you smarter than me, I guess," he said.

You killed your brother.

"I'm a lot smarter than you," Emma said. She knew how to handle him. Throw it right back at him. This was a good thing, because Blinky Dom had agreed to let Emma stay with him in Pleasantville where I thought she would be safer.

"Oh, you think so, do you?"

"My I.Q. is almost genius," she said.

"And what? I'm the biggest moron on earth?"

"Oh, yes, Papa. You're definitely the biggest moron on earth."

"See how she talks to her grandfather with such disrespect?" Blinky Dom cracked what was, for him, a smile. "Give your grandfather the moron a hug." He was equally unpleasant in his affection as in his anger.

Emma clinically obliged.

"So, you've got a date," Blinky Dom told me.

You killed your mother.

"Yes."

"Who is this creature?"

"Angela Vanni," Emma answered for me.

"Thanks, Emma," I said. "I was going to file it under None of Your Business."

"Vanni? The big guy's daughter? She's your client, I thought."

"I know. I had some guilt about that."

"Guilt? What do you know about guilt? Sure, there was that thing that almost killed your mother? With the thing she found."

This was the forensic difference between my father's and my take on the *Penthouse* incident. I thought I had killed her. He let me off easy with an *almost.*

"You're a smart little girl, Emma. I could do with a grandson. Someday, you'll get married and, poof, no more De Sestos. If your uncle could stop being selfish, chasing money-money-money and get his act together with a nice woman, we'd have somebody to carry on the name. And I'll be damned if my grandson will be a fighter."

I ran back upstairs when I realized I had forgotten my watch.

Angela had insisted on picking me up, believing that my hand wounds remained too serious to drive. I thought it was stupid for her to pick me up and drive me back to the Golden Prospect, but she insisted, and I didn't want to fight her. She scared me.

The doorbell rang and my father got it.

I heard Angela say, *"Piacere."*

My father responded, "*Piacere,* good to meet you." When I came back down the steps like a prom date, Blinky Dom was giving Angela a dissertation about me.

"My boy Jackie was a great fighter," he said. "Yes, he was. I keep all of his trophies down at the club. I'm awfully proud of him. I drive people crazy with all of the trophies and articles I show everybody. I'm sure your father was proud of you. You've done awfully well."

There weren't many great things about middle age, but there was one. By this point in your life, you know what you're not, and it's a relief not having to campaign in futility to better a self that's not getting any better. The ecstasy of giving up.

Case in point: Romance. I'm not a super-heavyweight in that department. *I could walk away from a murder attempt more pissed off than frightened,* but I always harbored the suspicion I was screwing up in the presence of Angela Vanni, who made me feel like I was in seventh grade. I dealt with it by sparring with her. That Angela did not seem to be repulsed by my strategy relaxed me a little, although it made me wonder what the hell *her* defect was.

Her apartment was ultramodern, the furniture blonde and sparse. The glass dining room table had been set up for two. This had been Mickey Price's apartment, which used to be decorated in dark, heavy furniture that had probably been stolen from the set of *Dark Shadows.* The only cluttered part of Angela's apartment was the section with numerous shelves filled with family pictures, many of them black-and-whites of Italian immigrants that she had probably never met.

"Do you want some wine?" Angela asked.

"No thanks, water's fine."

"You don't drink wine?"

"I'm not a big drinker."

"Are you a drinker at all?"

"Honestly, no."

Angela didn't appear to be surprised. "I'll get you bottled water."

She brought back two identical glasses, one half-filled with white wine and one with spring water.

"Andy in security told me you had a little talk with a hot-number card replacer," Angela said.

"We did. She won't be back."

"No visit to the Pine Barrens, I assume."

"Nah, we just threw her in the trunk of my car with a shovel and drove her around a while, get her thinking a little."

"No!"

"Okay," I droned, "We didn't."

There was such a nice breeze out on the balcony that we moved the place settings from the dining room to a table outside. Dinner was fusilli with shrimp.

"Where did you learn to cook like this?" I asked.

"I spent a semester abroad in Italy," she said. I envisioned Angela on a gondola in Venice.

"Never been there."

"Don't you find other cultures interesting?"

"No, I find central air-conditioning interesting."

"Ooh, you're awful."

"No, I'm honest."

Angela ran her hands along her collarbone. It made me wonder what her hands might look and feel like against *my* collarbone.

"Do I have something on my neck?" Angela asked.

"No, I was just watching your fingers on your neck."

"Why?"

"I like the whole fingers-on-your-neck thing."

"What about it do you like?"

"Oh, your fingers. Your neck-ular area."

Angela tried to suppress a laugh, but I saw her dimple surface. I reached out and traced my index finger through the little valley, and then withdrew it. "I had to do that," I said.

"You feel you've accomplished something?"

"I am a man of achievement," I said.

The breeze caused strands of Angela's hair to fall along her forehead. She blew the strands back up, extending her lips in a comic but oddly enticing gesture. The idea of something messing up Angela triggered a wave of speculation of all the ways I could dishevel her. She was usually so collected. The contrast between sleek Chanel-suited Angela and the very notion of an Angela who was breathing heavily, her heart drumming against my chest, was enough to block my sense of hearing. As she spoke, I heard nothing for a few moments. There was just the sight of her lips making shapes that I could not define. When I began hearing again, Angela asked, "One thing I wonder, Jackie, is how do you reconcile, you know, what you do?" She scrunched her nose as if she shouldn't have asked.

"My job?"

"Yes."

"I like my job. Just because my clients are businesses, it doesn't mean that they can't be hurt. I think the maggots that cause my clients' disasters are the bad guys."

"Well, sure, the con artists are, but when some big company has glass in their cereal . . ."

"What big company would *want* glass in their cereal? That's what kills me, this notion that companies have something to gain by hurting people. I just don't see it."

"You've never had a guilty client?" What was the shape her lips were making now? Trapezoid, I think.

"Of course I have, but more and more they're victims of a time when anybody who makes an allegation against them is treated like a virgin by the press. Not everybody that has a halo is an angel."

"What exactly do your other clients expect you to do for them?" Angela's lips rested in a rectangular position.

"They expect total cures, which is where they have it wrong."

"How so?"

"See, everything now is about wizardry. Nobody believes things just happen anymore. You'd think people have gotten smarter over the years, but they're just as naive to snake oil salesman as people were hundreds of years ago. Damage control is just the latest potion."

"So, you can't just make disasters disappear? Now you can't lie to somebody you've kissed," Angela warned.

"Not every disaster has a cure. Like you said, some clients are guilty," I said with Sally on my mind, perhaps unfairly.

"So, what do you advise?"

"You try to cure what you can't live with and, if you can't, you try to live with what you can't cure. I don't sell cures, I sell intervention. I sell little solutions. I try to ratchet up the odds in my client's favor. Sometimes I succeed, sometimes I fail, and sometimes I make things less bad. I don't know what else to say."

"That sounds wise to me."

"Wise like wise-ass?"

"No, really wise. Somewhere along the line, we were told that everything has a cure." Angela was really engaged.

"That's what America is all about," I said. "Go to the mall, buy a cure. If your marriage has trouble, get another one. Maybe that's not the move. You should know, Angela, your background . . ." I stopped myself. I sensed I was crossing a line.

"My background what?"

"How do you face up to your father?" I asked. There was no sense hiding.

"He was what he was. He took us straight, my brother, Chris, and me. I don't deny him, even though I don't approve of everything he did. I was called a Mafia princess my whole life."

"How did you feel about that?"

"Like you said, I couldn't cure it."

"So how did you learn to live with something you couldn't cure?" I asked.

"By diving into my work."

"What do they call that? Displacement?"

"Is that wrong?"

"No, actually. The things we do are reactions against other things. That's how you make things better, I guess. See something bad, build something better," I said.

"It works as well as it can."

"It can work, yeah. Did you ever talk to your dad about what he might have been if he hadn't, you know?" I reluctantly asked.

"Yes. It was one of the last discussions we had."

"What did he tell you?"

"It was incredible. After years of ranting about how he did it all for us, he just said, 'Angie, if I hadda do it over, I woulda been a wise guy.' I asked him why, and he said, 'Because I'm a wise guy.' We both laughed like it was a dumb joke, but I actually thought it was a pretty serious thing to say."

"Hmm. Mickey Price was a lot like that. Some of the low-down guys would talk about how the mob ran the world, and old Mick would just say, 'I'm a common gambler, for God's sake.' "

"My dad said that all his guys were two-nickel bums, including him. What do you think you are, Jackie?"

"A guy doing his job."

"Besides your job."

"I think I'm a father. To Emma, I mean. Even though I'm not her father, I think I'm her dad. Maybe that's why I never got married, because I'm not married to her mom."

"Her mom is dead."

"Yeah, women die on you."

"Men die on me, so there."

"Maybe we shouldn't think like that."

"You think how you think."

For dessert, Angela brought out profiteroles that she got from a bakery in Ventnor.

"Oh, geez," I said as she brought them out, "No thanks, I'm okay."

"No wine, no dessert?"

"That's okay."

"You're very disciplined."

"Or something."

"I'd love to know what that something is?"

"So would I," I said, sparing her my morbid fear of turning into Frankie Shrugs.

"Jackie," Angela asked, resting her long fingers on top of my knuckles. *Ooh, the first move is hers. Cool.*

"Yeah?"

"What is that thing that you can't cure?"

I didn't answer her. I kissed her on the balcony as Atlantic City melted into neon ice cream beneath us.

BOOK II

The Lord's Work

Those who make their living flirting with catastrophe develop a faculty of pessimistic imagination, of anticipating the worst, that is all but indistinguishable from clairvoyance.

—Michael Chabon, *The Amazing Adventures of Kavalier & Clay*

Victims of Sally Naturale

"The value of such a rumor was that what it lacked in credibility, it made up for in reach and resonance."

Sally Naturale had a penis, which grew as a result of exposure to the genetically-modified potions she used to make her gourmet food. Sally was the father of at least one of Jodie Foster's babies. Sally tripped on LSD. She worshipped Satan. A toddler got his head caught between the slats of a David Geffence and died. HyanniSportswear was made from the skin of aborted fetuses. Annen-burgers were made from squirrel gonads. Sally had a two-headed baby chained to a cinderblock wall in the basement of Cricket Crest.

These nuggets of horseshit were among the "Little Known Facts" posted on the website SallyNaturalesucks.com. The site was operated by a new grievance group calling itself "Victims of Sally Naturale." These victims included, of course, the ever-oppressed Murrin Connolly, and an assortment of characters whose plights included getting their fingers pinched in the hinges of Onassis Sunglasses and purchasing rotten Carnegie Melons.

A left-wing on-line nutrition publication called Silkwoodlives.com, which was named for the anti-nuclear activist some believe was murdered by energy industry operatives, claimed to have broken the mystery of Murrin's miscarriage:

NATURALE'S "REAL" MILK
FABRICATED IN RAHWAY

In an undercover sting operation executed by your intrepid comrades at Silkwoodlives.com, a vast fraudulent beverage processing system was discovered to be supervised by Sally Naturale herself. Comrade Schreiber of Silkwoodlives.com reverse-trailed Naturale's trucks from store delivery to their origin at a plant near Rahway Prison in Rahway, New Jersey.

> The Rahway plant, which is operated with the help of prison inmates, is located on the grounds of X-Rad Isotopes, the chemical conglomerate. X-Rad's waste chemicals were found to mimic the flavor of soy milk in our laboratory tests.
>
> For exclusive undercover photographs, click on our Death-Milk link below.

When I clicked on the skull and crossbones, the grainy photos popped up, one including a photograph of a woman vaguely resembling Sally pouring a green-brown liquid on the ground.

This was a textbook "flame," a false and damaging Internet-generated rumor. The value of such a rumor was that what it lacked in credibility, it made up for in reach and resonance. Within hours, Silkwoodlives.com was receiving tens of thousands of hits, especially from the proliferating cable commentators and comedians. One radio shock jock mentioned that it was his much-loathed mother-in-law's birthday, and that he had bought her a case of Naturale's Real Milk. While no blue-chip journalists picked up on the story, this didn't seem to matter. Within hours, political pundits were suggesting that the CIA slip Sally's milk to Saddam Hussein, a testament to the success of the flame.

Sally, expectedly, was overwrought and wanted to see me right away. Teapot Freddy and the Lord joined me for the forty-minute ride to Naturale's Earth. The Lord was eager to update me on some possible leads he had received on the attempt on my life, and the Teapot was planning a "covert interior designer's tour" of the big dome. While I met with Sally, the Lord would case the interior of Naturale's before the Teapot entered. For now, though, Teapot Freddy was in the back seat reading a Harlequin Romance novel featuring a cover photograph of Fabio gazing out over a burning orange sunset with a woman who looked like a slimmer version of him gripping his thighs. In other words, how Freddy wanted to see real life. The Lord and I talked things over in the front seat.

"So, Lordo, tell me more about your midget."

"A guy I know says he did a job a few years ago on a pawnshop in Deptford. He said he unloaded some knives on a midget."

"The midget was the fence?"

"Yeah, either a buyer or a fence."

"Anything else about him?"

"My guy said he's with some radical activist group called Pangea based out in the pines."

"What the hell would radical activists want with me?"

"Dunno. Maybe—if it's the same guy—he does contract work."

"Those two that I killed had that anarchist look, didn't they?"

"I didn't see them."

"Ratty-looking bastards. They haven't identified them yet."

"Ratty-looking, huh?"

"Yeah."

"Ever think they might be pineys?" Pineys were native Pine Barrens woodsmen. Some were quite normal. Others came straight out of *Deliverance.* The Lord waited for me to laugh at his absurd suggestion. I didn't.

Once I got off the ferry at Cricket Crest, Count Smartfarkle escorted me inside the house. Bebe waddled down the hall with a roll of paper in his hands.

"Hey, Jackie, just the guy I was looking for." I didn't know whether it was the comic style of his walk or the good cheer I felt when a rough customer seemed happy to see me, but I gladly extended my hand and said, "Hey to you, too, Bebe."

Count Smartfarkle stood back and Bebe excitedly waved his papers around. "Look what I got here, Jackie." He pressed the papers down on a small table in the hallway and pointed his stubby fingers down to hold them in place. "This here is the formula for our soy milk. And this page is the inspection that the authorities do to say that the milk is okay. You can have these if you need 'em."

"Geez, Bebe, this is great," I said. I didn't want to insult him by telling him that one of my guys had already been through the plant and inspected the milk, especially because he seemed so excited to contribute something. Having spent his career in his sister's shadow, his need made sense.

"These plant managers are a pain in the ass," Bebe said. "We don't actually own the plant, see. We have our people supervise the manufacturing of our stuff at a plant that produces all kinds of things. You can see it if you want. Anyhow, Jackie, we make good stuff. There's no way bad cloned crap gets in there."

Bebe held out his gorilla paws to hand me the documents, and I accepted them. "I really appreciate you using your leverage on this," I said, figuring a little gluteus smooch couldn't hurt.

"No problem. You here to talk to my sister?" he asked.

"Yeah."

"I'll get downstairs if I can."

Bebe saluted me and shuffled away.

Count Smartfarkle guided me to the "Throne Room." God. In the basement of the mansion, at the end of an interminable curved staircase, there was indeed a massive throne room. It was roughly the length of a bowling alley. The floor was pure white marble. The ceiling was about thirty feet high. There were marbled columns down each side of the room. Down the center was a crimson carpet with the repeating golden emblem of Cricket Crest—Lady Godiva riding a cricket and being chased by a couple of knights holding onto the backs of seahorses that appeared to have bagels around their necks. Sally sat alone on a raised throne wearing a tiara and reading an article about Ashley Judd's favorite curling iron in *InStyle* magazine. Neither Sally nor Count Smartfarkle found anything surreal about this, which made me wonder if I had unwittingly eaten mushrooms recently.

I shuddered because this place felt like a mausoleum. The antiseptic whiteness of the room validated the undercurrent of death, and I envisioned this being the room where Sally would be embalmed and lie in state in a glass coffin like Lenin or Snow White. Sally would probably have some mechanism to pump in cryogenic ointments that would give her corpse a futile but rosy glow.

"Jackie, did you see that web site?" Sally asked, looking up from her article.

"Yeah, I did, Sally. Your lawyers will be able to get it taken down in a minute."

"But it's already everywhere."

"I know."

"And you can't get the rumors back."

"I know, Sally, that's why they did it."

"So, they knew they'd have to take it down, but that it would get out?"

"Yes."

"Can we sue them?"

"Sure, if we can find them; but it won't take back those late-night jokes and E-mail rumors, which was the intention."

"So what do we do?"

"We track down the perps, which is what we're trying to do."

"I want you to get to the bottom of this, Jackie. Murrin lost her innocence the minute she got involved with this smear."

"We're looking into her big time, but we just got started."

"Do you know more about her husband?"

"We believe that he applied for a transfer a few months before they lost the baby."

"Why would he do that?"

"Don't know yet."

"Why wouldn't he take Murrin?"

"Would you? Anyway, we have to keep looking into them."

A sandpaper voice echoed from the hallway. "Who are we looking into?" said Bebe Naturale. He must have been out there listening. I cursed myself for speaking so openly without looking around.

The site of Bebe lurking in the back of the room only added to my feelings of insanity. He didn't seem remotely surprised to see his sister sitting on a throne wearing a tiara in a South Jersey basement. How could he be surprised at this point? He lived here and must have seen the blueprints to Cricket Crest. How does a client broach the subject of a throne room to an architect?

Sally appeared to be stricken by Bebe's arrival. I gave her a blank look. An order to clam up wouldn't have helped the cause.

"Oh, Bebe," Sally sighed, "I've asked Jackie to try to figure out who is doing this to us."

"Who's doing what?" Bebe barked. *Whoozdoonwhut.*

"The smear of our name, of our business," Sally said.

"Sal, you're overreacting, I think, with this dumb broad," Bebe counseled. "I just talked to Jackie and showed him our formula."

"That was really interesting," I said, widening my eyes at Sally, hoping she'd get the message that I didn't want her to let on that we already had the information. She got it.

"Overreacting? How can you say such a thing?" Sally was really upset. "These rumors are killing us. Our stock is at its all-time low. *You're* the money man, how can this not upset you?"

"It does upset me; but having Jackie to look into some whiny broad can make us look like the heavies," Bebe said, pulling off his Sam Giancana sunglasses so we could see the emotion in his eyes.

I don't want you scratching around Murrin, for some reason.

"Well, Bebe, I told Jackie to see what's behind this," Sally said strongly. I was proud of her.

"What do you make of this, Jackie? You think this is smart?" Bebe asked me.

"I do. We need to at least try. Most of these look-sees come up with nothing, but I don't think you should just sit and take it," I said.

"No, neither do I," Bebe said, trying to strike a compromise.

Yes, I think we should do nothing.

"Then why do you object?" Sally asked Bebe.

"Look, Sal, you've got this clean-cut, earth-broad reputation," Bebe explained, putting his sunglasses back on. "Suddenly word gets out we're ganging up on Murrin, we look bad. That's all I'm saying." He wasn't entirely wrong.

"What do we do then?" Sally challenged.

"I'm not saying I have a perfect answer," Bebe said, a tip-off by somebody who deep down wanted to do nothing.

"You don't think word will, uh, somehow get out, do you, Bebe?" Sally asked in a threatening way. She was sending him a message: Word gets out about our investigation, I knew it was you.

"I'm sick of fighting with you," Bebe said. "I think we ought to do some public education campaign, let people know about our formula, how we're inspected and all that. But do what the hell you want. What do I know? I said my piece. Someday if the *Bulletin* starts poking into us, don't say I didn't warn you." He turned to leave, and added, "Sorry you had to hear a family squabble, Jackie."

I wanted to experiment with Bebe. Besides, I was tired of being silent. I was hired to defend Sally, and I wasn't doing it now. "That's okay, but I know what I'd say if *The Bulletin* called," I said.

"What's that?" Bebe asked. *Whutzat.* "I'd admit it," I said, which elicited a maternal grin of pride from Sally.

"You'd admit it," Bebe repeated, as a fact, not a question.

"I'd admit it," I reiterated.

"Why the hell would you do that?" Bebe challenged.

"Because I think Murrin's dirty," I said. "I think this smear against Sally is dirty. I'd invite *The Bulletin* to team up with us and help us dig."

Bebe laughed. It was the first time I saw him laugh, and I found it to be the false laugh of a bureaucrat who had just been challenged—like he's taking the attack in stride, when he's scared shitless.

"You're the genius damage-control guy and you want to team with the media, the media that hates business?" Bebe said. "This is the advice you're getting, Sal? Why don't you just walk through Northeast Philly in a Ku Klux Klan robe, get it over with."

"I think it's a grand idea," Sally said. "That is, if we're challenged."

"Youse are nuts," Bebe responded, and waddled out.

Youse are onto something, and I better get my ass in gear.

I wasn't happy that Bebe had barged into our discussion, but I thought Sally and I played the bad hand we had been dealt pretty well. Guys like me operate best under cover of darkness, but when we're found out, it's usually best to challenge our challenger. The only thing that upset Bebe more than our investigation of Murrin was the notion that it could lead to an even bigger one. On one hand, he was being helpful. But when it came time to act, he balked.

Sally escorted me through the house. "He's not entirely wrong, you know, Jackie. This could get ugly if it got out."

"It won't get out, Sally."

"But what if it does. Those horrible reporters would love to say that I hired a spy to dispose of an inconvenient fat girl."

"That would be a good story, but I'm not disposing of Murrin, and our effort won't get out."

"If nothing ever gets out, what good is our program?"

"I didn't say that nothing would get out, I said that the idea that you're beating up on Murrin won't get out."

"You have that much control over the media, do you Jackie?" Sally rolled her eyes.

"I don't control the media, I feed them."

"I fed a tiger once on a safari. I'll never do it again. Even though it was sedated those teeth were something to behold. I don't want to get eaten, Jackie."

"You won't, Sally. Not by Murrin anyway."

"Something else, then?"

"We all get eaten someday."

"I understand that, but I don't want to be the lady that hired the cook that deep-fried her."

"You won't be. I'm very careful." I swallowed hard. Sally may have been nuts, but not all of her fears were. We arrived at Sally's sanctuary and the great window overlooking the lake.

"The view of the lake is nice," I said.

"I love it. It reminds me of Newport, Rhode Island."

"That's where all those big houses are?"

"Right. I lived in one of them when I was much younger."

"Uh-huh. We just stayed around here, growing up down the shore and all."

"Look, Jackie, don't worry about Bebe," Sally said, worried about Bebe, "He thinks he's a big *shtarker.* Just go ahead and do what we talked about."

Look Who's Got *Klee-es*

"This I will say, and heed me well . . ."

The Lord did his larcenous scouting of Naturale's Earth and pinpointed the suspect area to Teapot Freddy. He based his assessment on the existence of a centrally located series of doors, which, despite their convenience, none of Naturale's employees seemed inclined to enter.

Teapot Freddy's camera was in his glasses. It was one of the most expensive pieces of equipment I had ever purchased—about thirty large—but Freddy was so good with it that the investment paid off in a few months. The only problem was that Teapot Freddy, whose vision was excellent, wanted a variety of customized frames, which cost me another two grand.

Freddy, typically, agonized over what name he'd use as he posed as an interior decorator looking for ideas at Naturale's Earth for a client. He wore a blonde Olivia Newton-John circa-1975 wig and a fake goatee. At first, he wanted to call himself Hutch, after the TV series *Starsky & Hutch,* but he decided against it. He had been on a Scandinavian kick lately and had chosen the name Sven Pakkage.

The Lord and I viewed Teapot Freddy's line of sight on a little TV screen rigged up in my car.

The first fifteen minutes of Teapot Freddy in action was useless, intelligence-wise, but made for superb theater. In order to appear casual, Teapot Freddy cornered a salesgirl working in the section that sold bidets. He certainly knew how bidets were used, but enjoyed torturing Contessa Jane Delaney of Merchantville by making her explain the process of getting sprayed up the kazoo in vivid detail. Having established himself as a loose cannon, Teapot Freddy proceeded through a pair of swinging doors and followed a sterile white corridor. There were no doors along this corridor, only some kind of ventilation pipes. When Teapot Freddy turned a corner, an asphalt voice bellowed, "Whoa, Ace!"

Teapot Freddy swung around and his lenses faced a familiar local eyesore. Frankie Shrugs. I didn't shock easily, nor did the Lord, but both of our eyes froze open. My heart began to race and my fists automatically tightened.

"Who the hell are you?" *Whoduhelleryu.* Frankie Shrugs asked Sven Pakkage. His lip curled and he stood no more than three feet from Sven's face. Frankie Shrugs' bulging eyes filled the little screen. I could swear that I heard Sven's heartbeat through the audio system.

"I'm Sven Pakkage, the interior designer, and I'm looking for Count Smartfarkle," Sven said, aghast.

"Smartfarkle ain't back here. You ain't supposed to be back here." Frankie Shrugs moved forward again. My heart was still racing. The Lord rubbed his temples. We couldn't let Teapot Freddy get hurt, but we couldn't go in and blow our cover either.

"C'mon Sven," the Lord whispered.

"Lordo, we can't go in," I said.

"I know we can't go in."

Then I remembered. Of all of the Imps, myself included, Teapot Freddy was the most fearless, the most sure of who he was, which is why he was the greatest shill Atlantic City had ever known. Teapot Freddy was absolutely sure of who he was, even when he was being somebody else. That's because with every con, he was always Teapot Freddy at heart.

"Lookie here, Mr. Bench-press-a-hundred-pounds," Sven Pakkage began, "I don't know who you are, but in about three seconds, I'm going to show you some Kung Fu that'll make you sing to Quai Chang Cain for mercy. Then I'll drag your lame ass up to Cricket Crest and we'll have a little talkie-talk with Sally herself. *Howaaaaaah!*" he yelled, striking a martial arts pose.

After about five seconds of silence, Frankie Shrugs' guffaw echoed through the antiseptic corridor. The Lord and I joined in the release from our outpost in the car.

"Get the fuck outta here, Sven!" Frankie Shrugs said between breaths. "Bench press a hundred pounds, heh-heh-heh—I bench four hundred, heh-heh-heh!" Frankie Shrugs was hysterical, which meant he knew that Sven Pakkage-Teapot Freddy was no threat, precisely the message.

"This I will say, and heed me well," Sven Pakkage resumed, "Take me to Count Smartfarkle in peace and I shall spare you my wrath!" He appeared to have demonstrated a kick of some kind.

"Okay, Ace, heh-heh-heh, you win. Just don't hurt me."

"Very well then," Sven assured. "You have chosen your fate wisely." I could tell by the way the camera moved that Teapot Freddy had tilted his head up jauntily in victory.

Frankie Shrugs turned Teapot Freddy around, wiping tears from his eyes, and escorted him back through the swing doors. He pointed out a house telephone through the doors and instructed Teapot Freddy to "Press the O. They'll get you Smartfarkle."

"Can I ask you something?" Sven/Teapot asked.

"Sure, Ace."

Oh, no!

"Can you really bench press four hundred pounds?"

"Four-twenty."

The mafioso turned away and roared down the hall.

In the return ride to the shore, the Lord, Teapot Freddy and I reviewed the shock we had just witnessed. I could still hear every valve in my heart working savagely. This was unreal. While we had learned very little about the layout of Naturale's Earth, we knew a few facts of critical importance.

"Okay," I said at the wheel, "We've got Frankie Shrugs at Naturale's, and he's in a part of the building where he didn't want other people around."

"He seemed at home there," Teapot Freddy said, "Just strolling around."

"But security at the place is pretty weak," the Lord said, adding, "And the guy paid you a visit right before somebody tries to kill you."

"Very good, Lordo," I said. The Lord was a gifted burglar, but he tended to archly predict events that had already happened.

"So Jackie," Teapot Freddy said, pulling off his Sven Pakkage disguise, "Take it apart for your willing pupils."

"Sally sends me a packet," I began hypothesizing. "Frankie Shrugs and his animals get wind that she's reaching out for me. They pay me a visit to take my temperature, see what I'm up to. The skim gig was a ruse. I go and visit Sally and meet her brother. He's probably not happy to see an unfamiliar face, or somebody his sister hired without his knowledge. Bebe acts helpful the way most clients do when they feel like you've been dropped on them. He confers with Frankie Shrugs. I get back that night and somebody tries to kill me. The Lord and I spy on the place, security is weak. People who don't have good security probably figure that nobody'll tangle with them. They get arrogant."

"Sounds fair," the Lord said.

"Now Sherlocks," Teapot Freddy interjected, "There are a few questions we have to answer."

"Right," I said. "What didn't they want us to see? And there's another one: why does Sally lie about her background?" I said to no one in particular.

"What do you mean?" Teapot Freddy asked.

"When I first met her, she said she summered in Maine as a girl. Today, she said she had a house in Newport, Rhode Island."

"Maybe she's not lying," the Lord said, sweeping his hair away from his face.

"My narrow ass she lived in those places," Teapot Freddy said. "I once went there to a bed and breakfast—more bed than breakfast, if you get my drift—with an animal trainer named Cedric. Those aren't houses, they're hotels. Unless she's a Vanderbilt, she didn't 'summer' there."

"I don't think she did, either," I said. "Very odd chick. Very odd chick who's got gangsters in her shop, a hysterical Catholic broad who says she killed her baby, and railroad tracks on her property. Lordo, do you know anything about those tracks yet?"

"Not yet."

"Dig in hard on that one. If you don't find much . . . well, I've got an idea."

It was war.

Trouble at Lou's

"Somewhere down deep I'm still looking to be a star."

"We'll both have Reubens," I told the hostess, Beverly—known as Bevvy with the Chevy—who took orders from Trouble and me because Lou's on Ventnor Avenue was short-staffed. Bevvy with the Chevy, who had traded in her red Chevrolet for a new one every two years since the presidency of Calvin Coolidge, had been a restaurant hostess down the shore since, well, the presidency of Calvin Coolidge. She was the Yasser Arafat of hostesses, trotting across every restaurant on Absecon Island through bankruptcies, fires, walkouts, mob hits and changes in cuisine. Perpetually late-middle-aged, her trademark was a collection of Elton John-style, oversized glasses.

"Oh, dolls, they're excellent," Bevvy with the Chevy said. *Exslint.* She seemed really happy about the Reubens. That's what was so great about Bevvy with the Chevy, she was always enthusiastic, never bitter that she wasn't on the board of Microsoft the way everybody else seemed to be. She was glad that she had her Chevy, her job, and hawked her employer's wares with pride. This was one of my favorite traits in a person.

"How long have you been doing shifts here, Bevvy? I usually see you down at Murray's in Margate," I asked.

"Well, hun, I'm trying to earn a little more to go on a cruise with my sister, so these days I hop from restaurant to restaurant." *Restrint.* "You want soda or some water?" *Wudder.*

"Who's your sister, Patty with the Caddy?" I asked. "Listen to the smart mouth on him, wudja?" Bevvy with the Chevy said to Trouble.

"Water's fine for me," Trouble said.

"Sure, water," I agreed.

"Don't worry, dolls, these Reubens are the real deal. I don't want the police chief here busting me."

"I'd never bust you, Bevvy with the Chevy," Trouble said, holding up his hands, perp-style.

"I'm a law-and-order gal, huns. I've carried a little friend in my purse for years. I'm not a bad shot either. I don't take shit from nobody."

"Good for you, Bevvy," I said, "Now that I know that, I'll stop stalking you."

"You can stalk me any time, Jackie. Ain't it about time you got married?"

"Do you have to go on that cruise with your sister?" I asked. "I always thought we had a future."

"I'll pour a hot cup-a future on you if you're not careful," Bevvy with the Chevy said, walking away laughing.

"She's been here since at least 1967," Trouble said.

"I know."

"And, honest to God, she's always looked exactly like that. I bet she's sixty-five now. You know something? She was sixty-five back in 1967."

"When somebody knows your name, you always feel like a star," I said. "That shouldn't matter, but it does. Do you ever think about your track-star days?"

"Sure do. It was good being a star," Trouble said. "Somewhere down deep I'm still looking to be a star, break the tape for the cameras, but my wife reminds me that those sweet springtimes are long gone."

"That's rude."

"That's reality."

"I'm taking a strong stance on reality, Trouble."

"Which is?"

"I'm against it," I said.

"Very decisive."

Bevvy with the Chevy came back holding one Reuben, and another waitress set down another one. "Who's she?" I asked, pointing to the new waitress. "Rhonda with the Honda?"

Bevvy made like she was going to pour water on me, and the other waitress just walked away rolling her eyes. "If I ever saw a guy disturbing the peace"—*disturbinnapeece*—"this is it right here," Bevvy with the Chevy announced, pointing at me.

"I'll get on it," Trouble assured her as she walked away. "It seems to me, Jackie, that you wouldn't have called me here just to philosophize."

"That's not true, Trouble. I'm really very sensitive."

"You're a sensitive guy who almost got his ass shot off."

"What do you know about midgets?"

Trouble set the remaining half of his sandwich down. "Short people, aren't they? And they prefer 'little person.' Are you talking about the one from your house that night?"

"You're good, Trouble. Real good."

Trouble laughed. "What do you know now that you didn't know that night?"

"One of my guys says there's a midget out in the Pine Barrens who may be a fence of some kind. Likes weapons, may be tied into some activist group out there."

"Lot of wackos in those woods, Jackie."

"I know, but how many violent midgets affiliated with activist groups do you know of in the Pine Barrens?"

"I know there are a handful of communes around Lebanon State Forest up near Fort Dix. I can nose around. You understand, Jackie, that I'm a cop—and no meat-eater* either; I can't just report everything back to you."

"I appreciate it."

"And, Jackie?"

"Yeah."

"If you find anything out, you'll have the courtesy to let me know before you start playing Dirty Harry."

"I will."

"You know what Dirty Harry said, don't you Jackie?"

"What did he say?"

" 'A man's got to know his limitations.' "

*"Meat-eater" is wise-guy parlance for a cop on the take.

Shear Madness

"Then, of course, there's Father Dan."

Murrin Connolly got her hair done at a salon in Alloway called Shear Madness. The establishment was run by a hip, bearded stylist named Jerry, who had not gotten the memo that the 1970s had ended on New Years Eve, 1979. Jerry looked like, well, Jerry Garcia, and may have actually believed he was the legend's reincarnation. Everything Jerry said was *coooool.* An adequate hairdresser, but a disastrous business manager, Jerry was always looking for help.

Murrin's regular hairdresser, Bruce, had been having trouble getting into work at Shear Madness during the past few days. First, his Miata got a flat tire. Then his television cable went out. Once his tire had been repaired, somebody had siphoned off his gasoline. When Bruce got his tank filled back up again, he was called for jury duty.

Each of poor Bruce's tribulations was of course delivered courtesy of Allegation Sciences.

Jerry Garcia was relieved when Teapot Freddy happened to show up with his hairdressing portfolio. Jerry enthusiastically hired him on the spot and he was truckin'.

Teapot Freddy played Murrin beautifully, judging from their discussions that we recorded and analyzed. Freddy referred to her dirty blond hair as "golden tresses." Her tiny hyena eyes, the kind that mistook resentment for justice, became "stars." Her pasty, white-gray skin was now "alabaster." Her hefty body was officially "curvaceous," her snout of a nose became "pert," and her lifelong bad luck was romanticized as "your crucible."

Finally, somebody understood. Somebody who wasn't a threat. Somebody who had had hardships of his own, who had been misunderstood, harshly cast aside by a wickedly judgmental society. And, Murrin liked to talk, talk, talk.

"Tell me, my little Joan of Arc, who do you talk to? Who supports *you*?" Teapot Freddy asked Murrin.

"My husband's useless. He's stationed in Afghanistan now. He's in the Army," Murrin said.

"When did he leave?"

"A few months ago. He was recruited for a sensitive mission. They demanded he go right away."

"What about other family, child?"

"My parents are in the area. I have lunch with my mom all the time. My dad's not much of a talker."

"Men keep it all inside, the dogs!"

"My brother, Ryan, knows what's going on. He's not that way. He's pretty sensitive. He's a fundraiser, him and his causes, but he has a side to him that's sweet. Sometimes he just vanishes for weeks to do whatever he does. He was the first person I called after."

"After what, sweet love?"

"After I got sick from that milk."

"Oh, yes, that horrid, horrid milk."

"Then, of course, there's Father Dan."

"Father Dan?"

"Our priest. He's been a good outlet. Sometimes when my family is sick of me, he's the only one I can turn to," Murrin said, her voice trailing off.

"Oh, yes, it's wonderful to have a good clergyman. I couldn't get a priest on the phone even for last rites to save my whole life." Teapot Freddy's voice cracked. "You know, the way I am."

"But Father Dan wouldn't judge you. Maybe you should go to confession with Father Dan."

"Maybe I should try that. Maybe you're right-right-right. So you just go to confession, do you?"

"Yeah, I used to go once a week—but now that my heart is broken, I need to be in the church all of the time, even if it's not for confession. Father Dan knows what I'm going through and is always there for me."

"And you should, Murrin. You certainly should. So you go every day?"

"Father Dan is there almost every day, especially when he knows what a person is going through."

"That Father Dan sounds like such a love," Teapot Freddy echoed.

. . .

"So she drinks the milk, she loses the baby and she calls her brother, Ryan," I said to the Lord, thinking aloud. "The fundraiser."

"What a load-a shit," the Lord said.

"What's he raising money for, I wonder?" I asked. "See what you can find out on brother Ryan, boys. And I heard from my guy at Fort Dix that Frank Connolly applied for a transfer before they lost the baby—she tells the Fred-man he was recruited away."

"He may be involved," Nate said.

"Or he just hates her and wanted to get away from her," I said. "Do you know anything new on other fronts?"

"I've been checking the Port Authority and Jersey shipping records, Jackie."

"And?"

"Naturale's gets stuff from the Caribbean Islands."

"Right, Sally admits that. Lots of stuff goes through the islands. What kind of stuff do we know about?"

"It's vague."

"What does Naturale transport out?"

"Practically nothing."

"Maybe I'm an idiot here," I said to the Lord. "You're telling me that the Port Authority has records of Naturale's receiving shipments from the Caribbean, but Naturale's doesn't seem to send much out?"

"Right."

"The question, then, is what the hell are they getting, and where does it go?"

"Right."

"What does the manifest say is in the containers?"

"Food supplies."

"That makes sense, they sell a lot of food."

"Right, Jackie, but they don't process it in South Jersey. Their plants are in North Jersey, according to the packages."

"So they get shipments of something that they either do nothing with, or they do something with it that's some big secret. Who regulates that?"

"Port Authority, agriculture types."

"Is it possible that certain types of shipments are allowed to be vaguely labeled."

"Well, there's some sort of loophole for biological crap."

"What does that mean?"

"If something is thought to be dangerous like, I don't know, stuff that can be turned into weapons, special shipments are allowed to be marked differently, so hijackers and terrorists don't heist it."

I felt the Earth hurling through space sideswiping other planets.

"Jesus. If she's playing around with that shit, we've got a whole other problem."

"Yeah, like World War III. But it can still be other things. Illegal shit. Normal stuff. Don't go off on one of your save-the-world fantasies yet, Jackie."

"Okay," I said, shaking off my doomsday impulses. "Did you ever find out anything on the rails?"

"There's no railroads in the Pine Barrens. None on the maps or permits."

"When were you thinking of telling me that?"

"You're the big-picture guy, I thought I shouldn't detail you to death."

"That's a big detail. So there's a secret railway in the Pine Barrens?"

"Right. No records."

"Doesn't Swervin' Mervin still have that Cessna?"

"Yeah."

"Okay, book it."

"Where are we going?"

"Me? I'm staying on the ground. You're the one going."

"Where am I going, Jackie."

"The Pine Barrens."

"We're *in* the frigging Pine Barrens!"

"Hard to see the forest from the trees."

Angela's Recommendation

"He's a mind reader, is what he is, Jackie."

Angela and I were on my porch. There was a soft breeze that felt great between my toes. I was reading the newspaper. Angela was going over work documents. Blinky Dom had dropped Emma off, and she was inside playing with her toy horses. There was another poor-Murrin piece in *The Bulletin,* this one featured her giving a tour of the nursery where her baby would have played. It also featured a photo of a stalwart Frank Connolly in uniform that was taken just before he went to Afghanistan. Lovely, I thought, now the press is offering up a backhanded message that Sally's in cahoots with Al Qaeda.

"You've been reading the same page for a half hour," Angela said.

"I'm not really reading."

"I know you're not. You're obsessing."

"Look who's sitting in a nice breeze reading memos?"

"We're not talking about me, Jackie."

"Okay, so I'm the mutant workaholic, you're Miss Balance."

"I didn't say that. Don't bob and weave. What's on your mind?"

"It's this case. I'm on this Naturale job," I said, pointing to the stock photo of Sally, hands aloft, which gave the impression she was rejoicing at Murrin's misfortune.

"So that's what's been taking you away from the casino."

"I need other clients, Angie."

"I know you do."

No you don't.

Angela shot me dagger eyes that she tried to disguise with a grin. Didn't work; the broad was like her father. "Do you have some code of ethics, like psychiatrists, that prevents you from telling me anything?" she asked.

"No formal code, but, you know, I don't tell people what I do for the Golden Prospect."

"I appreciate that."

"All I can say is that it's a public opinion issue."

"That girl who lost the baby, right?"

"Right. Now, lots of people are coming forward saying that Sally's products did bad stuff to them, too. One minute she's the most popular person in the world, now everybody wants to kill her. It's strange."

"You don't think she makes bad products, do you?"

"I don't, Angie. There's something strange about Sally that I don't have a handle on yet. She's not who she says she is, but I don't think she poisons people."

"I think she's a lot of bullshit," Angela said.

"No doubt about it, but a lot of people build empires on bullshit. It doesn't mean they kill kids. Somebody's backstage fanning these rumors for some reason, and people seem willing to buy it."

Angela set down her paper and rested her chin on my shoulder. "You should talk to Jonah."

I took a long pause before responding. "Eastman?" Mickey Price's golden boy grandson.

"Yes."

"Why? He's a political guy."

"He's a mind reader is what he is, Jackie. You can investigate what's behind this Sally thing, and you'll probably find out. The public opinion aspect, though, you'll need help. You know, my father went to him a few years ago."

"I know."

"If it weren't for Jonah, I wouldn't have the casino. I don't know exactly what he did, but I know he did some polling that led to a big PR campaign. My dad loved him."

"That campaign got your dad killed."

"In his business, everything gets you killed. All I know is that he acted like a little kid whenever he talked about Jonah."

"Maybe you don't ask yourself hard questions, Angie. You don't like to look at your roots the way they were."

"Fuck you, Jackie," she said slapping her papers on the little bench beside her. "When did you get to be the Crown Prince of Naples?"

"I'm not. I just look at things as they are."

"Yeah, what are the things you think I ought to look at, Disaster? What evidence are you looking for to convict me?"

"Don't you ever look at some of the people who are from the same place as you, and they make you sick? Then you feel like a *strunz,* like you're trying to hide from your own people, which gets you asking, 'Who *are* my people?' Just because your grandfathers came from the same place, it doesn't mean you're brothers with some *goombah,* but you don't want to go around acting like the Dirk of Windsor either."

"This is your brain making noise, not mine, Jackie. I figured out who I was and wasn't a long time ago. I had to, given who my father was. You don't know what you want to be—a goodfella or a corporate guy."

"Bullshit, Angela. I don't want to be either."

"Well, Jackie, you don't know where you are in between, so you throw your baggage at Dirk and me."

"Ah, she rides to Dirk's defense," I said.

"I'm not defending him, I'm bitch-slapping you, *paisano.* That's your beef with Jonah, too, isn't it, Jackie?"

"I don't have a beef with Jonah. I hardly know the guy."

"But you know he's like me. He had a crook of a grandfather, and you can't take that he's clean now."

"I don't know how clean he is."

"Okay, Jackie the Monk, you're the only clean person in the world. Jesus died to pave the way for you."

"Jonah's all right, I guess. I shot the breeze with him a few times when he visited his grandfather at the casino."

Angela rolled her eyes and retrieved her documents. "His wife, Edie, is a South Jersey girl," she said, not looking at me. "They spend the summers at his in-laws place. They own property in Pilesgrove."

"Cowtown?"

"Uh-huh."

The Book of Jonah

"People need witches to explain why their own lives suck."

Every time I saw Jonah Eastman the thing that struck me about him was his height. He was not tall, about five-eight, but the image he burned in my mind was one of enormity. This was because I could not separate him from his grandfather, Mickey Price, who was a veritable troll, not an inch over five-two.

Angela wasn't entirely off base in her read of my sentiments about Jonah. I felt like an ass admitting it, but Jonah Eastman made me nervous. This may have been insecurity on my part, what with his Ivy League pedigree and legendary whiz-kid reputation in Republican polling circles, but I don't think that was it. What bothered me about him was that he was of two worlds, and I never knew which world claimed his loyalty. On one hand, I'd see the guy on television comfortably trading quips with other pundits. Then I'd see him out at a deli with his grandfather and these old-school gangsters, like Mickey's Sicilian partner, Blue Cocco and their fixer, Irv the Curve. While nobody had ever offered evidence that Eastman was mobbed-up, in the sense that he was part of the rackets, his comfort with the boys—Mario Vanni, included—made me wonder exactly what he was capable of.

Mickey Price had a similar trait—the capacity to quickly shift modes. One minute he'd be solemnly giving an order, the next minute he'd instigate mischief. Mickey used to carry around a little squeaker in his pocket. It was the size of a nail clipper. He would squeeze it discretely and it would emit a little squeak.

I remember sitting with Mickey up in his Golden Prospect apartment. He had a nurse named Odessa who helped him out practically round the clock. She was a huge black woman who could just as easily have been Mickey's bodyguard. Mickey lay back on his sofa and withdrew the squeaker from his pocket, and slipped his hand next to the cushions. He proceeded to make the thing squeak.

"What in the name if almighty heaven is that damned noise?" Odessa barked.

"I think it's from the air conditioner," Mickey said, glancing around with a straight face.

Odessa walked over to the wall, bent down, and proceeded to inspect the vent. Mickey began to snicker. Odessa's enormous ass was sticking up in the air, and Mickey's chest began heaving from amusement. I didn't know what to do, so I turned my head and faced the ocean. Mickey started squeaking again. Odessa fumbled her way to her feet and thundered, "Damn that noise!"

"Hmm," Mickey said, "I think it may be coming from that light next to the balcony doors. The electric current may be making it hiss," Mickey said.

Odessa hauled her freighter of a body over to the balcony and began examining the faux gaslight. Mickey commenced his squeaking, his hand still down by his side, obscured against the sofa's cushions.

"Mother-a-God!" Odessa blasphemed.

"Maybe it's the timer on that new Microsoft," Mickey suggested, darting his eyes toward the kitchen, feigning concern.

"Microsoft?" Odessa asked. "What are you talking about, old man?"

"The oven in the kitchen," Mickey said. "The Microsoft."

"Micro*wave*, you old fool. Microsoft is a contact lens you stick in your eye."

And so the futile charade continued—Mickey squeaking, Odessa searching, Mickey snickering like a second grader who had just cut a fart, and me looking in the opposite direction of wherever Odessa was so she couldn't see me laughing. This asinine activity was delivered courtesy, of a man whose obituary declared him to be "the most diabolical criminal mastermind of the twentieth century."

A subversive Jonah Eastman now stood with his back toward me, one arm draped over the top rung of the corral's fence, his opposite hand pressed against a cell phone he had strapped on like a pistol. He wore overalls, western boots, a baseball cap and a T-shirt, and was shouting "Heels down!" to his six-year-old daughter, who was posting on a draft horse. He also wore a Patek Phillipe wristwatch that I recognized as having belonged to his grandfather. It was a real motley look, which made Jonah infinitely more approachable than I had anticipated he would be. I don't know what I was expecting—an insult perhaps. Hearing my footsteps, he turned to greet me at his summertime getaway in Cowtown.

Only people from South Jersey are aware that there have been cowboys here for centuries. There are dairy farms, horse-breeding facilities and even an operating rodeo. I used to go to birthday parties here as a kid. Edie Eastman's father, who was part Lenape Indian, owned a lot of the land here, and had stables and a private corral of his own. Given that the place was a veritable summer camp, Jonah and Edie brought their kids up here for the season and lived in a guest house a few hundred yards from Edie's parents' place.

"Ah, the legendary Jonah Eastman," I said.

"It's true, Jackie," Jonah said.

"Do you think all your press clippings are true?" I asked.

"Of course they're true. I write them. Hey, Jackie, sorry if I don't look you in the eye for a few seconds, I'm watching Lily here try to canter." He shook my hand and smiled broadly. His grip was strong, his movements swift and hard, and I vaguely recall hearing he had been an athlete of some kind years ago. It was a shallow thing to admit, but I respected a guy much more at my age if he took care of himself. The thirties are when men start falling apart. When it takes you two months rather than two weeks to shed your holiday weight, there's a temptation to just give up, especially if you're already married and don't have to lobby to get somebody in the sack. I had never known that kind of comfort, and I sensed by the way he was stretching his shoulder muscles that Jonah, despite his marriage, was not prone to comfort, no matter what his circumstances were.

"My niece rides. Emma."

"You raised her, right?" Sadness fell across Jonah eyes. It was utterly sincere. The sunlight hit a few stray silver hairs on the side of his head. His vulnerability made me feel badly about the things I had thought about him. He was an orphan, too. Mickey Price had raised him after his parents died of something or other. It was a whole big mystery. Mickey and his wife had dragged Jonah out of the country for a few years when he was a teenager.

After college, Jonah went into politics. He did polling for Ronald Reagan, then he set up his own Republican polling company that was very successful, until his political enemies suggested that he do a poll that all but touched off a race war. After the poll was released, the right-wing Republicans said Jonah was too liberal; the moderates didn't want to look too lefty, so Jonah was out on his ass.

"I'm still raising her," I said.

"Someday—and I know the time's not now—you've got to tell me how you do it. How you do it *right*, I mean."

"I'm not sure I *am* doing it right."

"A guy like you, Jackie? Nah, a guy's called Disaster for a reason. A guy with a name like that wouldn't mess up a work of art like that kid. That's God's work." Jonah nodded, as if to convince himself he could do it, and turned back toward his daughter. "There you go! There you go! Way to keep him going, you little noodle!"

"You up for another client, Jonah?" I asked.

"You have one?"

"I think so. Do you have a staff to help you, or what?"

"No, just me, a Heeb with a cell phone."

Jonah led me up to the guest house and we sat down on the covered porch. I told him about the Naturale case and about the shooting.

"God, Jackie, I had no idea. I haven't been reading the local papers. I wouldn't have been so flip had I known."

"Don't worry about it. The police spun it as another A.C. homicide under investigation, so it didn't get much play. I just thought you should know there may be rough edges to this one."

"Well, Jackie, do you think revenge will get you into heaven?"

"No, but it'll give me something to do in the meantime."

Jonah laughed. "I think that way, too. It's awful. What do you think of Sally?"

"Her lack of shame appeals to me in a screwy way."

"I can understand that. At least she's honest in her desperation to be a player. I had a client once, a Hollywood type, who had me think of ways to keep him in the press by coming up with shtick to make it look like he was dodging publicity."

"Wait a minute. He wanted to *get* publicity by looking like he was *ducking* it?"

"Right. Shtick. Anyhow, I polled phrases like 'super-secretive', 'low-profile', 'un-Hollywood', 'reclusive', 'mysterious'. We wove those words into the lexicon with people in the community who owed him something. Before you knew it, he was on the cover of every magazine, talking about how press-shy he was. The strategy was, 'If I'm super-secretive, I must be running Hollywood.' "

"Was he running Hollywood?"

"It was like any business, Jackie—he was one of a handful of guys with power, but lots of guys run any town."

"Whatever happened to him?"

"He was knocked off by a younger, more super-secretive asshole."

"It's all about shtick, isn't it, Jonah?"

"Right. With your Sally thing, it seems like you've got a witch."

"Sally's not that bad. A little vain, but you know how these tycoons are."

"I didn't mean she's a bad person, just a witch, like, you know, in Salem."

"The witch trials, you mean?"

"Yes. Did you ever study those?"

"Just the basics. It was some crazy-ass Pilgrim thing wasn't it?"

"When they threw my grandfather out of the country I read all about the witch trials. I took a book out of the Ventnor library. I don't know, I was trying to connect it to what we were going through."

"Did you make a connection?"

"Not as much as I wanted. I wanted Mick to be totally innocent like the accused witches were, but I knew he wasn't. I always knew. But I learned something that helped me in politics and business."

"What was that?"

"People need witches to explain why their own lives suck. The average witch was just like Sally."

"I thought the witches were poor nut jobs."

"Eventually they were. At first, the accused witches were women who owned land, rich women. There was a lot of anxiety in Salem about which women would get the best guys and all that. This minister had a daughter who freaked out and started the whole thing. She was playing a game with her cousin and a babysitter, trying to predict who they would marry. They didn't think they would land anybody good, so they freaked out because they weren't rich enough. So, the minister's got a nut job of a daughter on his hands. He can't admit his kid's a kook, so he starts looking for witches. The first witches were rich women. Eventually, the rich women did what rich people do—they bought freedom. That's when they started hanging the poor women—people who couldn't fight back."

"So you're saying that Sally's not a witch, as in being bad; she's a witch as in she's a target."

"I'm saying that that's what we should poll."

"What's the best way to stop a witch hunt?"

Jonah shrugged. "Switch the witch."

Selfish

"Every sad family has its own brand of corruption."

Angela wanted to pick me up and do the driving—the injury thing again.

Blinky Dom was babysitting Emma at my place, because she needed to pick up some more clothing and collect some of her pens and pencils. He was reading *The Atlantic City Press* when Angela knocked on the door.

"So, where are you taking my boy, far away from his father?" I overheard him ask her. I was upstairs.

"Not too far, no."

"He's always got to go here and there. It's the way he is."

"He raises Emma, doesn't he?" Angela said.

"So he tells me. He's upstairs changing, him and his suits. He always has to look good."

"He always does look good."

"It's a selfish thing, I guess. I don't think much about looks, but when you're vain, you think about what you look like. I don't have that kind of selfishness. How are things at your casino?"

Angela hesitated. "Business is pretty good. All-consuming."

"Yes, business can suck the life out of you. You can't let it, though. Jackie always thinks about business. Sometimes it's too much already. You've got to look out for other things, like your family. When my son, Tommy, died, he only hoped that Jackie would be there, but business takes the president with him," Blinky Dom said. The president. As in Jefferson, Nixon, or Reagan.

I made my presence known by taking extra-loud steps down the staircase.

"Oh, look at you," Angela said.

"No, look at *you*." I didn't know what to call the suit Angela was wearing, but it was a real high-end number.

"It may be a late night, Dad," I said.

"Don't worry, I've got my things. I'll go to sleep in the guest room and won't bother anybody. Go about your business."

When we walked outside and past the window, I heard Blinky Dom say to Emma, "Maybe if those two with their fancy looks get together, they'll make you a brother." I snickered falsely, and allowed Angela to open the passenger door for me.

We went to a restaurant on the bay side of Absecon Island. The weather was right for us to sit outside and watch the boats bob along a nearby dock. I pulled out Angela's chair for her and kissed her from above as she sat. There was a middle-aged couple seated at the next table. The wife was carping at her husband about her "needs." He took it in passively.

As Angela and I listened to the harangue, I said, "Maybe that's why I never got married. You know what the spook in me thinks?"

"What?"

"He's listening to her yammer because he thinks it's his duty. He's going to go back home, page himself, make up some business emergency, and meet his secretary at the Econo-Lodge in Egg Harbor."

"That's terrible, but you're probably right."

When we were done eating, I took Angela's hand and brought her close to me, nose to nose. "What did you have in store for me now?" I asked with mock vulnerability. "It's early."

"Did you have something in mind?"

"I'm getting too old for diplomacy, Angela."

"What does that mean?"

"It means we need a place to be alone, and my place isn't available."

I held the door for Angela as she climbed into the driver's seat and then got in the other side. As we drove out, Mr. and Mrs. Needs left the restaurant. I sighed, imagining what their lives were like. Angela heard me.

"You know, I was thinking about why you weren't married," Angela said as she pulled onto Ventnor Avenue. "I was trying to come up with a theory."

"Lay one on me."

"It's just a theory."

"Go."

"A lot of men who become successful at midlife have some woman from their past, maybe from high school or something, somebody they couldn't get, somebody who didn't know he was alive, and now that he's made it and she isn't the alpha-chick anymore, she notices him and he thinks that just maybe . . . you know."

"So you think that maybe I'm waiting for someone who dissed me years ago?"

"Maybe."

"Nah, doesn't work."

"What doesn't work?"

"Those deals with women like that. They don't work."

"Why not, Jackie?"

"Because even if you can get her, you resent that she didn't take you when you were you—at your, I don't know the word."

"Essence?"

"Yeah, I guess, essence. You'd be with her, but you're thinking, where the hell were you when we were sixteen? You've got her on your arm, but uh."

I stopped myself, but I must have been wearing a wicked expression.

"You can curse, Jackie. Remember who my father was."

"Fine. So, you're with this girl, the one you couldn't get but finally do get, and you're thinking, I want to screw you, but what I really want is for you to go screw yourself."

Angela laughed. "You have thoughts that take hairpin turns like that, but you fish for a word like *essence?*"

This made me a little nervous. "Maybe I knew it, but wanted you to be the one to say it."

"Why?"

"It sounds better coming from you. You're prettier."

"Are you afraid that if you used the word that you'd sound . . . pretty."

"Not pretty, no. I'm all right with Freddy, guys like that. You are what you are. There are some things that I'd rather think than say."

"You're very good to Freddy, you know. He needs you."

"It surprises you that I'm nice to him?"

"A little."

"Why?"

"Ex-boxer, central-casting Italian? My father wouldn't have a guy like that in the same hemisphere if he could help it."

"I think of it like this: You're a little kid on the playground, right, and everybody's talking about sports and girls and . . . you're just not getting it, and you think you're a mutant because you've got this freak show going on in your head."

"And you sympathize with a freak show in your head?"

"Yeah, I do. Not the same show as Freddy, but I hated being a kid. Like in school, everybody was into tormenting the nuns, and I'm actually reading the Bible trying to figure out why Jesus is stirring up all this trouble and why God ices his own son. I mean, what the hell is that about? I'm actually trying to figure it out. Meanwhile, I've got Timmy Cahill and Pete De Marco talking about feeling up this girl or that one, and I want to punch their lights out for that kind of talk."

"Why did you think it was your job to punch their lights out?"

"Just my reaction, I guess. I don't know where it comes from. You can't help the stuff you think about. Everybody tells you to lighten up or turn it off, but the freak show keeps coming. I figure, if I've got this freak show and Teapot Freddy has this freak show, why torture the guy?"

"Why was being so interested in religion a freak show?"

"C'mon, Angie, around here? In my house, and the ass-kicking boxing way of life? Atlantic City in the seventies? The place was rotting. Guys getting a little under the boardwalk because they know nobody's walking above them because there's nobody there. Guys ferrying hash over from Somers Point. In 'seventy-eight, the casinos open and everybody's sneaking in to blow the cash they had. Or cash they didn't have. In the papers, the world is running out of gas, which has me freaking out. I had summer jobs working construction—restaurant repairs, stuff like that—after the casinos opened. Who runs the building trades? Little Nicky and his nephew Crazy Phil. It's in the water here, Angela. Look at our congressmen back then, those ABSCAM guys, strip-club owners who go to Washington to rep us. I should have just gone under the boardwalk with some Pleasantville skank and got lost in that."

"I remember that feeling, too, Jackie," Angela said, as she crossed Jackson Avenue from Ventnor into Atlantic City. "My parents' friends once asked me what I wanted to do when I graduated from high school. I said I wanted to go to college. One lady, Mrs. La Rosa—her hair was so big you could put a casino in it—looks at me and says, 'Why?' I looked around the room and said to myself, 'You're in hell, girl.' I couldn't just turn it off or let it go."

"That can be a good thing. I don't let Emma go. What about you? You believe in stuff."

"Sure," Angela said.

"I haven't been to Mass in years. I'm not religious."

"Yes, you are. You don't need to go to church to think about God. I think you think you're on a crusade. I think you see what you do as carrying out

God's will. You're a Catholic boy. You'll do business with the Devil, but you try to balance it out with faith."

Angela soon pulled into the Golden Prospect's lot. We got into a special elevator that Mickey Price had built years ago to ferry him straight up to his penthouse.

When the door opened into the penthouse hallway, I asked Angela "So, where do you fit into this missionary work? What we're doing isn't exactly pure."

"That's where you're wrong. What you have with your girls—it's holy to you." Her voice was breathy.

"How do you know I'm not boffing cocktail waitresses behind your back?"

"The very thought of it—and I don't doubt you have those thoughts—drives you into a state of mind that makes you ill. Like worrying about the world running out of gas."

Angela's utter confidence in her theory triggered a confession. It just spilled out of me. I told her about how, in the summer of 1980, a group of guys, including Nate the Great and me, rented a basement apartment on Baton Rouge Avenue in Atlantic City. It was a decadent summer, for the most part, with all of us having just registered for the draft. There wasn't a war, but with the Russians in Afghanistan and close to the Strait of Hormuz, the spigot for the world's oil, we were all nervous.

Nate the Great had a gorgeous girlfriend, a blonde named Janine. One morning, I woke up, and Janine was next to me in bed. In what was perhaps the most moronic question ever posed by a straight male, I asked her, "What are you doing here?" She answered in a throaty voice, "Friggin' Nate snores. Don't worry," she added, "Nate knows I'm here." And so, for the remainder of the summer, I woke up with a goddess next to me who I couldn't touch."

"Frustrating," Angela said, biting her lip.

"Yeah, Janine said I was a good sleeper."

"So what did you do?"

"There was a cashier I worked with at the White House Sub Shop."

"So you ended up with a girlfriend?"

"Not really. We were both paranoid about it for some reason. She wasn't somebody I wanted to show around and, it turned out, she was a Mormon who told me later that she was 'getting it out of her system' before she went on a mission. One thing I remember is how that summer, a Tom Petty song,

Even the Losers, was real big. It was always playing on the radio in the White House. I thought it fit the situation all right." I sung *"Even the losers . . . get lucky sometimes."*

Angela got the point. The whiff of scandal and damnation was never far away from the carnal thoughts and actualities of Saint Giovanni of Disaster.

Once inside her apartment, Angela opened the sliding glass door leading to her balcony. The sea air was cool and strong. It's strange how a person's senses have a memory of their own. The late spring air made me remember being eighteen, and how the exact same breeze had made me speculate how I could ever get to heaven when all I ever thought about was Janine and my girl on the side at the White House. I was utterly paralyzed by my conception of faith, but I managed to be euphoric at the very thought of the full Janine in bed, not just the woman who was dodging a neighboring snorer.

The lights in Angela's apartment were now out, although I had no memory of either Angela or me turning them off. Perhaps it was the ghost of Mickey Price wishing me luck. Angela sat beside me on the sofa.

"You scare me," I volunteered in the darkness.

"Why?"

"You see too much. I'm a badass, remember? Do you think your background somehow lets you see this stuff?"

"Every sad family has its own brand of corruption."

"That's true, Angie."

"Even though my father was what he was, I was never a target," she added.

"What does that mean?" I swallowed hard.

"You don't even see it, do you?"

"See what?"

"How your father treats you—he doesn't think anybody picks up on it."

"He's a harmless old man, Angela."

"I think he blames you for his wife's death, for his son's death, for having no male heir—why anybody would want that legacy to go on is beyond me."

"Look at your father! Look at what he was!"

"I didn't deny it, did I? I admitted it. I admitted it up front. Why is it that I can admit that my father was a murderer and you don't hear it, but you won't admit your father's a malignant old man who could suck the life out of anything?"

"The two are not the same."

"Maybe not, Jackie, but I can't believe you don't see it."

"You should see his fight shop, all of the pictures of me he has up."

"That's show business. That's to show the world his family feelings." She sneered the words "family feelings." "These old Italians—Jews, too—they believe in invoking family, 'blood is thicker than water,' when it wins them allies, but some of them can't play for money."

"Meaning what, Angela?"

"Meaning that they've never given any thought to their families, that they're not capable of it. Your father expects to be recognized as, well, a Don, in the Old-World sense, and he acts betrayed when he isn't."

"What do you want me to do, go break his ribs?"

"No, Jackie, that's what *you* want to do to him."

"Do you know what I want to do to you?" I asked, moving my hands slowly down her back. I wasn't in a fighting mood, unlike Angela, who often seemed to be.

"I think so, Jackie. It's not only taken you how many years to be able to say it?"

When Angela inched closer, the breeze had blown her top open wider than it had been before. A small freckle became visible just north of where her shirt closed in a "v." Still lost in my senses, I did something I had never done before in my life: I made no effort to disguise my intentions.

"Jackie," Angela laughed.

"What?" I said, calmly staring.

Angela closed her top just a little. I reached out and opened it again. She covered her mouth with her hand, incredulous. Another gust waltzed through the apartment. Memories of a girl I once knew in her cheerleading uniform. Memories of a girl I once knew without her cheerleading uniform. *Penthouse.* I am forty, but still intensely aware, if not obsessed with, the sensory imprint of my teens. Angela's theory about why I am not married is mostly wrong, but not entirely wrong. My circumstances of so long ago infuriated me, but rendered me determined to separate Angela Vanni from her clothing.

And then, two raps—fire and brimstone!—fell against my door.

Cafone

"Don't start with this now."

Angela sprang up and ran to the door. The visual made me feel like I was in a *Playboy* cartoon (a good thing), but the knock wasn't anything to laugh about.

Angela looked through the peephole.

"Dammit!" she whispered, running back to me. "It's Dirk."

Dirk Romella.

I clenched my fists. The turd knew I was here and was sabotaging me.

"Do you mean Dirk Uses-too-much-*gel*-a?"

"Jackie," she laughed. "Would you just slip out on the balcony while I talk to him?"

"No."

"Jackie!"

"He probably knows something's up with us by now, Angela."

"I know, but, uh, there's something . . ."

"Are you ashamed of me?"

"Don't start with this now. Please. Just for a second, go onto the balcony or into my bedroom."

"Cool!"

"Jackie, now. I want him to think he woke me up. I don't want him to think I'm a *putana*. Just hide while he's here."

I obeyed, and sat on the edge of Angela's bed in the darkness while she went into her bathroom and threw a robe on top of her clothing. Her bedroom was tidy, floral, and white. Family photos were all around. I couldn't imagine going at it with Angela on this bed—not that this had been proposed yet—with Mario Vanni glaring down at me shouting, "Get the fuck off my daughter you *strunz!*"

"What is it, Dirk?" Angela asked, opening the door.

"We were just robbed," Dirk said.

"What?"

"Two guys with guns and masks just used smoke bombs as a diversion to rob one of the cash kiosks, and then ran out."

"My God!"

"Your friend Jackie's one sharp private dick."

Dead man. Dead man. Dead man. Dead man.

"Shut up, Dirk!"

"He's the one who supposedly set up our scam-proof operation."

"This has nothing to do with him!"

"How do you know? He's supposed to protect you, not . . ."

"Not what, Dirk?"

"I've seen *guys* get whipped before, but women . . ."

That was *it.* I couldn't see any objects, just colors. Everything was red. Angela's white bed was red. I stomped down the hall on fire. Angela's eyes bugged open in horror when she saw me coming. "Hey, Dirk," I said furiously, "How'd your *Dago?*"

"What?"

I smacked the wussified notebook out of his hand and grabbed him by his collar.

"How'd your *dago?* You're *dago*-ing all right? Oh, yeah, it's nighttime," I said.

"Jackie!" Angela shouted.

Dirk tried to grab me back but failed to get a grip on anything.

"Jackie! Let go!" Angela cried.

Dirk was still trying to get ahold of something and scratched my collarbone with his fingernails. I slammed him on his cheek and let go as he fell against Angela's door.

"Aww," I said through my teeth, "Not a good day. Dirk's *dago* not good."

"Jackie!" Angela demanded, "Get out of here!"

"What?"

"Leave," Angela said, shaking.

"The guy accuses me of robbing you and *I* have to leave?"

"Leave, Jackie. I've got a crisis."

"This is my kind of crisis, Angela."

"You really helped tonight, *cafone,*" Dirk said.

Everything in Angela's apartment turned from red to laser-blue. *Cafone?* Meaning classless. Probably the only word he knew in his ancestral tongue. Angela gasped. I stepped toward him. He held up his hands to protect his tanned and bony face. I fell on top of Dirk and wailed on him until Angela pulled me off. I could have resisted her, but a surge of sanity shot through me.

Cafone.

"Leave, Jackie! I don't want your help."

I stared Angela down. She covered her mouth and began to cry when she saw my expression. I didn't know what that expression was. I reached out for her.

"No! No! Get out of here with that *animale* face!"

Animale?

I mouthed a non-word, and Angela covered her face and ran back to the sofa where we—or at least I—had been so happy moments before. Dirk stood up and approached the sofa. He would comfort her. Then what? What would happen after Dirk comforted her from the beastly *cafone?* Would he rut like an *animale* himself in her bedroom to the applause of Mario Vanni? Or would he be gentle? Oh, gentle Dirk, so sensitive, so *there for her.*

"Buona sera," Angela said to me calmly, and in the non-negotiable manner of her father. It actually scared me, especially when she pointed toward the door.

Cut your losses, Jackie D. Just go. You are not meant for this stuff. It's not supposed to work out with women. If God had wanted you to be with someone, it would have happened before you were forty years old. None of 'em want the panda. The world is full of Dirks who sand down their rough edges with a paper known as pedigree, and they always win. You can't break out. Hey, Jackie, I asked myself, don'tcha find the timing of all of this violence curious: How'd *your* Dago?

Focus on Sally

"She got phony."

The conference room where the focus groups would be held hadn't been redecorated since Hendrix put on his last acid bandana, judging from the style of the room. If you could even say that it had a style. The wood paneling was warped, the ripped vinyl seats were burnt orange, a color that I couldn't imagine the upholsterer had been proud of, and the meeting table was covered with a thin veneer of mahogany-swirl Formica. With the exception of the one-way glass that allowed for observers, the room was windowless. A folding table had been propped up on the side of the room stocked full of stale brownies and hideous cookies with marshmallows embedded like shrapnel. The drinks being offered were all artificial-fruit-flavored. All of these foods and drinks had been declared health hazards at some point during the Ford Administration, but no one had briefed the time-warped operators of this facility. Who knew? Maybe there was a reason this place was like this. Maybe it was supposed to be the Twilight Zone to throw people off.

We were in Cherry Hill, New Jersey, home of the great highway water tower bearing its name, and a trophy to America's capacity for metamorphosis. Cherry Hill was created by developers that were hell-bent on shedding the hick image that South Jersey had had during the first half of the twentieth century. In the early 1960s, Cherry Hill was ground zero for a consumer revolution that altered the nation—the first indoor megamall was built on the west side of town, a melting pot of Italians, Jews, Irish, Black, and mainstream Protestants, all determined to prove that Communism, however much it was gaining abroad, wasn't an option between the Atlantic Ocean and the Delaware River. By the late 1960s, Cherry Hill had become the epicenter of an earthquake of ambition—so much so that it eventually warranted an even newer water tower to be built across town from the old one. This tower read: "The Success Address," it's legs straddled apart as if to say, "You got a *problem* with that?" No, Cherry Hill didn't screw around, it's various ethnics asking civilization, "We made it, why can't you?"—which was why Jonah chose it as one of his main locations for focus groups.

I sat in the observation room feeling like a voyeur, which of course I was. There was something really unrespectable about watching honest people think out loud. At least when I spied on people, I was looking for crimes. Jonah sat beside me with a laptop that he used to communicate with the moderator. Jonah explained that while the participants on the other side of the mirror couldn't see us, we had to keep quiet because they might be able to hear us, which would make them uncomfortable. He had retained a moderator named Eliza Baird, with whom he had worked over the years. She was an attractive woman in her late forties who reminded me of my junior high guidance counselor.

The battery of focus groups would assess attitudes toward Sally Naturale, and then examine Murrin Connolly, and what it would take, if anything, to discredit her. There would be six focus groups. Given my professional obligations to Sally, I would sit in just this once and rely upon Jonah to report back the results of the other five groups.

There were eight focus group participants: Howard, a white, middle-aged attorney; James, a black pharmacy manager; Leon, a young Hispanic car salesman; Betty, a white grandmother; Kelly, a young white nurse; Marny, a thirty-five-ish advertising copywriter of vague ethnicity; Gigi, a restaurant hostess of Asian origin; and Gwen, a beautiful mocha-skinned store owner.

Dr. Baird opened with a broad statement of purpose. The way focus groups worked was that a general subject would be raised, and then the moderator would guide the group into a discussion about it. The participants would not know for a while that Sally Naturale was the subject. By the end of the session, the participants would most likely be aware that Sally was the client, but by that point, they already would have shared their views about her—too late to go back and edit.

Dr. Baird acknowledged to the group that interested parties might be observing the proceedings from behind the one-way mirror. Today, the ostensible subject was the reputations of community leaders. What made a leader admirable? Why were some leaders more inspiring than others? Why were we likely to forgive certain well-known people, but not others? What role did business success play in being part of the community? What was the price that a business leader should pay for that success?

Leon, the Hispanic car salesman, volunteered an observation about

George W. Bush, which was as good a place as any to begin. "See, here's where the Democrats blew it," he said. "They think that because the guy didn't know who the Vice President of Botswana was that the people gave a damn. In fact, people liked Bush better when he didn't know who the Vice President of Botswana was, because the rest of us didn't know either. You've got these nerdbags who live in penthouses in Rittenhouse Square who go to parties where they slap each other high-fives because they know who the Vice President of Botswana is. Let me tell you something, my friends, outside of Rittenhouse Square, nobody gives a rat's ass."

"I always thought that Bush was handsome," Kelly, the white nurse, said.

"Oh, please," said Gwen, the store owner. "He's a moron."

Dr. Baird asked Gwen, "Was there ever a chance that you'd vote for Bush?"

"Never," said Gwen.

"Why's that?"

"I never vote Republican. I don't like where they are on abortion."

"So," Dr. Baird probed, spinning her pencil between her fingers, "It didn't matter if he was smart or dumb, he wasn't going to get your vote no matter what?"

"It mattered, sure, but I was never going to vote for him," Gwen said.

"So you weren't inclined to give him a break," Dr. Baird said, as the group chuckled.

"If he were smart, I'd say so, but just wouldn't vote for him," Gwen concluded.

"I don't know, Gwen," Leon, the car salesman, cut it. "Everybody tries to say they're not biased, but we all are. You. Me. Everybody. We go into things with our experiences."

The discussion about Bush was bandied about for another ten minutes. I kept glancing over at Jonah, thinking he'd ask Dr. Baird to change the subject, but he just took notes, confident that she was doing the right thing. I didn't see where all of this was going, but my attention span didn't qualify me for this kind of work, so I let the pros lead.

"Are there business leaders," Dr. Baird asked, "Who you think are more likable than others?"

"Bill Gates has gotten better lately," Howard, the middle-aged attorney, said.

"How so?" Dr. Baird asked.

"He's given all of that money away to charity," Howard said. "Schools. Diseases. We're talking billions."

"Is it the amount of money that matters?" Dr. Baird asked.

"It's more than that," Howard said. "A few years ago, whenever you'd say Gates, it was always this doofy-looking guy on the cover of a magazine who looked like he was twelve-years-old, with an article about how he was worth a hundred billion and controlled our lives. That pissed people off—excuse me. When you see him now, he looks older, he looks like he's been knocked around a little with the anti-trust, and he's always talking about charity. You always see him with a starving kid or something."

"Same with Ted Turner," Gigi, the Asian hostess, said. "It's all that United Nations stuff. Didn't he give a billion to that? I'm from the Philippines, so we see that on the TV."

"Maybe it's all public relations," Betty, the grandmother, said. "Maybe they're just smarter about how they tell us things. Maybe nobody's really doing any real good. Maybe they just take better pictures."

Jonah tapped me on my knee. "Note, Jackie, that this comes from the oldest person in the focus group."

"Meaning what?"

"Meaning wisdom. But we're not here to learn for its own sake. We want to tell a story. These people will tell us how."

Dr. Baird asked, "Is there anybody closer to home, any famous business person, man or woman, who you think gives back to this community, makes people here proud?"

"Sally Naturale used to," Marny, the copywriter, said. A number of the others nodded.

"Tell me more," Dr. Baird prodded.

"She was cool when she started out. This ballsy woman, forgive me, talking about class," Marny said. "I remember being a teenager and thinking, 'This broad doesn't take any shit."

"I always loved that name, Sally Naturale, the way it rhymed," said James, the pharmacy manager. Everyone laughed.

"Why don't you feel the same way?" Dr. Baird asked Marny.

"She got phony," Marny said.

"Yeah, she did," said Howard, the middle-aged attorney.

"Phony how?" Dr. Baird asked.

"I took my wife to that place she's got in the woods," Howard said. "We're sitting there having lunch in this café they've got there. We're staring across the water at her house. She calls it Cricket Crest. Gimme a break. It was like all she wanted you to do was come and have lunch, buy her stuff with the stupid names, and see how big her house is. When somebody acts so perfect, it makes other people feel bad, people who aren't perfect."

"I have to agree," Betty, the grandmother, said. "I've lived here my whole life. I remember when she was on the way up, and seeing a Sally Naturale ad on TV. I'd think, 'That's my girl.' Now, though, I don't feel that way. Everything's so fancy. I'm at the point in my life where I know what I am and what I'm not, and when I've got those grandkids spilling Pepsi all over the floor, I'm glad it's linoleum. Sorry, but if that's cheap, it's cheap."

"What is Sally anyway?" Gigi, the Asian Hostess, asked. "She Italian?"

"I don't know," Dr. Baird said. "Does it matter?"

"No," everyone said simultaneously. It didn't matter. "Absolutely not," Kelly, the nurse, said.

Jonah chuckled.

"What?" I asked him.

"See those denials, Jackie?"

"Yeah."

"That means *it* matters. That means *it* matters big-time."

"She looked different years ago," Kelly said.

"That's true," Marny said. "When I was in high school, she looked Italian or Greek, or something. Then she started looking like a snob."

"A WASP," Jonah said to me.

"The people who go out there are snobs," Gwen said. "Cricket Crest. What the hell does that mean anyway?"

"She had that big I.P.O. a few years ago," James said. "That's when she put that cricket place up."

"What's I.P.O.?" Gigi asked.

"Initial Public Offering," James explained. "That's when she sold stock in her company and became a billionaire."

"No wonder she became a bitch," Gigi said matter-of-factly. The group laughed.

"The minute you make money, I guess you get nasty," James said.

"What do you mean?" Dr. Baird asked.

"There's that whole thing with that woman who lost her baby drinking Sally's Frankenstein milk," James explained.

The mention of "Frankenstein milk" triggered a flurry of cross-talk, with virtually every participant weighing in with fearful adjectives about genetic engineering.

"Cloning is just wrong," said Gigi.

"Something was bound to happen with that stuff," said James.

"Mother Nature doesn't like tampering," said Kelly. "And Mother Nature's got more pull than Sally Naturale."

"I wouldn't be surprised if a mutant soybean could kill somebody," said Howard. "Sally seems like the type who wouldn't give a damn."

Behind the glass, Jonah dropped his notepad and typed something frantically to Dr. Baird. I looked over his shoulder. CHILL THEM OUT, he wrote.

"What's going on?" I asked.

"The genetic engineering stuff is too hot. It turns them into a lynch mob against Sally," Jonah explained. "Whoever whipped up this witch hunt picked a winner of an issue. There's no room to maneuver on this point. We need to keep them on Murrin, away from genetics."

"Do they know that the milk caused it for sure?" Kelly said.

"It's not like I have evidence that the milk did the deed," James clarified, "Just that Sally's getting sued and whatnot by the Murrin girl."

"She's on TV a lot," Marny said, "The one who lost her baby."

"What does that say to you?" Dr. Baird asked.

"She's milking it," Marny answered.

"*Milking* it?" Kelly said.

Everyone chuckled at Marny's unintended pun.

"You know what I'm saying," Marny said, her cheeks turning red. "I'd be sad, too, but I wouldn't want to be crying in front of the whole world or anything."

"That's the lawyers at work," Howard said. "Believe me, I know. They get you crying on TV to get at the jury pool."

"That doesn't mean she didn't lose her baby," Gigi said.

"No, it doesn't," Howard defended, "But I'm just saying how the game works."

"Other people have lost pregnancies," Betty, the grandmother, said, "Including me. But you didn't see me yelling about it on Mike Wallace."

Jonah's leg bounced anxiously. "What is it?" I asked him.

"They don't like her, Jackie," he said.

"They don't like who?" I asked.

"Murrin. These groups usually go for victims," Jonah said. He began typing on his laptop: QUERY MORE ABOUT WHY THEY DON'T LIKE MURRIN.

Dr. Baird read the note as soon as it pinged on her laptop. "One question," she asked. "Why don't you feel more sorry for Murrin?"

Every member of the group rushed to deny that this was the way they felt. It was comical to behold.

Howard, the white attorney: "I was just saying how things work legally speaking. All of that religious talk Murrin does . . . there's something insane about it."

James, the black pharmacy manager: "She's very sad, no question about it."

Leon, the Hispanic car salesman: "We just don't have all the facts yet . . . is all."

Betty, the white grandmother: "Poor, poor girl, she seems confused."

Marny: "She's definitely suffering. You can't take that away from her. All the Christ stuff is a little much, though."

Gigi: "I didn't mean she wasn't really grieving."

Gwen: "There's no way to describe what she must be feeling. All I know is that we can't sit here and know for sure."

"Bull-fucking-shit," Jonah said under his breath.

As I listened to their words, Jonah studied their faces.

"What's bullshit?" I asked.

"I've been in thousands of these things. Thousands. People go for the mom. They don't question a mother. Murrin, whew . . . they don't like her, Jackie, and they won't admit why they don't like her, which means that the truth . . . what they're thinking is socially unacceptable."

"What does that tell you?"

Jonah sighed. He glanced down at the ground as if he were ashamed. "You can do a million surveys and test it out ten million ways, but it comes back to basic likability. Do . . . we . . . *like* you?

"*And,* Jonah?"

"They think she's a butt-ugly slab of white trash."

Bird's-Eye View

"We may not even need to get inside the dome at all."

The Lord met me at a bench on a boardwalk pier. We had been avoiding meetings at Allegation Sciences, because people who were capable of murder were also capable of bugging my office. I was also avoiding the hotel's interior, because I didn't want to run into Angela or Dirk Milhous Nixon. I alternated between feeling a morbid sense of loss over Angela and regretting that I didn't make a cripple out of Dirk when I had the chance. After all, it was his signature on the letter I just received severing the Golden Prospect's consulting contract with Allegation Sciences. I ripped it up and tossed it in a trash can. Fuck 'em, I was relieved.

The Lord slid his ass next to mine on the bench.

"I never want to go on another airplane as long as I live," he said.

"Neither do I. That's why I had *you* do it."

"I wasn't scared, it was just the noise of that single engine. I can still hear it."

I indulged the Lord as he explained to me how he had flown around South Jersey and Delaware for an entire day. I brought two little lifeguards into my line of vision as the Lord spoke and watched them twirling their whistles around on a little rope. Because I was wearing sunglasses, the Lord couldn't see that I was ignoring him. No matter how many times I told him how much I hated all of this process crap, he felt the need to tell me where he boarded, where the pilot flew him first, the color of the barge . . .

Thank God Teapot Freddy and Nate the Great found us. Something to get the Lord to focus on was exactly what I needed.

"Hey boys," I said, "The good Lord was about to tell me what he saw on his little plane ride." Teapot Freddy and Nate the Great sat on a bench beside us.

"From the Caribbean, Naturale's crates travel to the Port of Wilmington," the Lord began. "They're loaded onto barges, and go around Cape May and up the coast. They go into Little Egg Inlet and up the Mullica River toward Medford Lakes. The stuff is unloaded and put on the railroad cars that go through the pines and feed into the big dome."

"How the hell do you build a railroad in the frigging Pine Barrens and nobody knows about it?" I asked.

"Don't know," the Lord said.

"What about transports going *out* of the dome?" I asked.

"There aren't any," the Lord said. "Just small trucks and cars. No big-ass merchandise."

"Sally said that they don't actually make much there. But they sure as hell do something, judging from the Teapot's recent adventure," I said.

"Not impossible to find out," the Lord bragged.

"We may not even need to get inside the dome at all," I said. The Lord looked disappointed. He wanted to break in something fierce.

"How the hell can you find out what goes on inside a place if you can't get in?" the Lord asked. "Interview everybody that comes out?"

"No, Lordo," I said.

"Then how?"

I stood and walked toward the trash can where I had tossed Dirk's see-ya letter. I grabbed the top of the basket and held it tight. "We may find out what goes on inside by taking a look at what comes out. Trash, boys."

"Oh, puh-leeze," Teapot-Freddy said, holding his nose.

"Don't worry, Fred, it won't fall to you. If what I think is happening is happening, we'll need a scientist."

All eyes fell on Nate the Great.

The Aftertaste of Fucking Up

"The only thing people hate more than a rich bitch is a bad mother."

Jonah was obsessive about his family. He hated being away from them for even a day, which was strange for a guy who was so successful. It had probably cost him business over the years, but he somehow managed to make a living operating without a base—a Heeb with a cell phone. I thought about how much I'd like a life like Jonah's, and envied him for his ability to build and maintain a family. What brain function was I missing, I wondered?

After two days of focus groups, he had some conclusions. He asked me to meet him in Cowtown. When I got there at dusk, Jonah immediately gave me the lowdown on the focus groups. We sat at a picnic bench beneath a pine tree.

"I'll tell you, Jackie," Jonah began, "Your client lost her base the minute she put that house up."

"It sounded that way from the group I witnessed."

"It didn't get any better. People really know about that I.P.O. It wasn't the stock so much as it was all of the news stories about her being a billionaire that hit around that time. Then she moons everybody with Cricket Crest, which she never should have built. In other groups, I watched people go right from genetic engineering to wanting to tear down that house."

"The flash helped build the brand nationally, though."

"Maybe so, but it reamed her in her own backyard. I've seen this type of thing a lot. People like you when you're small, they like you when they feel like they made you. Once you get there, the knives come out. That's what happened with Sally. The genetic food is a hate-catalyst somehow."

"Do people admit the jealousy?"

"No. People would admit to murder before they'd admit to jealousy. Admitting to jealousy is an admission that you're, well, less. People won't do that, so they give it a principle to hide behind. Sally makes Frankenstein milk. Sally's a snob. Sally's got two dicks. Sally kills unborn children. Perfection made Sally's fortune, but it won't keep it."

"So what do we do?"

"*Im*perfection. Vulnerability. The aftertaste of fucking up, the revelation that Sally's a mess like the rest of us. Look, not only can't I make a soufflé or grow a decent garden, I don't know how to set the alarm on my watch or the cruise control in my car. I put a pre-made pizza in the oven for my kids and it comes out looking like somebody blew up a beagle. And I'm a relatively smart guy. If I can't do basic things right, imagine how some uneducated housewife feels?"

"Again, Jonah, what do we do?"

Jonah shrugged. "Sally has to give it back." He removed his baseball cap and ran his hands along his thinning hair.

"Give what back?"

"*It,*" he said, smiling broadly. His eyeteeth appeared exceptionally pointy today.

"What's *It*?"

"The house, everything. Sally has to pay her success tax." Jonah said this with a mild frown, as if it were no big deal.

"I thought you said that people hated her house."

"They hate that it's *her* house, Jackie. They don't hate the house. They *want* the house."

"How can she give back what she didn't take from anybody?"

"Do you know about mau-maus?"

"Africans or something?"

"Yes and no. Mau-mauing is confrontation. It's confronting people who have what you want, making them uncomfortable."

"Hell-raising."

"Right. Sally is a Have. She has *It.* The big banana. She's made it, and that's bad," Jonah said sternly, as if he believed that all success was ill-gotten.

"So, she must pay?"

"Right. The mau-maus want her to give it back."

"But aren't they . . . mau-maus, aren't they primitive for today?"

"No, not at all, Jackie. It can be anybody who wants but doesn't have."

"So, what, we make Sally a mau-mau?"

"No, Jackie, that's not doable. I need to think about it. The optics have to be right? How things look. The Kennedys were beautiful and their politics were correct, so we overlooked the criminal element, which took on a

Rat Pack groove, not the sense of total corruption, which, of course, it was."

"Sally worships the Kennedys. She has a huge picture of Jack and Jackie in her lobby." Jonah closed his eyes and snickered.

"Of course she does. This is good. She'll be comfortable with an illusion as long as it's dramatic." Jonah was hot, walking around in little circles trying to squeeze out a tactical pearl. I was getting bored, so I asked, "What about Murrin?"

"Ideally, we have to flip the villain," Jonah said, talking to himself I think. "We have to change it from Sally to Murrin. As I said, switch the witch. The problem right now is Murrin's got at least some victim equity. There aren't many options for Murrin. It's not like you can spread a rumor that she's a lesbo and the whole thing vanishes."

"Are there any options?"

"There's one, and I think you're already onto it. The only thing people hate more than a rich bitch is a bad mother. You think Murrin's a fraud, don't you?"

"Yeah."

"Prove it and you'll win."

"Okay, so your poll says we should take down Murrin if we can. She becomes the witch."

"Right."

"Where does that leave Sally? There still can be two witches, right?"

"No, there can't be two witches. But you're right in suggesting that stoning Murrin isn't enough. I mean, depending upon what you find out about her, we can give Murrin negatives, but Sally's still got negatives, too."

"Where's the answer?" I snapped. I was getting frustrated. I knew that Jonah was thinking it through himself, but I needed an action item.

"The answer is three centuries ago. Do you know how you survived a witch trial?"

"How?"

"You admitted to being a witch. You repented in the town square. You sucked ass with the public, told them they were right all along."

"Even if you didn't mean it?"

"Even if you didn't mean it. You join the people, return to your roots."

"In other words, you go slumming."

"Right. But you have to . . . I don't know, wrap it up in a religion or some mission."

"Religion . . . I don't know. I don't know what her religion is. I'm still trying to figure out her background. The public information about her is vague. It's all this royal princess stuff, which I don't buy. It's like she was conceived immaculately."

"Not likely, Jackie. I respect your religion, but . . ."

"All I'm saying, Jonah, is that I don't know if she Catholic, Jewish . . ."

"Well, Jewish wouldn't work," Jonah said, resigned.

"Why not? Jews don't repent?"

"No, we go to spas," Jonah nodded with comic timing. "Salvation through indulgence."

"But you're not like that? Spas and all?"

"Between my gangster grandfather and my part-Indian Methodist wife, the tribe threw me out a long time ago. No, we'll need to get Sally a religion with a pop feel. Catholicism is too Pope-y. Judaism is, uh, too. . . ."

"What? Ethnic?"

"Yeah, ethnic's a problem, but it's deeper than that. Jews have that whole ancient, biblical, plagues-and-locusts suffering thing that doesn't fly with mass audiences anymore. Sally, though, I can't believe she's a real WASP. Real ones don't act out the way she does."

I asked Jonah if he knew what *shtarker* meant, as if I didn't really care about the answer. He said it meant a rough customer, a badass. I didn't tell him that Sally had said it.

"So we need a Britney Spears religion, is that what you're saying?" I followed up quickly.

"That's not a bad idea. That tart wears a cross, right? What's she?"

"I don't know, she must be some kind of Christian," I guessed.

"You're on the right track, Jackie—you know, getting the cross without all the Christ."

"Whoa there, Jonah. I dunno," I said.

"Believe it or not, I read the Bible all the time. Old Testament. New Testament. Both. I don't admit it, especially not to media people, but I believe in some of it."

"Then how can you can be comfortable with what you're recommending? I feel guilty just thinking about it."

"I feel guilty about everything, too," Jonah frowned. His eyes suddenly looked like the eyes of an orphan. "All I'm saying is that I understand how you think. I always figured that my family was being punished for my grandfather's career. I've always read the Bible, trying to figure it all out, but I'm not an evangelist. I don't think you can spin a public that doesn't want to be spun. I don't think we're selling them religion. If I did, I'd feel guilty. I think this is damage control, positioning."

"In other words, I'm not going to hell for this?" I asked.

"My wife says heaven and hell are both lived on earth."

"That's not bad," I said. I really liked this theory. "What did you say Edie was, Methodist?"

"Yes. She's not religious, though. She thinks I'm a nut, the way I read the Bible."

"What about if we make Sally Methodist?"

"We'll test it and see." Jonah laughed. "I love the whole thing with Sally and the Kennedys."

"Yeah, she's obsessed."

"Mickey did business with Joe Kennedy," Jonah said.

"I'm not surprised. What did they do?"

"Kennedy couldn't load his whiskey off at the Delaware ports, so Mickey found a way to bring it through the Pine Barrens."

"Why the hell does everybody move stuff through the Pine Barrens?" I asked.

"Because there's nothing there. Everybody thinks the place is haunted," Jonah said, waving his fingers to mimic a ghost.

"Off-the-record, Jonah, Sally's got some activity in the pines."

I leaned up close to Jonah: "She's moving merchandize around by railroad, and there's no railroad—officially—in the pines."

"Jackie," Jonah said. "How'd you think Mickey used to move Kennedy's booze?"

"Mickey used rails?"

"Mickey *built* the rails during Prohibition. Joe Kennedy financed them."

"Who else would know something like that?" I asked, dizzy with enlightenment. "About the rails?"

"I know because of who my grandfather was. That should tell you what kind of people know about the rails," Jonah said with contempt. "You know, Jackie," he added, his eyes flashing caution, "nothing good every moved along those tracks."

The Benevolent League

"He really sticks to one cause."

Hello," Murrin said, answering her telephone shortly before lunch time. Normally, she went out this time of morning—either with her mother or to her church—but today she was home alone. One of our stringers reported that she was pacing around her house, clearly very bored or very lonely. Either one was good for our next maneuver.

"Good morning, I'm calling for Mr. or Mrs. Connolly," the confident voice said.

"This is Mrs. Connolly. Lt. Connolly isn't at home right now."

"I see. Well," the man continued, "I'll get right to the point, because I'm sure you're very busy."

"It's not a bad time, really," a lonely Murrin said.

"Aren't you the best? My name is Ronald Burke, and I am a professional fundraiser. I have been hired by the Community Service Benevolent League of Southern New Jersey."

"Oh. Uh-huh."

"As you've probably guessed by now, I'm raising money for the Benevolent League. Have you been contacted by one of our fundraisers before?"

"No, I don't think so."

"Good. You know, I have to ask that, because people don't like it when they get called too many times by the same group. Do you know anything about the Benevolent League, Mrs. Connolly?"

"No."

"It's a small organization that goes back to World War II. We sponsor soup kitchens for homeless people, among other things. Every summer the Benevolent League tries to raise funds for the homeless in plenty of time for the cold weather. A contribution of twenty-five or fifty dollars would be a tremendous help. Would you have any interest in making a contribution?"

"I'd like to, but this really isn't a good time for us. My husband's overseas and I'm watching the money."

"I totally understand. Do you mind if I ask you a question?"

"No."

"Are there causes you are interested in that we can send you literature on in the future?"

"I'm interested in certain causes, but I'm pretty well set on what I contribute to."

"It sounds like you've handled us pushy fundraisers before, Mrs. Connolly," Ronald Burke said, self-deprecating.

Murrin snorted, "My brother does stuff like that."

"Like what?"

"Fundraising."

"Really? Any particular causes, or is he like me, somebody who takes on a bunch of things?"

"I don't think he phones people. He's more of an organizer of events."

"Oh. You should ask him about the Benevolent League. Maybe he'd organize something for them."

"He really sticks to one cause."

"That's terrific. It's the best way to do things. You accomplish so much more that way. Do you mind if I ask what cause he works on? It's always interesting to know who my competition is," Mr. Burke said half-jokingly.

"He's an animal nut. He does all kinds of events for animal rights, protesting experiments and stuff."

"That's a very popular cause, especially in California. You don't hear much about it in New Jersey though. He's probably not local, is he?"

"He's in South Jersey. There's all kinds of habitats, or whatever you call it, around the Pine Barrens. You'd be surprised."

"How about that? I had no idea. Well, Mrs. Connolly, I may not have raised any money from you, but I certainly learned something today. I am grateful for your time."

"I wish I had more money so I could give some to you."

"Good things to good people, Mrs. Connolly. Thank you."

"Nice work, Nate," I said, after he played me the tape. "Now find the son of a bitch."

I had succeeded in avoiding Angela—and the Antichrist, Jerk Salmonella, for that matter—since we had had it out in Angela's apartment. I was able to con myself into being proud of the *vaffanculo* stance I had taken. I thought about telling Angela that I found the robbery to be suspicious, but she'd probably say "Duh!" Of course a robbery was suspicious. I envisioned myself trying to explain to her that I didn't do it *and* that it may have been tied to Frankie Shrugs or Petey Breath Mints or somebody, but all I had to buttress this was my own paranoia. I'd look worse if I tried to spin it. I took a walk on the boardwalk and tried to summon back a little swagger, but my sneer melted away after I walked a block.

I was drawn to an arcade in front of Trump's Taj Mahal where stuffed animals were stocked up all around targets at a water gun firing range. The vendor, a Popeye clone, looked at me anxiously, clearly hoping I would become the only patron he had probably seen in hours. His seasoned demeanor was rapidly becoming extinct, giving way to a generation of young retail mopes who confused a basic request for service with asking them to stick their genitals in a blender. Popeye's skin was an orangy tan, and when his mouth was fully closed, his jaw collapsed into his skull. He really did look like a cartoon.

"You wanna play, mister?" Popeye asked me.

"Let me see what you've got." On the second shelf, I spotted a little panda bear. "What do I have to do to win that panda?" I asked.

"The little one?" Popeye asked.

"The little one."

"Oh, you can do better than that," Popeye said. "A young fella like you."

"I just want the panda," I said.

"Well then, son, you gotta shoot the clown in the mouth and make the balloon on his head pop. I'll tell you what: If you can do it in fifteen seconds, you can get that big horse up there." The horse looked more like a donkey with brain damage. It had a lopsided grin that was disturbing.

"Well, sir, sometimes I feel like my head is nothing more than a balloon."

"Nah," Popeye said. "You look like a smart young fella."

"I'm the dumbest guy on the whole boardwalk."

"No, that would be Alfie over there." Popeye pointed to a younger version of himself who was standing behind another arcade. "He's my brother. Dumber than a bucket-a hammers."

I laughed, gave him a dollar, picked up the water gun, and began blasting the clown in the mouth. In about ten seconds, the balloon popped.

"Good for you, son. You get the big horse."

"No thanks. I'll give you five bucks for the little panda."

"Okay, Mr. Rockefeller," Popeye said swiping the five at lightning speed. "You enjoy that little panda."

I returned to the Golden Prospect and grabbed a piece of the hotel's stationery and an envelope from the front desk. I wrote Angela the following letter, thinking all the while what a candy-ass, wussbag pansy I was:

Dear Angela:

I didn't mean to embarrass you when I flipped out at Dirk. I guess I didn't like how he talked about me in front of you. You know what Joe Frazier said: "You got to remember that a man's dangerous when he's hurt." I've done some rotten things in my time, but I wouldn't do anything that would hurt you, like Dirk wants you to think. That doesn't mean I was right to let my hands talk the way I'm used to. In some things I go too far, in others not far enough. I will understand if you have had it with me, but I won this panda out on the boardwalk for you. They also had a big horse that looked more like a jackass, which probably would have summed me up better. Anyhow, sorry. Giovanni D.

I got a little box from the Golden Prospect gift shop, slipped the panda in, and left it with my note on Angela's receptionist's desk.

Rhetorical Passports

"Americans don't mind being lied to, Jackie, they mind being lied to poorly."

Jonah called me back two days later with the results from his latest rush poll. I met him at a diner in a nameless town.

"I did the poll, but I also polled about this thing the corporate types are calling Social Equity, because it may play a role for us," Jonah said.

"What the hell is that?"

"That everybody's equal."

"What do you make of it?"

"It polls pretty well. I say we go with it."

"Do you think everybody's equal?"

"Hell no, Jackie. Some people are geniuses, others are dumber than dog shit, but people tie the word 'equal' back to the Constitution. I see this time and again in my polls. They give it all kinds of meanings that it doesn't have. It makes people pump a fist in the air like they're at a ball game. Look, the attorney general can't come out and say, 'Bill Gates is smarter than you, he works harder than you, and he's luckier than you. So, let's break up his company.' So we go with equality, as if there's a common devil."

"So it has to have that power to the people whiff?"

"Exactly. Exactly," Jonah said, genuinely excited. "The bottom line is that you can screw anybody if it has the aftertaste of helping the little people. Americans don't mind being lied to, Jackie, they mind being lied to *poorly*. What you need, then, are rhetorical passports."

"English, Jonah."

"Sorry. There are certain words that poll really well. Tolerance. Diversity. Dialogue. Nurture."

"I wanna heave. What about 'empowerment.'"

"That came up, too."

"I hate 'empowerment.'"

"Who doesn't? Bear with me. If you invoke these words, the media are more likely to cover the story your way. But it's also optics. Take the Kennedys. JFK had it right when he said Nixon had no class. What kind of dung was 'I am not a crook?' He used the word 'crook'! And Nixon got personally involved with the dirty tricks. Kennedy left the strongarm stuff to his dad while he was out New Frontiering."

"To be honest with you, Jonah, I always liked Kennedy. My father used to talk about how Bobby spoke in Atlantic City in '64 like it just happened."

Jonah got a rare wistful look in his eyes. "Don't ever repeat this, but so did I. It worked. Mickey once caught me in front of my bathroom mirror—I must have been fourteen—and I was doing Kennedy's inaugural speech. He went berserk and started screaming 'That son of a bitch lost me Cuba!' "

"You know, Jonah, most boys that age get caught doing something else in the bathroom. I got nailed with a *Penthouse*."

"Well, I got nailed with *Profiles in Courage*."

We both laughed.

Sensing we might be slipping into the deep end of an emotional lake for both of us, I got back to the polls. "Okay, what about the religion part?" I asked.

"That gets tricky, Jackie. I'll need you to make an executive decision."

"Fine. What are my options?"

"Well, Catholicism has both high positives and negatives. I think it's too divisive for Sally. And, of course, Judaism is out, as I expected."

"What did the focus groups say?"

"Jews fire up a lot of resentment. It comes out as a lot of Israel-bashing, but if you read between the lines, what people are really saying is, 'They get all of the beachfront property.' Trust me on this, Jewish is not the way to go."

"What else do we have?"

"The net is this: Methodist sounds too Southern. With Baptist, the blacks are with you but you lose the Catholics. Presbyterian strikes people as being snooty. Lutheran seems too defiant, you know, like Martin Luther. Episcopalian has 'piss' in it, which conjures up that whole Mapplethorpe photo of the cross in the urine glass. Nobody up here's heard of Disciples of Christ. With Mormon you've got the whole polygamy thing, which the dock workers think is cool, but that doesn't help us. Quaker makes good cereal, but people don't link it to Jesus. Amish . . . well, you know, those are field-trip people. (Nobody can get past the *Witness* flick.)

Mennonite—one guy thought it was an aftershave; a woman thought it was the thing that makes Superman go weak. That leaves us with Unitarian."

"What makes people like Unitarian?"

"Nothing. It's just that it doesn't piss anybody off. Unitarian's the backdrop, Jackie, not center stage. I mean, it's got the whole church thing going on, without it being overly Christian."

"I'm okay with Unitarian."

"Then we go Unitarian. It's a neutral position. Now, Sally will need to do something unassailable, something so incredibly good that people attack her at their peril. If there's bad stuff under her fingernails, we'll have to dump it all out there, hammer the public with it before Sally repents. This way, when she finally repents, nobody'll give a damn. They'll be so exhausted with the negatives that they'll be open to her repentance. That's what they did with Clinton during the whole blowjob thing."

"Clinton outright lied."

"Yeah, he did. Then he used the time he bought with his lie to dig up dirt on his enemies. When he finally came out and said, 'Okay, I lied', people said, 'Well, yeah, tell me something I don't know'. When there's shit everywhere, nobody wants to sift through it, they just want to get out of the shit."

"Vivid, Jonah."

"Honest, Jackie."

"This thing Sally does, does it have to be genuinely good, or does it just have to *look* good?"

"The public rewards attempts at charity, and doesn't punish do-gooders who fail. The attempt and the rhetoric are everything."

"The polling aside, tell me what your gut tells you."

"My gut tells me to go back to Sally's beginnings."

Fragile Merrill

"Jesus isn't here."

I rarely ever get in the ring anymore, but I liked giving my boxing skills the weekly polish. I had a heavy bag chained to a beam beneath my porch at home, but didn't have a speed bag there because it made too much noise. I tried to go to a little club on Jerome Avenue in Margate where they had a few speed bags every Tuesday before work. I'd work the bag for about fifteen minutes, which isn't easy, and then skip rope for another fifteen. The place wasn't officially open until nine, but the owner, an old pug called Apples, had given me the key.

I went through my routine and added ten minutes of stomach crunches on the rancid gray mat. I never showered at the club, because I hated lugging all of my stuff around in a bag. Besides, I kept sweating for about a half hour after a workout, and didn't want to sit around this dump cooling off. I carried my duffel bag, which had bottled water, my wallet, keys, and Beretta, into the locker room.

The place sounded quieter that usual.

I walked to the sink and rested the duffel bag on the counter. I splashed my face with water and watched in the mirror as it mixed with my sweat and rolled into the drain. As I looked into the mirror, I shivered. I loved my routines, which I carried out amid the familiar sounds of the shore. The room sounded different, and I was getting irritable. I backed up a few paces and looked at the few rows of lockers, when it occurred to me: the little window above the back row of lockers was closed. Apples usually kept it open to keep the place aired out, and I could always hear the hum of the occasional car zipping by on Jerome.

I went back to the sink to get my duffel bag feeling very anxious. You're not always wrong, Jackie Disaster. My heartbeat was urgent. It was an otherworldly urgency—not that of a man in a temporary rush, but something more definitive, like the ref slapping canvas. Done. Over. No split decision I kept my hand in the bag around my gun and proceeded slowly around the first row of lockers. My God, it smelled in here. As I rounded the first row of lockers, I felt the rush of corrupt air and then a cold pain against my scalp, right above my ear.

Petey Breath Mints, swinging down with a knife.

I dodged to my right and swung my duffel bag around, which entangled but did not stop his second stab, which reopened the wound on my left hand from my last ambush. I squeezed the trigger of my Beretta while it was still inside my bag. The shot missed Petey, but was close enough and unexpected enough to startle him. In the nanosecond that Petey flinched, I withdrew the Beretta, which I held down low. I pulled the trigger again and heard a simultaneous crack of gunfire accompanied by a splitting of bone and a cry from Petey Breath Mints, who fell back against the locker. As he fell, he tried to hold onto his knife but was so stunned by being shot—people always are—that he lost his focus and dropped the knife. Petey, hyperventilating, lurched his head to the side, wincing, trying to see where he had been hit.

It was a hip shot. Right into the bone. I pointed the barrel of the gun toward his eye and Petey yelped "Jesus, no!"

"Jesus isn't here, Petey," I said. "I wanted a midget, but you'll do. I brought the butt of the gun down on his temple until I drew blood. Then I crouched down beside him, rolled the half-conscious killer onto his side and smashed him in his ribs. The ribs are thinnest around the back, one of the first things you learn as a boxer. I broke at least three of them and was still unsatisfied. I slammed Petey in his jaw until I heard a snapping sound.

The sun was rising a little too fast for my liking. I dragged Petey Breath Mints out of the back of the club, lifted him up, which was damned hard, and locked him in the trunk of my Cadillac. There was a black Range Rover in the corner of the lot, which I imagined belonged to Petey. I went back into the club and cleaned up the blood, mine and Petey's, took his knife, and went back to my car. I popped the trunk, where Petey was still unconscious, reached around in his pants pockets, and found his keys. Range Rover indeed. I took a rag and jammed it in his mouth.

I began driving north on Ventnor Avenue, nice and slow. Jackie, you're a professional. You're a smooth guy. Unflappable. Keep telling yourself that. I'm just driving along down Ventnor Avenue minding my own business. You're Bruce Willis or Vin Diesel in a Bruckheimer flick. Willis is from

South Jersey just like you, right? Get that smirk on, the one that makes the guys in the audiences think, "Whoa! To be that confident!" The one that makes the girls think, "Whoa! To be *with* somebody that confident!" It's not like there's a gangster with halitosis hemorrhaging in my trunk with a gunshot wound, a bleeding temple, a broken jaw, and multiple fractured ribs. Why would anybody think that?

Then, I got behind *her.* The old lady with the blue-tinted helmet hair driving the AMC Pacer, the second ugliest car in history after the El Camino. *Look at the size of that watermelon head.* She was leaning forward with her pendulous boobs practically draping over the steering wheel. I couldn't pass, because the garbage truck in the left lane was going so slowly it might as well have been backing up. *Look at that cranium. Like Jupiter. Where the hell is she going this early anyway*? I was frothing. My heart was thumping to the rhythm of some awful disco song from the 1970s. *Turn the Beat Around.*

I roared into the first side street I could find, to shoot over to Atlantic. *Holy shit!* It was a one-way, and a St. Bernard's tongue hung like a wet beach blanket on my grill. The affluent accountant (he had that look) walking the St. Bernard shouted: "What, are you crazy?" He jumped back five feet and pulled the St. Bernard with him. I was looking for blood. My chest hurt, and I was thinking heart attack. My breath was short. The accountant approached and I tried to shift my car into reverse. I ended up rolling down my window instead. I could knock this guy's head off in three seconds, throw his ass in the trunk, along with the St. Bernard and bury them all in a shallow grave near Rancocas Creek in the Pine Barrens. *How shallow is a shallow grave?* I couldn't figure out if I was angry with myself for losing my cool, angry that the accountant didn't recognize that he was screwing with a guy who could kill him (He *should* know this, right?), or angry because the accountant had every right to be pissed off at me. *He* was the one walking his dog, I was the one with a killer bleeding in his trunk.

C'mon back, Bruce Willis. Direct me, Bruckheimer. I backed up slowly after raising my hand at the accountant in apology. *He was* right *there, Jackie. Your anger doesn't make you right and his weakness doesn't make him wrong. Back up slowly.* I did. I edged back out onto Ventnor and drove north to the only place I could think of going.

Fragile Merrill was the biggest black man in the history of the Delaware Valley. Fragile was so huge that the sight of him tended to cause troublemakers to drop a load in their pants, which was convenient, since Fragile directed the flow of waste at the Atlantic City Sanitary Commission's sewage processing plant just north of the city, on Absecon Inlet. Fragile weighed about five hundred pounds and, statistically, should have keeled over of a heart attack years ago. But he didn't, because when Death came calling, Fragile sat on him.

Fragile was an intensely moral man, who I met during a series of grab-ass pickup basketball games that local churches had set up for underprivileged kids. Fragile coached a Baptist church based in Atlantic City, and I sometimes coached for Our Lady of the Low Tide in Margate. After one game, Fragile asked me what I did for a living, and I mistakenly told him that it was a hard thing to explain. I think he took it as an insult to his intelligence. I felt bad about it, so I told him what I did. With eerie prescience, Fragile asked me what I did with bad guys, people I needed to get talking, but who wouldn't. My first instinct was to play dumb like I didn't understand what he was talking about, but I sensed I had found an asset, if not a believer, so I said, "What do you suggest?" His face broke into a charismatic gap-toothed grin, the kind that belonged exclusively to men who had been sent from Mount Olympus to handle inconvenient justice. The ironic thing about Fragile was that he wasn't a violent guy, he was able to get people talking by just looking at them. Oh, and something else. Very few things could get a man talking faster than ending up in the wrong pipe at a sewage treatment plant.

I pulled into the plant at about seven o'clock. I knew Fragile got in early, and I tapped on the door of his dungeon—an entrance that sat at the foot of a gravel road near the great swamp that opened out into the Atlantic.

Fragile slowly opened the door. His smile lit up the sunrise.

"You want a Range Rover?" I asked.

"Hmm, let's see, Disaster. What color?" Fragile's voice was velvet.

"It's black now, but you'll need to change it if you're wise."

Fragile backed up and ran his hands over his continent of a body. "What color do you think goes with my figure?"

"I'm thinking hunter green."

"A nature-boy look, huh? Yeah, I like that. How will I earn it?"

"I brought you a visitor."

"Aren't you charming?" he said, singsong.

"Very few people appreciate how adorable I am, Fragile."

"Not me, boss, you're my little yellow rose."

"It was like West Side Story when we first met on that basketball court. Tony and Maria. Why don't we just run away and get it over with?" I said.

"Why? Let me tell you why. 'Cause your narrow ass is driving down to a sewage plant at the ass-crack of dawn, and you wouldn't be doing that if something intrepid wasn't going down."

"You're a man of vision, Fragile. I just banged around a gangster who tried to kill me. He's in my trunk pistol-whipped, broken up, and a little shot."

"Just a little?"

"Just a little."

"Why does everybody try to kill your ass? I heard about that little scuffle you had. We're proud of you, but I was worried— thought I wasn't going get any more annuities."

"Annuities. That's a very financial word."

"I'm a man of finance, Disaster—in addition to being a man of justice."

"And you will be financed." I pulled out the keys to Petey's Range Rover and handed them to Fragile.

"Sweet."

"You'll have to paint it, sell it or something. This guy's bad bad."

"Mafia?"

"Crack-dealing Mafia."

Fragile scowled. It was a religious, hell-grown scowl. "This guy dead?"

"We may be able to revive him. He came at me with a knife where I train. He probably wanted to make it look like a mugging. Maybe it was his idea of being Machiavellian."

"That's good. Very organized."

"I imagine he'll deny everything when we start asking him questions."

"Yeah, they're all virgins until I dip 'em in the doodie."

Fragile had me back up my car into a storage area adjacent to the processing chamber. I popped my trunk. When it swung open, Fragile didn't flinch at the scabby sight of a barely moving Petey.

"This dirtbag is Petey Breath Mints," he said.

"I know."

"He works a crack gig down in Ducktown."

"That's what I was telling you, Fragile."

"Remember that little tiger, Lamont, on my b-ball team?"

"The real little kid?"

"Yeah, younger than everybody else."

"Right."

"He got ahold of some of that crap and almost died last winter."

"Is he okay now?"

"Yeah, but, you know."

"I know."

Fragile grabbed Petey Breath Mints by his neck. The gangster groaned as Fragile threw him over his shoulder like a sack of mulch. Fragile pressed a button that closed the mechanical door of the warehouse and threw Petey down onto a concrete floor beneath a giant glass wall with hundreds of controls on it. The glass separated us from Atlantic City's sphincter. A sterile, tiled room (why they bothered with a tile pattern was beyond me) sprawled on the other side of the glass and featured a basketball-court-sized river of sewage. It flowed from a waterfall of human waste at the extreme left of the room and ended up at giant fan-like contraption at the right that propelled the sewage into some other realm I could not imagine.

"You look at this all day, Fragile?" I said, twisting my face in horror. I had never been in this part of the plant, usually taking troublemakers to a smaller, more remote location that wasn't doodie-obvious. One look at Fragile was usually all it took to get folks talking.

"Yeah, I look at it all day. And sometimes I have to put on a big-ass moon suit and go in there when the valves aren't working."

I crossed myself.

"Why, Disaster, didn't it ever occur to you that Atlantic City had an asshole?"

"Of course it occurred to me, but, you know, I never pictured . . ."

"Yes, it's a real place. Now, I'm gonna strip Mr. Breath Mints down, shoot him some gay talk to get his juices going, and lower him in that river Styx and see what he'll say. That all right with you?"

"Yeah, but what's on the other side of that big fan thing?"

"It's chemicals. Chemicals that kill the bacteria. Can dissolve a block of concrete in about thirty seconds."

"Then what?"

"Then, once it's purified, it goes out to sea."

"We swim in this?"

"No, man, we don't swim in this. We swim in what it turns into."

"Do the chemicals work? Do they kill the bacteria?"

"Disaster, man, do you want me to whip out a Periodic Table of the elements, or do you want this man to talk?"

"Talk."

Fragile ripped Petey's clothes off, which woke him up good. Naked, I could see that the bullet had smashed the protruding part of his hipbone, which created quite a visual spectacle; but, if he could live with his ass breath, he could live with a nicked hip. He screamed comically when his eyes rose to capture the full beauty of Fragile.

"You ain't a bad looking boy, you know that?" Fragile began. Fragile hit Petey with the fear harbored by most Caucasian hoodlums, which is to be in confinement and raped by a gargantuan black man. "You got ass breath, but I could take a run at you, mm-mm-mm."

Petey Breath Mints looked at me and shook his head as if it had all been one grand misunderstanding. "Jackie, it was just a scare job, swear-ta God."

Fragile reached down and grabbed Petey's ass. "Nice round ass, you got."

"Whatever you say," I said, bored.

"It was just a scare job," Petey said again.

"What? The job on the Golden Prospect, or the thing at my house?"

"They were scare jobs."

So, the Golden Prospect holdup that cost me Angela was somehow part of this. I wanted to go and tell Angela, but since I dropped off the panda, I figured that the next move was hers.

"So, now we got two scare jobs, one of them with hollow point bullets that almost killed my little niece?"

"That wasn't me," Petey said.

"Let me ask you a question, Petey," Fragile said. "When you're out murdering somebody, do you ever bother to think what that person feels like? I mean, Lordy, you seem shocked that you're going to die like the Dark Ages."

"C'mon, honest, it was a scare job," Petey begged.

"He likes that scare-job thing, doesn't he?" I said to Fragile.

"He does, Jackie, he really does," Fragile agreed. "He must think we're a couple-a dumb Mongoloids. You know, man," Fragile said to Petey Breath Mints, "I think I've seen you around A.C."

Petey said nothing.

"You spend time in A.C.?" Fragile asked.

"Sometimes," Petey said, waiting for the big man to say something else.

"Tell him about some of your sales and marketing accounts, Petey," I said.

"What do you sell in A.C. Petey my man?" Fragile asked.

"Look, I do what they tell me."

Fragile stomped on Petey's head and he began spitting teeth. "Looks like Petey here isn't responsible for anything he does. No free will with this man. He's a victim. That Mafia dragged him right outta his mama's tummy and made him sell crack in A.C. to the young brothers, and then try to kill you."

"There's something to be said for forgiveness," I said.

"I think we'll let God and the devil sort that out," Fragile concluded. "Now, Jackie, you leave me here with my bitch, and we'll see what he knows."

"No, guys," Petey said, coming even more alive, bleeding again from his head. "I got money." I walked behind an enormous generator of some kind and listened.

"And where is that money?" Fragile asked.

"I've got some in my house."

"This here the keychain?" Fragile asked.

Petey nodded *yes.*

"Jackie, I'm gonna look smooth in that Range Rover, huh?" Fragile said. "Where's home, Breath Mints?"

"Are you gonna kill me?"

"Y-M-C-A!" Fragile began to sing in a fey voice. "Naw, we're gonna have some fun, you sexy thing."

"Oh, Jesus, just kill me."

"You don't find me attractive?" Fragile thundered, jilted.

"No, please."

"I think I'll dip you in a little sauce before I eat you all up," Fragile said.

"Jesus!"

Fragile opened up a large drawer, the same size as the kind used to store corpses in a morgue. He picked up Petey by the neck and the leg and threw him in the drawer and slammed it shut. He then hit a button, which prompted a hydraulic whir. Fragile worked a few more controls, and in about thirty seconds, Petey Breath Mints emerged in a square metal crate that moved on a conveyor belt twenty feet above the sewage river. He was retching from the smell. I was on the other side of the picture window and, while I couldn't smell anything, I retched in genuine sympathy for this dope pusher and murderer.

With another flick of a switch, a cable attached to the crate began lowering Petey into the orange-brown shifting mass.

"C'mere, Disaster. Here's the microphone. Ask away."

"Petey, who sent you to kill me?" My voice echoed into the chamber where the guy hung with the sewage. Fragile jerked the crate lower.

"The guys said you were screwing around with something. That you should know better. Ngh. God."

"Does Frankie Shrugs know more?"

"He's my skipper, but, honest, they don't tell me the whole deal. You know that, Jackie, they keep the top protected. They said you were screwing around with something."

"The big dome in the woods. Sally's place?"

"Yeah."

"Why do the boys care about Sally? Are they shaking her down?"

"I don't know!"

Fragile jerked the crate down a notch again. Petey screamed as he hovered inches above the waste. He may not have been lying before. Top mob guys didn't always tell trigger men like Petey the whole story. This way, they were insulated from prosecution. But I had to keep at him.

"You're a busy man for somebody who doesn't know anything."

Fragile dropped the crate into the river. Waste flowed over Petey, who screamed and gurgled. After about fifteen seconds he raised the crate.

"If you don't know any more, Petey, tell me something you don't know for sure, but you think you know," I asked.

Petey talked, and what he suspected was a hell of a lot more interesting than what he knew.

Fragile glanced at me with puppy-dog eyes.

"Do you have any idea what this guy will do to us if he ever sees the light of day?" I said within range of the microphone. Petey was screaming himself hoarse.

"Worse than this?" Fragile asked.

"Certainly not better."

Fragile released the lever, which sent the crate down into the river again, and he left it there for about ten seconds.

I flicked the mike off. "Fragile, let's bank this guy. Here's a little tape recorder I carry around. Hold him for a while. Make sure he doesn't get away. Have him tell you everything he knows about everything. Tell him that if we think it'll impress our friends in the endeavor of law enforcement, we'll drop him off somewhere more sanitary."

"What if he lacks further insight?"

"Something tells me that's not going to happen. I've got to bank this guy, Fragile. Clean him up, have him talk. When he doesn't tell you anything of value, dip him. The back and forth of it all should spark revelations."

Later that day, after I played the tape that Fragile had made of Petey, I didn't have anything close to the whole story about the plot against Sally and me, but I knew Murrin's younger brother was into more than four-legged animals.

The Holy Cannoli

"Repentance has to be about more than business, son."

Olga's Diner sat at the intersection of Routes 73 and 70, the large scripted "O" in the sign welcoming the residents of Camden County, and pointing them down the shore with the tail of the "s." The Marlton restaurant had been run by the same Greek family that opened the place in ancient times. Okay, maybe not, but it had been here forever, and, to their credit, the owners never felt compelled to remodel the place in accordance with the community's nouvelle poses. That Mario Vanni had been assassinated here only added to the diner's prestige.

I saw Bruce Springsteen in there once. It was in 1978, after I got my drivers license. Earlier in the evening, he had walked into Kaminski's Ale House in Cherry Hill unannounced (he did things like that), played *Because the Night,* a song he wrote with local girl Patti Smith and left with Steve Van Zant. I had gone to Kaminski's because I had a crush on a Cherry Hill girl with whom I hoped to have a well-choreographed accidental meeting. She didn't show, but Bruce did. When he left with Little Steven, I tailed them to Olga's. Springsteen and I were hip to hip at the urinals, and he said something to me I never forgot: "What's up?"

I thought this was huge, and remember interpreting what Springsteen might have meant by it throughout my entire euphoric ride back down the Shore. I remember being further awestruck by the similarity of our builds. We were both pretty average in height, which I thought suggested a life of phenomenal achievement for me. On the way out of the rest room, while Springsteen and I washed our hands, I said the only thing I could think of: "I'm, uh, Jackie De Sesto."

"Okay, Jackie D," Springsteen said in his perpetually hoarse voice, and walked out. I'm pretty sure my speedometer hit one-twenty on my ride home. It's a really embarrassing thing to admit, but for the next year, I hoped that Springsteen would release a boxing anthem called Jackie D. I scribbled some lyrics to the song (as if they would somehow be transmitted telepathically to Bruce) which I stupidly left on my parents' kitchen table. Blinky Dom asked me about them, and I explained to him, idiotically, that I had met Springsteen at Olga's and had a fantasy he'd write something about me.

"You meet this Spring*stein* in the pisser and think he's gonna write about you?" Blinky Dom barked. "He forgot you before he dried his hands." Cruel, but probably true.

From my booth I could see Father Ignacio pulling up to Olga's right on time, which wasn't a surprise, given that a free lunch was in store. Known in local circles as "the Holy Cannoli" because of his capacity to vacuum down the many meals to which he had been invited (or not), he had been my family's priest at Our Lady of the Low Tide for as long as I can remember. He was about seventy now, with thinning white hair, a crimson face, and a paunch that had diminished somewhat since he had a stroke last year. He looked more Irish than Italian, something that never made sense to me.

The Holy Cannoli was driving a Cadillac Escalade, one of America's most corpulent sport utility vehicles. I never questioned my Franciscan friend about the origins of his motorized beast, but I was aware that he had been known to perform last rites for the kind of South Philly gentry that tended to bleed to death from gunshot wounds on street corners. Something told me that Buddha Vic, Nicky Bones and Chickie Boy had not, in fact, accepted the Lord Jesus Christ as their savior on Passyunk Avenue, but you never knew. Vow of poverty aside, I assumed that the explanation for the Cadillac Esplanade lay therein.

Father Ignacio always made me anxious. For one thing, he knew all about my boxing, and I think he may have thought I was stupid. He always wore an expression of disappointment; it was something I couldn't see on his face when he was with other people, just with me. He also tended to bring up my father whenever I saw him. Blinky Dom had a one-dimensional genius, which was to identify and mobilize allies who would repeat his mantra that other people, people like me, were selfish and neglectful of him. This drove me into a rage. I was always hoping somebody would come along who would not be manipulated by this, but it never happened. People saw Blinky Dom as a helpless old man, and inevitably bought his vaudeville act and slammed me in the face with it.

I told Father Ignacio on the telephone that I wanted his advice about something, and that I wanted him to meet a client, if he was willing. I was vague. After we met with Sally, my intended target, I planned to spend the afternoon with her, at her request.

Heads turned as the enormous priest rolled into the diner in his black habit. His red face looked like an explosion against the whiteness of his collar. The Holy Cannoli slid into the booth facing Route 70, and asked about the stitches in my scalp.

"I'm accident-prone."

"Funny, so are many of my parishioners. Are you still reading those shipwreck books, Jackie?"

"That's my dad. I was into pirates."

"Right, pirates. I remember you getting out every book you could on pirates."

"South Jersey was crazy with pirates."

"I thought that was down around Nag's Head."

"There, too. When the pirates were chased out of Cape May by the Brits, they moved north, right near us in Ocean City. They set up taverns and everything. The locals didn't exactly object until people all over the country found out that pirates were welcome in South Jersey."

"Not a lot has changed, has it? We've still got pirates and problem children." I couldn't tell whether or not he was making an oblique reference to me and I spun back at him, perhaps too defensively.

"Well, you know, Father, there were pirates and there were pirates. Take Captain Kidd. Everybody knows him as a pirate, but he was hired by the colonial governors of New Jersey and New York to protect merchant ships from pirates."

"Takes one to know one, I suppose," Father Ignacio harrumphed.

"Yeah, but the government and big shippers trusted the guy to chase down the pirates that were trying to rob them," I explained. "Kidd became a successful legitimate businessman. He ran docks and had taverns all over Jersey. He lived on Wall Street.

"I thought they hanged him," Father Ignacio said.

"Eventually, they did. His clients thought he was ripping them off. He saw the noose coming down, though, and he supposedly buried a whole lot of loot in Ocean City."

"Are you looking for it, Jackie, or do you restrict your searches to lower truths?"

"You remember that talk? No, Father, I'm not looking only for lower truths. By the way, a lot of people who study pirates think Kidd was framed."

"Well, bless him then."

I decided to terminate the history lesson, since Father Ignacio was chronically reaching the wrong conclusions. I sighed. Father Ignacio waved over a waitress and ordered pancakes. I ordered a tuna sandwich, light on the mayo.

"So, Jackie, why are we here?"

"Repentance."

"For your father or something?"

"What do you mean, for my father?"

"He says things to me."

"Like what?" Big mistake.

"He says you ignore him, Jackie. He says you've—how did he put it—*forsaken* him."

"Oh, Jesus."

"Watch it, Jackie. The man is all alone."

"He's been singing that tune for years. He was singing it when my mother was alive, and when Tommy and I were running around the house. If I hear that word selfish one more time, I'm going to kill him myself and get it over with."

"You've got a lot of anger, son."

"And you can listen to his confessions and then go back to your quiet rectory. I have to live with it."

"Maybe we should all sit down and talk, vent some of this anger."

"Maybe we should talk about the Church getting its own rectory in order."

"That's not necessary, Jackie. Although I think the Church could use your services."

I wanted to lash out at Father Ignacio. I wanted to say, *did it ever occur to you that you're being used? Did you ever think that Blinky Dom is exploiting you because you're in the compassion racket? Did you consider that everybody dies on him, or flees from him for a reason, and that by carrying his spit bucket, you are being the opposite of compassionate—you're cold to the suffering of those who don't act out?* But I didn't ask any of these things, because I needed the Holy Cannoli for Sally.

"I can't make my father better any more than you can stop bad priests from doing what they do."

"I didn't mean to get into this."

"Neither did I. I just don't believe you can talk to everybody. Talking doesn't answer everything. When you talk, you have to split the difference, and I'm not meeting Dom halfway."

"That's very closed-minded. You need to work through this anger."

"You can only keep your mind open for so long. When enough maggots crawl in, it's time to close it."

"Very well, tell me about this repentance you seek."

"I'm not seeking it. It's for a client, and I'll name her if you promise to hold this in total confidence."

"That's my job. Is this client a Catholic?"

"To be honest, I don't know."

"You don't know who your client is?"

"I know who she says she is, but I think she's hiding something."

"What do you want me to do?"

"I want you to talk to her about cleaning her life up. Well, repentance. I think she needs to hear it from a Christian perspective."

"Since when have you been such a missionary?"

"I'm in business, Father, and I won't lie and say I'm not. Even though I'm not totally sure where I'm going with this, I know cleaning up her act is a part of my program."

"Who is she?"

I exhaled slowly. I could hear my heart beat, a sense that I hated. One would think a person would be encouraged hearing his own heartbeat, but I wasn't. If I could hear it beat, I could hear it stop. That's how I reasoned it out. "Sally Naturale."

"The woman from TV?"

"Uh-huh. There's trouble because a woman is suing her."

"Does she seem like the repenting type?"

"She's the business type. If repentance is good for business, she'll do it."

"Repentance has to be about more than business, Jackie."

"I sense it will be, but somebody has to lay it all out for her."

"Not all faiths share the Catholic view on salvation."

"I know that. I'm not picky at this point. I wanted somebody smart who can discuss how it works, I'm not looking to make it through one religion or another."

"Do you have any sense of what she believes?"

"Yes, she believes in defending her name."

"I meant religion-wise."

"I don't know for sure, Father. She's said a few words in Yiddish."

"Then why doesn't she just come out and say she's Jewish?"

"I don't know if she is, Father. Lots of non-Jews use Yiddish words."

"Sally sounds like she's from around here."

"I agree with you."

"Do you know my friend, Ravioli?"

"Did you say 'Ravioli'?"

"No. *Rabbi* Oli. It's what I call my friend Rabbi Wald. We kid each other."

"He was friends with Mickey Price, right?"

"Right. You may want to check with him, Jackie. It sounds like a little mystery you've got going on."

"I agree. Would you at least go with me to talk to Sally, Father?"

"Of course."

Sally Fidgets

"Maybe I took my eye off the road just a tad somewhere along the line."

Father Ignacio followed me for a few miles in his Escalade to Naturale's Earth. He had never been here before. On our march through the store, and then across the ferry to Cricket Crest, his eyes widened to take in the spectacle. People always insisted they weren't impressed with huge homes, but they were. I admit that when I first saw the place, I had thoughts about how Emma and I would live here. Then I had a panic about not being able to find her in this flagstone excretion, and my little brick place in Margate seemed about the right size for me. In a small house everybody's closer.

I was only being partially truthful with Father Ignacio about why I wanted him to meet with Sally. It was true that she kept invoking redemption, and that this would be a critical theme in our damage control program. But I wasn't entirely sure that she *got* the concept. I also suspected that something was gnawing at Sally's conscience, and I thought Father Ignacio might be able to shake something loose. He always had that effect on me, so maybe he'd have it on someone else.

I put on a baseball cap I had in my car to cover my scalp slice. Sally entered her sanctuary much in the same way that she had when I met her—as if she were on a dolly. She gestured to the chairs with absurd drama like a ballerina, and we were seated. Her back was toward the great window that overlooked Naturale's Earth.

"So we're going to save my soul," Sally began with a grin.

I said nothing, and I didn't plan to. I was here to listen.

"Well, Ms. Naturale . . ." Father Ignacio said.

"Sally."

"Well, okay, Sally. Jackie told me you were interested in learning about the concept of redemption. He didn't get into your soul. Jackie is godly in his own odd way, but I didn't sense this was missionary work."

"You never know with Mr. De Sesto."

I sat like the naughty boy I had been cast as in this session.

"Very well, Sally, how do you define repentance?"

"Wiping the slate clean," she said immediately.

"Wiping it clean to what end?"

"To be cleared. To be redeemed. To have people stop saying these wretched things about me."

"It sounds like we are talking about two different things. One is your image, for your business. The other is your soul."

"I'm hurt, Father."

"Are you hurt because your business has been damaged or because there is something going on within you?"

Sally thought. I could tell by the tightness around her eyes that the merchandiser in her was test-marketing the right message, but not necessarily the right moral.

"Of course I am suffering, Father."

"Suffering why? Suffering how?"

"To be accused of being a monster, after devoting my life to this business, is devastating."

"That is both a business problem and an emotional one. Jackie says you are concerned about repentance. I am a priest. I can help you understand repentance. I cannot help you with business."

"What are you asking me, Father?"

"I am asking about your interest in salvation. Jackie has been frank with me that his interest is on the business side. Are you interested in speaking with me to gain a strategy or to reflect on your life's choices?"

"I would say both."

"Thank you for being honest. Now, tell me, since I don't know much about business, is there something in your life you might have done differently?"

"Of course."

"Like what?"

"I'm an old salesgirl. There are others who run the business with me. Maybe, I don't know, I took my eye off the road just a tad somewhere along the line."

"How did that choice cause you trouble?"

"Things we did, people we, I, brought aboard. I probably focused on growing the business at the expense of other things."

"You do have wonderful things, I'll say that much. I was quite taken by the scent of your Upper Crust Pizza."

"I'll make sure you don't leave empty-handed," Sally said.

The Holy Cannoli bowed. "But tell me more about those other things?"

Sally fidgeted. It occurred to me that the puffy chair she sat in resembled a crocodile's mouth. One snap and Sally was lunch meat. "Oh, I can't review every business decision I ever made, Father."

"I'm not asking you to. Pick one that haunts you."

"I think I focused so much on public image—which I had to, by the way—that I lost track of what happened on the inside."

"On the inside?"

"I just don't know. I just don't know."

She knows. She knows.

Father Ignacio sighed, but not too dramatically. I knew this sigh. It was the sigh of the priest who wasn't getting anywhere, but who knew there was, in fact, a *there* to get to. "Sally, this isn't a confessional," he said, perhaps softened by her promise of a doggie bag. "In fact, I don't even know your faith. Would you mind if I asked you if are active in a faith?"

"No. I'm not religious."

"Were you raised in a faith?"

"Yes, Success," Sally chuckled.

"Okay, okay, Sally. I accept your feelings that you are troubled. I also sense that you have some things to work through, but I cannot pressure you to share with me things that are not my business the way your accountant would. I can pressure you, though, to share with yourself things that *are* your business. Only by addressing these things can you begin to make things right."

"There is so much to lose, Father." She held her hands aloft like Yul Brynner in *The King and I.*

"What would you lose?" he asked, his red jowls wobbling.

"I don't know. This is all so much . . . heartache. I don't know."

She knows.

"Well, Sally, you think about these things. All I can say is that sometimes you have to lose something big to gain something bigger."

"But so much?" Sally sighed.

. . .

When I walked Father Ignacio down the stone steps to the ferry, he said, "You're right, Jackie. This is a woman with a secret."

"Uh-huh."

"Oh, and Jackie?"

"Yeah?"

"Talk to Rabbi Wald."

"I will. Oh, look, Count Smartfarkle's bringing your pizzas."

The Holy Cannoli licked his lips.

Brawl

"I just go berserk."

Did you bring your exercise gear?" Sally asked me when I got back to her sanctuary.

"You asked me to, so I did," I said, holding up my gym bag.

"Are you up for a run? I thought we'd combine a run through the woods with a meeting."

"Sure."

"You can change in the restroom down the hall. I have to take a call, but I will meet you in fifteen minutes on the patio."

"Okay."

I changed into my running gear, including a bandana to cover my head wound, and trolled around the patio. I began to hear the crickets. I followed the sound, which was driving me crazy. I ran down the first visible path into the woods that appeared to go to the lake, stopping as the sound became louder. Glancing around, it dawned on me that despite the sounds crickets were not usually visible. What did I expect to see? With a few steps lower into the woods, the sound became louder still. I looked down through the brush. There was a brown wooden post with a box attached. I bent down to examine it. It contained a speaker encased in a wooden mini-cabinet. I pretended to be stretching, and listened. It was the cricket sound. They were piping cricket sounds in through speakers. Why the hell would they do this? I didn't have time to think this through, so I ran back up to the patio, the chirping of the crickets growing more faint. My vanity was my investigator's instinct, but I was stumped on this one.

Sally emerged, trim and toned. She studied me fleetingly as I studied her. It was strange the way people checked out one another, even if they had no intention of acting on anything. Sally was the age my mother would be if she had lived, and I certainly wasn't thinking sexually. Nevertheless, I couldn't say that I hadn't noticed or been impressed by the way Sally took care of herself. I felt strange exercising with a woman. It wasn't a sexist thing, rather, it was a free-floating sense of further betraying Angela. I hadn't heard diddly from her. My sentiments dissolved from rage to abandonment, an emotion I was used to. I still felt like a candy-ass though.

We ran in the woods for about a mile and came to a clearing where a boom box sat under a wooden canopy. Sally turned it on. A Simon & Garfunkel song was playing—*Bridge Over Troubled Water.*

"I like to run then stretch, run, stretch," Sally explained. "Is that okay?"

"Sure," I said. Truthfully, I wasn't a big stretcher, tending to see it as a waste of time, but I complied.

As Sally stretched—and I pretended to stretch—she began singing along with the duo: *"Sail on, Silverberg, sail on by . . ."*

I couldn't restrain my laughter.

"What?' Sally asked.

"Sail on, *Silverberg?"*

"What's wrong with that?"

"I'm pretty sure that it's 'Sail on, silver bird'."

"Oh, maybe it is. I just think of this family I knew once that had that name."

"When you grew up?"

"Oh, no, they rented an apartment from us in Cape May, where we once had a summer house. *'Sail on, Silverberg,"* she sang on, jittery.

Sally began to run again, I sensed as a diversion from her Silverberg faux pas and asked, "So, what are your politics anyway?"

"Why do you ask?"

"You've got this humble background, which, of course, is fine, but you work with these big companies."

"I don't think I have politics. I did when I was little."

"Like what?"

I couldn't help but laugh. "I called myself a Billy Jack liberal."

"Billy Jack?"

"Don't you remember those movies? Early seventies. This guy Billy Jack used to go around punching out white people to save the Indians. I would walk out of the movie—I must have been twelve—all pumped up, going, 'Billy Jack! Yeah!' "

"So?"

"Well, when I got a little older, I realized that I didn't give a damn about the Indians, I just liked that this badass was beating people up and trashing department stores and thinking it was all a great cause."

"Maybe Billy Jack believed in the Indians."

"Maybe he did, but I sure as hell didn't, and neither did the kids who went to the movie with me. We were kids from the shore for God's sake. That's what the sixties and seventies were when you think about it: a bunch of real lucky white kids pumping their fists in the air while Billy Jack beat up a cop. C'mon. The poor guy's just a cop doing his job, and we're all thinking we've got a cause. I remember a line he said that I thought was so cool. *I just go berserk.* I had never heard the word before, but I ran around saying it for a year—for no reason, either. My mom would say, 'Eat your lasagna,' and I'd push back from the table and say, 'Sometimes, I just go berserk.' Whenever I said that, my mom would just look at me like I was a total nimrod. Because I was."

"Would you go berserk on a rich old lady?"

"What are you talking about?"

Sally ran ahead and stopped at another clearing. She opened a cabinet and retrieved two pairs of boxing gloves.

"Let's spar," she said, slipping on her gloves.

Now what did I do?

"Sally, I don't think this is a good idea," I said.

"Why not?"

"I boxed, seriously."

"Oh, did you?" Sally leaned back and executed an impressive roundhouse kick. I felt its wake, as I moved my head back.

"Okay, for a few minutes," I agreed. I put the gloves on and moved away from the cabinet. I began to bounce. Sally threw a few punches, which I ducked. Then she threw one that I didn't duck. In fact, it hit me on the chin, which pissed me off.

"C'mon, Jackie Disaster," she said, bouncing.

I bounced, too, but really just flicked my hands at her playfully. The idea of making a fist and hitting a woman, even lightly, was abhorrent to be. Sally bounced a little more and moved toward me with a right hook. I dodged it. The second I became pleased with my speed, Sally nailed me with a left jab right in the nose. It stung badly. As she approached again, within seconds of her successful jab, I instinctively drew my left elbow back and smashed the little bitch on her nose. She fell back several steps, blood spurting from her nostrils. Sally ran a finger beneath her nose and studied her blood. The next thing I remember was Sally's glove inches from my eyes, and then I was flat on my ass, the back of my head hitting a rock.

When I came to, my head was in Sally's hands. She was laughing. I sat up, terrified and unaware of my surroundings until Sally shushed me and laid me back down.

"What the hell happened?" I asked.

"You hit me in the nose. I think you broke it. So I decked you," Sally said.

Indeed, Sally had darkness beneath her eyes. She saw that I was looking, and she ran her finger beneath her nose again. A few flecks of dark, dried blood fell onto her knuckle.

"You said strange things, Jackie."

"Like what?"

"You said 'Goddamned farce.'"

"I did?"

"Yes," she laughed, "you did. But I assure you, this was no farce. I decked you." Sally was proud. "What does it mean?" she asked.

I sat up slowly. My head throbbed, especially in the back where it had hit that little rock. I exhaled and kept blinking because my head felt like it was tilted off its axis.

"It was something my mother said to me," I surrendered.

"What did she mean, Jackie?"

"I'm not sure."

"When did she say it?"

"Right before she died. I thought she was in a coma or something, delirious. I was just sitting there, then she talked. I never took it seriously."

Sally scooted up closer to me and sat Indian-style. "How long before she died did she say it, Jackie?"

"Day or two."

"She was telling you something."

"She was dying, she was babbling."

"What else did she say . . . when she babbled?"

"That my father's got this goddamned farce about how proud he is of me."

"Your mother didn't believe he was proud of you?"

"No." I laughed like a nerd. "She said he wanted to kill me." I did the nerd laugh again.

"Why would he want to kill you?"

"She wasn't into psychological stuff and neither am I," I said angrily.

"Some people are what they are."

"My father, you mean?"

"Your father. Other people. People are what they are. Do you think your father wants to kill you?"

I sat up straight and wiped my nose to see if it was still bleeding. It was. I laid back down flat again. I gurgled a little when I tried to speak.

"Yeah." I looked away, but Sally pulled my head back and made me face her.

"It's one of those things you just feel, isn't it, Jackie."

"Yeah," I said, thinking of how annoyed I had been at Angela when she began psychoanalyzing me about my father. The difference here was that I had no intention of diverting the subject by making out with Sally in the woods.

"There is no drama more painful to watch than that of a man coming face to face with his limitations," Sally said. "With his smallness."

"Do you mean to tell me that my dad is limited to ranting at me? How can he come off so sad and helpless to everybody else?"

"Everyone finds a . . . a hook for survival. When you get down to it, Jackie, we're all specialists. Your father's specialty is leveraging sympathizers through his misery and attacking you in private."

"So what the hell am I supposed to do, kill him?"

"That's not in your nature."

"Sure it is. Look at what happened to the two guys who broke into my house."

"You have an exquisite sense of justice, but you're a lamb with people you care about. You want to wipe out all of the nasty little souls."

"If I lightened up on Murrin, I'd fail you as a consultant. I know she's sad, but she's dirty, Sally. Why does being sad have to be a badge to take somebody strong down? Mercy doesn't pay my mortgage."

A stream of blood fell from Sally's nose, as if it were a biological reaction to my comment. I handed her the bandana I had on my head, which she placed beneath her nose. Perhaps my scalp stitches were less visible than I had thought because Sally didn't say anything.

"I can't believe my shot connected that way," I said. She chuckled, surprisingly unconcerned for such a vain woman. Maybe she thought she deserved it.

"Oh, it connected," she said.

"I was just being playful."

"I saw that face, Jackie."

"What face?"

"When I first got you on your nose," she said through the towel. "Your face changed. I knew there was that side. Maybe I needed to see it."

"What side, Sally?"

"The boy-who-survives side. You may not think you wanted to hit me, but you wanted to hit me. You snarled at me, Jackie. It was an animal face, like a panther."

I swallowed awkwardly. "I don't know, maybe it was instinct, or . . ."

"Maybe I provoked it on purpose, to see who I had on my side. I don't know what I did," she laughed.

Thank God she was laughing. That's all I needed, a headline in the *Camden Courier:*

DOILY QUEEN FOLDED BY
SOUTH JERSEY BRAWLER
Sally Naturale KOd by Aging Welterweight "Jackie Disaster"

When she removed the bandana, her nose had a bump on it. I imagine that it looked the way it had before she had it sliced lean like corned beef.

"Sally, let me ask you something."

"Yes, Jackie."

"Why are there cricket sounds coming in through speakers?"

"Oh, you heard them?"

"Yes, I did."

"If I told you, you'd think I was crazy."

"But, Sally, I already do."

"Oh, you're awful. When I was much younger, I was very, very lost. I ran away from home, and lived in the woods for a time. My only friends were the crickets. Do you believe me?"

"If anyone else told me that, I wouldn't believe it."

"But do you believe *me,* Jackie?"

"Somehow, I do."

I only half believed her.

Moonpie

"I need a little buzz in the financial community about an attractive stock."

Every so often in life you meet someone whose personality is appealing in a way that you can't separate from his geographical origin. Chris "Moonpie" Byers was such a man, which was why I harbored a secret fantasy that I had hailed from Oxford, Mississippi, as he did. Moonpie was a gallant golden-haired man with a broad, earnest face, an oversized teddy bear demeanor, and a flair for subversion so profound that I was never able to reconcile it with my vision of a sunny Boy Scout who had once ignited dog shit in a paper bag on the front porches of the South.

Moonpie was now a stock analyst with an investment house in Philly. I got to know him when he hired me to figure out why analysts at a competitive firm were trashing a biotech stock to the financial media. The affair was causing Moonpie career trouble, because he had been pushing the stock, and he suspected something was dirty. He was right. It turned out that these analysts were "connected" guys who were spreading rumors about the stock, and then shorting it for a Trenton mobster. I uncovered the scheme and alerted law enforcement and the media. Moonpie was vindicated, and the biotech company rebounded. Moonpie was grateful, and now I needed him and was happy to have him in my bank.

I took the train from Atlantic City to Philly. Given the scheme I was noodling with, I didn't want to be tracked, which is why I took the train. It was easy to lose a tail in a train station, especially since it was outside of my travel routine.

I hadn't been on a train for years and my heart was pumping at an engorged gallop. For one thing, I didn't like the train because I was not driving it. There was a wiry and greasy-looking man in a tank-top standing at the front of the car holding a ceiling strap and displaying maximum armpit. It was not an attractive look, and it set me in a mood that was to last throughout my ride. Then there was the yuppie broad sitting next to me, talking to Myrna on her cell phone. She was loud. I don't know everything about Myrna yet, but I became aware that she prefers pads to Tampax. I was not pleased to learn that, but I was somewhat more pleased than I was to overhear from the guy on the cell phone in front of me that Willoughby in accounting screwed up the transfer papers with Amato in St. Paul. My jaw was tightening and I was wondering if my chronic rage was becoming a medical issue, as opposed to a quirk.

Next, the guy across the aisle made it clear to the dude sitting next to him, not to mention everyone west of Portugal, that there was no way he was going to cooperate with Vince in marketing. He meant *no way.* The other guy thought this was gutsy, and laughed loudly.

There was a veritable variety show going on around me, with characters using cell phones to announce their significance to the world. Perhaps some of these talks were necessary, but I doubted it. Wasn't it possible to speak softly? Sure it was—but this was wireless showtime in America's commuter vaudeville. *It's the "Me" Show!* Everybody's a player, a star in his own drama that's broadcast via cell phone.

I stood and stepped over the chick next to me talking to Myrna. I wore the Disaster snarl. I wore sunglasses. Against all my better instincts, I stood in the aisle and pulled back my suit jacket just far enough for the chick and the two guys to see that I was heavy with Señor Beretta. I sucked in my breath and took a step back so the other dude yammering on the cell phone about Willoughby could see me. I looked at him. "The Bolsheviks are everywhere!" I said angrily, nostrils flaring, my eyes darting around like a mental patient. "I must stop them! I must!"

The Myrna chick whimpered. The other cell phone guy shut up. The two guys congratulating each other over how one of them won't cooperate with Vince recoiled. Their eyes became tiny oval screens in which they reviewed their lives. I smiled the smile of the brainwashed. I sat back down in my seat as they craned their necks at me, terrified. I looked out the window and quietly sang Glenn Campbell's *Rhinestone Cowboy.* The others ceased talking and were perfectly quiet until the train rolled into Philadelphia.

I met Moonpie at the food court in 30th Street Station. We each grabbed a hoagie and a soft pretzel and sat down among the throngs at grated tables. Moonpie looked like he was twelve, but was about thirty-five. He thanked me over and over again in his courtly way for helping him out a few years ago, which made me feel a little guilty about springing this request on him.

"So, Moonpie," I said. "What's going on with your bad self?"

"How'd you get banged up?" he asked. There was a new scrape on my cheek from my Sally KO.

"Sparring."

"Against who?"

"An old lady."

"Yeah, yeah, yeah. How's your niece?" Moonpie asked.

"You need an intern for summer work?"

"Hah! Isn't Emma ten or something?"

"Yeah, but she's smarter that both of us combined."

"I have a son now who's real smart. He's three and he knows all the presidents."

"All of them, huh? Even those James Buchanan guys, all them?"

"Honestly, Jackie, he does. I'm surprised you know James Buchanan. You don't strike me as the kind who dives into history books."

"You'd be wrong. I just act like a hard ass, but I read all kinds of books."

"You'd never know it."

"I need a certain act in my business, you know, like when Columbo acted like a nitwit? If I came up against one of the scuzz buckets I run into and started going, 'Hey, did you know that James Buchanan was the only president who wasn't married?' they wouldn't open up."

"Is that true about Buchanan?"

"Oh, yeah, Buchanan's my friend Freddy's favorite president. He thinks he was gay like him."

"What does he base that on, that Buchanan wasn't married?"

"See, Freddy thinks everything means somebody's secretly gay. It's how he sees the world. If you talk about a president, any president, he starts with Buchanan. If you talk about the Middle East, he starts telling you Arafat is gay."

"Arafat?"

"Oh, yeah, he's big on Arafat being gay. He says the wife's a beard. He's obsessed with it. What are you going to do?"

Moonpie fiddled with a few potato chips. "It sounds like you need me for one of your endeavors, I guess?" He was a bit nervous.

"I need you to kill Arafat," I deadpanned.

"What?" Moonpie looked genuinely terrified. I really think he thought I killed people.

"I think we can make it look like a love triangle thing, you know, a Gianni Versace deal."

I smirked at Moonpie and he spit out a few potato chips, hysterical.

"No, look," I said, "I need a little buzz in the financial community about an attractive stock."

"Is the stock really attractive?"

"Yes, no, maybe, maybe not. This isn't really about money."

"Seriously, Jackie, you're not talking about a trading scheme because. . . ."

"No, honestly Moonpie. There's no insider trading. Nothing like that. I just need some kind of buzz."

"What's your game if it's not money?"

"Human behavior. I want to rock somebody's world to see what he does. I've got some folks . . . I can't tell what side they're on. This may help. If you need some money, I'll pay."

"No, best if I don't take anything. What are we talking about?"

"E-mails. Internet message boards. People thinking big news is coming down."

"That's pedestrian enough."

"Exactly. We're not looking to rock the markets, just see how naughty boys react."

I told Moonpie about my lunatic stunt on the train ride into Philly. He laughed his ass off, but felt a competitive need to match my shameless immaturity. We concluded our meeting with Moonpie deciding to torture a poor service worker of unclear ethnicity at the food court. He asked the attendant in his genteel manner, "Is there a rest room nearby?"

The young man said yes and pointed the way.

Moonpie waved him in closer as I sat back to enjoy the entertainment. Moonpie darted his eyes around conspiratorially and asked the attendant, "What can I do in there?"

The attendant asked, "In the bathroom?"

"Yes, sir," Moonpie said politely.

I covered my mouth.

"You, uh, do what you do in a bathroom, I guess," the attendant said.

"Hmm. I'm a little confused. You're saying I can do anything I want in the bathroom?" Moonpie asked, eyes widening, pervert-style.

"You can do what you do in a bathroom," The attendant reiterated.

"Hmm," Moonpie muttered pensively as the attendant walked away.

When he was gone, Moonpie howled at having completely mind-slammed the guy.

"I'm going to look forward to working with you again, Pie," I said.

"It'll be fun," Moonpie said snickering off to the restroom.

My campaign was throttling up.

On the train ride back to Atlantic City, my cell phone rang. I answered it and walked onto the platform in between cars, because I didn't want to bother anybody. Nate the Great had been on assignment rifling through Sally's trash to follow up on my hunch.

"Yo," Nate the Great said.

"Where are you?"

"I'm in a goddamned wet suit inside a goddamned dumpster you know goddamned where."

"Keep it vague, buddy."

"Little Miss Silk Panties seems to throw away a lot of high-octane chemicals for a nature-girl."

"What kind of chemicals?"

"Naughty chemicals. Boom-boom chemicals."

Over one weekend in mid-June, Internet message boards were ablaze with rumors that Naturale's Real Living was ripe for a takeover. The buzz even bounced up to the mainstream news media, as stock analysts began calling Naturale, the company's potential suitors, and their contacts in the business media to see what they knew. This roundup story ran on the following Tuesday morning in *The Bulletin:*

NATURALE SHARES SURGE

Shares in Naturale's Real Living surged on speculation that the company might be a target for takeover by Millennium Taste Lifestyles, the Los Angeles-based conglomerate. Naturale shares rose by 9¾ points to close at $35.25 per share.

In a company statement, CEO Sally Naturale denied that the company was on the block. "We're not for sale," Naturale said. "This doesn't mean that we would never entertain a reasonable offer, but we are not in discussion with Millennium Taste Lifestyles."

> However, according to an E-mail received by *The Bulletin*, Sally Naturale had, as of last Friday, scheduled a meeting with Harry Welman, chief executive of Genuine Article, the Kansas City-based gourmet housewares company.

Somewhere on a golf course on Philadelphia's Main Line, Moonpie was having a Margarita.

Bebe Has a Heart

"So, Jackie, it's your job to take out the garbage of American business, is that it?"

The Lord had been supervising a freelancer we had tailing Frankie Shrugs, who had gone back and forth between Naturale's Earth and Vincent's Friggin' Hardware Store in South Philly twice in one day. During that day, Frankie Shrugs also met with Bebe Naturale at Pennypacker Park in Cherry Hill. I had abandoned any guilt that I once harbored about initially judging Bebe Naturale as a squat thug. This is precisely what I suspected he was, albeit a squat thug capable of low-rent charm when it availed him.

One time, Frankie Shrugs and Bebe were conferring with a well-dressed middle-aged dude. We didn't recognize him, but our freelancer snapped his picture. We had no way of knowing what they were talking about, but they seemed uptight. During their furtive meeting, Frankie Shrugs had answered his cell phone twice and sighed mightily both times. Somebody was giving him grief, and that somebody very likely worked out of Vincent's Friggin' Hardware Store.

When the reports came in, I decided that a chance meeting with Bebe Naturale was in order. I wanted to study the guy and get a sense of what he was worried about. I'm not being entirely honest here. I wanted to screw with him because, ever since *The Bulletin* broke its story about the impending takeover of Naturale's Real Living, the Beebster had been going nuts. The question was why.

My objective in fabricating the Naturale takeover with my friend Moonpie was not to engage in stock fraud, but just to watch what Bebe and the boys did. Having watched Petey Breath Mints in action for years, I was inclined to believe him when he said, hovering over his scatological fjord, that his involvement in these escapades was limited. While he had certainly intended to kill me, it was plausible that he didn't know exactly why he had been given the order. One of the few things that I learned when I was with the A.C.P.D. was that when an investigation was standing still, it never hurt to "shake the trees" to see what flew out. Even if you didn't know what you were looking for, disruptions tended to provoke paranoia in bad men, and paranoia in turn provoked careless behavior.

By introducing the variable of a takeover, I thought I could disrupt Bebe and Frankie Shrugs, and that something vital would emerge.

I wandered through Naturale's Earth and inquired about Bebe's whereabouts. When Viscount Selkirk said that Bebe was about to take the ferry over to Cricket Crest, I ran into him accidentally on purpose. Bebe was waddling toward the ferry in an all-white jumpsuit. He looked like a clump of walking laundry.

"Hey there, Bebe."

"Yeah, Jackie. What are you doing?" *Whatcherdoon.* "Here to see Sally?"

"I was in the area and thought I'd stop by. Anything interesting happening here?"

"Nah," he said after a hesitation. He pulled at his pants. "I'm a little worried about my sister. She's obsessed with this Murrin thing."

"How do you feel about it these days?"

"I'm worried. This stuff never helps the image of the company, and we're all about image, you know?"

"Sure."

"I go back and forth, Jackie. Sometimes I get so angry at that bitch Murrin that I want to let you go full steam ahead. Other times, I wonder if the cure isn't worse than the disease. I'm not trying to be a pain in the ass."

"I know, Bebe. It's your business. You're torn between the ways this could go."

"Just go gentle on Sally. She's not always all together, you know."

"I was going to ask her about the merger," I continued. "I hadn't heard anything about it and was taken off guard."

"Uh-huh." He bore in on me. "Whattaya think?"

"That's how people make fortunes."

"You a shareholder, Jackie?"

"No, I don't buy stock in client companies."

"No? Why not?"

"Because sometimes I have sensitive information and I don't want to ever be accused of trading on it. If I don't own stock, I can't be accused."

"Uh-huh."

"I'd love to be in a position to retire. You're lucky, Bebe. You're all set."

“Whattaya know about being all set?” he asked.

“Nothing,” I said. “Just thought you’d be happy.”

“When you build a business from nothing, you love it like a kid.”

“I guess that’s true.”

“It’s not all about money, Jackie.”

“I know.”

“He knows,” Bebe said to a tree. “So, Jackie, it’s your job to take out the garbage of American business, is that it?” he said with a false laugh that he hoped would sound spontaneous.

“That’s only part of it.”

“Yeah, what’s the rest?”

“I not only take out the trash, I bury it.”

“Yeah? No shit. Just do me a favor, don’t push Sally too hard, huh?” Bebe waddled away onto the ferry like an albino penguin with gas.

I thought of Bebe as a slob, the kind of guy who wanted the degenerate life, something that a rich buyout would have yielded. Sure, it was plausible that he didn’t want to lose control over a business he built, but I now believed he had something going on with Frankie Shrugs and the boys, where an acquisition meant trouble. They wanted to control Naturale for some other purpose, and that purpose was sufficiently important to render the millions that would be earned in a takeover irrelevant.

There is an intangible moment when two people decide they are enemies. That moment is based less on a specific declaration than a mutually intuitive recognition that agendas are on a collision course. That moment had just come for Bebe and me.

A good-looking Naturale sales girl waved to Bebe from the ferry. I watched as Bebe came to life, sucked in his gut and asked her how things were going.

BOOK III

A Lower Truth

It is a shameful thing that you should mind these folks that are out of their wits.

—accused witch Martha Carrier, executed in Salem, Massachusetts, August 19, 1692

Baked Upper Crust

"When I saw all of the black smoke,
I knew we were dealing with a whole other gig."

At first, the patrolman thought that the smoke rising above Naturale's Earth was a result of garden-variety fireworks and high jinks. It was, after all, the early morning of July 4th and for decades wooded Medford Lakes had been a gathering place for South Jersey kids prone to celebrating freedom by blowing things up with M-80s, including the occasional house pet. Somehow, blowing things up had managed to become a constitutional right, if the testimony from local court proceedings offered insight into the local mindset.

Officer Hank Vargas radioed in to the Medford Fire Department when he smelled smoke. He also alerted the New Jersey State Police. The scent invited his cruiser toward the gated driveway of Cricket Crest. As is customary for the recently gilded, Sally Naturale's monstrous house could be seen from the road. The idea behind the wrought iron entrance was to pose for privacy when shameless exposure had been the real objective.

Cricket Crest rose in the summer sunrise, gaudy, flabby with its turrets and moats, but intact. The enormous black mass that floated above it like a Satanic halo suggested a catalyst other than a handful of zitty punks with liberation from King George on their minds.

The blackened dome of Naturale's Earth imploded beneath the helicopters of the Philadelphia-area network television affiliates. This happened at about eight o'clock in the morning, which would have been rush hour, had it not been for the holiday. Traditionally, holidays are a slow news time, but on Independence Day, the news often focuses on traffic. Traffic is covered via helicopter. Helicopters are always ready to go on holiday weekends, desperate for action.

So it was that their high-flying camera crews captured the Armageddon at Naturale's Earth from the first radio report from Officer Vargas to cinders collapsing on the stadium-sized retail center filled with David Geffences and well-done Upper Crust Pizza.

The morning after the fire, *The Bulletin* ran with an article under the banner headline—

NATURALE'S EARTH DESTROYED BY FIRE.
GOOD TASTE DOYENNE IS MISSING
Sharon Hahn
Staff Reporter for *The Bulletin*

Medford, N.J.——An early morning fire reduced to ashes Naturale's Earth, the South Jersey mega-shopping complex developed by America's doyenne of good taste, Sally Naturale. Despite the enormity of the fire, according to local authorities, no bodies have been found in the wreckage. However, Ms. Naturale remains unaccounted for. According to her brother, Bebe Naturale, she was not at their palatial estate, Cricket Crest, which is across a small lake from the one-million-square-foot shopping mall that bears their name.

Firefighters were called to Naturale's Earth at approximately six o'clock on the morning of July 4th after a police cruiser reporter seeing smoke in the vicinity. Within the hour, dozens of fire trucks from Burlington and Camden counties were on the scene.

It took six hours to bring the blaze under control. Hundreds of Medford-area residents gathered behind police lines to watch as the dome caved in with an enormous boom that echoed for miles, sending the "golden woman" statue (Ms. Naturale once described her as the Goddess of Refinement) atop it plummeting through the roof and into the cinders. Ash spewed into the air and virtually covered the lake that separated the megaplex from Cricket Crest.

"When I smelled smoke," said Officer Hank Vargas, who was first on the scene said, "I figured it was the fireworks pranks we've gotten here for years. But when I saw all of the black smoke, I knew we were dealing with a whole other gig."

Captain Fred Squires of the Medford Lakes Fire Department said that authorities have no idea at present what might have caused the fire and have not ruled anything out.

Among those watching the facility burn was Bebe Naturale, who was too shocked to offer comment. News cameras recording the fire captured a dazed Naturale staring at the fire from

> his stone porch at Cricket Crest until the smoke became too thick and he was encouraged to move indoors.
>
> A spokesman for the company, Nancy Straub, indicated that Sally Naturale, a notorious workaholic, was known to ferry over to her office in the great dome early in the morning. A habitual user of cellular phones and walkie-talkies, it is highly unusual for her not to check in frequently with her colleagues, explained Straub. "We're very, very concerned," she said, adding that Naturale had not been planning any trips out of the area to her knowledge.

The article went on to give a history of Naturale's Real Living, along with the usual adjectives that Sally had hammered into her mystique—secretive, private—and, of course, the obligatory, but vague allusions to her privileged childhood on America's "golden shores."

The Devil Calls

"I know the truth about your baby."

As ash from Naturale's Earth rained down on South Jersey, I became consumed with worry. In anxious times, the most potent therapy I knew was work. Despite the uncertainty of Sally's fate, we had been instructed—and funded—for continued work. The Lord plopped himself down on one of my guest chairs and smirked nervously at me. Air from the vent above him blew his hair around.

"Okay, Oswald, what did you kill?" I asked him.

"Nothing. I went through the money records I swiped from Naturale's storage center," the Lord said.

"Anything interesting?"

"Sally was charitable."

"That's not surprising."

"Here's what's bugging me: She gave ten million to some college a few days before she took Naturale's public."

"Ten million?"

"Ten million."

"What college?"

"Beaver."

We both laughed.

"What do you know about the place?" the Lord asked.

"Suburban Philly. It was all girls, but they changed the name a couple of years ago."

"Wise choice."

"Did Sally go there, Lordo?"

"Don't know. And there was no publicity around the gift. Not a building named for her, nothing. So I had this chick I know call the school and say she was doing a story on successful women entrepreneurs who attended local colleges. The kid at the school said they had no record of Sally Naturale going there."

"Hmm."

"What do you make of it, Jackie?"

"Sally put her name on everything she does. Why not this?"

"That's a good question."

"I put Sally in her mid-sixties now. That would have made her a college graduate in the late 1950s or early 1960s. Until we get her real name, we can't get an exact date of birth."

"Yeah, so?"

"See if you can find out where that school keeps its academic records." The Lord smirked again, this time, a little less nervously.

Murrin's phone rang early in the morning. She answered it in the kitchen.

"Hello?"

"Murrin Connolly," a deep voice accused.

"Who's this?"

"I know the truth about your baby."

"Who is this?!"

"I know the truth." Click.

A Little Confession With-a Father Vic

"I feel like people are looking at me like they think it's my fault."

Murrin was hysterical. I could see she was crying. She had thrown on an unflattering green sweatsuit that had pant legs that were too short. The sun reflected off her blinding white calves as she wiped her nose with a crumpled yellow tissue that she had pulled from her handbag.

I was wearing a clerical collar, a long-haired wig, a faux mustache and wire-rimmed glasses. I was aiming shamelessly for *Saturday Night Live*'s Father Guido Sarducci, the hipster priest who could be forgiven for not knowing what he was doing, perhaps because he had just done a doobie in the back of his van. In a sting, sometimes slick is a liability, and idiocy is genius. I tilted my head at Murrin, sensitively, as she entered St. Thomas Aquinas parish in Salem County. Her eyes expressed abject betrayal when she saw that Father Dan was not on hand.

"Where's Father Dan?" Murrin asked.

"He's not-a here, Murrin," I said.

"I don't remember you," she sniffed. Her eyes were darting around in search of Father Dan.

"Why, I'm-a Father Vic," I said gently. "I'm from St. Thomas More in a-Deptford, and we met at last-a Easter's picnic. I was-a the bunny rabbit." I held up my hands to my chest like a moron bunny rabbit. "I sometimes fill in-a for other priests when they're having the commitments."

"There were so many people there. I don't remember the bunny."

"That's-a to be understanding. Who can always remember a bunny? Bunnies must-a be anonymous 'cause it's a costume, like-a Halloweening. What is wrong-a, Murrin?"

"I've been coming to confession a lot."

"Would you like to come back-a tomorrow when Father Dan is here?"

"Yeah. I mean, no. I need to talk to someone."

"I'd-a be pleased to speak-a with you," I said, taking her hand, "but I wouldn't be offending if you would-a rather meet-a with Father Dan. I was just-a blowing the balloons up for a picnic. I'm always afraid they gonna pop-a like a balloon. That-a scare-a me for the reasons."

"Can we go inside?"

We proceeded into the church and sat in one of the pews. There was no one else in the sanctuary.

"It feels weird talking to someone I don't know," Murrin said.

"Talking to somebody you don't-a know makes you feel like a wing-a ding. I always am thinking confession is-a strange for that reasoning. Why-a would a person go into a little phone booth and tell-a everything to a stranger? It never made-a sense to me. But then-a, when I came to America, I learned about having faithings in people, and it made-a more sense."

Murrin laughed and studied me curiously. By confirming her discomfort, not to mention throwing in a pinch of lunacy, the threat was defusing.

"I'll-a tell you what, Murrin," Father Vic continued. "If you're-a worried about what's on-a your mind, make-a up some of your tellings. That way, you get to feel-a better. It'll be like-a story time, not a confessings."

Murrin snickered again and clucked out an, "Okay. I did, uh, I may have done something very bad."

"Go on."

"My baby," Murrin said.

"What's a matter with-a the bambino?"

"The baby died."

"Oh, no! How does this-a happen to a nice-a girl? This is what gets-a me so mad. It makes-a me wanna scream at the churchings. How old was the baby?"

"The baby was in me."

Long hesitation.

"The baby was not-a yet born, Murrin?"

"Yes."

"Was there a sickness?"

"No. Not that I know. No."

"How far along in babyness were-a you, Murrin?"

"Four months."

"I have-a to ask you this-a, Murrin. You did-a not . . . terminal the baby?"

"No, I did not terminal. I mean, you know."

"Then-a why do you take the responsibilitings?"

"Yes, I do feel guilty."

"Why is that, Murrin?"

"I don't know, I just do," she cried.

"Bambinos can-a be lost sometimes, and the mother has grievings but doesn't always think-a she's done the fault."

"But I do."

I sighed. My sigh was audible and followed by a pause. I felt moisture around my scalp.

"Murrin, did-a you do something you want to tell me for?"

"I just feel responsible. I feel like people are looking at me like they think it's my fault."

"Other people, they are-a so goofy. They think-a this. They think-a that. They think-a they see Elvis Presley at-a the Donald Trumpet Casino. How can-a they see-a Elvis? He ate a hamburger with-a peanut butter and he-a died. Donald Trumpet probably never knew-a Elvis Presley. I was in college in Napoli. Then I come to America and-a they say in the paper that Elvis is-a working in a Burger King in-a Pittsburgh. So why would-a you even listen to the silly people?"

"You're very funny, Father Vic. You make me laugh. I don't laugh a lot lately."

"But-a this is my job. Everybody-a says I have the funny bones, but I just listen and say-a what comes into my earlobes. You know-a what I think? People think-a you had ablution to the baby and-a it gives you the crazings."

"No. No, I did not have an—I did not do that."

"But-a you feel at faultings?"

"Yes, I do."

"If you did not-a terminal the baby, but you feel-a like you hurt your baby, what did you do to make you feel-a like you did?"

"I am so sad. I feel like I hurt my baby, but I have always been sad."

"Even before the bambino went away?" My breath began to feel short. As my eyes bore into Murrin's, while I thought she was lying, I also began wondering whether or not the harm caused by my campaign might be outweighing whatever her crime was.

"Were you sad-a when you were pregnataled?" I continued, fanning myself with a prayer card.

"Yes."

"Did you tell-a your doctor?" I asked, removing a handkerchief and wiping my brow. I felt as if my moustache might be slipping, so I held it in place, trying to pass it off as an odd gesture by an odd man.

"I didn't talk to the baby doctor."

"You talked-a to another doctor?"

"Yes."

"What-a kind of doctor?"

"You know, for your feelings." Murrin wailed and ran from the church. I followed her into the parking lot as soon as I realized that she was not coming back. She climbed into her car and sped away. I swallowed hard behind the rented van where the Lord was waiting. Swervin' Mervin radioed in from his Cessna: "She's heading for her mother's."

"You don't look so hot, Jackie," Nate the Great said. I was meeting with Nate and the Lord over a soda at the counter at Ponzio's in Cherry Hill. We were planning to go into Camden on the Naturale matter after sunset.

"I think the chick's dirty," I told them.

"You thought she was guilty before," the Lord said.

"My stomach's bothering me," I said.

"He heaved up his lungs at the church," the Lord told Nate.

"I don't want to talk about it right now," I said.

"Do you think she's lying about how she lost the baby?" Nate the Great asked.

"Maybe, maybe not. It's this whole doctor thing that's gnawing at me. It looks like she went to another doctor, maybe a psychiatrist."

"Maybe she's embarrassed about her situation," the Lord suggested. "She's paranoid. She thinks everybody's talking about her."

"That's because she's guilty of something," I said. "She's keeping secrets from everybody that she should be honest with. If she edits with her priest, she probably edits with her doctor. She ran out of the church when I started on her with the doctors."

"You know when my patients lied to me?" Nate the Great asked.

"When?"

"When they weren't following doctors orders."

"Okay," I said. "But she was seeing two doctors. Whose orders wasn't she following?"

"Jackie, some patients think if they don't say anything, all's well," Nate calmly reasoned.

"It's like, if they don't go to the doctor, they won't get sick, that kind of crap?" the Lord asked.

"Right," Nate the Great explained. "It could be a contraindication kind of deal."

"What does that mean?" I asked.

"Say you've got a heart attack patient," Nate began. "He takes something to lower cholesterol, but he still wants to treat his body like hell. So he takes the cholesterol medicine *and* he keeps smoking and eating eggs, but he tells his doc he's a good boy. Or, say, you've got an athlete who has a Doc Feelgood giving him steroids, but tells his team doc he's clean."

"Okay, Nate, it makes sense, but what about a miserable pregnant woman?" I asked.

"Miserable and pregnant, guys, is not a good combo," Nate said authoritatively.

"Why?" the Lord asked. "You don't eat right and it screws up the kid?"

"Not so much," Nate the Great said, solemnly, "If you drink too much or take certain medicines when you're pregnant . . . bye-bye baby."

Going In

"Homeowners assume that because garage doors are large and noisy, they won't be used."

Maybe I've been warped by the odd business I'm in, but I'm convinced that the key to survival in millennial America is audacity. Audacity is virtue; subtlety is a crime, which is why we chose to break into Murrin Connolly's house in broad daylight.

The house in Salem County was a three-bedroom rancher. The van out in front with fraudulent tags read "Salem Utility." I changed into jeans and a Salem County utility top, identical to the one that the Lord wore. He also wore a fake beard and a baseball cap with a fake ponytail attached.

First, the Lord killed power to Murrin's street by climbing up a utility pole and doing something unknowable to a transformer at the end of the block. This would serve two purposes. It would disable the brand of automatic garage door opener that Murrin had at her house (the Lord had taken zoom lens shots of the apparatus the prior week as Murrin pulled out), and it would keep the neighbors inside their homes waiting to see if their power would come back on.

The Lord always went for the garage door first. Homeowners assume that because garage doors are large and noisy they won't be used. This is true in the nighttime when it's quiet, but not in daylight. The other thing people forget is that the inner door that separates the garage from the house is inevitably the most vulnerable because of the dual—and false—assumptions that the garage door will not be used at all, and that burglars would have to go through the hassle of getting through two doors versus one.

The Lord proceeded to the garage door wearing workman's gloves. This brand of opener shut itself off during power outages and allowed residents manual control. It had something to do with past injuries and deaths when the immobilized garage door created a firetrap. I waited in the back of the van.

The Lord pivoted with his back against the door and did something to the handle that made it turn. He lifted up the door about two feet, and in a deft gymnastic move disappeared beneath it and shut it behind him. "I'm in," he said into the little mike he had clipped onto his shirt.

Murrin had not bothered to lock the inner door of the garage. The Lord moved through the house, first to the kitchen. In rapid-fire, he listed the contents of the refrigerator in accordance with the products I told him I was looking for. I took notes. He moved to the downstairs pantry and powder room and repeated his list.

I fell over after a loud banging hit the rear of the van a few feet from where I was huddled inside.

"Motherf—" I whispered.

"What's wrong?" the Lord asked.

"Somebody just banged on the van," I said softly.

"Shit."

"What do you think I should do?" I asked.

"Shit."

"Big help!"

"Okay," the Lord composed himself, "If you answer it, they'll know somebody is in front of Murrin's house."

"They know that now."

"But not *in* her house."

"They may have seen the garage deal."

"Let's keep going. Here's what we're gonna do. I'll move upstairs, go through the routine but won't exit through the garage. I'll go out the back and I'll meet you up on the street behind us."

"What if it's a cop out there?"

"I just shut the power down, how could it be a cop this quick? It's probably a neighbor who saw a utility van. Let's keep going," the Lord said.

"Okay."

"Pull out slow when you go."

"Got it, now move upstairs," I said as quietly as I could.

I heard the thunk of the Lord's gazelle leaps up the stairs.

"Guest bath," the Lord said. He fired off the products in the bathroom.

"Got 'em," I said. He moved to the master bath.

"Master bath," he said. Product list.

"Okay," I said. "Hit the dresser."

Another damned bang on the van door. The shadow of a great big pumpkin head appeared in the driver's side of the window. I decided to choke it down and ignore it. In my headphones, I heard the sound of a drawer opening inside the house and the Lord mumbling, "What a cow." He shook something that sounded like a baby rattle, and read me the name of the product.

"That'll be all," I said after uttering "The Lord's work is done."

The operation lasted four minutes.

I climbed from the rear of the van into the driver's seat. In my side mirror, I saw the confused expression of a middle-aged woman with helmet hair and needlepoint, almost certainly a neighbor who had knocked to inquire about the power. If I peeled out, it would signal guilt. I had my Father Vic wig, moustache, and glasses in a bag on the passenger seat. I slapped the wig and the moustache on, but used my regular sunglasses. Helmet Head knocked on the window. I grabbed the walkie-talkie I had been using to communicate with the Lord and turned it up. I rolled down my window and Helmet Head appeared with her scrunched up little face.

"What's the matter with you, are you deaf?" she asked me, waving her needlepoint at me.

"I'm sorry Miss," I said employing a Southern accent. "Was that you knockin' against the van?"

"Who do you think it was, Julia Roberts?"

"Sorry there, Miss," I said loudly over the screeching of the walkie-talkie, which I had changed to a neutral channel that would loudly make white noise. "I had on headphones and I was talking to my boss who was checkin' out the colonical wire that goes back to the valvitator." I thought it was wise to give her too many details to stress what a nonentity I was.

"Are you the one that caused the power to blow out?" Helmet Head asked. I studied her eyes. They were the eyes of a bored and powerless busybody for whom gratuitous confrontation was the climax of her day. What's the strategy here, Jackie boy? The tiny cogs in my brain wrenched into a higher gear. Let her win, Giovanni. Let her go to her Garden Club and let everybody know that she had reamed out a loser.

"I sure as heck hope not," I said. "I just pulled over here because I was trying to find the house of somebody needing a satellite wire re-link. See, I do freelance work on the side, but my boss, Mr. Peterson, sometimes he don't tell me when he has my regular punch-work scheduled."

"What's going on with the power? We don't have any power! Did you do something to knock out the power?"

"I sure do hope not. I did examine the transformer down the block to see what kind of current receptor you had. See, sometimes neighborhoods like this use the three-twenty B model, and other times they use the three-twenty B *junior* model. All I did was take a look, honest."

"I don't care about any junior model, I just want my power back."

"Well, that's the county, Miss, that handles power . . ."

"I don't have time to get caught up in that mess. You do something, do you hear me?"

"I'll tell you what I'll do, Miss. I'll go right back to that transformer and check it out. If it's not right, I'll radio into the county myself."

"You better. I have the name of your company and I'll make so much trouble for you that . . ."

"I think I can fix it, Miss. Really, I think I can." I swallowed hard so she could see my fear.

I slowly drove away and picked up the Lord on the next block. We couldn't have Helmet Head calling the authorities, so we pulled up to the utility pole, and the Lord hustled to the top and returned power. Presumably, the return to normalcy gave Helmet Head the power surge she needed.

Petey Confesses, Too

"He'll know what is going to happen to him if he fails to carry a tune."

My Internet chat room name was Boardwalk. Before lunch, I logged on to Bermudatriangle.com, where celebrity sightings were discussed with passion but no reliability. Chat rooms played an important role in disinformation, because anybody could log on and pretend to be an expert on a subject. Trafficking in false information had a way of migrating into the mainstream media as if it were fact.

BOARDWALK: Friend with Jersey cops said brother Bebe was asked for DNA sample.

ASBURY: Holy shit!

LOSERDOG: They think her brother did it?

BOARDWALK: Not sure. Said he was into bad stuff.

PORNSTAR: Word on this side of Delaware that he's in mob.

REGIMUS: You're all wrong. Sally took a vaca. Homes all over the world.

BOARDWALK: Then why are fuzz all over South Jersey talking to dentists?

ASHBURY: They're looking for dental records?

BOARDWALK: Looks like it.

CONEHEAD: What's up, gang?

REGIMUS: Yo Cone.

PORNSTAR: Where you been, Cone? Hear about the insider-trading thing with Sally?

BOARDWALK: Heard that, too. Something about brother involved with giving Mafia types stock.

REGIMUS: All true but Sally escaped. She was gonna blow the whistle on those scuzzbuckets. She's in friggin' France.

CONEHEAD: How could she not know sleazebaggery is going on in own shop? Like that Enron guy Lay didn't know. Boolsheeeat.

BOARDWALK: She's the face of the company, not day-to-day manager. That's her brother.

ASHBURY: Cousin met her at Earth opening. Says she's sweet little thing. A little wacky, but sweet. She fell in with a bad bunch of MFs.

CONEHEAD: Maybe. Whole things sounds funky. Heard something that Naturale deals arms.

PORNSTAR: Not worth having a big old house if they're gonna kill your ass in the end.

REGIMUS: I'll say.

GODSON: Just logged on. Guy I know with Newark crew said Bebe is a Ecstasy fiend. Supplies him.

BOARDWALK: Heard same kinda stuff, Godson. Bad crowd. Cesspool out in the Pines, huh?

GODSON: You said it, Boards.

REGIMUS: I see on my screen that they found an E-mail from Sally. Whoa!

Jonah's chat room name was Godson.

The Bulletin's website reported that same day that the authorities had discovered correspondence on the company's off-site server indicating that Sally Naturale had sent one of her communications aides an e-mail on the morning of the fire. The E-mail read: "I'm afraid we will have to take up this matter in another life. As far as I am concerned, the Sally you know doesn't exist anymore."

The Internet came alive with speculation about what these words meant, the two primary theories being that it was a suicide note or that Sally feared for her life.

While I was waiting for Trouble on the boardwalk outside of the Golden Prospect, my cell phone rang. It was a guy I had inside of the Delaware River Port Authority.

"What do you have?" I asked.

"The guy in that picture you sent me? With the goons? In the park in Cherry Hill? Name is Thelmont. He's with us."

"Thanks. Nice work. You will be remembered with affection."

"I always wondered why Thelmont dressed so good."

"Now you know."

. . .

Trouble was late for our boardwalk meeting and I was getting antsy. A little boy about three years old walked beside me holding his mother's hand. He wore a stupid denim hat with the Phillies' insignia, presumably to protect him from the July sun. His eyes were wet and sad looking. I had this horrid impulse to jump up from the bench and shriek at him—*Grraaaahhhhhh!*—and push his mother onto the sand so he couldn't run to her for cover, show him what the boardwalk was all about. Stunned and ashamed of myself beyond belief, I set my cell phone down, crossed myself and prayed for forgiveness, hands clasped and everything. I hated all of that Freudian crap, but I was pretty sure I knew where this stuff came from. Here's this little kid who is lucky enough to have his mother and I'm thinking how all my mother did was left me with Blinky Dom's venom and tragedy. If nobody in my family gets protection, why should this little guy? What am I doing? Running around dressed like Father Guido Sarducci trying to squeeze out a confession from a miserable fat girl.

Trouble finally walked up and startled me. "Say one for me, would you?"

"Say what?"

"A prayer," he said.

"Did I look like I was praying?"

"Yeah, you did."

"I'm very spiritual," I said hoping a comical admission would be more effective than a stone-faced denial.

Trouble had a mischievous look on his face.

"Jackie," he said, "Why is it that every time I get together with you I get the feeling we're going to toilet paper a house?"

"You think that's a crazy reaction?"

"Do you?"

"Nah, it's rational. But tp-ing a house, that's small time. I'm more of a light-a-bag-of-dog-shit-on-fire-then-ring-the-doorbell-and-run-away kind of guy."

"You bring any dog shit?"

I took out my little tape recorder and played Trouble a morsel. In the preview, Petey was saying, *"All I do is distribute. I don't know where it comes from. I handle A.C. and the whole island. Ventnor, Margate, Longport. Frankie Shrugs is my skipper."*

Trouble's eyes widened. "Is that Petey Breath Mints?" he said, sounding like a kid who had just gotten a glimpse of a *Playboy*.

"Yup."

"How did you get this?"

"Petey tried to kill me a little while ago. He jumped me down at Apples' Gym early one morning and tried to knife me. I shot him in the hip, not serious. You want to know more?"

"Holy Moses. Just what I need to know."

"He, uh, volunteered to talk. I volunteered to listen and to tape. I convinced him he'd be safer with you, become Flipper the Dolphin, but you'll have to play a little game. If he decides not to repeat this stuff, just tell him that things are starting to smell. Sniff a little. He'll know what is going to happen to him if he fails to carry a tune."

"Sniff, huh?"

"Yeah, sniff. I really believe Petie's just a button, not a strategy guy. But I think he can give you Frankie Shrugs and maybe even more. I've got other stuff going that should produce bigger, and I'll let you know."

"Need more of a hint, Jackie."

"Mob guys and corporate types in Jersey. Crooked Port Authority types in Philly . . ."

"Whoa, across state lines! That's a federal pinch."

I didn't need to tell Trouble that a federal takedown would be a great career move for him, but volunteered, "Just think, Trouble, it took a former Secret Service agent turned Atlantic City chief-of-police to crack it."

"I didn't crack a damned thing yet. Where do I find Petey?"

"You know that Korean market on Indiana Avenue?"

"Tee Kim's?"

"Kim's got some funky meat hanging in the storage locker."

Changing the Definition

"Some people lie because it is who they are."

I called the Holy Cannoli to see if he was in the mood for some honey-roasted peanuts.

"Honey-roasted, huh?" How's the cholesterol on those?"

"I don't know, I don't eat them. I figure they're worse than apples and better than whipped butter."

"A reasonable compromise," Father Ignacio said. "It's hard to park where you are."

"Tell the valet you're with me. I'll take care of it." The magic words. I called down to the Golden Prospect's valet service and told them to comp the Holy Cannoli.

We took a walk on the boardwalk. Father Ignacio was dressed in classic Franciscan attire—the baggy brown robe, the sandals. I bought him a bag of honey-roasted peanuts, which he dove into like Greg Louganis.

"You want some, Jackie?" he asked, his face getting sticky.

"No thanks."

"You've got to enjoy God's treats more."

"I'm not a big enjoyer."

"That's got to change. I'm not suggesting a life of sin—just eat a little more."

"I'm afraid of getting, uh . . . I like to keep in shape."

"You're a diplomat suddenly? You meant you didn't want to become fat like me."

"I like to keep in shape. I was a boxer."

"So was I," Father Ignacio said. Everybody's a boxer. "What do you worry about? Your health? Or is it another fear?"

This was as good a time for confession as any. "I don't want to become just another boardwalk *cafone*. You're a priest. Nobody'll think you're a goon."

"There are skinny goons."

"It's just the image . . . the image of a big Italian goon. It drives me crazy. I don't know why."

"So, if given the choice between sacrificing food and foreswearing the mischief you do in your career, you'll hold back on the food?" he asked.

"I never thought of it that way."

"Every now and then a priest can have a worthy thought," Father Ignacio said, slamming a handful of peanuts into his mouth and swallowing them without chewing much.

"I agree. I have a question for you about something I'm working on. Father, why do you think somebody would lie about something stupid?"

"Maybe it's not stupid to them," he said. A lone peanut dropped onto the boardwalk and rolled away. Father Ignacio mournfully watched it drop between the slats.

"Say you asked me what I had for breakfast. In real life, I had cereal. Why would I say, 'I had scrambled eggs'?"

"You wouldn't."

"But a certain type of person would."

"A liar."

"Right. But why lie about something so stupid?"

"You have to look at the essence of a person. Their soul."

"I don't get it."

"Some people are corrupt in their core, deep inside. Anything that flows from such a person is then corrupt."

"But there's no reason to lie about something when it doesn't give you any advantage."

"That's what I mean by essence. When something unholy is in your core, you don't need a reason. Think of the word 'reason.' To be reasonable is to engage the real world. If you have a black soul, you are with the devil, you are not with God, in His world. Some people lie because it is who they are. It is their nature. It is what they know. May I ask you who is lying? Is it someone other than our unfortunate friend with the big house?"

"Sally was lying all right. About her background."

"Many self-made people do." Father Ignacio bore in on me, trying to glean something about Sally's fate. "Who else is lying?" he asked after he got nothing.

"A woman who is going after her."

"What is she lying about?"

"The circumstances of her baby's death. An unborn baby."

"Is she a Catholic?"

"Yes."

"Then she terminated the pregnancy." He said this automatically, as if there could be no other explanation.

"She denied it."

"Maybe she's lying."

"She was asked directly."

"By you?"

"Basically, yeah. I'm not going to confess any more to you. I'm in a rough business, Father."

"So you obtained this information in an unsavory manner?" Father Ignacio shook his head regretfully and crumpled up his empty bag of peanuts. I sensed I wasn't getting absolution today, the Holy Cannoli being a believer in punishing the punishable, not the hardcore sinners. I had no doggie bags for Father Ignacio. Besides, he probably figured that, with his gangster friends, he had no shot at a real redemption program, but with me he'd at least succeed in making me feel like hell.

"Treachery. At least I'm being honest with you."

"Thank you for that partial confession—which, by the way, is what I think this young woman is doing with you."

"What? Partially confessing?"

"Yes. Perhaps she didn't have an abortion under the traditional definition, but she may have aborted the child in a manner that allows her to call it by another name."

"The devil has all kinds of names."

"Indeed he does. And, Jackie?"

"Yeah?"

"You are not forgiven."

"I didn't think I would be," I said, feeling ash in my eyes.

Cavities

"A little man pulls the strings."

The art of kicking somebody's ass has fallen victim to the speculation of countless chuckleheads that have never been in a fight. This is not to say there aren't an array of techniques, however, only one has paid consistent dividends for me. The three-step process will be outlined here.

STEP #1—DECEPTION

I don't like to be conceited or fruity, but I wasn't a bad looking old woman. Sinewy legs, eyes with assorted colors offset by a shock of cottony white hair. I was a spry thing, and was hoping this wouldn't go unnoticed as I sat in Dr. Feinberg's waiting room at his dental office in Hammonton. Vanity has a way of transcending circumstance.

After all, we didn't want Ryan Murphy, Murrin's brother, to recognize me prior to his checkup with everybody's favorite dentist. Between Murrin's loose lips, the Imps' investigative work, and our own piney network, we drew a bead on brother Ryan by monitoring his phone calls, one of which was placed to Dr. Feinberg's office.

I put brother Ryan in his late twenties. He had dirty brown hair that was most likely this shade because it was dirty. He sported one of those anemic goatees that have become the signature of those who were born in the 1970s and 1980s, but wanted to convey the impression that they had been on the front lines of the 1960s. I imagine the thirst for the sixties was so intense because the clothes were so cool, exchanges of bodily fluids were mandatory, and so much stuff got wrecked, not to mention smoked. Debauchery gets framed in the moral box of social justice, which I loved somehow.

Brother Ryan was thin and pixie-ish. He had round, ponderous hazel eyes. I could see how his gimmick could easily win recruits to the causes Murrin had suggested he believed in. He carried a green backpack that didn't appear to have much in it, which was good, because within ten minutes I would personally stuff his fucking head inside of it.

Dr. Feinberg and his assistants wouldn't be in the office today, having been scheduled for a seminar on new whitening techniques, which was conveniently being held at the Golden Prospect with complementary chips drawn on the house. Brother Ryan's appointment had been deleted from all computer records. Why would Dr. Feinberg and his staff have scheduled an appointment on a day when they were all out at a seminar? Silly brother Ryan.

Behind the reception counter sat Teapot Freddy in a surgical face mask and a crisp white medical shirt, which he had emblazoned in fire engine red with a name he had chosen for himself (with considerable focus-group support from the Imps and yours truly). Today, the Teapot was known as Thorsten Bulgessen.

"Yes, sir," Thorsten said to brother Ryan. "Are you here for your two-thirty with the doctor?"

"Yeah," brother Ryan said, lazy.

"Oh, good. That's spectacular." Then Thorsten turned to me. "Mrs. Pinsky," he said, "The doctor is looking at your X-rays and will be with you soon."

"You said that ten minutes ago," I said.

"You've been very patient, Mrs. Pinsky," Thorsten said reassuringly. He disappeared from the reception window.

"I'm seventy-four years old," I said to brother Ryan. "When I came in I was your age."

Brother Ryan half-smiled.

"What do you do, young man?" I asked. I spoke with a creaky, old woman's voice that, truthfully, sucked.

"Uh, I'm a graduate student."

"Where do you go to school?"

"Um, Rutgers."

"A fine school. My grandson, Haywood, goes there."

"Oh."

"Do you know him?"

"What's his name again? It's a big campus." I took a hard look at his eyes, which were bloodshot from lying.

"My grandson's name is Haywood. Haywood Jablowme."

Brother Ryan glanced up at me in disbelief. "Come again," he said, hip.

"Haywood Jablowme," I spoke softly. "You got shit in your ear?" I shouted in my real voice. I rose, slipping on my knucks. Brother Ryan's eyes bulged out, but he remained seated. I smashed him on his cheekbone. He fell back.

STEP #2—FALSE HOPE

The first punch would hurt brother Ryan, but would be surmountable. It would give him confidence, despite his injury, that he could escape. Well, he wouldn't—but the head game was critical in order to cycle through the range of emotions that would allow Step #3 to be effective.

STEP #3—DESPAIR

I grabbed Ryan by his throat with my left hand and slammed him in the face with my knuckleduster until his nose was flat. Blood was rolling down his shirt as he cradled his head, wailing. I locked the outer door to Dr. Feinberg's offices and stomped down hard on his crotch. As he cried out, I pulled off my old lady wig and jammed it in his mouth to muffle his screams.

Nate the Great and the Lord burst in the waiting room wearing medical face masks and helped me pick up Ryan. We carried him down the hall. He was dripping blood onto the linoleum floor.

"Don't worry about them," Thorsten said to Ryan, trailing us with a mop, "They're in public relations!" We dropped brother Ryan into a dental chair. As we restrained him with fabric straps, he spit out my wig. He looked up at me and screamed at my wigless head, which offended me.

"I thought I looked pretty good," I said.

"I would kill for legs like that when I get to be your age!" Thorsten said to me, jamming a towel in Ryan's mouth.

"Thank you, Thorsten. No matter how old you get," I said, "You never lose your desire to be recognized for the sexually vibrant being you are."

"Jesus Christ," the Lord said. With that, Thorsten shut the door behind him and shook his head sorrowfully at me.

I reached down and grabbed brother Ryan's throat. He was crying now. "Do you know who I am?" I asked. "Just nod."

He nodded in the negative. I moved back about a foot and punched him hard in the groin. "Do you know who I am?" I asked again.

He screamed something, which was muffled. "Just nod, brother Ryan. Do you know who I am?"

Brother Ryan nodded in the affirmative.

"Let me tell you why we're here. Some of your Pangea buddies tried to kill me. My ten-year-old niece was in the house. I know that. That's not something we'll be debating today. What I don't know, brother Ryan, is why. We're here so that you can tell me. I want you to think about this as Dr. Lecter works on your cavity."

Nate the Great put a dental drill up to brother Ryan's ears and made it whir. Brother Ryan screamed into his rag and his eyes rolled up into his head. Tears streamed down his cheeks.

"Is there anything you want to tell us?" I asked.

Mildly, brother Ryan nodded yes. "Don't scream now, brother Ryan, promise?" He agreed. Thorsten removed the towel from his mouth, which was caked with blood.

"I don't know why," brother Ryan said in between sobs.

"You don't know why," I repeated in a factual monotone. Ryan nodded no. "Do you know somebody tried to kill me, brother Ryan?"

"I knew there was a shooting," he said catching his breath.

"And that's all you know?"

"That's all I know."

"Before we begin, just know that you can make this stop at any time."

"Begin what?"

"Begin work on your cavity," Nate the Great said. "You have one, don't you? That's why you scheduled this appointment."

"You're not a dentist," Ryan said, his eyes broadening in terror.

"Don't worry about it," Nate said, whirring the drill and approaching brother Ryan. "Say, ahh." Ryan shook his head away from Nate the Great. The Lord stood behind brother Ryan's head and pulled his mouth open. Nate put down his drill and pulled down brother Ryan's lower jaw and slipped in a device that prevented him from being able to close his mouth. Then Nate raised a padded clamp on either side of Ryan's head so that he could not move it from side to side. He was paralyzed.

Brother Ryan frantically tried to say something, but wasn't at his most articulate.

"You're probably wondering about anesthesia," I said, leaning against a wall. "Don't worry about it. We know you're an animal rights activist, brother Ryan, and we respect that. We know that anesthesia is tested on animals and would never want to administer something that ran contrary to your principles."

With that, Nate the Great pulled out a shiny silver tray containing a variety of medieval-looking dental implements and held it up for brother Ryan to examine. His face became ashen; he looked like the men I killed as they lay on gurneys in the morgue. Angela popped into my head, and I tried to imagine what her expression would be if she saw me supervising a scene like this.

"Opposing animal research. That's your bag, huh?" I sniffed.

Brother Ryan was trying to catch his breath.

"Tell me what you know, brother Ryan, or we start in your mouth and move slowly south. Do we have to get disgusting here?"

Brother Ryan attempted to shake his head no. I ordered Nate the Great to remove the mouth clamps.

"I don't know why," brother Ryan said. "I swear, I don't know why. I know it's Pangea. It's Pangea."

"This is good, brother Ryan. A third man got away. He looked like a dwarf or something. He was driving an El Camino, an ugly-ass car."

"They've got a little man," brother Ryan sighed. He squeaked out another cry. "A little man pulls the strings."

"Who is he, brother Ryan?"

"I swear I don't know his name." I grabbed brother Ryan by his *cajones,* hard, and was horrified to discover that he had wet himself. Brother Ryan yelped, "Aw, God, aw, God."

"Jesus, brother Ryan." I rose and washed my hands in the sink. "C'mon, brother Ryan, tell me about the little man."

"He's called Mr. Leeds. You can do anything you want to me, but I don't know where he gets his orders. It's layered. I just raid the animal research clinics. I'm not a killer."

"Those labs you blow up with medical research, you don't think you kill people?"

"I told you what I know."

"Leeds was the family that spawned the Jersey Devil," Nate the Great said.

"No shit?" I said, turning back to brother Ryan. "What do you know about the Jersey Devil?"

"I don't know about that."

"When you met Mr. Leeds, where did you reach him, where did you meet?"

"He called me."

"Where does he operate from? You don't answer this, you die in a real bad way."

"In the pines. Pangea has a place in Lebanon State Forest. A training camp. I swear it's all I know."

"Why would a mobster know you, brother Ryan? Tell me."

"I owed some money," he said.

"So we've got mobsters and midgets and an animal rights activist who wants me to believe that he don't know nuthin'," I said mockingly. "I withdrew my Beretta and pointed it at brother Ryan's eye. "Give some thought to the big picture, boy, because I'm still not getting it."

Slowly, during the next ten minutes I began to get it.

Yiddish Lesson

"Did this woman, her younger brother, her family, just up and vanish maybe in the early fifties?"

Jonah described Rabbi Wald as a *shtarker* himself, and someone who would probably like a guy like me. I could see from his swagger, his deep tan, and the toothpick in his mouth that I may have found a new friend.

"I heard good things about you from Jonah Eastman," I said, after the rabbi sat down at a table at Ozzie's in Longport. I could see when he crossed his legs he was wearing Western boots. Here was something—a rabbi with a little yippie-ky-yay. He was built like an aging wrestler. I put him in his late sixties. The last I had heard, he didn't have a formal congregation, but operated an *ad hoc* temple for aging racketeers in the boiler room of the Margate Jewish Community Center, *Vilda Chaya* Reform.

"How is Friar Schmuck?" the rabbi asked.

"Excuse me?"

"We call each other names. Father Ignacio is Friar Schmuck. I'm Rabbi Oli, like ravioli."

"Father Ignacio mentioned that."

"I married Jonah. That Indian girl of his"—*gurlahizz*—"is a doll. Quiet but tough. I was a friend of his grandfather. Used to visit him all the time at the Prospect and, before that, his taffy shop."

"Mickey made good taffy," I said.

Rabbi Wald laughed, revealing a deep set of dimples and great white Chiclet teeth, and then leaned in furtively. A rich tuft of gray chest hair surfaced from the opening in his polo shirt.

"So why do they still call you Disaster anyway, you don't fight anymore, do you?" he asked.

"No. It just stuck with me. My clients have disasters, my last name's De Sesto . . . I don't know."

"I guess it's better than people calling you Gaseous Clay," he said laughing at his own joke. "I'd like a name like that: Rabbi Disaster. You know, I got into a little trouble years ago. I don't have a normal congregation. Mostly guys who can't get into a regular one."

I knew this, but shrugged my shoulders as if I didn't.

"I had this understudy, you know, a junior rabbi. He was into all this sensitive stuff. He encouraged all of the Bar Mitzvah boys to give a speech about world peace at their ceremonies. He started with alla this make-peace-with-the-Palestinians bullshit." The Rabbi flicked a fresh toothpick in his mouth.

"So what happened?"

"I kicked the piss out of him. They threw me out of the congregation. The only people who took me seriously as a religious man were Mickey Price and his boys. And, a-course, my girl, Doreen. She was a showgirl at the Taj Mahal, but, man, she surprises me with what she knows about the New Testament. So, Father Ignacio says you got a case, maybe I could help you out." I could tell that he really wanted to do it, which concerned me a little. Sometimes amateurs could be trouble on cases like this, because their real goal was to go out and yap about the cool stuff they were mixed up in. That they might be in danger only made the endeavor more appealing

"Can I start off by saying something insulting?" I asked.*

"Why the hell not?"

"This is sensitive stuff I'm working on. It involves law enforcement, possible litigation, and I don't want to put you in any jeopardy, have you put under oath, that kind of thing. Are you good at keeping secrets?"

"I'm a rabbi, aren't I?"

"You are. But what's that Jewish word for somebody who talks a lot? You don't know anybody like that, do you?"

"Yenta?"

"Yeah, yenta."

"Nah, I'm no yenta. How could I be and have hung with guys like Mickey Price? You ask Jonah about how I keep secrets."

"I did. He said that you could."

"There you have it."

"Okay, then. You grew up in South Jersey, right?"

"Yeah, Camden."

"Do you know the word *shtarker*?"

*Contrary to conventional wisdom, discretion is more effectively urged with a gentle prod. A threat is seen by knock-around guys as a device of amateurs.

"Sure, it means tough guy."

"Do you mind if I ask how old you are?"

"I'm sixty-seven."

"Did you know any women, maybe a few years younger than you, who had a younger brother? This woman may have had a friend or neighbor named Silverberg. Now, here's the weird part. Did this woman, her younger brother, her family, just up and vanish maybe in the early fifties?"

"Sounds like *The Twilight Zone.*"

"You're right, it does."

"I'll need to think about this. Any other clues?"

"Not many, Rabbi. I suspect that the woman may be a little nutty. Her family may have been nutty."

"You mean mentally ill?"

"Yeah, crazy."

"Are these people big *machers*?"

"Sorry?"

"Big shots."

"Yes. The woman is famous. Please hold this real tight."

"Who am I gonna tell?"

"Do you know any Silverbergs?"

Rabbi Wald grabbed a pickle that sat on a plate in front of him. "Son, if I throw this pickle over my shoulder, chances are I'll hit a Silverberg. Not a wonderful clue, Dr. Watson. Any other clues?"

"Yeah," I laughed.

"What?"

"The woman might have gone to Beaver College."

"Arcadia. They changed the name. Obvious reasons."

"I'll say. So you'll keep me posted."

"Sure." Rabbi Wald snickered like the Lord. I couldn't tell if he was onto something or was caught up in his own inner drama.

Substitute Teacher

"Jackie Disaster was a brochure."

I sat at my desk and read the news summary for the fourth time that day.

NATURALE PRICE RISES
ON SETTLEMENT TALKS

(American Commerce Wire—Philadelphia, August 3) Shares in Naturale's Real Living rose yesterday on speculation that the company is close to reaching a settlement in a class action suit brought against the company by consumers who claim to have become ill as a result of drinking Naturale's Real Soy Milk. Lead attorney for the group, which informally calls itself Victims of Sally Naturale, Ruth Marx-Levine, said she had received no official word about the settlement but was optimistic.

Sources close to the company have said that the recent destruction of Naturale headquarters and disappearance of Sally Naturale have prompted the company to engage litigants.

"Fire or no fire, the consequences to a consumer product company of poisoning people with genetically-altered soybeans are serious," Marx-Levine said.

Naturale attorney, Geoffrey Klein dismissed the Victims of Sally Naturale's suit as "despicable grandstanding designed to exploit a horrible situation."

This is the second time in one month that shares in Naturale surged. In recent weeks, the market has swirled with rumors that Naturale would be acquired by Millennium Taste Lifestyles, speculation that intensified after retail industry analyst Stuart Marsh said that the company's stock price had essentially been discounted by the litigation.

The phone on my desk rang. A husky voice spoke:

"Look at these nice poems up here on the wall," the voice said.

"Who is this?" I asked instinctively and stupidly, proving that there's no such thing as a professional when the well-being of people you love is on the line.

"The kid can write. Nice poems up here on the cork in Miss Truitt's class. She ain't here today. I'm subbing."

Click.

"Emma!" I whispered. The speed with which tears sprung from my eyes surprised me on a biological level. I ran to the outer offices. None of the Imps were here. They were out on assignment. I cursed myself for sending them out on assignment. I vowed never to send them out again.

I called home. No answer. Hell, Emma was staying with Blinky Dom. I called Blinky Dom. No answer, just his normal message—Dom barking, "If I was home I'd answer!" *Beep.* What time did she get home from school again? Jesus, for the life of me I couldn't think what the right time was. I vowed never to forget the right time again. In times of crisis you vow a lot.

I said Emma's name again while I stared at my useless fighter hands. I tore out of my office not bothering to lock it. I avoided the elevator down to the garage fearing I'd get stuck. In the past few weeks, I worried about running into Angela, but not now. I thought about who to call. What could I promise God? I was in Hell. Was this retribution for my Father Vic-Confession job? I had been on the receiving end of a vile prank call, but the one I had orchestrated against Murrin had been less vile because it was done in the pursuit of justice, right? Right?

I got in my car and screeched out of the Golden Prospect garage. I believed in God. I didn't believe in God. If Emma were all right, I'd believe in God without question. If Emma had been hurt, I would desert God.

If Emma was all right, I'd desert God, because God never gave a damn about her until now. And now was a little late. If Emma had been hurt, I'd become a monk.

I dialed up Trouble. I got his cell phone's voice mail. Great cop—voice mail, which might as well have said, "I'm sorry if you're being defenestrated by a psychopath right now, but I'm unable to take your call . . ." I don't remember exactly what I said, but it was something like, "Emma. Poems. School. Frankie Shrugs."

I remember nothing about my ride down Atlantic Avenue, but I have every confidence that I did not stop at any red lights and almost certainly endangered the lives of many. But those lives weren't important. No one loved those people. There was only one person in the universe, and that was Emma.

Emma was not home. I fell to the floor. I prayed and cursed, prayed and cursed, my loathing of God having converted into a form of faith. I punched walls, not even caring that there was no such thing as Jackie Disaster. Jackie Disaster was a brochure.

I heard a car door slam. It was Blinky Dom in his De Ville (a toaster with wheels, honestly)—not who I needed to see. The moment he caught my eye, he reached for his chest and winced as if a shooting pain had shot horizontally through his lungs. If I just blew him away, maybe I would have gotten off on an insanity plea. Or maybe I'd go to jail and just not give a damn. Without Emma, would I really care about getting beaten and raped in prison? Hell, why wait for prison, just clip Blinky Dom and ice myself in the surf.

Then I saw Emma climb from the passenger seat of Blinky Dom's car. I ran out like the garden-variety hysterical mother you see on those real-life cop shows when she gets her kid back. I was breathing very hard. I lifted her up and ran with her into the house. I must have kissed her a thousand times. My tears were all over her face, which was growing redder from kiss burn.

"Where were you?" I asked.

Blinky Dom tromped in. "What the hell's wrong with you?"

I thought about lying for a second, but couldn't do it. "Somebody called and said they were at your school, Emma. I thought they had you. I thought they had you."

"We were out watching fights at my club! Jesus Christ!" Blinky Dom said.

"Why were you doing that?" I asked, wiping my eyes. Emma began to laugh at me.

"I wanted to see what they looked like," she said.

Gone

"Good yontiff, Pontiff."

I drove Emma to school the following morning and was met there by an off-duty A.C.P.D. cop that Trouble had referred, a sinewy woman in her late twenties named Cookie. She would stay with Emma during school hours for the foreseeable future.

When I got back to my office, I was manic. It was the first time in weeks I hadn't fretted over Angela. I hadn't reached a verdict on God, but I was euphoric over Emma's safe return and decided to celebrate with a run. Mid-way through my exercise, near where the boardwalk ended, a stocky figure wearing Western boots began waving me down. At first, I thought he might be waving to someone behind me, but I recognized him when he started looking over his shoulder as if he were about to make a dastardly handoff. It was Rabbi Wald.

"Look at you with that bandana on your head," Rabbi Wald said. *Loogitchu.* "You look like Captain Morgenstern the pirate."

"You mean Captain Morgan?"

"Ah," Rabbi Wald swatted, "They all shorten their names when it serves them. Hey, Jackie, you're Catholic, right?" the rabbi accused.

"Yeah, Rabbi, I am."

"You know what you say when if you see the Pope on the Jewish high holidays?"

"No."

"You say, 'Good *yontiff,* Pontiff'." The rabbi laughed. My sweat dripped off me and was absorbed by the wood on the boardwalk. I felt my heartbeat slow down behind my sternum. I did one of those I-don't-get-the-joke-but-I'll-smile-anyway looks. "What, you don't get it?"

"Sorry, no."

"Good *yontiff* means happy holiday. So *good yontiff, Pontiff* is wishing the Pope a good Rosh Hashanah or something. Now do you get it?"

"Sure. I'll remember it next time I run into the Pope at the JCC in Margate."

"You never know . . . I called your office . . . they said you went for a run. I got something for you. On the *meshugganahs.*"

"*Mesh* . . . crazy, right?"

"Right."

"What do you know?"

"There was a family, just like you said. I talked to every Yid who ever came outta Camden. I checked out the Silverbergs in my yearbook. There was a rich family with that name. They may have been related to people like the ones you talked about. I wrote down the name here on the back of this." He handed me a matchbook from Ponzio's restaurant.

I took a look at the name. It made sense. "Good for you. Good for you, Rabbi," I said, genuinely excited.

"If this is her, she was a few years behind me. Gone"—the rabbi collapsed his hands together and then launched them apart as if to say *Poof!*—"by the mid-fifties or thereabouts. The only thing that isn't right is the look. The girl doesn't look a thing like the big *macher,* so we may have dead-ended."

"Hmm."

"Anyhow, all I could find out is how they were pulled out of summer camp, then"—the *poof* gesture with the hands again—"gone!"

"Summer camp, huh?"

"Yeah."

"Was it in Maine or Lake George by any chance?" I asked, thinking myself very sleuthy.

"Nah," the rabbi said, which deflated me. Then he conjured up a delinquent grin. "The camp was right here."

"Here, like down the shore?"

"Nah. Nah. Pine Barrens. Out in Medford Lakes."

The Memorial

"Where I'll be safe."

Public relations stunts only work when the audience wants them to work. This was not a concept that I expected Bebe Naturale to understand. Bebe decided to hold a memorial service for Sally on the stone porch at Cricket Crest. Count Smartfarkle had alerted me the day before the service. If for no other reason than curiosity about the mind of Bebe Naturale, I had to go.

Bebe invited the media and had local notables get up to say a few words about Sally. Of particular note was Bebe's choice of co-mourner. Sitting at his right was none other than Frankie Shrugs. Bebe was outing himself, at least partially. By showing he knew tough guys, what could his detractors do? Accuse him of knowing tough guys. I grudgingly admired the maneuver, but I viewed it as an acknowledgement that Bebe knew he was in somebody's crosshairs.

I had suggested to the Count that he could appear loyal to Bebe (which he would need to do to keep his job, with Sally gone) by providing black ribbons that the mourners could wear. I had Nate the Great grab a bunch from Glick's Funeral Home in Atlantic City and drive them to Count Smartfarkle at Cricket Crest. In one of them, the one I instructed the Count to give Bebe, Nate had inserted a transmitter.

Bebe and Frankie Shrugs were dressed in black. Frankie looked as though he might explode out of his suit. Every move he made prompted a tsunami of muscle and fat to ripple beneath his clothing. Frankie Shrugs sported a pre-cancerous tan, which was offset by drips of fat gold jewelry on his fingers and wrists. I could tell by how slowly he moved that he was feeling pretty damned good about himself, which pissed me off.

A photo of a beaming Sally rested on an easel next to a podium. At the latticed entrance to the ceremony each mourner was given a red rose and encouraged to place it at the base of Sally's portrait.

I took a red rose, bowed my head, and joined the procession. Bebe eyed me cautiously and scratched his chin with one of his knuckles. It was a Brando move, I thought. Then it hit me when I dropped the rose at the foot of the easel. The roses, the scratching gesture—in Bebe's kaleidoscope mind he was reenacting, albeit with some variation, the funeral scene in *The Godfather*. I could work with this.

The photo of Sally looked familiar. It was the tiara. This was the photo of Sally and Princess Diana, only the dead princess had been cropped out. If Sally had had any say in the choice of photo, Diana would have surely remained. Diana was the whole purpose of the photo. See me, Sally, Phlersey elocutionist extraordinaire, wearing a tiara *next to the princess,* who is tiara-less. I knew Bebe had cropped Sally to be nasty, and even though Sally's desperation made me nauseous, it ticked me off at Bebe nonetheless.

After dropping the rose, I made certain that Bebe and Frankie Shrugs saw me standing on the side. Brainstorm: I ostentatiously waved Count Smartfarkle over to me and whispered to him. I wanted Bebe and Frankie Shrugs to see me whispering.

Count Smartfarkle then approached Bebe and asked him if he could have a word with him. Bebe rose and walked with the Count to beside the podium.

"Bebe," the Count said, "Jackie Disaster just approached me. He said he wants to meet with you so you can work out all of your problems." I could hear the discussion through a tiny receiver I wore in my ear.

Bebe's eyes widened in a mixture of surprise and delight.

"He said that?" Bebe asked.

"Yes," the Count confirmed. "He said you can pick a place where you'll feel safe and then let me know. I can take care of the arrangements."

"Okay," Bebe said softly. I waved from across the way. Bebe nodded back and returned to sit beside Frankie Shrugs.

"I know how he's gonna come at me," Bebe said to Frankie Shrugs.

"Yeah, how?" Frankie asked.

"I'm supposed to pick a place to meet. Where I'll be safe," Bebe added sarcastically.

"You need help?" Frankie asked.

"No. I'm gonna handle this myself."

Frankie Shrugs' eyes popped open wide in genuine respect for Bebe's adventurousness. Bebe was almost certainly sporting wood about now.

"You know, Bebe," Frankie Shrugs said, "I always thought it would have been Petey Breath Mints."

"No," Bebe muttered sagaciously. "Petey was stupid, and don't get me started on his breath. It's a smart move. Smartfarkle was always, uh, smarter. But I never knew until this very day that it's been Jackie Disaster all along."

The moment I heard Bebe's words echo in my earpiece, I cupped my hands over my nose and mouth and pretended to suppress a sneeze so that Don Calzone and his *putzigliere,* Frankie Shrugs, couldn't see me laugh. "Jesus Henry Kee-rist," I spoke into my hands softly.

Not softly enough, evidently, because a peculiar young woman standing next to me, whose features were all concentrated in the center of her face, put her arms around me and whispered sensitively, "It'll be okay."

Feigning a stricken expression, I nodded, left the service, and drove back down the shore in my bitchin' El Dorado at ninety miles per hour laughing uncontrollably. I had no expectation that a Bebe-Disaster summit would ever take place, but once you discover a man's delusion, he's yours.

Give Him Something Juicy

"Bebe's a snake, and, given time, he'll eat his own tail and swallow himself."

I've been stewing on what to do about Bebe," I told Jonah as we walked along the boardwalk. Jonah was wearing a Brooks Brothers polo shirt, khaki pants, running shoes and a baseball cap. He looked like a kid, and there was something uncharacteristically vulnerable about the way he was straining not to look at his grandfather's old hotel as the thickly sweet scent of burning saltwater taffy followed us.

"This is the brother, right?"

"Yeah. He's mobbed up tight."

"Is he a made guy?" Jonah asked.

"Trouble says he doesn't think so," I said.

"So he's been earning all of this money for the boys for all these years and they didn't make him?"

"Guess not. He must be an associate."

"He's a fat slob associate and his sister's a skinny little WASP wannabe—who speaks Phlersey," Jonah said.

"It doesn't compute, Jonah."

"Yeah, you'd think they'd make a guy like that after all this time. Well, look, my grandfather spent his life in it, but they never made him. Not that he wanted it, but, you know . . ."

"Uh-huh. Sally exercises to *Fiddler on the Roof.*"

"Are you serious?"

"Yeah, I heard it playing in the workout room the day I met her."

"How can you work up a sweat to *Sunrise, Sunset?*"

"Don't ask me. I listen to *Rocky,*" I said.

"Who doesn't?" Jonah responded. I think he was serious.

"Yeah, well, I'm already screwing with Bebe, but I'd still like to rattle him and some of his wiseguy friends, keep them off balance, Jonah. My sense is that Bebe's a snake and, given time, he'll eat his own tail and swallow himself."

"Given time? You don't have much time, Jackie."

"I know. Any thoughts on how to get him to eat his tail?"

Jonah closed his eyes and kept them closed while he speculated. "Well, of course, one way is to let him start swallowing before he knows it's his tail, give him something so juicy that by the time he realizes what's happening, he's almost all gone."

"You know, all those guys are paranoid," I said.

"That's true, they are. What are you thinking?"

"If my hunch is right, that fire already scared the piss out of some bad guys. But they could always be scared some more, I suppose."

"That's true," Jonah said. "The local racket guys, going way back, are always thinking that New York or the Russians or somebody is going to move in while they're weak. Tweak that. But what about getting Bebe to start nibbling on something juicy?"

"Maybe not some*thing* juicy, Jonah. Maybe someone juicy."

"Those are always nice."

I met the Lord next to the slot machines, which appeared as if they had lined up, military style, to promise fortunes to the saggy-faced old women who were dancing with them. The slots were erect and sleek like young soldiers, and the ladies' eyes were desperate for remunerative romance. "Lordo, do you know Frankie Shrugs?" I asked.

"You wouldn't let me slap a homer on his ass," the Lord said, dejected. "I'm still pissed about that."

"What does he drive, you know?"

"In the summer, a gold Jag convertible. Always parks it away from everybody so it doesn't get scratched. You ready for the homer?"

"No, I want you to take out his car."

"With explosives, like?"

"No, with Gummi Bears. Of course with explosives."

"Not with him in it, right?"

"Of course not."

"Boom-Boom Weber is available," the Lord said. "What's your beef with Frankie Shrugs?"

"He's ugly."

Big Man Thursday

"You're Bebe Naturale, aren't you?"

As hard as it was to figure out what had driven Sally Naturale, her brother had become a cinch. Once we began tracking him more intensely, Bebe proved to be very much a man of workaday routines. Every Thursday night he held court at Braddock's Tavern in Medford. He usually brought a guest with him—today it was a young aide from his office—but he kept one or two seats open because he liked to invite a random gawker to join him. It may be hard to fathom anyone gawking at Bebe Naturale, but this was South Jersey, U.S.A., where money—or at least the perception of its possession—made a slob like Bebe appear positively svelte in the eyes of those who were predisposed to equating money with arrival.

According to Swervin' Mervin, our favorite tracker, there appeared to be a correlation between those who sucked up to Bebe at Braddock's Tavern and those who moved up in the Naturale organization. He held his liquor well, but tended to loosen up after a few glasses of wine, usually red. After three glasses or so, Bebe's eyes tended to wander around the restaurant; and, if there was a young hottie waiting for a friend at the bar, she often found herself invited to share the table with the great man. I didn't know how far Bebe actually went with women, but his interest in young attractive ones could not have been more obvious.

What happened next wasn't particularly sinister, but it was an amusing spectacle to behold, if for nothing else than its insipid consistency. Bebe began by flattering his guests. It took the Imps a while to figure out how it worked, but the objective of Bebe's flattery was to set up his guests to flatter him in return, not unlike the way a volleyball net-man gently sets up a shot for his teammate to spike. The Lord and Nate the Great had been hysterical when they described the maneuver to me.

"Oh, Nate," the Lord mimicked, "Your kielbasa is huge."

"If mine's huge, good man," Nate the Great responded, "Yours is positively gargantuan."

"No-no-no," the Lord said, "If mine's gargantuan, you're is positively, uh, mammoth."

I cut off the exchange not because I was offended, but because I knew that the Lord was running out of words for *really big.*

The climax of the suckfest, at least for Bebe, occurred when the stray offered to pay for her meal, and Bebe would loudly protest, *"Don't be ridicculus, I'll take care of it!"* And the Bebemeister would "take care of it." Big gangland conspiracy implied. Then Bebe would squeeze out a wad of cash and do the thing that many locals admired more than any act of God: he'd pay. If this had been a play, the chorus would emerge at this point in a fountain of confetti.

On this edition of Big Man Thursday, there was an achingly beautiful blonde sitting at the bar in a very short skirt showing tanned calves. She sipped Chablis as she paged through a travel book about Italy. Occasionally, she glanced toward Bebe's table and then looked down at her book coyly. A shy one. Beautiful but shy. Rare.

"You goin' to Italy, doll?" a relaxed Bebe, supported by his chorus, eventually asked.

The woman touched her fingers to her cleavage. "Me?" She brushed her hair aside and smiled like a coltish Girl Scout who did not know she was beautiful. Her teeth glistened.

"Yeah, honey, you got the book on Italy," Bebe said. *ITly.*

"I was planning a trip there this fall," the beauty said.

"C'mon over and join us," Big Man Bebe said.

"That's okay, I don't want to interrupt."

"You're not interrupting anything, honest."

"Honest?" she said cutely, with a bite of her lower lip.

"Right, honest."

"You're Bebe Naturale, aren't you?"

Orgasm. "Who wants to know?" the Big Man heaved.

"Rena D'Amico."

"Pretty name."

"Northern Italian."

"North, south, it's all good."

Bebe thought he was Mick Jagger.

The Thing With Angela

"I saw my father."

I saw a shadow next to the doorway of my office. It was a reluctant and willowy shadow.

"Freddy?" I asked.

"No," another feminine voice answered.

"Angela?"

Angela stepped in side my office. She was wearing a red outfit that made her look sexy and tired at the same time.

"Hi," I said.

"Hi. I wanted you to know I got your note and the panda."

"I wasn't sure it got to you. I haven't been here much, and your offices are on another floor and all. It's been a few weeks, I guess."

"I got it. Thanks," she said, appearing fragile. "I wanted to think a little."

Both of us were silent. I remained seated. Angela stood. "That makes sense. What did you think of the panda?" I asked.

"It was cute."

"Where did you put it?"

"On my desk."

"What about the note?"

"I'm glad you wrote it."

"I had to. Even if you hated me, I couldn't just let everything sit. You were a client and all."

"So the note was account management, huh?"

I thought about taking the James Dean route, something I would have done a few years ago. Distant. Complex. Brooding. I was on the verge of Complex when one of the more reasonable voices in my head surrendered: *You're forty, panda-buyer.*

"No, Angie, it wasn't account management. I've got plenty of business.

I'm relieved not to be working for you, no bullshit. I suggested it, remember?"

"I know. It's better this way, even though I know you didn't rob the casino."

I stood up and walked a few steps toward her. "I said I was sorry in writing, and I'll tell you in person. I'm sorry that I did things that way."

Angela threw her arms around me. "I don't know, Jackie, I looked at you and I saw my father. I thought to myself, I thought I got away from that *pazzo* life, and here I am back in it. Can you understand that?"

"I guess. Dirk called me a *cafone* in front of you."

"After you decked him. What do you care what he called you?"

"I care what he called me in front of you."

"And you thought I'd listen?"

"Worse. I was afraid you'd believe it. I was afraid maybe you did believe it when you threw me out."

"That's not what I think of you, Jackie. It's what you think of yourself."

"You think I think that?"

Angela backed away from me and met my eyes. "Yes, I think you think that." She didn't say it in a mean way, though. I didn't know what to say, so I stared at one of my pirate ships.

"About the robbery, Jackie," Angela said, "Whoever did it didn't get very much money."

"I don't think money was the point, Angie."

"Either do I. You hit a casino, you don't hit it for six large in a bank sack."

"It was a message job. I don't want to sound conceited, but I'm pretty sure whoever did it wanted you to be pissed off at me."

"You're not suggesting . . ."

"Dirk? Nah. I mean, you never know, but I don't think so. I don't know if it's that he loves you or hates me more, but either way, he's got too much to lose. Whoever did it played us pretty good, if that's what really happened."

"They knew you had a temper," Angela said sternly.

"They were right. I had a temper. I have a temper."

"You don't need to be insecure about Dirk."

"I'm not insecure. I'm just stupid."

"Jackie, you're not stupid. You and Dirk bring out the worst in each other."

"I knew he talked subversive about me."

"Well, you talk subversive about him, don't you? He's like oil, and you're like a lit match. Kaboom!" Angela brought her hands together slowly and sprung them apart quickly.

"He wants you in the sack, Angie."

"No he doesn't. He wants the casino. He wants to build it up and sell it and become chairman of the parent company."

"He wants both."

"What do *you* want, Jackie?"

"A prize fighter who gets a girl a panda? He wants the girl he got the panda for. Getting you that panda is as big a risk as a guy like me takes . . . Look, Angie, maybe it does mean I'm something like what you said. Maybe I'm not secure about everything, but I kind of felt like you were trying to hide me and keep the door open for Dirk, too. Some women are like bond traders, always looking at the screen to see if there's a better buy. I'd like to say that there's no way anybody can be a better bargain than me, but I know that would be conceited. It's not like I'm sixteen anymore, and if things don't work out, I can just meet somebody new on summer break. Maybe that's what got me going. It's corny and all, but the stakes are higher now."

"I know, Jackie."

"Can we try this again?"

My official reason for not pursuing Angela Vanni had always been that she was a client, but I realized that I had a darker dis-incentive: the woman liked me. Despite her Mafia pedigree, Angela was a bit of a nerd. She was capable of being sleek, what with her Chanel suits, but you could tell—I could tell—that she didn't get around much, and struck me as the kind of girl who would rather read some dumb-ass, musty book on a Friday night than go out somewhere. Even though I wasn't exactly Johnny Nightlife, was it possible that I hadn't pursued Angela sooner because she wasn't cool enough in the high-school sense? And, was it possible that my paralysis was due, in part, to a fear that maybe, under all the Disaster show business, I was afraid of finding out that I was part dweeb, too?

These were the thoughts I was thinking when I got done kissing Angela in my office.

I walked her back to her suite. I didn't hold her hand—I didn't want to push things.

"How's your dad doing with Emma staying at his place?" she asked.

"Okay. I was thinking lately. You weren't totally wrong about him."

"What wasn't I wrong about?"

"The way he is. Sometimes, when things are going well for me, he has medical incidents."

"Like what?"

"Vague stuff. But scary. Chest pains he thinks are heart attacks, headaches that he claims a doctor called suspicious."

"Implication being brain tumor?"

"Right."

"What do you do when he acts out like that?"

"Take him to doctors, take him to dinner, listen to him rant."

"Maybe you should stop."

"Good sons don't do that. Besides, Father Ignacio starts giving me grief. I'm a coldhearted bastard who lets his father suffer."

"That's your father talking."

"I know, but he has a gift for finding ambassadors."

"Ambassadors who don't want to hear him rant, who want you to, ah . . ."

"Suck in the poison."

"Yes."

Angela ran her fingers through my hair, right above my scar. I shuddered. I hadn't told her about the Petey murder attempt. She thought the wound was from the midget hit attempt, and I did nothing to disabuse her of her theory. "Do you have any idea how not-tough you really are?" Angela asked.

"What should I do?"

"Take that snarl that served you so well in the ring, not to mention your business, and tell your father and his asshole ambassadors to go fuck themselves."

It was startling to hear Angela curse. It was as if she shouldn't know bad words. Nevertheless, she did, and I kissed her because it was very sexy—not just how she looked when she said it, but the words she chose.

You Are What You Are

"The first governor of New Jersey wore a dress."

The Lord and Teapot Freddy returned from their adventures at lunch time. They brought up a few hoagies from Macko's and we sat down to eat around a small meeting table in my office. I rejected the Coke Teapot Freddy brought me in favor of tap water. I hadn't been exercising as much as I usually did, and was afraid I'd turn into Frankie Shrugs by Labor Day. An electronics expert had just swept Allegation Sciences for bugs and pronounced us clean.

"You know where that college, Beaver, uh, Arcadia, keeps their records, Lordo?" I asked.

"Yeah, I do."

"You know," Teapot Freddy interjected, "Why change the name? I mean, you are what you are."

"Not everybody likes crude-sounding titles, Fred," I said.

"Well," Teapot Freddy argued, setting down his Diet Pepsi, "If I had gone to the University of Gay, I wouldn't lobby to have the name changed to, I don't know, Parthenon College."

"But, Fred," I said, "What if it was Pansy College or Light in the Loafers University?"

"Or Queer-ass U?" The Lord added, helpfully.

"That's not necessary, Lordo," Teapot Freddy said. "Although, it's a miracle our fair state isn't called New Queersey."

"Huh?" the Lord asked.

"The first governor of New Jersey wore a dress," Teapot Freddy said. This was true. He once showed me a passage in a book where this was mentioned. He actually went to the library and researched this stuff.

"Get outta here!" the Lord said. "I didn't think they had gays back then."

"What do you mean *they had?* It's not like we just came into inventory. His name was Governor Cornbury," Teapot Freddy asserted.

"Should have been Governor Cornhole," was the Lord's retort.

I slid a napkin across to the Lord with a woman's name on it. "See if they have any files on this Arcadia graduate right here."

"Why does it matter at this point?" the Lord asked.

"I want to know who she was."

"Why? I don't get it." The Lord shrugged.

"I think it's possible that whatever happened back then triggered what's been going on in that dome. It may be nothing, but it may tell us what's really going on," I said.

"Okay," the Lord said. "What then?"

"Then, depending upon what we find, we'll have the Chancellor of Gay U here cozy-up to the Dean of Beaver College, and ask what she knows about this particular graduate. If she turns gray, we'll know we've got our girl."

By dazzling an Arcadia campus policeman with his adventures in the CIA (utterly false), the Lord had been able to determine over a late night drink that the old academic records of Beaver/Arcadia were kept in a warehouse in King of Prussia, Pennsylvania. There was nothing especially valuable about them, so few security precautions were taken. Setting off fireworks in a building elsewhere on the property diverted the attention of the warehouse's security guards, for whom the Lord's little spectacle had granted the greatest excitement they had had in twelve years. As the facility's two guards inspected the premises, fantasizing they were Delta Force commandos, the Lord got inside by maneuvering a garage door lock. It took him about an hour to find the box containing the records of a long-forgotten class at Beaver College. The records for the Class of 1960 were there, but the files for the graduate whose name I had jotted down on a napkin were not.

The following weekend, Teapot Freddy attended an Arcadia fundraiser. He posed as a representative of an association of college publishers. He used the name Dave Toma, who had been a cop who wore disguises to get his man. *Toma,* the TV show, had lasted only one season in the early seventies.

At the fundraiser, "Toma" sidled up to Dean Robin Enright and got her talking about successful businesswomen. Teapot Freddy asked Dean Enright what the most generous contributions to Beaver/Arcadia by an individual had been. She mentioned a few names that Teapot Freddy didn't recognize.

"What about that ten million dollar donation?" Teapot Freddy mentioned casually.

"Ten million dollars?" Dean Enright asked.

"Yes, the donor was a friend of mine," Teapot Freddy said sadly. He then dropped her name.

"Are you sure?"

"I'm positive. She was Class of 1960."

"Oh," Dean Enright said.

"Surely, you must know about her contribution," Teapot Freddy said. "All that money, and there's not a building in her name."

Dean Enright fiddled with a chain around her neck.

"Odd," Dean Enright said. "Oh, would you excuse me, one of my trustees just arrived?"

"Absolutely," Teapot Freddy said.

In the car ride back from the fundraiser, Teapot Freddy called me speaking in vague terms. "The lady was nervous when I mentioned the name," he said.

"Did she deny it?" I asked.

"No. See, Jackie Boy, these Ivory Tower types aren't from our world. They don't have our flair for lying. The lady couldn't wait to be rid of me."

"Then she knows," I said.

"She knows, honeycomb."

Jackie, I Think You're Gonna Be a Little Pissed

"They make 'em, like, identical."

The Lord and Boom-Boom Weber slipped nervously into Mack-o's Subs where I waited for them. We were the only patrons. A nervous-looking teenager behind the counter was cleaning the grill and watching his biceps move as he did it. He gazed out the window with every other stroke, I presumed because he was waiting for a girl.

Boom-Boom looked like the gas station night manager that he was—tall, greyhound thin, and greasy. He had enormous hands with ropelike veins carrying what I presumed to be motor oil through his system. The only trait that didn't go along with his low-rent appearance was his flashing blue eyes, which were very much alive and in search of something to detonate.

I could sniff a botched job from a hemisphere away, and a botched job against Frankie Shrugs wasn't a good thing.

The Lord hung back near the entrance. He had clearly persuaded Boom-Boom to take the pinch, so here it went.

"Jackie, I think you're gonna be a little pissed," Boom-Boom said, averting his gimlet eyes.

"Did you do the car, Boom-Boom?"

"I did a gold Jag." The muscles in his face were twitching.

"And?"

"It wasn't his. An old, retired-looking guy came out of the restaurant where we was at. He was all upset after he saw his car all blowed up." Boom-Boom's head sunk low on his shoulders, and he leaned forward until his forehead touched the table.

"You think?"

Boom-Boom sprang back up. "Yeah, we did his car. The guy we were after put his car, the same damned model, out in back of the place. It wasn't my fault, Jackie."

Wait. This was going to be a masterpiece.

"You blew up the wrong car and it wasn't your fault?"

"No, it's like, they make all these Jags look alike."

"Who's they?"

"The Jaguar people." Boom-Boom held his hands apart, as if this would emphasize the obvious rightness of his analysis.

"So it's Jaguar's fault?"

"They make 'em, like, identical."

"Yeah, when did they start doing that, yesterday?"

"I don't know."

"Did Frankie see what happened?"

"Yeah, he drove around after the thing went up, so he knew somebody did a car just like his."

This may just have been enough.

"Okay, Boom-Boom, listen to me. The Lord will give you a little something. It's best that you go away for a while."

"I have a brother in Jupiter."

"The planet?"

"Florida."

"Well, go to the planet. It'll be safer."

"So, you're pissed at me, Jackie?"

Out of Respect for Our Guest

"She thinks she's going to be a diva or something."

During my career I have witnessed an executive piss in his pants precisely twice. One time, I was sitting in a chief executive's guest chair watching him pace before a vast window overlooking Independence Square when his secretary buzzed him with the following jewel: "Your wife is on line one. Reverend Jesse Jackson is holding on line two."

Psssssssssssssssss.

The man was wearing khakis, so, believe me, I could see what he did. The company was soon propelled into a "diversity" scandal that had been triggered when the company's personnel chief was accused of calling a black vice-president "that slutty moolie." The exec rebutted the charge, claiming that he had denied a request to give her a raise by saying "That's a lotta moolah." No deal. The personnel chief and the CEO lost their jobs, and the company shelled out about two-hundred-million dollars to the aggrieved, once Rev. Jackson called his news conference. Praise Jesus!

The second time I was party to an award-winning loss of executive bladder control was when I watched the head of PR for a locally-based conglomerate drench her seat when Philadelphia's most notorious investigative reporter, Al Just, asked her if her company employed child labor in Bangladesh. Just, he of the furrowed brow, forced her to look at photographs uncovered by his nationally syndicated muckraking program, *America Betrayed,* of children working at the company's plant outside of Dacca. Her answer (in a frighteningly inappropriate Southern sorority-girl drawl) was: "You and I might define 'children' differently." Just dropped his jaw in astonishment. He kept his mouth open, staring at the woman in horror. This was an interviewing technique called the Pregnant Pause, which was designed to get the interview subject to say or do something stupid.

Psssssssssssssssss.

In a fit of journalistic discretion, Just informed his audience in his doleful baritone that "Out of respect for our guest, Ms. Stafford, we have edited out the footage of her urinating on her seat." Out of respect for his guest. Soon after the bootlegged urination footage began turning up on the Internet, Ms. Stafford became a "consultant" to the conglomerate, the first time in recorded history when a high-ranking corporate official had been sacked for wetting herself on prime time.

When I returned to the office, there was a voice mail from Al Just, simply stating: "De Sesto, I'll be there in your office at one-thirty to talk Naturale." Today it was my turn to be a "guest," and I didn't find the prospects for my own public drowning to be nearly as amusing as the misfortunes of the others who had, quite literally, pissed away their careers. I instinctively ran out of my office to the rest room where I had the impulse to do something other than rest.

Al Just had been an investigative reporter for KBRO-TV in Philadelphia for about thirty years. In his sixties now, Just still fancied himself the region's premiere muckraker, part Bob Woodward, part Indiana Jones. Sporting a distressed leather jacket throughout the year, and a thinning ponytail that resembled the flow from a spigot before the water ran out, Just's beat had been the mob for most of his career. His career had peaked during the 1980s, when the mob sponsored a murder a day, or so it seemed, and the evening news was filled with the cinematic deaths of Tony Bananas, Pat the Cat, Chicken Man, Mickey Diamonds, Chickie, Rocco Marinucci, and Salvy Boy. Just liked to position his nightly bloodbaths as cutting-edge investigative reports, but all he was really doing was standing in front of liquid-crimson windshields and devastated front porches brow furrowing, and hoping that viewers would see his poses as journalistic risk-taking.

In the 1990s, things quieted down with the mob. Mario Vanni had wisely moved his syndicate underground where it belonged, and street corner massacres slipped from fashion. Just enjoyed a brief resurgence at the millennium, when Vanni was assassinated outside of Olga's Diner. And then, nothing.

I had provided Al Just with stories over the years, and the fact that we both knew what the other one was had been a source of mutual respect. As an investigative reporter, he tended not to have much sympathy for my clients; but I was able to back him off of a lynching, once in a while when I had evidence to prove that one was unwarranted. He didn't take my goods out of any tenderness toward my clients or me, but because he knew that I wouldn't hesitate to use the vindicating evidence I had uncovered to embarrass him with competing media. My sit-downs with Just were never contentious, not a threat ever was uttered. I simply laid down my cards and came to an understanding about how bad the story would or would not be. For my part, I recognized when I had a dirty client with a weak case and never punished Just when his coverage reflected my client's untenable position. Nevertheless, an investigative reporter, by the very nature of his trade, had to—had to—screw somebody. And I knew as well as I knew the Hail Mary that Just would vaporize me in a heartbeat if it meant a couple of ratings points.

Osama Disaster

"The question is, does Jackie Disaster clean up messes or create them?"

Al Just showed up faster than I thought he would, dressed in full Indiana Jones regalia, beard stubble and all. He looked tall and tired, like an aging lizard. Tired meant desperate, and desperate wasn't good for me. He sat himself down in my guest chair without shaking hands. Al Just was Billy Jack, ready to go berserk on The Man on behalf of the little people.

"What brings you to our fair boardwalk, Al?" I asked, hiding behind my desk for protection. I fantasized about having a Batman-like device that would allow me to catapult Just into the ocean

"My nose itches." Just carried his esses too long, at least off camera. *Itchessss.*

"Would you like a tissue? I have the kind with aloe, which softens the blow and cuts down on flaking," I added helpfully.

"No, I'd like enlightenment."

"I'm flattered that you think of me as a source of light."

"Sometimes light, sometimes darkness. You know how it is with us, good and evil."

"How can I help you?"

"A birdie whispered in my ear that you're on the Naturale case."

Bebe. Frankie Shrugs. One of my own guys stabbing me in the back. The CIA. The Mossad. The Vatican. The world was plotting against me.

"That's true," I acknowledged.

"That birdie said you were the one to discover Sally's final e-mail."

"I suggested that the authorities check Sally's server, that's all. The cops actually found it."

"Did you know I did a feature on Sally a few years ago?"

"Not really."

"We had a nice interview."

"Sally was great on camera."

"Do you know what she told me in that interview?" Just left his mouth open—the I'm-just-dumb-old-Lt.-Columbo look.

"That she was a man trapped in a woman's body?" I suggested.

"No, Jackie, she told me she didn't know how to use a computer."

"Uh-huh."

"Do you see what I'm getting at, Jackie?"

"That you're a woman trapped in a man's body."

Just sighed. "If she didn't know how to use a computer, how could she have sent out an e-mail?"

When faced with an allegation of which you are guilty, it's one's natural impulse to begin rattling off alternative theories that prove it wasn't you. It's hard to be guilty and silent simultaneously. My mouth craved action, but my brain was still computing my options. I could actually feel my brain spinning. How would an innocent man react to what was being implied?

Outrage. You'd want to kill this *strunz.*

"What are you suggesting, Al? I'm a little fucking slow."

"Look, Jackie, I've worked with you for years. I know what you do, you know what I do. We're guys who do what we do. But—where my producers are going with this . . ." *Thissssss.*

"Your producers, not you?"

"Where my producers are going with this is worst-case scenario—murders, arson, kidnapping, God knows what else. The question is, does Jackie Disaster clean up messes or create them? I'm not saying you'd do stuff like that. . . ."

I'm saying you'd do stuff like that.

"But," Just continued, "you may know something that could help me out here."

"Fuck you, Al!"

"Jackie, hold on a minute, I'm not accusing. . . ."

"Fuck you! Yes you are. Don't be cute with me. Look, you. . . ."

"Jackie . . ."

"You don't like what I do for a living. You spend your life hunting new moose heads for your wall."

"Jackie. . . ."

"My clients are the mooses. You don't like my clients so you want to nail me for repping them."

"Jackie, would you let me talk for a minute?"

"Go do your murder and mayhem story. Link me to terrorism. Call me Osama Disaster."

"C'mon, Jackie. I didn't say you did all this stuff, I only suggested you'd know something. You put two guys in the A.C. Morgue, for Christ's sake."

"I'm the one they tried to kill. Don't you think I have questions, Al?"

"Of course. I thought we could get answers together."

"Oh, goody!" I bounced to my feet. "Teamwork. Like friggin' Cagney & Lacey."

"Jack . . ."

"What do you want from me? Do you want me to admit I chopped up Sally in the Pine Barrens? I'm in the middle of this thing just like you are."

"That's enough, Jackie. You made your point with your antics." *Anticssss.*

So he wasn't totally buying.

"Sally brought me in to look into these milk allegations, Al."

"That's it?"

"That's it for now."

"All right, Jackie, I'll be frank, I see your hand in some of this. Don't insult my intelligence. You're not above creating disasters, Jackie. You're going to get into my story either sitting up or lying down, but you're getting in. You've got twenty-four hours to sing me a song, or I'll write my own and sing it."

And he would, too.

The lead-in to the story began with stock footage of Sally amidst her cornucopia of high-status products, as the camera panned back to catch the hugeness of Naturale's Earth. The screen froze on Sally's smiling face, then cut, horrifyingly, to the dome after the fire. Ashes.

Al Just's voiceover was oblique. "The fate of Sally Naturale remains a mystery, but in the ruins a clue emerges. A telltale E-mail, allegedly from Sally . . . but is it?"

The screen showed Just's interview with Sally from several years ago. A previously unreleased segment featuring Sally saying "Oh, I can't use those computer contraptions for the life of me."

Al Just, in studio, alone. He was thinking, Lt. Columbo: "But how could a woman who could not use a computer send an E-mail?" Just's right eyebrow raised. He held his cocked eyebrow in position for what seemed like two weeks.

Maybe she learned later, asshole, I thought.

Just relaxed his eyebrow. "The eyes of the nation are on the mystery man who discovered the E-mail, a shadowy operative for big business, a man known as . . . Jackie Disaster . . . when we come back, on "America Betrayed."

Psssssssssssssssss.

The show hadn't actually run, nor had I actually soaked myself. This was my projection of were Al Just was going. He would "link" two truths. Number one, Sally vanished under mysterious circumstances. Number two, I was on the case. The implication of the link? Try these:

1. I killed and/or kidnapped Sally.
2. I torched Cricket Crest.
3. I was working at the behest of a sinister force, such as S.P.E.C.T.R.E. (the Special Executive for Counterintelligence, Terrorism, Revenge and Extortion, from the James Bond series) or the Mafia.
4. I discovered the telltale e-mail and had released it in order to appear as if I was helping in the search for Sally, when I really killed and/or kidnapped Sally, and torched Cricket Crest at the behest of a sinister force such as S.P.E.C.T.R.E. or the Mafia.

I was cool. A cool guy would throw air punches in the window as he scouted the ocean for answers. Finding none, I touched my desk to confirm that my success had once been real, and then nauseously imagined myself, a turbo-*cafone,* working for Frankie Shrugs in the back of a fetid social club in Ducktown.

Like Solozzo

"You're a little fuzzy bunny rabbit."

Rena D'Amico slipped cinematically out of the pool and approached Bebe, to his astonishment, on the stone porch at Cricket Crest. Water fell from Rena like the tears of a thousand men she had tortured, on purpose or unwittingly, during her brief life. A thinner Bebe dipped shrimp in cocktail sauce and gulped blush wine. He wasn't diet-thin; he was worry-thin. Rena sipped merlot.

"You seem preoccupied," Rena said dutifully.

"I am, doll."

"With what?"

"With my plans."

"What plans? The ones about the business?" Rena leaned forward and balanced her heart-shaped head in her hands. On their last date, Bebe had alluded to changes at Naturale, changes where he would finally be recognized. He was furtive, hinting at "deals" and "power plays."

"Yeah." Bebe gulped more rosé.

"Is there something else wrong with the business?" Rena cocked her head to the side and frowned.

Bebe puffed out his chest. "Not really wrong, no. Stress. See, Rena," Bebe explained, "There's things the public sees. People the public sees. Like my poor sister. But there's things people don't see. People see the flash, but not the power, who runs things."

"You run Naturale, don't you Bebe? Everybody says that."

"What do they say?"

"They say Sally's the salesgirl. You're the brains. You're going to rebuild it, once and for all." Rena made a light gesture of applause with her fingers.

"Aah. Don't believe all you hear," Bebe said.

Believe all that you hear, as long as it's what you just said.

"It's common sense, Bebe. Everybody knows there's the front and there's the power," Rena said, rubbing his knuckles. "You should go on TV. You should tell people there are new plans for Naturale. You can be tasteful about your sister."

"I'm not a TV kind of guy."

"Neither was Michael Corleone. But he talked about his business. He was Machiavellian, and he fooled everybody."

"It ain't . . . it's not that easy. Problem is, sweetheart, there's always partners, people you need to cut in. And some of my partners aren't happy with a guy they think is screwing with us."

"What is this guy doing?"

"Nosing around. He was working with my sister."

"You don't think he had anything to do with the fire, do you?"

"This guy's a killer, Rena. He may have killed my sister."

"Oh my God!" Rena covered her mouth and tapped her fingers against her collarbone in a gesture of palpitation that was aimed to prompt masculine reassurance.

"That's the real world, sweetheart. Sorry you have to hear it, but it's the real world. You don't know what goes on in . . . our life."

"What do you mean, our life?"

"The world I'm in, you know."

"You mean . . ." Rena bit her lower lip, "The Mafia?"

"You shouldn't say such words," Bebe said, suppressing a smirk.

"Why not?" Rena said, giving him a poke. "Mafia," she giggled. "Everybody knows you're in with them."

"What the hell do they know? They know what they know, and they know nothing," Bebe chuckled.

"What do you call it then, if not Mafia?" She ran her fingers along her cross.

"I dunno . . . the Thing. Nothing really."

Rena ran her fingers along Bebe's. "So what are you going to do about this man?" She took Bebe's hand and kissed it. She then held his hand against her heart. His eyes twitched. He could feel her heartbeat and the glorious rise of flesh just above it.

"Nunna your business, young lady."

"But you're not really like *them?*"

"What do you mean?" Bebe asked, deflated.

"You're not, you know, tough like that."

"I'm a businessman," Bebe said with a snarl, as if he were an actor playing Bebe in a mob movie.

"But you're not made like them—violent like them. I mean, you're smart, but you're not, like, I don't know, the real guys."

"What real guys?"

"The real Mafia guys. I mean, you're a little fuzzy bunny rabbit." Rena poked him in his jelly belly. Bebe, mortified, backed up in his chair and almost fell out when one of the legs caught in a wedge in between the stones.

"You don't know what I am!"

Rena's lower lip quivered. She fiddled again with her cross, and grew a pair of spaniel eyes. "I'm sorry, Bebe." She looked down, scolded schoolgirl-style.

"I didn't mean to yell, I just . . ."

"You don't have to explain. You don't have to make yourself into something that you're . . . never mind."

"Something what?"

"Something that you're not comfortable being."

"I can't tell you what I do, Rena. You don't want to know. Just because I don't tell you things doesn't mean things don't happen."

"Would you . . . could you . . . make this awful man . . . go away." Rena tugged at her lower lip.

"Who knows?"

"But you don't do things personally."

"Whatever."

"I had an uncle in Newark who worked for Richie the Boot," Rena said.

"The Boot, sure."

"He used to talk a little bit, not specifics. I know what he'd say."

"What?"

"He'd say a guy like this one doing the things to you would have to be in a place where he felt in control, safe. Like Solozzo."

"Solozzo?"

"Solozzo in *The Godfather*."

"Oh, him."

"My uncle explained that scene to me when I watched it with him in high school. They're in that restaurant," Rena said slowly, making her voice more kittenish. "And Solozzo thinks he's safe because he's got that policeman there, and Michael Corleone goes into the bathroom and he reaches around for that gun, and he's so sexy when he's just waiting there for the right moment, and those thoughts are racing in his head. Wow!"

Rena sprung to her feet in a dramatization of an orgasm, and fell into Bebe's lap.

Not Impervious to Nervous

"His loyalty is to his career."

Let me be clear: you can be the toughest guy in the world, but you still don't want Al Just on your ass. After air-punching in my office for an hour, fantasizing about bankruptcy and disgrace, I decided to visit Jonah. Just had relentlessly dogged Jonah's grandfather for decades and, I suspected—but did not know for sure—that Jonah had tangled with Just during his days working for Angela's father.

When I drove up to the ranch in Cowtown, Jonah was stretching against a fence preparing to run. He was understandably startled to see me. Feeling intensely paranoid, I was temporarily swearing off the telephone.

"I don't think I've ever seen you look nervous, Jackie," Jonah said, looking worried himself. "I always thought you were impervious."

"Impervious to nervous? No. Jonah, what do you know about Al Just?"

"Everything. Why?"

"He came to see me. He wants me to be his guest on his program."

"What a wonderful host," Jonah said knowingly.

"He's looking into me, Jonah."

"I've been there."

"Were you guilty?"

"Hell yeah! Are *you*?"

"I didn't do everything I think he thinks I did, but, uh, I'm a virgin like Madonna's a virgin."

"Madonna? The deity or the singer?"

"The singer."

"Okay, so you've got a problem. You think Just will pinch you on everything from Naturale to militant Islam."

"That's about it."

"What was your tone with him?"

"Fuck you."

"Fuck *me,* or you took a fuck-you tone?"

"The tone."

"Good. Do you have anything to give him?"

"Not yet."

"If our other efforts pay a dividend, you'll have something, right?"

"That's the idea."

"Good. You know Jackie, he doesn't want you."

"What does he want?"

"He wants a story. His loyalty is to his career."

"I know that, Jonah," I said, feeling a bit patronized.

"But the answer lies in that."

Jonah looked off toward the corral momentarily and then met my eyes with the twinkle of a man who held Fate by the gonads. I never thought of Jonah as resembling his grandfather, but when he showed his teeth, I discovered a familiar expression. Mickey Price was not a big grinner, but, examining Jonah's dimpled laughter, I recalled Mickey's occasional bursts of mischief.

Epiphany: "What if I give Just everything, Jonah," I said.

"Everything and everyone," he agreed, as if the idea had been mine and mine alone. "Buy him off with a scoop. Not immediately though, but you've got to give him an appetizer soon."

"We're close on Murrin."

"Pretty hefty appetizer."

"Don't be mean, Jonah."

"Sorry, Mr. Feelings. Make sure he knows Murrin's an appetizer, then promise Al he'll break a story that'll make ABSCAM look like a couple of kids soaping up windows on Halloween. If Murrin goes well, he may be your bitch."

"I had been planning on giving out pieces of the story to different media. One gets Murrin, another solves the Naturale riddle."

"Things change. You may have to put your retirement in one stock."

"You've got goods on Just, don't you, Jonah?"

Jonah glanced at me coldly, and then winked. "When you see him next, hint to him that you know he's had a history of getting help with his homework. You don't need to, or want to, know more, Jackie. Guys like Just live in fear of getting caught trafficking in innuendo the way we do. There was a scandal years ago with a *Washington Post* reporter that made up a story about a poor little boy. She won a Pulitzer, until it all turned out to be bullshit. Reporters make up stuff. We make up stuff."

"They're allowed to. They're reporters."

"Jackie, any reporter that's been around as long as Al Just knows in his heart that he's another businessman, and all businessmen cut corners."

"And that businessman's option, Jonah, is to fry my ass no matter the size of the appetizer."

Jonah nodded. "Feed him an appetizer. Don't look scared. Imply you know he's winged it in the past."

Chat

"She said no, and they burned down her place."

The following came from an Internet chat room intercept during the third week in August. Normally, I would have been excited that my cyber program was going well, but it was hard to feel good about anything with Al Just lying in wait. Guaranteed, he had a team of interns checking out everything on the Internet. Success on the disinformation front meant trouble on the Al Just front, because it gave him more of a story about corporate skullduggery . . . that is, if I didn't feed him a prime rib cut of Murrin fast.

ASBURY: Did the cops ever get the dental records for Sally?

LOSERDOG: Don't know for sure, but Boardwalk said they got the records but don't have any remains.

CONEHEAD: Wouldn't you be hiding too if the mob was trying to kill you?

LOSERDOG: Hell yeah.

REGIMUS: That's what I've been saying. She's hiding because they're trying to kill her.

BUBBLES: She must be scared to death.

PORNSTAR: Get this: A buddy of mine with somebody at the gaming commission said the mob wanted to use Sally as a front to get a casino license. She said no, and they burned down her place. She knew it was coming. She was scared in that E-mail they found.

REGIMUS: It's gotta be something like that.

ASBURY: What about the ShoreWatch web site article that feds found Sally's body and are getting evidence from an informant who's talking?

BUBBLES: Where did you hear that?

ASBURY: Was on ShoreWatch, can't you read?

BUBBLES: Sorry. Any idea where ShoreWatch got it?

LOSERDOG: They have sources with cops.

Absolutely Exclusive

"Do you want a clean sting for your program or not?"

I called Al Just and told him it was time for a visit.

"Do you have my story, Disaster?"

"Part of it."

"Don't give me striptease."

"Do you want a clean sting for your next show or not?"

"Was Sally a naughty girl, Jackie?"

"Someone else was pretty naughty."

"No Sally dirt?"

"I've got some, but not for release yet."

"Don't jerk me around!"

"A little birdie told me you have a history of not wanting to do your homework. Do you want to air a home run and then look like a jackass when it turns out you didn't touch all the bases, or do you want to start with an honest triple?"

"Are you shopping this triple to others?"

"No, Al, my intention is to give the triple *and* the home run to you, but if you break my balls with this G. Gordon Liddy position you're taking on me, I'm going to City Line."

This was a reference to Al Just's arch competitor, Sheila Stockwell, a sharp young muckraker from a network affiliate on City Line Avenue in the Philly suburbs.

"Sheila and I are old friends."

"Mr. Nielsen says she's up your sphincter, so I'm sure you spend a lot of time making out in Fairmount Park. Do we really need to play this game? All I want is to get you off your Jackie Disaster-runs-the-underworld shtick. I'm trying to be a grown-up here."

Just sighed. "Gimme an hour."

Al Just stood in my doorway, leather jacket a-hangin', ponytail a-danglin'.

"Looking for the lost ark?" I asked him.

"Huh?" Just snarled.

"The lost ark. Where's your whip? Oh, I'm sorry, I thought you were somebody else."

Just tugged at his ponytail, which shed dandruff onto his bomber jacket. He had one of those unfortunate noses where the septum in the middle was longer than his nostrils on either side, so I could see up his nose. If we ever got on good terms again, I'd buy him a Remington nose-hair trimmer. But we were far from that point.

"So, you've got Sally Naturale as a client?" Al began with a wink.

"Her estate at least, yeah."

"You think she went down in that fire?" he asked.

I had expected this question. Implicit in our arrangement was that I would never lie to him.* "Hard to survive an inferno like that."

"You don't happen to have her hidden in the casino's basement, do you?"

"Nah, not in the basement. I've got her disguised as the maitre d' at Olga's Diner."

"Good plan."

"What I can tell you for sure is that Murrin Connolly, who has been going after her, is a bad girl."

"How so?"

I slid over a thick envelope. Just opened it up and took out the videotape and the papers. "Hmm, looks like somebody's had a busy summer," he chuckled.

"It's all yours," I explained. "Absolutely exclusive."

"As opposed to partially exclusive?"

"No, Al, absolutely exclusive. If you like it, use it as you want. If you don't like it, let me know after you review it, and I'll shoot it to *Dateline* or someplace. Take a look at it here in my office."

"I can't suck up to Sally, Jackie, if there's nothing in here to vindicate her. I can't knowingly traffic in dirt about Murrin," Just warned.

"Of course you can't. I don't expect you to. What I hope is that the material you have will be enough to shed some light onto what's been going on."

*This did not mean that I was obliged to answer uncomfortable questions directly. Cute answers were acceptable under our ground rules, provided the cuteness was obvious.

"What's Murrin expecting?"

"We softened her up for you. She thinks she's going to be a diva. I can't tell you how to do your job, but you may want to play that."

"You know, the public thinks she's the victim. If I show otherwise, it'll have to be pretty strong, not just 'Murrin smoked pot in college.' "

"It's strong. And everything you'll report is totally honest. If this report goes well, there should be some stuff breaking soon afterward that's a lot bigger."

"Like where Sally's been?" Just asked.

I shrugged my shoulders.

"You're going to give up your own client?" he asked.

"I'm loyal to my clients."

"I know, that's why I'm surprised."

"Well, Al, it'll have to be a mystery for a few more weeks. I'll set you up in our little meeting room where you can read the file and look at the tape for as long as you want."

"Will you draw me some chips, too?"

"I'm not an authorized casino operator, Al. And you know how fussy I am about right from wrong."

Prep Time

"Don't forget to show us a smile."

MurMur." This is what Teapot Freddy had taken to calling Murrin. It was an endearment that she liked, and the boys of Allegation Sciences were convinced by her tone of voice on the tapes Teapot Freddy made that Murrin was well under his spell. Al Just had bitten on an initial *America Betrayed* episode on Murrin. I felt that it was time to get Murrin prepared for her interview. Poorly prepared. I wanted an unmitigated flameout.

Teapot Freddy suggested to Murrin that he train her at a studio on Rittenhouse Square in Philadelphia. When he laid out the froufrou arrangements—lights, cameras, personal makeup and styling, a catered lunch—she bit hard and swallowed.

Teapot Freddy made up Murrin conservatively. Her hair looked rather straight on the remote monitor the Lord, Nate the Great, and I watched in my office. Murrin appeared almost corporate solid, which worried me until I realized what Teapot Freddy was doing: he wanted Murrin to think that this was how she would be made up for her star turn, which, of course, she wouldn't be. As Teapot Freddy explained to her, "We're just experimenting to get a sense of how the camera adores you."

And now, the mock interview. Teapot Freddy sat in the interviewer's chair. A small screen had been placed at Freddy's left, which allowed him to check out how Murrin appeared on camera.

"Oh, MurMur, you should see yourself."

"How do I look?" she asked, coquettish.

"Like Gwyneth Paltrow!"

"Get out!" Murrin said, recognizing but appreciating Teapot Freddy's trademark hyperbole.

"Okay, are you ready for the interview, MurMur?"

"Let's go."

"Remember, show sensitivity when I hit you with trick questions, and don't forget to show us a smile."

"Okay." MurMur was feeling good.

"Murrin, tell us all, what did Sally Naturale do to you?"

Murrin smiled. Murrin showed sensitivity. "I know she's missing and all, and I feel bad about coming out at a time like this, but I feel like I can't hide my story."

"Why not?"

"Because I don't want other people to suffer the way I've suffered."

For the next forty-five minutes, Teapot Freddy lobbed Wiffle Balls at Murrin, all of which she smashed like Mark McGwire.

Things We Deserve

"Murrin was not alone in her material jubilee."

I looked up from my desk and saw Angela standing in the doorway. She was holding the panda. It was the first time I had actually seen her with it.

"Do you think I should give him a name?" she asked.

"Sure," I said, setting aside surveillance reports that I decided could wait the moment I saw the freckle that God had chosen to place six inches beneath Angela's neck. She was wearing a cream-colored business suit with very sleek lapels. That did it. I stood up and shut the door to my office. I kissed her and backed up, homing in on that freckle as if it were the proven origin of all cosmic matter, the Big Bang, as it were. Angela stood there.

"Angela," I said. "Would you take that off?"

She removed the jacket and tossed it at me. I sat on the sofa.

"What about the shirt?" I asked.

"What about it?"

"I don't think it should be on now," I explained.

"Why not?"

"We talked before, Angela. And we'll talk later. I want you to take your shirt off."

She stepped toward me. "No one has ever asked me to do that."

"I'm asking," I said, reaching up and slipping my forefinger between two buttons on her shirt.

"Do you want to do it?" she asked.

"No," I said. "I want you to do it."

She removed everything above her waist, let it slip to the floor, and fell on top of me. I recognized quickly that I still had my entire suit on, and hadn't even loosened my tie. Angela tried to loosen it and succeeded only in cutting off my air supply. She bit my upper lip lightly.

"Now you listen to me, Disaster," she said. "After what you put me through, you're going to stand up right there in front of me and take that suit off. I mean everything."

"Angela . . ."

"Don't argue with me! You are going to lose," she reiterated. She rolled over on the couch, removed her skirt swiftly, and fell back. "Now!" she said.

And now it was.

Murrin wasn't too good with a stick shift, but she could learn. The wildness in her eyes suggested determination. Some of the Lord's minions (after the Boom-Boom debacle, I didn't ask for names) had been getting back to us reliably with scoops of Murrin dirt. Murrin bought the Porsche Carrera, putting down ten thousand dollars that she had transferred from her Reliable Mutual Fund, account number 723-6619-2, via telephone. It was illegal to invade a person's financial records, but, if you happened to have a friend at the phone company who happened to mention who a person had been calling (slightly less illegal), and a certain Salem County Porsche dealership didn't own a shredder, motivated parties might be able to—legally—sift through abandoned garbage and produce a record of the transaction.

According to the talkative salesman at Stanley's Porsche, who was convinced by a certain disgraced South Jersey plastic surgeon that he was in the market for a Porsche, Murrin had said she *deserved* her automotive treat.

Murrin was not alone in her material jubilee. Other charter members of the Victims of Sally Naturale "support group" were splurging, too. Like most culturally-sanctioned extortionists, they were greedy and stupid. These qualities were bad for them, but good for me. Dana Lewis of Audubon contracted to remodel her kitchen despite her husband's layoff from DuPont last spring. John Blanton got himself a new Boston Whaler at the Beach Haven Marina on Long Beach Island. He had been haggling with the dealer for a while, but some turn of good fortune recently pushed him over the edge. Harriet Cordova just threw herself a big party in a suite at Harrah's. Despite our sleuthing, we were never able to determine the occasion that prompted the celebration, but a waiter at the event—Teapot Freddy, calling himself Reed Milloy—said that the cocktail wieners were really plump.

BOOK IV

The Theater of Repentance

The whole of humankind having no desire save the opportunity to participate in having a clean slate, an empty canvas, an unburdened sky.

—South Jersey's Patti Smith, *Patti Smith Complete*

Prime-Time Poodle

"It's not your business!"

Teapot Freddy began the day of Murrin's big interview with Al Just by taking her to the spa at the Rittenhouse Hotel in Philadelphia's Center City for a massage, facial, manicure, and pedicure. Later, he beautified her in a room at KBRO's studios. Teapot Freddy did her hair as a derivative of a trailer park mullet. Waves of stringy hair fell around her shoulders, capped off by a puff of yellow hair that stood straight up. Teapot Freddy applied golden eye shadow, dense mascara, and a thick smattering of rouge that contrasted sharply with her pale skin. Teapot Freddy justified the makeup with a lecture about how studio lights are better absorbed by this particular application of cosmetics. He dressed Murrin in a lime-green jump suit one size too small, explaining that the camera tends to slim women down when they're wearing pale citrus colors.

Murrin looked like the love child of Hulk Hogan and a poodle.

Al Just, a man who had once interviewed a two-headed half-llama man, recoiled when he first saw Murrin. Just established *America Betrayed*'s ground rules, namely that, outside of Murrin, the camera crew and himself, there could be no one else in the room. He didn't position this harshly, or in a way that Murrin would have found threatening. He described it with a roll of his eyes as a technical matter. Murrin agreed, after all, she and Just were comrades united against the wicked House of Naturale.

"And we're rolling," a cameraman said.

Just began the interview gently, tilting his head to the side, as if he were Murrin's sweet Uncle Al, and she had a boo-boo. His ponytail slid against his collar, snakelike, which conflicted with his Mister Rogers tone. He was wearing a soft, pinkish shirt, not his bomber jacket. His hair was freshly shampooed, which cut back on his usual reptilian sheen.

"What happened, Murrin?" Just asked, frowning sympathetically.

Murrin smiled per Teapot Freddy's bad instructions.*

"Well, I was a few months along in my pregnancy—we had just seen the baby in the sonogram. I bought Naturale's Real Milk, the soy milk. The ads said that the protein was good for pregnant women, little babies." She choked back the word *babies,* but not too much. Then she smiled again.

"That's a natural thing to think, right, that protein is good for babies?"

"Yes."

"Did you hold an opinion of Sally Naturale before all of this happened?"

"I saw her on TV, but never thought about her much. She seemed like a nice enough lady."

"Given what's going on, with the fire and Sally's disappearance, how does criticizing her make you feel?"

"I don't enjoy it. I don't wish bad things on anybody, but I think the whole thing seems fishy."

"What does, the fire and Sally's disappearance?"

"You said it, not me."

"You're sad, aren't you Murrin?" Just said softly.

"Of course I'm sad," she said with the right amount of vulnerability.

"When were you the saddest?"

"After I lost the baby."

"Were you sad before you lost the baby?"

"I don't understand."

"Were you ever sad before you lost the baby?" Just widened his eyes, the primate signal that there was no threat here.

"Oh, no, I was very excited."

"After you lost the baby, would you say you were depressed?"

"Very depressed, yes. It was awful."

"Did you seek help for your sadness?"

"I talked to my priest sometimes."

"Did you talk to him before you lost the baby?"

"Sometimes. I'm Catholic, so I go to confession." She said this buoyantly, while holding out her cross as if she was a cop flipping a suspect a badge.

"Do you tell the priest your deepest feelings?"

*Somewhere along the line, it became conventional wisdom that smiling on camera was a good thing, when, in fact, smiling when discussing serious matters is repugnant to viewers.

"Oh, yes."

"Do you tell him the truth?"

"Oh, yes." Her calm face suggested that she knew that Just was on her side.

"Is the priest the only person you tell your deepest feelings to?"

Murrin raised her eyebrows quizzically. "I talk to people in my family sometimes."

"What about a doctor?"

Murrin shifted in her chair. "My doctor was a big help to me after I lost the baby," she finally said.

"What kind of doctor was he?"

"A baby doctor. I forget what you call them. Obsessions, or something like that. My husband and I spent every last dime we had trying to get a diagnosis, to figure out what went wrong."

"What did the doctor say?"

"The tests couldn't be sure, but he thought, uh, that something toxic got into me. The only thing that I had eaten that was out of my normal routine was the milk. The doctor thought that could be it, especially when he heard about the genetic stuff in it."

"I see. Did you ever discuss your sadness with another doctor?"

"I don't think so."

"What about, oh, a psychiatrist? Did you ever discuss your depression with a psychiatrist?" Despite the sibilants contained in this question, I noticed that Just did not hiss.

"I, uh—oh, I don't think that's any of your business." Murrin darted her eyes around searching for allies. But there were none there. No "golden tresses" or "alabaster complexions" today.

"But you've been sharing your innermost feelings with the public for months on television, your deepest pain."

"It's different."

"What's different, Murrin?"

"You are asking me private things. I just want to help people."

Still slowly, feigning confusion not anger, Just said, "But you were willing to admit that you were depressed—that you went to a priest for confession. But you believe my question about a psychiatrist is personal?"

"It's too personal."

"Did your baby doctor ever tell you about things you couldn't do while you were pregnant?"

"I don't know, maybe."

"Have you ever heard of a drug called Centrilex?"

Murrin shifted in her chair again and looked around the room. With the exception of Just and two cameramen who were neutral to her torture, there was nothing in that room with the capacity for compassion. She was starting to feel very much alone.

"I think I've heard of it." Beads of sweat broke out just south of her pompadour.

"Do you know what it does?"

"Why are you shouting at me, I'm not a doctor?"

"Trust me, Murrin, I'm not the devil. Do you think I'm the devil?"

"Devil? No." She readjusted herself in the chair yet again and blew a stray hair from her forehead.

"Do you know that Centrilex is a drug that treats depression?"

"I think I've heard that."

"Have you ever taken Centrilex?"

"I don't think so. I don't know the names of medications. I don't have to tell you about my personal . . . about medicines and doctors and all."

"You admit that you've been depressed, isn't that right?"

"Anyone who lost a baby would be depressed after."

"Yes, but not everyone would be depressed *before* they lost a baby."

Murrin leaned forward now, her lip was quivering as she spoke: "You said before, back there, that you believed me. You said!" she repeated childishly.

"Oh, I did, Murrin, back there, but out here you've gotten me thinking. Have you taken Centrilex?"

"I know I took something after I lost my baby."

"What about *before* you lost your baby?"

Murrin was rocking now, and her poodle-do was deflating. "I took vitamins and medicines like all pregnant people, things that the doctor said were okay."

"Which doctor."

"A w-w-witch doctor?"

"No, Murrin, not a witch doctor, but *which* doctor told you to take vitamins and medicines?"

"My baby doctor."

Murrin rocked forward and remained in an attack position in her chair. Just then leaned into her, which caused Murrin to flinch.

"What about Dr. Manion?" Just asked.

"I don't have to tell you who my doctors are."

"You didn't feel that you had to tell your obstetrician who your other doctors were, did you Murrin?" While Just's body position was in full attack, his voice was soft, sad even, with a boo-hoo tone. Just knew how sinister men can appear when they become hostile toward women on camera, so he performed his lean-in like a concerned father not a predator. "You didn't tell your baby doctor that you were seeing a psychiatrist, and you didn't tell your psychiatrist that you were pregnant."

"It's not your business!"

"But sweetheart, you've been calling Sally Naturale a baby killer. You have taken a sympathetic America into your womb, and now you're throwing out all of the people who care about you."

"I just wanted to help people," Murrin whimpered.

I wanted to be on TV.

"I'm not so sure about that, Murrin."

"You're not being fair!" Murrin buried her face in her hands, then bounced up again stone-faced when Al Just began to deliver his anchor punch.

"Okay, Murrin, you don't have to answer any more questions. Let me tell you what I think happened. I believe you went to Dr. Manion, the psychiatrist, last winter during the initial stages of your pregnancy. I believe you did not tell him that you were pregnant. I believe you took the Centrilex without telling your baby doctor." Just removed a prop prescription container and shook it. The pills inside quaking against the plastic sounded like a baby rattle. "I believe you did not want either doctor knowing about the other, because any responsible doctor would not have allowed you to take Centrilex while you were pregnant. I believe that the Centrilex terminated your pregnancy, and that you could not admit the secret you were keeping and that you chose to blame Sally Naturale's soy milk."

"My doctor thought it was the genetic milk!"

"He wouldn't come on camera with us, Murrin, and his deposition did not indicate genetic milk as a cause. He said that, sadly, miscarriages happen, and that sometimes it's impossible to tell the cause. Naturale's milk isn't made to be any different from many products on the market that people have been eating and drinking for years without incident."

"I'm going to sue your ass!"

"How will you pay your attorney? With the money you get from selling your Porsche?"

"What does *that* have to do with anything?"

"You said moments ago that you spent every dime you had on doctors."

Footage of Murrin in her Porsche ran across a small monitor in the studio that allowed Murrin to see it.

"I'm going to sue you," Murrin said righteously.

"I have no doubt that you will," Just nodded, feigning hurt. "After all, that's what you do. I also believe you'll reconsider when you, not to mention millions of others, take a look at what we've got."

When Murrin returned to KBRO's green room, she found a note from Teapot Freddy reading: "MurMur, it was too painful for me to watch them do this to you. We must both be strong. Adieu. Adieu. Your friend, Jack Tripper."

Jonah had conducted three sets of surveys. The first, conducted in the early weeks of Murrin's stardom, assessed her believability. Over sixty percent of those surveyed were inclined to believe her, a figure Jonah felt was soft, given her misfortune. Roughly the same amount believed that Sally Naturale's genetically-engineered milk was to blame.

The second survey—it was a focus group, actually—looked into the circumstances under which the public would change its mind about Murrin—in other words, disbelieve her. The answer was unusually clear for a focus group: if Murrin was perceived to have had any complicity in her unborn baby's death, she was toast. Jonah felt that there was an intangible revulsion of Murrin that couldn't be measured, but could come in handy in concert with evidence of complicity. The complicity card was the one we had to play, and play it we did, once we were able to prove it.

The final survey was what Jonah called a benchmark. Its purpose was to measure the extent to which opinions about Murrin had changed. On the evening that *America Betrayed* ran, only eighteen percent—probably committed Sally Naturale-haters and media-bashers—believed Murrin's story. Murrin's Warholian brush with fame was over. But *my* unwanted brush with notoriety would soon begin, if I didn't bag bigger game for Al Just pronto.

Shvitz

"That poor girl got flambéed."

Both Father Ignacio and Jonah wanted to see me. I decided to have lunch with both of them at the same place, Murray's in Margate. I would just eat two light meals in a row. Murray's was part delicatessen and part restaurant. It was located at the base of an apartment building in Margate, a block from Lucy, the giant six-story elephant that had once been Mario Vanni's headquarters.

I had an ulterior motive for stacking the two appointments. With the Holy Cannoli, there was always a rebuke of some kind. While I routinely snapped back at him like a tough guy, his needling about my father ate away at me in a big way. With one witch, Murrin, out of the way, my conscience had freed up room for Blinky Dom.

The Jonah visit, on the other hand, was something I welcomed. Not only had he delivered on our Murrin program, but I liked the way he could get me thinking about things. He was like me, after all, in the sense that he was capable of balancing ruthlessness with reflection. And besides, with the Imps still scattered throughout the region out on the Naturale assignment, I wanted someone to scheme with, especially with Al Just slithering at my heels.

Father Ignacio was prompt. He was wearing a greenish warm-up suit and white loafers and looked like a walking lime wedding cake. I ordered a cup of cabbage soup. Father Ignacio got the tuna melt hoagie, an order of bagel chips, a bowl of chicken-noodle soup and an apple Danish. He had watched Al Just's evisceration of Murrin and asked me if I saw it.

I nodded cautiously, but didn't really want to get into the Murrin caper with him. He knew I had been involved, and I knew that he knew.

"That poor girl got flambéed," Father Ignacio said.

"She provoked a grizzly bear," I said matter-of-factly.

"No, she provoked a very sharp ex-prizefighter and a ruthless old woman hell-bent on survival."

"Should I feel guilty?"

"Do you?"

"About Murrin?"

"Yes, Jackie."

"No. She's a looter."

"So she is," the Holy Cannoli said, suggesting sympathy nonetheless.

The lunches came.

"Have you talked to your father?" Father Ignacio asked. Hell.

"A few days ago. He's got Emma."

"Well, I stopped by his club a few days ago." The Holy Cannoli pursed his lips in disapproval.

"Oh yeah? How was he?" I asked, like the biggest idiot on earth.

"You know, how he always is." Father Ignacio laughed and wiped his mouth. "We got to talking about you and Tommy as fighters. He said your niece keeps pressing for details on how her father died."

"Really?"

"She wanted to know who Tommy was fighting, where the fight was, things like that. Your dad said you were quite a fighter."

"Me?"

"Yes."

"Funny, he never told me that."

"He said that Tommy did a lot of show business."

"He said that?"

"Why does that surprise you?"

"Show business was always a negative thing with him. He meant it like . . . 'empty suit.' "

"Well, he said Tommy wanted trophies, but you really wanted to fight."

This statement hit me like a brick through plate glass. What now? Does the lens dissolve into soft focus and Jackie the hard-headed Beast melts away to become the sensitive, hibernating Prince with flaxen hair? Everything is one big misunderstanding that can be resolved with one simple insight that, silly me, I should have known all along. The angry son had been the better fighter after all, and his mental hunchback of a father couldn't express it. . . . *The hills are alive* . . .

In the course of a nanosecond, my range of emotion ran from feeling flattered to feeling manipulated. First, the old bastard comes at me through his clerical surrogate with guilt. When that fails, and I find Angela—and contentment—he tries sucker-punching me with my boxing greatness, juxtaposed, of course, with my fabled brother's. Was I going insane? Was there a Machiavellian maneuver behind everything? Was it possible that I should be taking all of this at face value?

"Father Ignacio," I said.

"Yes, son?"

"Is there a piece-a snot hanging from my nose?"

"No, why?" he said, puzzled.

"Do you ever feel like you've got a dry one hanging there, and no matter how much you scratch around you still feel like it's there?"

"Uh, yes. Jackie, did you hear what I said?"

"Yeah."

Father Ignacio looked at me with that such-a-complex-child look. He wanted to heal me with pop-psych, and all I wanted was my cabbage soup.

Ostensibly, Jonah wanted to meet me to hook me up with a few of his contacts for the final phase of our program, but I sensed there was something deeper to his pursuit of a meeting.

Jonah hurried through business. "You're fixed for Internet contacts, right, Jackie?"

"Right. I've got guys who go back to your grandpop's day."

"Good. Now, we're going to need media friends, folks who'll show and tell without asking too many questions."

"I'm pretty strong there, too."

"What about on the entertainment side? We'll need to get some of those old news documentaries aired everywhere."

"Do you have a suggestion?" I asked. "I'm not sure about that one."

"Call my friend, Cindi, in PR in Cherry Hill. She's wired pretty well at some of the networks. She may be able to get a roster of the documentaries they've got in the can."

"We'll have to just make sure the networks get them ready. They won't actually air them until Trouble makes his announcement and Al Just drops his big one."

"Right. Right," Jonah agreed, fiddling with an onion on his cheese steak.

"Ah, the world of spin control," I said.

"We don't sell spin," Jonah responded sharply.

"What do we sell, Jonah?"

"Big-ass, butt-ugly truth."

"Jonah, my man, you look distracted."

"Mickey took me to this place for years, Jackie. He'd bring me here with his guys."

"I know he liked Murray's," I said. "You know what they used to do that was funny? He and his guys—Irv the Curve, Blue Cocco—used to eat like horses. Corned beef. Pastrami. Sandwiches taller than the Island House. Stuff with more cholesterol than you could imagine. Then—this is the great part—they'd go back to the Golden Prospect to the damned sauna!"

"Taking a *schvitz,* they called it."

"Right, but the thing was, Jonah, they thought that the *shvitz* undid all the bad eating. They thought it was exercise. They'd sit there eating all of this stuff and then say they had to go work out. It was like Catholics going to confession: you sin then you confess. These old guys would chow down on fat, and then they'd sit in the sauna for twenty minutes and leave happy that they were in good shape!"

"It's an ironic thing, I think, that they deluded themselves that way," Jonah said philosophically. "I always thought that the reason why these crooks survived is that the world thought they had all of this power, but they knew they were just boardwalk mopes. They all lived into their nineties, you know, Jackie?"

"I know, that's the thing," I said, truly awestruck.

"And here we are going for runs, we get tested for cholesterol . . ."

"When we should be taking a *shvitz,*" I said.

"Maybe not, though." Jonah frowned.

"Why not, Jonah?"

"Those guys were made from something else, I think. We agonize over everything, we wonder what it all means. I don't think they did. Things were what they were. Look at September 11, the attacks. You've got people out there who wonder whether we brought that on ourselves. Can you believe that? Back then with Mickey and his guys . . . they were old school, they'd say, those hijackers were the enemy. Period. End of story." Jonah sliced the air with his hand. His green eyes went cold and a vein near his temple pulsed. It was as if he was trying to impersonate his grandfather and convince himself that he, too, could survive into his nineties.

"So you're saying that we think too much, Jonah."

"Yes. We're out there in that part of the sky that starts out gray but ends up blue as it goes up, like around sunset, when you get clouds with all those colors."

"Yeah, I guess so. I'm always wondering what color I am, too," I acknowledged. "Ah, who knows, maybe Mickey and his guys wondered about it, too, and just didn't let anybody know," I suggested.

"Mickey worried plenty about Al Just, Jackie."

"Good, because every time I talk to Just, I'm a wiseguy on the surface, but I need a change of underwear after he leaves."

Jonah laughed. "Was anybody in your crowd involved with that life?"

"Not that I know. They were all laborers. People think, I guess because I'm Italian, that there must have been something going on back then; but there wasn't, I don't think. The De Sestos weren't a success story, but were of good, honest stock.

"The Jewish and Italian boys managed to make a go of it, didn't they? It was like that all over the country. With every Italian crew, there was a little Jewish guy in the corner going, 'Put away your guns, boys, here's how we're gonna do it.' "

I laughed. "Eventually, the Italians learned to put down their guns on their own. Except the few *jamooks* we've still got."

"Right, until this new generation started watching the movies—guys our age. But do you know why the Italians really outlasted the Jews in the rackets, Jackie?"

"Why?"

"Better nicknames. Italians had Carmine the Snake, Lupo the Wolf, Sammy the Bull. The Jews had Benny the Hypochondriac, Sol the Worrier, Morty the Procrastinator. How scary is it if somebody comes up to you and says, 'Watch out, Morty the Procrastinator is gonna break your kneecaps . . . if he gets around to it'?"

"Hah! Some of the old Yids—Mickey, Lansky, Siegel—were pretty tough."

"I know they were, but the stereotypes outlived the old buzzards."

"Our age isn't as young as it was, huh, Jonah?"

Jonah removed his baseball cap and ran his fingers through thinning black hair. "No." He felt around his scalp as if he had expected there would be more hair. He appeared to be shaken by what he felt.

Warlock

"Sickle cell? That's what they *get, the* colored.
I can't have that!"

The call came shortly after I got back to the office. Blinky Dom was at Atlantic City General Fucking Hospital (not affiliated with Vincent's Frigging Hardware). His assistant, LaMont, said it appeared to be a stroke. I was at the hospital inside of ten minutes and parked illegally after placing an ancient "Police Business" card on top of my dashboard. Emma was out at a summer art camp in Ventnor.

When I got to my father's hospital room, he was lying in bed on top of the covers in a hospital gown. He wore an identifying tag around his wrist like the Purple Heart. His head was turned toward the door.

"So, you went and had a stroke," I said, attempting buoyancy.

"They dunno," Blinky Dom said with a swat.

"What actually happened?"

"I'm at my desk having a goddamned bagel, reading the paper. I get dizzy all of a sudden and the paper blurs up. I fall, like, in front of myself and my head bounces off the desk." Blinky Dom came alive with enthusiasm. "I start sweating and sweating, so I called for LaMont. LaMont comes in and he calls the hospital. The medics come and strap me into this stretcher. Everybody's looking at me. The fighters, the people on the street. Everybody. It was embarrassing as hell. So, I get here and they start with the poking and the poking, like I'm an animal. . . ."

"What did the doctors tell you?"

"Ah, the doctors don't know anything. They know how to rob a man. Then I'm sitting here all alone by myself, and eventually you get here. What are you snarling at?"

"I'm not snarling."

"Yeah, you are. You're snarling at a sick man."

I whirled around and left the hospital room. I was sweating. I approached a nurse. "Can somebody tell me about my father?" I asked loudly.

"Which one's he?"

"He's the son of a bitch in one-twenty-three."

"There's no need for that kind of talk."

"Would somebody tell me exactly what happened to him?"

The nurse spoke to me like I was a mental patient. "What is his name, sir?"

"Dominic De Sesto."

A doctor about my age, maybe a little younger, overheard me. "De Sesto? You the fighter?"

"Uh-huh."

"I saw you fight years ago. You fought under 'Jackie Disaster'."

"So, how'd I do?" I asked, purposefully hard.

"You were pissed. You broke the guy's jaw."

"Maddox. That was the Maddox fight."

"Right, Maddox."

"Look, I don't want to break any more jaws, but I just might if somebody doesn't tell me what happened to my father."

"Sure, I'll get Dr. Schwartz who looked at him."

Inside of a minute another young doctor emerged from a back room. "I'm Craig Schwartz," he said.

"Jackie De Sesto."

"Jackie, we have to run some more tests on your father."

"What does your gut say?" I interrupted, probably scaring the guy.

"I think he may have had an anxiety attack, or something like that. His blood pressure was high, his heart rate was fine. It may have been slightly fast, but that happens when doctors are working on you. We gave him a tranquilizer and some aspirin after we drew blood."

"So you don't think he had a stroke?"

"We're not sure yet."

"What about a heart attack?"

"It doesn't look like it, but again . . ."

"I know, you have to do tests."

"Right. Look, these things happen when a man gets older."

"How about when a man is younger? How about three times a week when he's thirty three?"

"I, I can't . . ."

"Calm down, Doc, you're doing your job. Sorry to hassle you."

I deserted the trembling doctor and returned to Blinky Dom's room.

"Well, Pop, I think we know what it is."

"You do?"

"It's cancer."

"Cancer?!"

"No, I mean it's tuberculosis."

"How the hell could it be tuberculosis? They don't even have tuberculosis anymore."

"Well, they do now. They brought it back for a special promotion. You can get tuberculosis and a Happy Meal with a coupon. Do you have a coupon?"

"What the hell's wrong with you?"

"You've got malaria, pop, I'm worried about you."

"Malaria? What are you saying?"

"I'm saying you've got polio. Do you know how serious that is?"

"I had a vaccination a hundred years ago."

"Not for sickle cell anemia, you didn't. That's what the doctor said you had."

"Sickle cell? That's what *they* get, the *colored.* I can't have that!"

"Yeah, *you* do. The doctor said you had sickle cell. Who would-a thought?"

"Something's wrong with you. Always has been."

"So, Pop, is this stunt because of the time I'm spending with Angela?"

"A course not! Go be selfish." Blinky Dom stood and shuffled toward the window. "You should live and be well with that gangster's money, now that it's been polished up by his Ivory League daughter."

"What's with Vanni as the source of all evil in the world?"

"The man was a gangster. What a name he gave the Italian people!"

"I've known you for forty years and you never gave a shit about the Italian people!"

Blinky Dom was stunned by my tone. He stood and rubbed his chest—the heart attack maneuver—a gesture I had grown tired of it by the time I was a fetus.

"A gangster!" he said.

I grabbed Blinky Dom by the light blue gown he was wearing and shoved him against the wall. "You don't hate that Vanni was a gangster, you hate that he was a *successful* gangster, a gangster who looked out for his children despite his day job."

When I spoke the word *despite*—not a word I used a lot—I spat on Blinky Dom's face. It may have been intentional, I don't know. His eyes bugged out. Behind his glasses they looked huge and desperate like a goldfish that had just realized he had jumped out of his bowl onto the countertop. Not a lot of options . . . I let go of his gown and pushed him toward the bed. His pale white ass was hanging out of his gown. I laughed. He took off his glasses and wiped my venom off the lenses with a tissue. Without his glasses his eyes appeared to be tiny, like holes left by drill bits.

I walked to the door. Blinky Dom sat on his bed and looked at the floor as if he had been weighed down by a load of camel manure that had been lowered onto his head.

"I tried to do everything the way I thought was right and good," he said as I opened the door. "I can't help it if I've been forsaken."

"Don't spin a moral on it, Dom," I said, realizing for the first time how the man defined *selfish*—it meant an unwillingness to be abused. "You are what you are."

Five Gorillas Loaded for Bear Versus a Midget

"How did you think it would end, Mr. Leeds?"

There are places in the Pine Barrens where the sand is white. One theory is that the whiteness is caused by a chemical interaction between the soil and a massive fresh water preserve that has slept beneath the state since the Ice Age. One such place where the sand is white is a wooded commune called Penny Pot.

As vast as the Pine Barrens are, the community of pineys is rather small. Between brother Ryan's confession during his unfortunate dental appointment and the network of pineys I had cultivated over the years to scare casino cheats, we located the midget, Mr. Leeds, in Penny Pot. Until we picked up the little man, we had been keeping brother Ryan under the watchful eye of Fragile Merrill.

Bad men tend toward arrogance. They believe that because they create mayhem, God endowed them with divine capacities. Nevertheless, we didn't want to take stupid chances with Mr. Leeds. Swervin' Mervin had pinpointed the commune by air when he flew over last week. Nate the Great, disguised as a piney, ambled nearby just before dawn several days ago and located the El Camino in a lean-to next to Mr. Leeds' cottage, which was surrounded by other cottages. Mr. Leeds also drove a late-model Honda Accord, which he had presumably been using since the attack on my house. Nate, with the help of some piney allies, determined that Mr. Leeds watched the evening reruns of *Seinfeld* and *Friends* on a battery-operated TV, smoked a pipe on his porch, and then retired for the evening. Nate hadn't noticed booby traps of any kind. The small cottages around Mr. Leeds did not appear to be occupied, and were presumably used for the temporary housing of anarchists. Given Mr. Leeds' wanted-man status, it made sense that he wouldn't want too much traffic these days.

We came in two vehicles. In the van was the Lord, Nate the Great, and

Swervin' Mervin. Fragile drove Petey's Range Rover, which had since been painted silver. We parked about a quarter mile away from the cottage. Swervin' Mervin walked ahead and confirmed via radio that there was some activity in Mr. Leeds' house. There did not appear to be others in the neighboring cottages. Just in case, we were armed with Berettas and stun guns, the kind that can shoot a bolt of electricity for a few yards and really ruin somebody's boxers. Five gorillas loaded for bear, versus a midget in the Pine Barrens. I loved it, and, more importantly, I believed I was justified.

Mr. Leeds stepped out onto his porch at 8:01 shortly after the *Seinfeld* rerun finished. My gang was standing about thirty yards in front of him, but lurking in the woods so that he couldn't see us, taking advantage of dusk setting in. He carried a small plastic bag and a meerschaum pipe, and sat down on his rocking chair. I got a look at his face, which was, all things considered, rather benign. His beard made him appear elfin, rather than the wicked troll-like look I had expected. During the past few months, his mythology had given him the appearance in my mind of those gross munchkins in *The Wizard of Oz*. The munchkins had always scared me more than the wicked witch or flying monkeys because they looked as if they were going to explode. Mr. Leeds wore an Irish-style-cap, a flannel shirt, and overalls. I put him in his mid-forties. I couldn't say for sure that he was the midget I saw that night at my house, but how many midgets with El Caminos could there be?

Nate the Great crept beside one of the guest cottages and Swervin' Mervin backed up against the other one. Their role was to stop anyone who might come charging out of the cottages to help Mr. Leeds. I bent down and made my way beside Mr. Leeds' porch. I sniffed. Pot. The guy was smoking pot. I don't know why this surprised me, as if I thought midgets would disapprove of drugs. Fragile would remain about thirty yards directly in front of Mr. Leeds until I gave him the word to go. With all of the boxing strategies I had mapped out over the years—how to take down big guys, wiry guys, stocky guys—I had never given any thought to how I'd take apart a midget. So many of my take down blueprints assumed that my opponent was my size or larger. I knew the effects of a level shot to the nose and the upward arc of a hook to the ribs of a bigger man, but had never considered what I'd do to a man as small as Mr. Leeds. I had considered the possibility that Mr. Leeds would be able to compensate for his size with extraordinarily efficient strength. I would soon know.

Calm down, Jackie. It's not vengeance time yet, it's business. Your job right now is to capture the little prick. "Go," I whispered to Fragile into my two-way radio. The giant ambled out from the woods slowly toward Mr. Leeds. I could see Fragile's steps from where I huddled. He walked slowly with his arms swaying beside his tattered clothing. He wore a slight smile, as if he were sending the signal to Mr. Leeds to relax, that he was a gentle giant.

Startled, Mr. Leeds set aside his pipe, rose from his rocker and stepped back toward his door as he studied Fragile, whose smile grew brighter as the sun fell. I hopped over the porch's railing. Mr. Leeds turned toward me and emitted a random syllable of fear.

"Mr. Leeds," I said, "Jackie Disaster."

Faster than I could have imagined, Mr. Leeds dove between two slats in the porch railing.

"Son of a bitch!" I said. I began to run after him, jumping over the rail. Mr. Leeds' legs shot out from his sides as he ran looking like a penguin on amphetamines.

"C'mon!" I shouted to the rest of the boys who were soon behind me. Mr. Leeds wove expertly in between trees, his little ass cheeks bouncing up and down like grapefruits as he ran. When he veered to one side, he nearly stumbled, allowing me to move in closer. As he recovered his initial speed, I withdrew my stun gun from my pocket, extended my arm, and blasted him in the back with a purple bolt. He shrieked and fell to the ground. I jumped on top of him. He managed to roll over and punch me in the face. Shocked by his coordination—and the fact that the stun gun proved ineffective—my jaw fell open.

"You little prick," I said, and smashed him back in the nose with my left hand. I then zapped him again with my stun gun, this time in the groin. Mr. Leeds yelped.

Then I kneeled on his chest and punched him repeatedly in the face. The rest of the boys caught up with me as I knelt, winded, on top of the midget—who kicked me in the shins as I stood up again. This time, we were all on Mr. Leeds, who still had some supernatural wriggling left in him. He was kicking, cursing, and spitting until Fragile growled like a grizzly bear, gripped Mr. Leeds' throat and squeezed him until he was almost unconscious. After Fragile finally let go, he rose and knocked Mr. Leeds out with one kick to his large skull.

Teapot Freddy was waiting for us at the stable near the shore where I took Emma to ride from time to time. Emma and I didn't actually own horses, but we went there so often over the years that we considered two of the horses "ours." She rode a draft horse named Mystic and I rode an old thoroughbred called Buckin' A. For a modest fee, the Mexican guys that operated the stable let us have the place for the evening and into the morning.

Fragile carried Mr. Leeds under his arm like a sack of mulch, then dropped him in the central aisle that separated the two rows of stalls. He managed to stand.

I walked up to Mr. Leeds and rained hate down upon him with my eyes. Fragile, Teapot Freddy, the Lord, and Nate the Great stood around us. Each had stun guns and Berettas, save Freddy. Swervin' Mervin was on guard outside.

My hate had layers like fireworks. Every time I thought the last burst of new color had shown itself, another explosion radiated from nowhere, displaying hues, levels, and velocities that had been unimaginable moments before.

"Have you ever been horseback riding, Mr. Leeds?" I asked.

"No," the midget responded. He had a normal adult voice. "Well, maybe once when I was a kid." I tried to imagine Mr. Leeds as a child. Couldn't do it.

"Well, we're going to see if we can bring back some childhood memories for you."

"What are you going to do?"

I bent down and faced Mr. Leeds eye to eye. "I'm not going to tell you what I'm going to do. I'm going to tell you what *you're* going to do."

"And what is that?" Mr. Leeds asked with an annoying calm.

"You're going to tell us who your sponsors are and what they want. We will ask politely first. First, do you know Murrin's brother, Ryan?"

"I know no one with those names," he said, confident.

Fragile kicked Mr. Leeds to the ground and I stepped hard with my boot heel onto his neck.

"Listen to me, you frigging smurf!" When he caught his breath, Mr. Leeds' smugness evaporated.

Fragile brought Mr. Leeds to his feet. The Lord pinned Mr. Leeds' hands behind his back while Nate the Great removed his clothing.

Teapot Freddy glanced studiously at Mr. Leeds naked groin. "Interesting," he said.

"What's interesting?" I asked.

"Pretty normal below the Mason-Dixon," Teapot Freddy summed up.

Mr. Leeds gazed downward at his privates.

"You seemed pleased," I said to Freddy.

"Fascinated. It makes me look at dwarfism in a whole new light."

"Do I want to hear this?" I asked, as Nate the Great and the Lord bound Mr. Leeds' hands behind his back.

"Well," Teapot Freddy began professorially, "There's an optical advantage to being a midget if your doo-wang-dang is normal sized. Take a tall drink of water like me. Undressed, my thing is a smaller percentage of my body than his."

"Uh-huh," I said, deeply regretting that I had asked the Teapot anything.

"But a midget! Think of the possibilities. His bishop is a greater percentage of his body than a normal-sized man. I mean, really, there's got to be a way to parlay that into a selling point."

Teapot Freddy turned to Mr. Leeds. "Is this making any sense to you?" Mr. Leeds again looked south for a revelation.

"I never thought about it," he finally surrendered. "Little people try to stick with other little people."

"Oh, how closed-minded is that?" Freddy said. "Look, before we do our little thingamajig, are there, I don't know, any midget magazines or web sites that would walk me through this, or do you only get the killer-dwarf rags?"

"You're misusing the terms. We call ourselves little people."

"Would you just stop with that," Teapot Freddy ordered.

"That'll be enough for now," I said. "Time to string him up."

Fragile walked Mr. Leeds down the central aisle of the stable where the Lord and Nate the Great waited by Buckin' A. Mr. Leeds stumbled when he saw the freshly-tied noose swinging from a rafter, grazing gently against Buck's back. We helped Mr. Leeds up.

"How did you think it would end, Mr. Leeds?" I asked.

"Not like this."

Mr. Leeds dropped to his knees again and his dead weight caused Fragile to drop him. He tried to run, but the Lord kicked him in the head as he attempted to get up. "You're *hanging* me?!" Mr. Leeds cried.

"Well, you *did* check off hanging on your activities card," Teapot Freddy said.

"It's weird," I said. "When you shoot a guy, he says, 'You shot me.' When you hang a guy, he says, 'You're hanging me?' What's up with that?"

All five of us grabbed the hysterical, naked midget and, with considerable struggle, propped him up on the back of Buckin' A. Teapot Freddy was almost in tears himself. As soon as Mr. Leeds was atop the horse, Freddy walked down the aisle wiping his eyes. Nate the Great climbed a short ladder and slipped the noose around Mr. Leeds' neck. "I'm a doctor," he assured the midget. "I'm pretty sure this'll be quick."

"What is your real name?" I asked.

"Does it matter now? I'm a dead man."

"Not yet. Do you believe in God?"

"No. I have other masters."

I stomped my foot loudly. Buckin' A spooked and shifted sideways. Mr. Leeds screamed, and I restrained the horse with his reins.

"Thoroughbreds are jumpy," I explained. Mr. Leeds sobbed. "What is your real name? I'm giving you a chance at redemption. It doesn't have to end this way?"

"Terry Lack."

"Who do you work for?" I stomped my foot again. Buckin' A spooked. Terry Lack yelped as I restrained the animal again.

"Pangea! The activist group! Pangea!"

"Why did you try to kill me?"

"Fuck you!"

"Welcome to Hell, Terry Lack. You'll answer your masters there." I withdrew my Beretta, pointed it skyward, and pulled the trigger. Terry Lack screamed "*Nooooo!*" and the horse sprinted forward, leaving the midget's fate up in the air.

Spectacular Justice

"I don't want you to think that everybody gets killed, not even all bad men."

We didn't kill the little bastard. The hanging rope hadn't been fastened tightly to the rafter. When I pulled my Beretta, the Lord shot Terry Lack in the back with a stun gun. When he fell to the ground, Nate the Great injected him with sodium pentathol, the truth serum.

We knew everything now, including the first names of the Dutch-anarchist Pangea hitmen that I killed at my house, Meindert and Johann.

Trouble arrested Terry Lack early the next morning. As a favor, a police photographer snapped a Polaroid of Trouble putting Terry Lack in back of a squad car. Lack was wearing only his underwear, and was still hallucinating from Nate the Great's potion. He looked Trouble straight in the eye and asked, babbling, "Where did the albino put his nostrils?"

"Up your ass," Trouble responded.

"I already looked there," the midget said calmly, attempting to turn around and look at his ass, but failing.

"You'll have plenty of time to find your ass in prison," Trouble said.

"That's good," the midget said. "I need more time with my ass."

Trouble shook his head in disbelief. The Imps, Swervin' Mervin, and Fragile had left. Trouble drove me back home where Emma was staying with Cookie the Cop, who I hired after the Frankie Shrugs scare. After Blinky Dom's hospitalization, I had to make a change of plans.

The moment Trouble and I pulled up to the house, Emma ran out. I sat next to Emma at the kitchen table.

"Emmalina," I said. "Do you remember that they said there was a midget that night at our house?"

"Yes."

"He was arrested this morning. I got him."

"You did?" she asked, more impressed than I imagined she'd be. Then she looked sad. "You didn't, you know . . . kill him?"

"Why do you think I kill everybody, Emma?"

"Did you, Jackie?"

"No, Emma, I did not." I handed her the Polaroid of Trouble and Terry Lack. "You see Trouble there, don't you?"

"Yes."

"He's a policeman. You saw him drop me off, right?"

"Yes."

"I caught him, kiddo, but I didn't kill him. I wanted you to see that."

"Why?"

"I just wanted you to see me do the right thing," I explained. "I don't want you to think that everybody gets killed, not even all bad men."

"Why did he try to kill us?"

"He was working for some very bad men who were afraid that I would find out the bad things they were doing. Pretty soon everybody will know why they did what they did."

"You found out the bad things they were doing?" Emma asked.

"Yes, I found out what they were doing, Em, and I worked with the police to get them."

"Did you get all of them?"

"Almost. There's one left."

"There's still a bad man out there?"

"Yes."

"When will you get him?"

"Soon."

Electric Justice

"How are you holding up, Bebe?"

I gathered with the Imps at my house. We ordered pizza. Emma was at a sleepover at a neighbor's. Tonight, Al Just was interviewing Bebe Naturale in a "retrospective" on the life of his sister.

When *America Betrayed* aired, Just began with old ads and interview snippets featuring Sally. The screen then showed the taped footage of Just and Bebe walking through the ruins of Naturale's Earth. Just wore his trademark bomber jacket and khakis. Bebe was dressed more conservatively, in loose-fitting black slacks, and a business shirt that was open at the collar. He was not wearing his Sam Giancana sunglasses. Bebe came across like a sad sack, which was problematic, because the American public accepted weakness at face value. *If he's sad, he's for real,* logic that didn't help my strategy.

Just began questioning Bebe softly. Bebe was sitting in Sally's puffy white chair, which he filled up, as opposed to Sally, who seemed to swim in it. But he stayed soft, and the Imps began shooting glances back and forth. I fidgeted. While it wouldn't be wise to screw the guy who brought you the story, one option was always to make the guy who brought it to you the object of coverage:

Sleazebag corporate troubleshooter digs up dirt on grieving mother and tries to ambush the mourning brother of an American icon who is believed to have just died horribly.

"How are you holding up, Bebe?" Just began.

"You want the honest answer or a TV answer?" Bebe said. He was gruff, but somehow it worked.

"The honest answer."

"I'm not doing so great. I don't have Sally. Even though we think we know what happened, we don't know what happened, officially. I can run a lot of the business, but she's the soul."

"What do you plan to do?"

"I'm going to keep hoping, for one thing."

"Are you hopeful?"

"Honestly? No. Not about my sister. I've seen her every day practically my whole life. If she's not here, something's wrong."

"What about the business?"

"We'll rebuild. Maybe not right here right now, but we'll rebuild."

I felt sweat roll down my back. I ran my fingers through my hair and was surprised at how much sweat had poured out. I pulled a bandana from my back pocket and ran it across my forehead. Nate the Great bounced. The Lord craned his neck from side to side. Teapot Freddy did something with his hands that made him look like he was playing an invisible piano.

"Did you watch my interview with Murrin Connolly?" Just asked.

"I did."

"What did you think?"

"I think she's sad. But I've got to tell you, I wanted to throw something at the TV. The way a person can just make up things, and I don't mean to be critical of the media, but the media just picked up on all her lies over the summer. It made me sick. Even if she's sad, I can't say I'm not bitter."

I stood and began to pace. Bebe was handling this deftly. What most novices do is *express compassion,* thinking that's what the audience will relate to. Not so. Audiences want to see intuitive human rage, and they don't believe people who are overly magnanimous. It was as if the bastard had been trained. Nate the Great got up, too, and started walking around the couch.

"I've got to ask you this, Bebe," Just said, as if it were a throwaway. "As I prepared for this story, some people I talked to said you had mob connections."

Bebe shrugged. "Whenever somebody's successful and they have a vowel at the end of their name, that's what they get."

"Do you know the name Ryan Murphy?"

"No," Bebe said, hesitantly.

"He's Murrin Connolly's brother."

"Okay," Bebe said, nodding blankly.

"Do you know the name . . . Peter Serano?"

"Peter what?" Bebe asked.

"He goes by a nickname. Petey Breath Mints?"

"What a name! Wouldn't want to know somebody with that name."

"Terry Lack. Does that name ring a bell?"

"No, Al. Who are these people?"

"They're people who work with a guy known as Frankie Shrugs," Just mentioned matter-of-factly.

"Frankie Shrugs?" Bebe said. "I know Frankie Shrugs."

"You do?"

"Sure. He's a union guy. Shipping and whatnot. I've known him for years."

There are moments when every channel leading to a man's reservoir of paranoia catches fire. As the saying goes, *all of your friends are false, all of your enemies are real.* I glanced around the room, suspecting everyone of betrayal.

The problem was that Bebe was being consistently—and plausibly—honest. It was quite possible that he didn't know Ryan or Terry Lack, but he sure as hell knew Petey Breath Mints. Then again, maybe he didn't know everything Petey had been up to. Scams happen in layers. Just because Bebe was dirty overall didn't mean that he handled every facet of the operation. This is something that reporters never get when they cover corruption—that not everybody who is sleazy masterminded every aspect of the sleaze. And now Bebe was acknowledging knowing Frankie Shrugs, something he had been preparing for since Sally's memorial service.

My mind rattled around for my betrayer. I wondered if Bebe might not be clean, after all, but I didn't care. I needed him to be dirty. My world wouldn't make sense any other way. I prayed for a turn in the interview.

Then, hope. Just removed a photo from his file—a photo I had given him. "Is this a picture of you and Frankie Shrugs?" he asked. The camera focused on the color photo.

"Yeah. What's this about, Al? I told you I knew the guy."

"Yes, but why would you meet with him in a park?"

"I do that a lot. Get away from the office."

"Do you know that the F.B.I. says that Frankie Shrugs is a made member of the Vanni Crime Family of La Cosa Nostra?"

"The F.B.I. has an agenda. They want scalps. I've never heard that about Frankie."

"Why would your sister give ten million dollars to Arcadia University?"

"Arc . . . who?"

"Arcadia University."

"Never heard of it."

"Do you know any midgets?"

"Midgets?"

I turned to the Imps. "He's dizzying the guy," I said hopefully.

Dizzying was boxing slang. It meant to throw so many shots at an opponent without provocation that he becomes disoriented, physically, and in the strategic sense. The disorientation wouldn't be caused by the power of any particular blow, but the act of a professional swinging inconsistently screwed with a guy's mind. Mid-fight, he'd have to re-evaluate everything he had been taught in training. He'd question his trainer. He'd become angry that he wasted his time prepping when nothing he learned mattered. Everything that had worked before was failing now. All was becoming chaos.

"We have confessions from a South Jersey mobster and two associates, who allege that you were involved in a scheme to drive down the price of Naturale's stock."

"Why would I do a thing like that?"

"So that you could buy it through fronts and take over the company."

"My sister and I were very rich. Why would we do something stupid like that? You're crazy, Al."

Just signaled for the technician to play a tape. The camera zoomed in on Bebe, magnifying his every pore, while the voice of brother Ryan reverberated across America. "The idea was to drive down the price of Naturale stock so Bebe and the boys could buy in cheap and drive Sally out. They thought her profile was too high."

Bebe's face was tight. He shrugged and conveyed a puzzled expression. "Bebe," Just asked, "What would have been the goal of taking over from Sally, when you had so much money? And what were 'the boys' worried about?"

"You're the one with the doctored-up entertainment. You tell me," Bebe ordered.

Just nodded to the technician who delivered the coup de grâce: "Naturale's was a big front," the voice of brother Ryan said. "The company's real business was drugs. When Sally's legitimate business brought too much attention, it was time for her to go."

Just ended the interview by informing his audience that they had heard the voice of Ryan Murphy, the brother of Murrin Connolly, who had presented the soy milk scheme to Bebe Naturale and the mob for the purpose of ending Sally's reign.

Bebe snarled. He didn't fidget. He didn't sweat. A threat was bubbling up from his lips, but the one he uttered wasn't violent. "Hope you don't mind unemployment, Al, because when my lawyers get done with you, you and your whole network will be waiting in line on Arch Street for welfare checks."

"Sounds familiar."

Bebe snarled again.

"Where's Sally, Bebe?" Just asked.

With that, Bebe rose from his chair and got a few steps until he became tangled up in the microphone and wires clipped to his shirt. "Those microphones are nothing but trouble," Just said.

And Bebe only knew a fraction of what we had on him. Just, of course, had proven nothing against Bebe in the legal sense—but this was about transmitting disturbing images, images that conveyed a simple, if unsubstantiated message: *This guy's a bad man. I don't like him. And anyone who claims to have been hurt by bad men must be telling a terrible truth.*

I went to the freezer and happily ate a half pint of chocolate gelato, confident that it would *not* turn me into Frankie Shrugs.

Trouble Scores

"Dirty laundry always turns up."

SWEEP LED BY ATLANTIC CITY POLICE CHIEF
NETS DELAWARE VALLEY DRUG KINGPINS
Hartwell Says Naturale Fronted Narcotics Ring

Hours after Al Just's interview with Bebe ran, this was the headline that blazed across the evening edition of The *Bulletin.* It was the Thursday before Labor Day Weekend, prior to the region's final migration to the sea. That evening, a combined strike force headed by Trouble Hartwell fanned out across the Delaware Valley and arrested two dozen organized-crime figures and government officials linked to the distribution of narcotics in the region. Among those captured in the sweep were Frankie Shrugs, his boss; Vinnie "The Ratchet" (proprietor of Vincent's Friggin' Hardware); Deputy Inspector of the Delaware River Port Authority, Arthur Thelmont; Burlington County Solicitor, Seth Seidlin, and a host of lesser lights, such as anarchists Terry Lack and Ryan Murphy. At a news conference in Atlantic City, Trouble, flanked by federal law enforcement officials and state prosecutors, stated plainly that the arrests were based upon overwhelming evidence, including the sworn testimony of a Mafia turncoat, that Naturale's Real Living was being used as a front for a "long-standing, deeply entrenched narcotics enterprise."

Trouble took questions from the throng of dazed reporters at the headquarters of the Atlantic City Police Department.

QUESTION: Was Sally Naturale involved?

TROUBLE: We do not know.

QUESTION: Do you suspect she was involved?

TROUBLE: We do not know.

QUESTION: Was the fire tied to the drugs?

TROUBLE: Most likely.

QUESTION: Do you believe Sally was murdered?

TROUBLE: No comment.

QUESTION: How long has the drug ring been operating?

TROUBLE: We believe since the 1970s.

QUESTION: Did Al Just play a role in busting the ring?

TROUBLE: His investigative work was important, yes.

QUESTION: Was Sally's brother involved?

TROUBLE: No comment.

QUESTION: Was Bebe Naturale arrested?

TROUBLE: No.

QUESTION: Will he be arrested?

TROUBLE: No comment.

QUESTION: Why is the A.C.P.D. leading the investigation?

TROUBLE: Our officers uncovered the ring.

QUESTION: How did Naturale become involved with drugs.

TROUBLE: This will come out in court.

QUESTION: Who approached who, the mob or Naturale?

TROUBLE: This will come out in court.

QUESTION: Where is Bebe Naturale?

TROUBLE: We believe he is in the area.

QUESTION: Is he under surveillance?

TROUBLE: No comment.

QUESTION: What was Naturale's role as a mob front?

TROUBLE: To provide a respectable shield for the processing of narcotics.

QUESTION: What kind of narcotics?

TROUBLE: Cocaine, hashish, marijuana, and Ecstasy.

QUESTION: Were the drugs grown on Naturale property?

TROUBLE: Drugs were mostly grown in Central America and processed here.

QUESTION: How many people were involved in the operation?

TROUBLE: Surprisingly few. It was well-layered. Very few Naturale employees were involved.

QUESTION: What about public officials?

TROUBLE: Some public officials played a role in importation and facilitating distribution, allowing certain shipments from the Caribbean to go unrecorded.

QUESTION: Do you have any information on the fate of Sally Naturale?

TROUBLE: None that we can share at this time.

QUESTION: Will any of the things we're asking come out?

TROUBLE: Dirty laundry always turns up.

QUESTION: Could Sally have been about to come forward?

TROUBLE: This is one theory.

QUESTION: Before the fire, I mean. Did they want her silenced?

TROUBLE: We're looking at this.

QUESTION: Is it possible that Sally Naturale is alive?

TROUBLE: Anything's possible.

The Weekend of the FOAFs

"Sally didn't stand a chance."

Possibilities are fugitives. They escape quietly under cover of darkness, and, by the time civilization learns of the escape, the fugitive is deep into the heartland. Trouble's obtuse and unhelpful answers were widely interpreted as a bold declaration: Sally Naturale was a victim. She had either been murdered, or the fire had been set to send her a message. That Sally might have been a player in the drug ring, well . . .

A malevolent Sally Naturale was not an option. The vile Murrin had been exposed as a fraud. Sally's life's work had been destroyed in the pines. She no longer saturated the airwaves with the question that hacked at the rawest nerves of anxious middle-class Americans—*is this class?*—while making them sleepwalk in their HyanniSportswear like Gore-Tex zombies to buy more, more, more—just in case it was, in fact, class. The authorities had arrested gangsters and corrupt public officials. The busts had led the news. *They* must have done it to her, after all, the Delaware Valley had once rooted for Sally, and good people don't root for drug pushers, they—we—root for people like ourselves. *They* stole Sally Naturale.

We couldn't leave any room for interpretation, and the best declarations of certainty are made during moments of vagueness. We hammered our narrative on-line: Sally found out about the drugs and was ready to blow the whole thing open. Then they killed her.

After Trouble's news conference, I set on-line chat rooms on fire throughout the Delaware Valley by dipping into a pool of cyberpunks I routinely used to spread rumors about the macabre fate of casino cheats. Cited as evidence in many cases was information gleaned by a "friend of a friend," or FOAF, in cyber lingo.

BIGBULL: A buddy of mine who worked at Naturale said Sally knew the hit was coming down and she took off to an island she has someplace.
GANGSTA: My boys say their posse clipped the bitch and my boys know some shit.
VINELANDVINNIE: The mob runs everything. Why is everybody so fuckin' surprised? They run the pizza parlors and they run the corporations. Sally didn't stand a chance.
MASTERMIND: In the old days, the boys like Vanni wouldn't have whacked Sally. They didn't kill women. Ever since Vanni died, the old ways went out the window.
ITALIANSTALLION: A friend of mine who's in with the borgata says they're gonna find Sally face down in an alley with a rat in her pie hole.
FOXYBITCH: She was a snob and she had it coming.

Speculation about the wicked motive for Sally's disappearance moved from the Internet to the pundits on local and national television, who inevitably spoke with great confidence about the little they knew. A hiss-less Al Just was interviewed by the likes of Larry King, furrowing his brow as he absorbed compliments about his investigative fortitude, and worried on the air about Sally's fate.

There was my buddy, Jerome Janove, a former Treasury agent and "security expert" who said on one national news program: "High-profile figures are more and more vulnerable to penetration by kidnappers and other criminal elements. If Sally had been my client, she would have had round-the-clock protection. It's a travesty that she didn't."

Criminal justice Professor Hal Bart of Burlington County College—we used to go running together—observed on MSNBC: "The mob needs to corrupt legitimate businesspeople like Sally Naturale, and they do it either by force or the threat of force. It's a frightening position to be in, and you're really trapped."

An Atlantic City drug dealer I busted—and banked—after a Golden Prospect scam years ago, made his way onto CNN (his face digitally mixed to be unrecognizable) to explain: "When I used to deal, the big guys always hid behind solid citizens. The citizens usually didn't know that they were being used as fronts. We once used a catering company—totally legit—to run deliveries. I mean, who thinks that there's gonna be a pound of hash under the pigs-in-a-blanket? But there were. When the owner found out, he went ape-(*bleep*). We had the guy running the ring pay a visit to his kids at school. He got humble quick. Maybe Sally didn't."

A corporate forensic psychiatrist I retained over the years didn't need much prodding to pitch her insights to a popular cable talk show to explain the mindset of an executive under siege. Dr. Barbara Warner said: "Based on my experience, one of two things may be happening here. First, you may have an executive whose company grew so fast that it was impossible to track the activities of thousands of people. Remember, while people in the media like to believe that chief executives know everything, it doesn't take many people to run a rogue operation like this. Sally Naturale may have been on the verge of discovering this when she was murdered or fled. The other possibility, I think, is that she had known about the narcotics ring for some time, but had her ego so tied up in the business that any acknowledgement of these activities would have not only threatened her life, but would have caused her tremendous psychological pain. So, she may have been in utter denial in addition to her outright terror."

KBRO ran numerous retrospectives of the Philly-South Jersey underworld's most audacious capers involving legitimate enterprise, including a scam to corner the macaroni market and the vending industry. AI Just gave tremendous play to mob boss Nicky Scarfo's murder of a New Jersey judge who didn't rule his way, not to mention an earlier hit on a roofer's union boss who ran afoul of the boys.

Through Jonah Eastman's connections, we got one of the networks to air an old documentary about Jimmy Hoffa on Thursday night, the thesis of which was that Hoffa was murdered because he was about to come forward and expose mob control of the Teamsters, in a return bid for the union's leadership. Several other networks picked up on our the-mob-runs-the-world narrative and ran old documentaries about the Kennedy assassination, with an emphasis on the investigators that had concluded that the mob did the job because of Bobby Kennedy's investigation of the rackets.

The Worldwide News Network released the results of their Worldwide/Eastman poll on Saturday, which appeared in thousands of daily newspapers and television news broadcasts, including the updates during sports programming. The results were as follows:

- 86% believed that the Mafia had taken over Naturale.
- 74% believed that Sally Naturale was dead.
- 72% believed that the Naturale fire was due to arson.
- 68% believed that the Mafia had burned down Naturale's Earth.
- 71% believed the Mafia had investments in Fortune 500 companies.

- 16% believed that Sally was actively complicit in her company's compromise.

While Jonah hadn't cooked the results, what Worldwide had failed to share was that the poll, while statistically valid, had been conducted in the Delaware Valley, the region we had most heavily bombarded with messages about Sally's fate.

Pain in the Ass Innocent Bystanders

"That blonde sure made you stupid."

Bebe Naturale was hiding out somewhere, maybe in the Pine Barrens, maybe in some other vessel of his own delusions. He contacted me from his cell phone and stated with false humility that he needed my assistance in the current controversy. I was skeptical, and I told him so.

"What are you worried about, Jackie? *I'm* the hunted one!"

The exact phrase Solozzo used when confronting Michael Corleone.

"I've had two attempts on my life this summer," I said.

"Two? I know of the one, the thing at your house."

"Well, Bebe, there was another one."

"What happened?"

"I'm fine. Nothing happened."

"Can we talk, then? We've gotta straighten this whole mess out. I'm aging a hundred years a minute out here."

"Where are you?"

"Never mind where I am."

"Well, where do you want to meet?"

"I was thinking Lenny's."

"I don't know it."

"It's in Westmont, near the train line."

"Okay, I think I know where it is—but I want to go early before crowds. I don't want to have to scan a hundred faces."

"I'll pick you up at five-thirty then, at the Crystal Lake Shopping Mall," Bebe promised.

Bebe was right on time, which made me trust him even less than I already did. He pulled up in a Ford Explorer. I double-checked the backseat to make sure a Clemenza-wannabe wasn't waiting with a garrote. I opened the driver's side door and scanned the side of Bebe's seat for a weapon. Clear. I swept my hand under Bebe's seat and the dash. Nothing. I felt around Bebe's ankles and shins and his sports jacket. O.K. It was clear, so I climbed into the passenger seat very conscious of the short path between my hand and my Beretta. Bebe parked on the street in front of Lenny's and we walked cautiously along the sidewalk toward the awning. My throat was dry from nerves and I had a rancid aftertaste in my mouth. It was still hot outside, but there was something about the position of the sun—it seemed father away than it had a week ago—that suggested autumn. The roar of a high-speed line train shook the awning.

Bebe and I said nothing to each other as we walked. He appeared to be much thinner than when I saw him last, still soft and pudgy, but no longer obese. He reached into his pocket, and I immediately grabbed his lapel with my left hand.

"Jesus, Jackie," he cried, holding up his hands, "I just wanted to click my car shut." I allowed him to slowly withdraw his key chain and lock his truck with a chirp.

Lenny's was a small, family-style restaurant. The floor was a black-and-white patterned tile. The tablecloths were red-and-white checks. The lighting was dim, and a long old-fashioned bar ran along the left side of the wall. About a dozen round tables were evenly spaced along the floor.

I looked Bebe over closely as the host approached us. I was not pleasant to the poor guy, checking out his apron and pants for metallic bulges.

"Geez, Jackie, you're not the trusting sort," Bebe (my buddy) said, witnessing the tension in my face.

We were seated at a small table in the center rear of the restaurant, and we were the only customers in the entire joint.

I scanned the menu. "Do you have a recommendation?" I asked Bebe, who was fidgeting with a breadstick.

"Have the veal," he said. "It's the best in town."

"I'll have it," I said.

The waiter came by with a bottle of red wine and began making small talk with Bebe as he poured it. Bebe was visibly annoyed with the banter and said to the waiter, "Do you mind if I talk to my friend here in private for a minute?"

The waiter shuffled away, looking scared.

Bebe sighed. "I don't know how things ever got this far."

"You're in a dangerous business," I said.

"It wasn't a business that concerned you, Jackie."

"Your sister hired me."

"And what did it get her?"

"That's what I'd like to ask *you.* Do you know where she is?" I asked.

"If I knew where she was, would I have gone on that TV show? I don't know where the hell she is. What's more, I see your fingerprints."

"How's that?"

"There's a lot of nonsense going down. Private dick stuff, pranks. Reports on the news. The fire. I'm not a total fucking idiot."

"I never thought that you were. You did quite a number breaking up my girlfriend and me with that casino stunt."

"You got cute. We got cute."

"Was Dirk Romella involved?"

"Not everything's a conspiracy, Jackie. Some people can piss you off just by being alive. Romella's a preppy piece-a shit, not a conspirator."

"So where do we go from here, Bebe?"

"I don't need to know what you did and what you didn't do. I just need you to guarantee that it stops."

I hesitated before responding, thinking that maybe Bebe would ask me if I knew anything about Sally's whereabouts.

"What kind of guarantee can I give you?" I said. "The cops may be making a case against you, but I'm the one being shot at."

The waiter came by timidly and took our order. Bebe got the veal, too. "This whole thing is gonna give me an ulcer," he said. "Do you mind if I go to the bathroom?" he asked.

Feigning excitement at the antipasto that had just been set before us, I said, "You gotta go, you gotta go." I speared a curl of salami that was closest to him, just to step on his turf a little.

Bebe left. My eyes tracked him into the bathroom, and I turned my chair slightly to get a better view of his path. I didn't touch the antipasto. I removed my Beretta and rested it on my lap. I then covered it with the tablecloth. Bebe emerged from the restroom in about two minutes. He stopped at the side of the table, sighed, and sat down.

"The antipasto is terrific," I said enthusiastically.

"Yeah," Bebe said, unable to hide his hatred.

"I'll tell you, Bebe, I can't remember the time I've ever had antipasto this good. I'm really glad you took me here. I can't wait to come back with some friends," I said, a touch giddy.

An incoming high-speed-line train shook the building. Bebe was sweating. He appeared to be on the verge of vomiting. I reached beneath the tablecloth with my right hand and gripped my gun. I kept talking about the antipasto, gesturing with my left hand, trying for some combination of annoying and oblivious. "I mean, Carmine's down the shore has good antipasto, and there are a few places in South Philly that have good antipasto, but this stuff is incredible! It's even better than the antipasto I once had—"

Bebe rocked in his chair and then stood, his fat hands swinging his sports jacket aside. As he did, I shoved back my chair and drew my Beretta. The hammer of Bebe's gun got stuck in his belt and, as he tried to yank it out, it went off, sending a streak of smoke up from his pants. Bebe cried out in horror looking crotchward. I kept my Beretta trained on Bebe as he drew his hands up toward his face. I squeezed the trigger and the bullet took off the upper rim of Bebe's ear. He cried again, falling to the floor, dropping his gun. The waiter hid behind a far table.

"You shot me!" Bebe shrieked. He was now in the fetal position alternating his hands between his bloody ear and his belt.

"Better make sure you didn't shoot your dick off," I said, nonchalantly standing, my gun trained on him. I had meant just to fire beside his ear to shock him, but was glad I drew blood. "Keep your hands up by your head, you dumbass." I didn't want to touch his gun, it being evidence.

Bebe was hyperventilating. I knelt down beside him. "You didn't listen," I scolded him.

"What the fuck are you talking about?" he cried.

"Clemenza specifically said you should come out of the bathroom blasting. Two shots in the head apiece."

"Huh?"

"The movie, dumbass. *The Godfather.* This little reenactment. Look, you grabbed the gun—the one that your clowns left for you—behind the toilet like a good boy, but you came out and sat down. After you shoot, you were supposed to drop the gun, not get it caught in your pants. I assume you made it 'real loud to scare away any pain-in-the-ass innocent bystanders'? That blonde sure made you stupid."

"What blonde?"

"She's something, isn't she?"

"Rena?" he asked, betrayed like the dork at a prom who should have known going in that the quarterback was going to bang his date on the beach.

"Rena? Is that what she's calling herself? See, I haven't spent that much time with her since she went blonde. I was walking into walls when I first met her, too, but, I didn't act on it. Anyway, I knew her by a different name. She had dark hair and was running a little card replacing scam in my casino."

The police and medics, headed by Trouble, burst into the restaurant with the Westmont Cops. The medics attended to the gelatinous Bebe. An officer read him his rights for his life's crowning achievement, a racketeering pinch. Trouble inspected Bebe's gun and snickered as he confirmed that the Lord had succeeded in replacing Bebe's bullets with blanks just in case he proved to be a good shot.

The officer stood Bebe up. I approached him, grabbed his cheeks, and, to his horror, kissed him. "You broke my heart." I backed away laughing.

The cops and medics restrained Bebe as he cursed me from his meltdown.

Naturale's Revival

"It was the reverence of a savvy throng of hustlers who knew but respected a good swindle when they saw one."

"Will you go in the water?" Reverend Smoky Sharpe shouted on Labor Day from the Camden soundstage, which rose from the gray shore of the Delaware River. The City of Brotherly Love rose unrepentant at his back. The steeple of One Liberty Place appeared to sit on Reverend Sharpe's shoulder, parrot-like. He was dressed in a white suit. Tall, very young and Hell-serious, the evangelist's shaved head was the color of crude oil, the orange sun paying its toll and crossing over the Ben Franklin Bridge, reflecting angrily on his white linen suit. "Will you *go* in the water?" he asked again.

The crowd—a few thousand, sitting on the fresh, soft grass—answered him with cries of "amen," "yessir," and "Hallelujah!" Most of the faces were black or otherwise swarthy, with the occasional brave paleface mixed among them.

Reverend Sharpe was the pastor of Camden Unitarian Defiance, a parish that had open and folded dozens of times since the middle of the 1800s. It had first sprouted as a makeshift church for the men who toiled to build the Camden and Burlington County railway line, and had since become South Jersey's religious chameleon. Its latest incarnation began as a black evangelical church at the turn of the millennium with the charismatic, then-twenty-five-year-old local child, Smoky Sharpe, at its helm. Sharpe, a former high school basketball star, had shrewdly raised the money to refurbish his church from the numerous corporations that populated the Delaware Valley. His fundraising style was innovative, and I remember admiring it when it first made the news. Reverend Sharpe would arrive on corporate campuses on the day of Board of Directors meetings with the Defiance Gospel Choir in tow and praise Jesus as the big shots were filing in. As a shareholder of the company in question, the Reverend had politely placed a resolution before the Board to contribute to the reconstruction of Camden Unitarian Defiance. When the vote came down (inevitably) the right way, the Defiance Gospel Choir praised Jesus even more loudly, not to mention the "progressive thinking" of the corporation in question. Not one threat had ever been uttered.

Today, the Defiance Gospel Choir drifted in fuchsia slowly toward the stage and stopped in a crescent at the corner.

"Will *you* go in the water?" Reverend Sharpe changed emphasis.

"Hallelujah!" answered the multitudes and the choir.

"You know, I have a question for you, every one of you."

"What's that, Brother?" the crowd answered.

"Will you go in the wa-ter?"

"That's right!"

Despite the sweat that poured from Smoky Sharpe's scalp, it wasn't as hot as past Labor Days. Reverend Sharpe probably sweated like this in February; it was part of his trademark. The temperature was in the mid-eighties and the humidity was low. The breeze was soft, and I couldn't help but think that all of the country should be here and take in the cradle of liberty, even though the Camden buildings immediately around us were crumbling.

To the north, an old warehouse sat ostentatiously decaying. It may have once been the RCA plant, or maybe Van Sciver's furniture. It didn't really matter anymore, but I vaguely remember my grandfather telling me that he laid the bricks when he was a teenage laborer. It's the only thing I really remember my grandfather telling me. In his thick Italian accent and singsong voice, he'd lovingly recount it all, not one word in his simple description running over one syllable: "We mix the mix and put it on the brick when it's still wet. Then we hold the brick and squish it in real-a snug."

Why my grandfather, with his flat little cap that made him look like a mushroom pressed down by the heavens, thought that his workaday description of bricklaying would fascinate a little boy made no sense at the time, or for many years afterward. Today it did. The multitudes along this unadorned riverbank were just like my grandfather. They came to Camden having been promised nothing, and they still managed to hope, in a vacuum of evidence, that there would be something to sing about. In my grandfather's case, he couldn't believe how lucky he was to find work as a bricklayer, and he saw the rise of those buildings as being the essential footings of America. Moreover, when the Nazis and later the communists began rattling their ammunition, the same simple man who rejoiced over bricks would willingly enlist to smash the armies of those who would threaten his freedom. I never really knew Ettore De Sesto, but as these peaceful people awaited a message from Reverend Smoky Sharpe, he became my hero, and I missed him.

"I know who will go in the water," Reverend Sharpe shouted. "Do you know who will go in the water?" he asked.

"Yes, we do!" the crowd answered.

"Will Sally Naturale go in the water?" he asked.

Silence. A few quizzical expressions. Some even laughed, as if Reverend Sharpe had cracked an inside joke in urban code, which he hadn't.

"I asked you, Will Sally Naturale go in the water?"

A few inaudible syllables.

"Let me tell you something people," Reverend Sharpe continued, with a laugh in his voice. "Sally Naturale *will* go in the water. I know because she told me."

Everyone looked around at each other, hoping someone could make sense of the spectacle. Al Just and other media battalions faced Reverend Sharpe with their cameras and microphones like a firing squad.

"You see," Reverend Sharpe continued, "There's a problem here. These shores on which I stand were once sacred, prosperous shores. This was the home of Walt Whitman. Across the river—right over there—was where Benjamin Franklin flew his kite one rainy night and found something that had been here all along—electricity. Do you believe in electricity? Why, you have to, because it's real. You can't *not* believe in electricity. God created it for man. He created it for you. Here in Camden, we once led the way. We made the *Mmm-Mmm, Good* food for America to eat, we made furniture for America to rest its aching sinews after hard days of labor, and we made the sights and sounds of music and human voices echo through wires, screens and amplifiers. That's right, you hear all about the future, people, but you can't see the future unless you know where it started, and it started right here in Camden. Yes it did. Walt wrote the poems, Campbell made the soup, Van Sciver made the furniture and RCA made the sights and the sounds of America. Right here. Right here.

"Now, I asked you if you'd go in the water. I asked you that, did I not?" The *t* sound at the end of "not" skipped across the still Delaware, ricocheted off the granite of Philadelphia and echoed softly back to Camden.

The audience clapped, but still glanced around because they were not sure where Reverend Sharpe was headed.

"But before you can go in the water, you need to see someone go in the water before you, someone who hasn't seen water in a while. But she has seen fire, oh, yes she has.

"You remember what happened last Fourth of July, you remember that." The Reverend stated this as a point of fact.

"Yes we do, that's right," the crowd uttered. Heads poked up and down, in and out, all around the assembly. They were looking. They sensed that the Reverend Smoky Sharpe would put on the show of shows—but, had he lost his mind?

"Fires blow in and fires blow out. Fires damage, they cause heartache, and they leave homes barren. But fire is no match for water, is it Sally?" Reverend Sharpe's gaze swept over the crowd. The only audible sounds were the rippling of the Delaware and the autumnal drums of a high-school marching band rehearsing in an innocent suburb somewhere east of Camden.

"Is it, Sally?" he repeated. Reverend Sharpe lifted up his hands and opened his eyes wide. Softly, he repeated, "Is it, Sally?"

A fragile woman with steel gray hair and a white choir robe rose in the crowd, not bothering to adjust the robe as she approached the soundstage. The bottom of the robe clung to her pale, toned legs, but then separated from her flesh at the hint of an autumn breeze. Reverend Sharpe held out his hands in a ceasing gesture and the little old lady stopped as the congregation took her in.

"The reason why you will go in the water is because you've returned from the fire," Reverend Sharpe said.

I made my way from the back of the crowd out toward where it petered out upriver. The woman standing alone in the crowd in a choir robe was Sally Naturale, her natural gray hair held back by a simple white bandana, the kind sold by any street-corner vendor. She wore little makeup, but her skin was the blush red of a farmer's wife, especially her nose, which sported the slightly witchlike bump that I had restored for her. She wore no jewelry.

"You'll go in the water to soothe you from the fire," Reverend Sharpe continued. "We need not know where you have been, Sally, because we know you have returned, and we know why. This is your home, Sally Naturale. It always was. These are the grounds where you ran as a little girl. There was soft grass here then. Then it went away. It turned to hard mud and dust, and became the grounds for drug deals and hate. It became ungodly. Ungodly!" Reverend Sharpe whispered in a way that managed to be loud.

Reverend Sharpe waved Sally toward the stage. The crowd parted, scanning her with magnetic eyes, searching out possible malignancies. Reverend Sharpe jumped down from the stage, revealing the athleticism that had first won him notoriety. He towered above Sally, who appeared to float in the receding summer. Sally struck me as the kind of woman who might have looked exactly the same thirty years ago, and who might look the same thirty years from now.

There was perverse reverence in this crowd. It was the reverence of a savvy throng of hustlers who knew but respected a good swindle when they saw one, and did not resist because they sensed that this swindle might just deliver something lasting.

Reverend Sharpe placed his web of a hand atop Sally's head and told her where she had been. "You have been in fire. You sensed it coming, and you knew it was a righteous fire. But you ran, because fire is frightening, because it was stronger than you were. Sometimes, when we achieve success, we find it hard to believe that anything is stronger than we are. Just like Ben Franklin may have been wise and strong, he only received those currents through that old kite of his because God gave him those currents."

The crowd nodded thoughtfully.

"You came back Sally," Reverend Sharpe said. "You went away, but you came back. You came back because we need you here, and He knows we need you in Camden. You know what Mr. Springsteen said, 'Everything dies, baby, that's a fact, but maybe everything that dies someday comes back.' You are bringing it back."

"The money that once created great private wealth for only you now comes down the river, barge after barge." Indeed a huge vessel with construction equipment glided slowly by. "You have promised, Sally, to rebuild your business with this money. The rebuilding has begun, and within months Camden will see the dividends, because Camden will be the home of Naturale's Revival. It will be a thriving enterprise, with hundreds of millions of dollars pouring into this once proud city that will be proud again. Naturale's Revival!"

"Now, let me ask you again, Sally, will you go in the water?"

"Yes, I will," Sally said.

The clergyman and Sally proceeded slowly to the banks of the Delaware, where the sun drew a bead on a section of ripples.

Reverend Sharpe removed his portable microphone and handed it to the deacon. In his magnificent suit, he walked into the water with Sally. He took her in his arms and gently swung her backward into the filmy Delaware. When he brought up the tiny soaking creature, she glistened in the retreating sunlight.

"Hallelujah! Welcome home, Sally," Reverend Sharpe said.

Count Smartfarkle slipped beside Sally, embraced her, pursed his lips in disgust at the rancid Delaware River, and handed his purified icon a Naturale's Classware cup filled with spring water, and a tablet of Cipro. She drank it down and acknowledged the crowd, aping precisely Queen Elizabeth's stiff little wave.

Optics Rule

"Camden rotted, and I rotted."

The Bulletin's coverage led with a montage of photographs above the fold, featuring one in the center with a waiflike Sally in her choir robe, redemptive, at the river alongside a forgiving Reverend Sharpe. The photos around Sally the Waif were far less divine. There was one of Bebe in his Sam Giancana sunglasses being cuffed and stuffed. There were mug shots of Frankie Shrugs, Petey Breath Mints, the smarmy looking Port Authority crook, Thelmont, and the midget, Terry Lack. Frankie Shrugs was winking in his photo. The burning cinders of Naturale's Earth belched into the sky in another photo. The remnants of the blown-up Jaguar—the one that was supposed to belong to Frankie Shrugs—also made the montage, along with the photo caption, "A Message From the Big Apple?" An article about the region's bloody gangland history appeared below the fold with the requisite assassination photos of Vanni, Bruno, Narducci, and Salvy Testa. Finally, another article appeared adjacent to a smaller photo of a larcenous and corpulent Murrin Connolly crying for the camera as she falsely accused Sally of killing her baby. The police mug shot of her amply dazed brother, Ryan, appeared on the inside jump.

The visual juxtaposition of an aged and angelic Sally against a horde of predators in sunglasses, mug shots, gutter-strewn corpses, Armageddon hellfires, and—the cherry on top—a repugnant aborting extortionist. Well, it was impossible on an optical level to see Sally as anything but a dazed and unwitting victim in a vast corruption beyond her ken.

"Excuse me, Al. My hearing's been going," Sally said to Al Just as the camera began to roll for his exclusive.

"I asked why you hid?" Just asked.

"Oh, I was afraid and I was ashamed," Sally explained for the *America Betrayed* broadcast to run that evening. The ground rules I negotiated limited Just's interview to ten minutes, which had to be aired unedited. It was to take place immediately after Sally emerged from the water. Her hair was slicked straight back, drops of river water occasionally falling onto her forehead or onto her robe.

"Were you inside Naturale's Earth when the fire broke out?" Just asked.

"No," Sally said. "I was at home exercising. I smelled smoke. I looked across the lake and I saw the fire. I felt like they were coming for me. I sent an E-mail—I just learned to use the computer—to a colleague. I wasn't sure if I did it the right way or even if it went anywhere. I ran to my car and I drove and I drove."

"Where did you go?"

"I went deep into the Pine Barrens. I had a sleeping bag. I stayed in the woods for weeks thinking and thinking. Once I accepted my new life, I began to build Naturale's Revival in Camden. In disguise."

"What did you think about?"

"I thought about why the Lord had entered my life. Why the Lord had burned down all I had created."

"Did you get an answer?"

"Excuse me?" Sally said, leaning forward and pointing to her ear.

"I said, did you get an answer?"

"Yes, the Lord gave me an answer."

"What was it?"

"The Lord told me—in his own way, of course—that I deserved the fire, that there were unholy things going on."

"What unholy things?"

"I cannot say. All I can say—and I believe I owe the public this—is that I knew bad things were happening at Naturale's Real Living. I knew. I didn't do anything about it because I was afraid. I was afraid that the devil was stronger than God. I was afraid that I would be harmed. And I was afraid that I would lose everything that I created. It was a selfish fear, the last one. But when the fire came, I knew that the fear was more than selfish. I knew I was in danger."

"Are you still afraid, Sally?"

"No."

"Why not?"

"I have accepted that I will lose what I created, that it cannot be solely mine, that I have to give something back. We need to embrace diverse communities. I lost my roots, which are here in Camden. Camden rotted, and I rotted. This is where I am from, and this is where I'm going to stay. I want to have dialogue with the people who are a part of me and rebuild my company as a monument to diversity. People here felt I was fooling them, and all along I thought I was being me. This was a form of intolerance, and it was wrong of me. Everybody wasn't wrong though."

"Will we ever know what the unholy things were? You are being candid, Sally, but not completely candid."

"I can only confess to my sins. I cannot confess to the crimes of others, even if I know about them. Everything will come out soon."

Following the Just interview, we took Sally by van to Medford Lakes where the newly-minted senior citizen walked through the cinders of Naturale's Earth holding a handkerchief to her nose, and cameras captured her tears as she knelt by the charred statue of the toga-clad Goddess of Refinement that had once capped the great dome. *The South Jersey Journal* led with an article about Naturale's Revival.

SALLY NATURALE RETURNS TO CAMDEN

Vows to Revitalize Birthplace as "Monument to Diversity"

After a nearly two-month absence, good-taste doyenne, Sally Naturale, returned to Camden yesterday to be baptized in the Delaware River by Reverend Smokey Sharpe of the Defiance Unitarian Church. Naturale, who became an icon of material success, stunned thousands of onlookers as she rose from the crowd appearing markedly different from the pitchwoman known in ubiquitous television commercials.

Naturale, whose once-raven hair was gray, promised to rebuild her headquarters, which was destroyed in a fire in Medford Lakes last summer, this time along the Camden riverfront. In an interview with KBRO-TV's Al Just last night, Naturale pledged her entire fortune—that despite the recent collapse of her company's stock is estimated at seventy-five million—to rebuilding her company, that will focus on a variety of products made in New Jersey and will serve as a "monument to diversity." The products already being manufactured will include Jersian Rugs for the home, Asbury Parkas for winter, Hackensack Wear for bedtime, Garden State Cuisines, such as Cam-Dinners, Teaneck Tea and Short Hills Shortcake (which will be made from home-grown New Jersey natural resources, such as cranberries, blueberries, and Cumberland-County-grown wheat), Wild-water (bottled from fresh water reserves beneath the Pine Barrens), and Nep-Tuna Fish, from schools caught off the New Jersey Coasts, spices such as Cinnaminson Cinnamon, Nutley Nuts, Rumson Rum, household goods including Tenafly Swatters, New Bruns-Wick Candles and Free-Holders for hot beverages.

Selma, Queen of the Pines

"Sally Naturale did not appear to have been born at all, she just emerged."

As tales of corruption continued to make headlines in hard news reports, lifestyle reporters, with my guidance, began examining the question that had preoccupied me from the first time I saw Sally Naturale on television. Who was she?

When outsiders judge crisis management, they inevitably focus on the bad advice they believe the client was given by handlers. What the armchair pundits don't realize is that all clients have seemingly irrational points on which they do not budge, which complicates the resolution of the crisis. Sally's sticking point was her true identity. She was more concerned with people finding out about her humble origins than learning she had been mobbed up since the birth of her career.

In a series of tense discussions, I made a deal with Sally: she could keep her name and her pop nod to Christianity, but she would not directly discuss her background with anyone. She always wanted the option of saying that the papers got it wrong. No matter how many times I explained to her that she couldn't claim to be a native of Camden and not acknowledge who she once had been, she always wanted me to stage-manage hocus-pocus that would make the thud of her past sound like a choir. So I discreetly briefed a few loyal reporters and plagiarized for Sally the Reaganesque gesture of pointing to her ear and squinting whenever she heard a question she didn't want to answer.

Selma Natelman was born the eldest child of Morris and Yetta Natelman, the furriers, in Camden, New Jersey in the blistering summer of 1940. As the decade of war rolled on, many in Camden prospered and drifted purposefully west to Philadelphia and, if they were truly blessed, even farther west to the Main Line suburbs of Bryn Mawr, Haverford, or Gladwyne. Other families were not so lucky. The collapse of Natelman's Furs served as a social-Darwinian blow to the noticeably unfit little family.

What went on in the Natelman household during the 1940s and 1950s can only be imagined, but this much is certain: Selma and her younger brother Bernard were unceremoniously yanked out of summer camp in Medford Lakes one midsummer, never to return. Little Selma suppressed her hysterics on her way out of Camp Summit. Tubby little Bernard blubbered, and was dragged into the Natelman family car carrying the tattered stuffed bunny rabbit he called Bun-Bun, its fluffy guts hemorrhaging onto the piney dirt. The implication of the aborted camp season became gossip. According to the few who remember the family, the Natelmans had money problems. In all households, this is regrettable. In the Natelman household, it was catastrophic.

No one knows exactly where the Natelmans went, but the death certificate of Morris Natelman in Vineland, New Jersey in 1952 suggests that they didn't go far. Yetta Natelman spent at least one summer as a housekeeper at the Cape May, New Jersey mansion of a wealthy family named Silverberg. The Lord had uncovered an old deed in the Cape May Courthouse for a family by that name. Genealogical records pegged Morton Silverberg as Yetta Natelman's first cousin. Ashamed that her children would see her as a housekeeper—for cousins no less—Yetta arranged for Selma and Bernard to spend the next few summers with other families that had vacation homes throughout the East, including the coast of Maine, Newport, Rhode Island, and Lake George, New York. Sally admitted to me that she and Bernard were essentially household servants, however, they also became friendly with the children of their employers. Despite her humiliation, these experiences were seminal in forging in young Selma a belief that living the high life was the noblest goal of human existence.

In 1956, sixteen-year-old Selma was found wandering in a bed sheet in Wharton State Forest by patients and staff of Ancora State Mental Hospital, which bordered the huge pine woods. Selma spent the next few years in and out of Ancora, where she combusted her psychotic delusions into a mid-level deity she called Selma, Queen of the Pines. Selma had been the Joan Baez type, according to Rabbi Wald, who found some of her records in the files of a Camden Jewish social services organization that had had some involvement with the Natelmans.

. . .

The morning after Sally's re-emergence at the Delaware River, Rabbi Wald and the Holy Cannoli met me for coffee at Ozzie's. The rabbi was wearing all black—including his western boots. Father Ignacio ambled in wearing a cream-colored bathing suit, matching shirt, and an enormous straw western hat.

"You look like a blintz, padre," Wald greeted.

"Good morning to you, too, Rabbi Oli," the priest said, sitting beside the rabbi.

Father Ignacio waved down a waitress. "Gimme the special omelet, sweetheart," he said. Rabbi Wald was already working on a corn muffin and I was carving away at a grapefruit. "By the way, Jackie," Father Ignacio said as he adjusted his massive body in the little chair, "I just talked to your dad."

Shit. Shit. Shit.

"How's he doing?" I asked.

"He's fine. You know, the doctor said they studied some of his blood work and he may have actually had what they call an 'episode'. That's a small stroke."

In other words, I had beaten the shit out of Mr. Magoo. My father no less, who had just had a stroke. In a way, I think Blinky Dom viewed the stroke as vindication. For anybody else, it would have been a scare, but for him it was the culmination of a seventy-year crusade to certify that he was a gravely ill man. I was on the Concorde to Hell.

"My father *is* an episode," I barked.

Sensing the tension, Rabbi Wald recalled for me one of his visits to Ancora long ago, his toothpick dancing in his mouth, "Sally was calling herself Queen Selma," he began. "She gave other patients a tour of the 'Executive Mansion', the only problem being that the tour had taken place in the woods and everyone, including Queen Selma, was stark naked. "Hell of a body on her back then," he said.

First Lady Jacqueline Kennedy had, of course, given the American public a tour of the White House in February of 1962, which was broadcast to a record forty-seven million people, including guests of Ancora.

"Queen Selma asked me to play the role of the news guy, Charles Collingwood," Rabbi Wald explained. "I did it, too, because the social services people called me up and said they thought it would mean a lot to Sally to see somebody from the outside on her big day. Here I am in the middle of the woods next to this nuthouse and this crazy piece-a ass is giving me a tour. The man in me is thinking, *get a load of this piece-a ass.* But the rabbi in me is thinking, she's a lunatic? How the hell can I wanna bang a lunatic?"

Father Ignacio shot the rabbi a disapproving look.

"Millions of people like her, Rabbi," I said.

Like any queen, Selma had a court—dukes, viscounts, countesses. In addition to devouring books on commerce, Selma, the sixties earth mama, had learned a thing or two about growing the mind-numbing plants she richly needed in Ancora's gardens and greenhouses, plants that proliferated throughout the affluent Delaware Valley in the 1960s and 1970s. Hemp, poppy, coca. One of the Ancora's most lucid mental patients, Selma applied for special admissions to the regrettably named all-female Beaver College in Glenside, Pennsylvania, just outside of Philadelphia. Somehow—perhaps the Dean of Admissions was looking for diversity—she got in.

By the time her flagstone estate was built on a rise that overlooked the camp where she was so humiliated, Selma Natelman of Camden, New Jersey had shed her coarse cocoon, endured radical plastic surgery, and completed her metamorphosis into Sally Naturale of Cricket Crest, USA and points west.

As the rabbi spoke, I retreated into my own recollection of events. Before the Imps and I blew up Naturale's Earth, the Lord had broken into Sally's financial records and swiped a handful of them, which was when he found the ten-million-dollar contribution to Beaver College shortly before her company went public. I knew there had to be a link, one that the Lord found when he went into their old academic records. Every graduate of the Class of 1960 had records in her file except for one Selma Natelman. When Teapot Freddy approached Dean Enright at that fundraising cocktail party and dropped his friendship with Selma Natelman, the expression on her face and the tone in her voice suggested that Sally and Selma were likely one and the same. The dean's silence had surely been part of the contribution deal.

Sally Naturale did not wish to appear to have been born at all. Rather, she wanted people to assume that she had just emerged. When "Sally" did emerge from Ancora, she carried with her fantasies of a building a consumer products company filled with Carnegie Melons and Onassis Sunglasses.

If the arc of Sally's life aspired heavenward, her younger brother, Bernard, now calling himself Bebe, looked to the underworld for protection from his indignities. While Selma was in Ancora, Bernard appears to have spent those years in a Vineland orphanage. The pudgy "Bebe" decided he would become an Italian gangster, thus the Romanesque surname, Naturale. One would think that Sally, left to her own devices, would have chosen a last name like Winthrop or Fenwick, but Sally needed her brother's *gonif* sensibilities, and had accompanied him to the courthouse in Camden where they changed their names in the winter of 1964.

Bebe's lowdown aspiration wasn't entirely unusual. Plenty of Jewish boys sought to be Italian, Jonah Eastman once told me, but he had yet to meet an Italian boy who wanted to be Jewish. It was Jonah who had shrewdly smelled something rotten when I told him about Bebe's behavior. He had grown up with this drama, having seen his grandfather, Mickey Price—the last great Jewish gangster—become a cult figure. It was, pure and simple, a warped issue of masculine identity. Bernard Natelman had blubbered on his way out of Camp Summit, a perfectly normal response that in his frightened little mind he must have interpreted as being a shameful trait that could only be addressed by becoming a Mafiosi at a time when most Italians were distancing themselves from those that shamed them. Simply put, Bebe was a Falsetto—a wannabe.

It wasn't hard to convert Marty Collins into Rena D'Amico and mobilize her against Bebe. She turned out to be an enthusiastic Impette. Marty pushed all of Bebe's fantasies and psychic buttons, effectively peeling him apart by tapping into his bunny rabbit trauma at Camp Summit so long ago, one tidbit of many we had fed her during our intensive briefing sessions.

Sally needed financing to build her empire in the pines. No legitimate bank would underwrite the barely functional Naturales and their loony-bird dreams, which is where Bebe came in. Bebe had gone to a unique bank, the kind of institution that had been built on the fortunes of the local dispossessed: The Bank of Fuggetaboudit, the Mob.

"The scheme was simple," I told my God-squad of two: "The Naturales could have their classy, hallucinogenic kingdom, but the mob would control it and use it as a beard for their own manufacture of drugs. Sally could grow her weeds on the perimeter of Cricket Crest and whatever 'organic' farms she owned in the Caribbean, but the boys would do their thing deep on the inside, where nobody was looking."

"Kenahora!" Rabbi Wald said, which probably meant *"Madonn'!"*

Bebe Naturale imported marijuana, hashish, and cocaine. The crates coming in from the Caribbean also contained enough legitimate food and agricultural products for Naturale to operate its front business. Once the raw drug materials arrived at Naturale's Earth, they were refined inside the dome and delivered to the street by a handful of couriers who posed as regular shoppers just a-coming and a-going with small, unsuspicious parcels, thus another benefit of the retail façade.

"As Naturale's grew," I explained, "It snagged the eye of investment bankers who liked what they thought Sally was peddling." The idea of being a publicly traded diva appealed to Sally's grandiosity, not to mention her ambitions to build a legitimate enterprise. Because of her increasingly high profile, not to mention all of the discreet groundwork for the initial public offering that Sally had advanced, Bebe and the boys went along. For a while. "Eventually, the legit operations were successful enough that Sally saw her chance to go completely straight."

"Under it all she had a good heart," Father Ignacio said, perhaps to justify his involvement in my end of the scheme.

"Bebe and the boys weren't happy about it," I said, "But Sally had become a high-profile rainmaker. She had to be accommodated."

Sally, being Sally, began believing she was the real thing—a high-class billionairess. Nevertheless, the higher her profile rose and the more public her company became, the more scrutiny she invited in the post-Enron era. Not good, if you're really a dope pusher.

"The *meshuggah*!" Rabbi Wald said.

"She figured she could hire me to get Murrin, but that I'd be either so loyal or so stupid that I wouldn't find anything else out," I said.

"See, Jackie, this is what happens when you get too successful," Father Ignacio warned me. "You're so used to everybody kissing your behind that you really think you're smarter than everybody else. You lose your ability to be self-critical. These people live in a bubble after a while."

"Who knows," the rabbi shrugged, "maybe it's not such a bad thing to keep getting your ass kicked. That way you stay sane."

"You know, Rabbi, I wondered now and then why she even hired me, but you just hit on it," I said.

"Sally was used to telling vendors to make her napkins whiter, and give her tomato sauce less garlic," the rabbi said. "The next thing she knew, she had whiter napkins and less garlic-y sauce. Just look what happened to that Hollywood agent, Ovitz. Most powerful Zeus, most powerful Jupiter, and next thing you know, he thinks he can move Heaven and Earth. Boom! Out on his ass. I'll tell you something, given Sally's experience, it was reasonable for her to assume you'd be another wind-up-and-point kind of guy."

"Charming people are the most easily charmed," the Holy Cannoli frowned.

"Imagine what happens when they're psychotic," Rabbi Wald said, finishing off his corn muffin.

Bebe and the mob couldn't just kill Sally. An investigation into the death of health nut Sally Naturale would yield nothing but, well, disaster. The boys, however, could discredit her and weaken her, using a technique that had been growing in popularity, as deep cultural resentments colluded with a vengeful legal system and a witch-hunting news media: The Smear.

"Along comes Murrin's brother, Ryan," I explained, "Who owed the mob money." During the course of disquieting discussions with his burly creditors, Brother Ryan had referenced Murrin's troubles. Together, they cooked up a scheme whereby the loss of her baby would be attributed to Naturale's Real Milk. The bad publicity would depress Naturale's stock price. Brother Ryan's debt-paydown contract was to recruit Murrin, who was quite receptive to fanciful notions of how she had lost her baby. He had acknowledged during his dental confession that he had taken Murrin to the Bistre-a-u, where she had an epiphany about Sally's killer soy milk as she watched the clouds line up like servants atop Cricket Crest.

Indeed, as the summer swaggered on, Moonpie had confirmed that large blocks of Naturale stock had been purchased through less-than-blue-chip investors, information we handed over to Trouble.

During Sally's missing weeks, we had hidden her in a small house in a piney village called Tabernacle. The house belonged to Bevvy with the Chevvy and her sister, Rhoda with the Toyota.

"Why did Bevvy agree to do it?" Father Ignacio asked.

"Like all good people, Bevvy and Rhoda see the divine in small rewards," I answered. "I paid for their cruise."

Sally spent her days with Rabbi Wald and Father Ignacio—both well-paid consultants—confessing to her long-standing pact with the Jersey Devil—in other words, what crimes she had committed in the name of upward mobility. Together, the two of them coached her on the rhetoric of repentance and the realities associated with paying a price.

Trouble came to the house in Tabernacle, too, as did some of his contacts with the F.B.I. There we cut our deal: Sally would tell the authorities everything she knew about the Naturale operation in exchange for immunity from prosecution. She would be portrayed in the media as an unwitting victim of a sinister force beyond her control.

Teapot Freddy would visit and experiment with Sally's hair and makeup styles. We were looking for a Jersey look, but not so Jersey that Sally couldn't live with herself. We settled on Sally's natural thick gray hair with the rationale that Jersey was real, and nothing was more real than one's own appearance.

I provided Nate the Great with a college yearbook photo of Selma Natelman. He cross-checked it against her current photos with his computerized face gizmos. "She had her face changed to look like Jackie Kennedy," I told the dazed clergymen.

"She didn't look that much like her," Father Ignacio said, smearing white toast with raspberry jelly, presumably to make it look more like a donut.

"She didn't look exactly like Jackie Kennedy," I said, "Because my doc friend said there are certain, uh, skull basics—distance between eye sockets, nasal and oral cavities—that can't be altered."

Of course, there were aspects of my program that I had no intention of telling Father Ignacio and Rabbi Wald.

The purification of cocaine requires an incendiary combination of chemicals, including sulfuric acid, potassium permanganate, and, get this—*kerosene.* We knew Naturale's Earth possessed many of them in serious quantities because that's what Nate the Great had been searching for—and testing—in Naturale's garbage. When dumped into the water, the byproduct of these concoctions leaves a heavy, greasy discharge, which is what the Lord and I saw that night when we prowled the lakeside of Naturale's Earth.

The Lord's gift for burglary came in handy on Independence Day, as did Boom-Boom Weber's gift for arson. Teapot Freddy's flair for distraction caused the two hoodlums who were processing the drugs inside the dome to give chase when Freddy ran through the laboratory naked, save a ski mask, leather chaps, and a full salute. *That* kind of full salute. "Yee haw!" Teapot Freddy yelled as the hoods gave chase. When they left the room, Nate the Great and I, also masked, shot them with taser guns. As they writhed on the ground, Nate the Great injected them with powerful sedatives. As the Lord, Freddy, and I dragged the thugs outside and scoured the huge building for workers, Nate the Great mobilized his science skills, distributed the volatile chemicals throughout the building, and, with Boom-Boom's help, proceeded to blow the hell out of the coke lab.

My buddy, Moonpie, came in handy later in the summer when I decided to leak the lie about Naturale planning to settle with the Victims of Sally Naturale. My objective was to get some of these "victims" to start spending the settlement money before they got it, thereby validating that they had leveled serious allegations against Sally because they were greedy hustlers, period. We closely monitored the men and women of VSN, and recorded their shenanigans for evidence and future broadcast.

By bathing in the broth of social justice and repudiating her wealth, Sally confirmed for the riverside masses and the media alike the immovable ethic that success was corrupt and dispossession was virtuous. While none of us, Sally included, believed in this as an operating philosophy, by reincarnating Naturale, Inc., in the form of a communal revival*, we validated Sally's persecution at the hands of violent narco-criminals, and gave decent people the hope that we needed them to absolve her.

Still, there was one thing that didn't make sense to me. "Rabbi," I asked, "I know Sally told you about going to Camp Summit and all, but did she ever say anything about crickets?"

"Crickets? No. What, are you going nuts on me now?"

*The Reverend Sharpe didn't come cheap, but he was a growth stock. Fragile helped distribute "walking around money" for the Defiance Gospel Choir and other rented revivalists.

The Perpetrator as Victim

"Sally and I were like Mother-Son vaudevillians each entertainingly and successfully full of shit."

I was standing about six feet from Sally on Market Street in Camden when I saw that poodle cranium puff out above the others. Murrin was under investigation for perjury, but she had not yet been charged with any crime (the courts, like the media, are quite protective of those who make allegations) and was free to haunt South Jersey.

The knife glinted in the sunlight. It's a strange thing about my nature: I am anxious nearly all of the time, just not in the actual face of disaster, which is when I am most at peace. As the blade came down toward Sally's temple, I saw Murrin's terrier teeth grimace. Only in the movies can a man draw a gun in a split second, and I was not made of quicksilver. My voice, as soft as I could deploy it, was the next sound that Murrin heard. "Go to hell, Murrin," I said, like a cherub fluttering at God's shoulder. It was the easy smile that accompanied my directive, I think, that befuddled her.

Sally heard me, though, and turned. As her head turned, Murrin brought the knife down. It missed Sally's head and pierced her shoulder blade instead. I pushed Murrin aside. Like most victims made strong by their victimhood, there was power in that loose white flesh, and my confidence softened as I struggled to push Murrin back. Murrin swung at me wildly and I felt the slender knife tear open the tiny scab that Petey Breath Mints had made in my scalp when he came at me weeks before. I yanked Murrin back by her mullet and bit her on the shoulder. It was a girlish thing to do, I know, but this close, my teeth were all I had. She screamed and fell back. I kicked her behind her knees, causing her to buckle. As she fell, I stomped hard on her upper arm, near where I had bitten her. She screamed again, which made me stomp another time, forcing Murrin to let go of the knife.

Rabid in her commitment to destroy Sally, the witch from Salem County managed to rise. Her victimhood was her religion, and she apparently equated its abandonment with godlessness. She began to charge like a rabid boar, not at me but at the chosen object of her life's ruin, Sally, who sat in an eerie calm on her side as a geyser of blood spurted from her back. I jumped between Murrin and Sally, and smashed Murrin in her pig nose. While she cried out from the blow, she also tackled me and wailed away at me on the ground.

As I tried to wrestle Murrin off of me, my breathlessness was complicated by a narcissistic take-down—Jackie Disaster had been sacked by a chick whose spandex ass routinely knocked over the *National Enquirer* rack in the supermarket. I turned my head and fleetingly caught sight of Sally sitting calmly behind me, her shirt now looking like putanesca sauce. It occurred to me how absurd this spectacle was, and I actually croaked out a laugh, which elicited a belch of some kind from Murrin. Then Springsteen at Olga's popped into my head along with one of his lyrics I never understood: *Suspended in my masquerade.* It was a cool assembly of words that described both Sally and the tired part of me that was the unsinkable bad boy, Jackie Disaster. Sally and I were like Mother Son vaudevillians, each entertainingly and successfully full of shit. Amidst this chaos, it struck me that frauds actually have to be better than originals, because everybody's watching us closer. As I began to choke Murrin, two bystanders pulled her off of me. I crossed myself on the hot pavement and policemen subdued her. Murrin's lifelong struggle was over. And, aging welterweight that I was, it took me a shove, a punch, a trip, two stomps, and a sissy-ass bite to bring this sad girl down. My legend deflated rapidly in my own eyes.

Sally saw me coming, but lost consciousness before I got to her.

Flexible

"The best crisis-management case studies are the ones nobody ever hears about."

I found my car and began tailing the ambulance, when I saw police lights swirling in my rearview mirror. I checked my speedometer. I wasn't speeding with my traditional abandon. I pulled over and sighed.

I turned around and got a direct look at the patrol car. It was an unmarked cruiser with a portable light. Trouble emerged from the driver's side. He was alone. I smirked, Bruce Willis style, and prepared for light badass banter, but Trouble wasn't smiling. He wore the expression of a perp.

When he got to my car, I asked, "Have another caper for me?"

"I was wondering if you had one for me," he said, grim.

"Always," I said. "What do you need?"

"The joint strike force keeps asking about the Naturale fire, Jackie."

"Why wouldn't they?" I said.

"Petey Breath Mints is singing like Tony Bennett, but he doesn't know anything about the fire. Jackie, he's singing on murders, dope, the Naturale connection, but he draws a blank on the fire. Why would he admit to all of this stuff, but not the arson?"

"Maybe he wasn't involved with it. Maybe he's lying."

"Maybe. We're under pressure to mount a case on the fire. It caused about fifty million in damage, a real disaster. Nobody can account for *you* that morning."

"I can't account for myself. I may have been out running, or at Apples' place, out on assignment, who knows? You know I have a theory, Trouble . . . all of the things we think are conspiracies aren't, and all of the things we don't, are."

"Hmm. Maybe. Petey thinks it was you, Jackie." Trouble frowned.

"Petie's a *jamook,* Trouble."

"He's a *jamook* with a lawyer who will do what it takes to reduce his sentence. I won't screw with you, Jackie. We can't ignore the fire, even with all you've done. We can't overlook that none of the mob informants say they know anything about Frankie Shrugs' car. And there's nothing leading back to New York or the Russians either. This was done by a special kind of arsonist."

"Special how?"

"An arsonist with a conscience."

I laughed. "A kinder, gentler arsonist, huh?"

"People worked in that dome at night, Jackie. They were taken out before the fire. About an hour elapsed from when the security company got the entrance codes and the fire started. Whoever lit the place up put a value on human life. The midget and those wiseguys shot up your house when there was a child inside."

"What else you got, Trouble?"

"Not much. I know you've been talking to Jonah Eastman."

"He did some polls."

"He's also the master of diversions."

"You think Jonah did it?"

"Nah," Trouble swatted. "Jonah's a strategist, he's not a button."

Trouble was baiting me here. He wanted me to say, "What, I'm just a button? I don't have a brain?" I kept quiet and followed Trouble's line of vision nowhere in particular.

"What would you have me do, I'm a cop?" he pressed on.

Time to push back. "You're a cop on the rise. You're a hero now. You know like I do that any implication I was involved with any of that stuff is bullshit ranting by vermin. It's desperate silliness. What isn't silliness is an allegation that a supercop who cracked the case was somehow complicit in an . . . I don't know . . . Machiavellian damage-control strategy, where a handful of guys with agendas got together and did their thing. That's where Petey would take this. Al Just would take us all down for a bump in the ratings—even if we didn't do anything. You've got to look at where the car will skid, not just where it is when it slams on the brakes, Trouble."

"That would be a damned mess," he said, knowing that I was not threatening as much as I was projecting a mutual destiny that would be catastrophic.

"You know, the best crisis-management case studies are the ones nobody ever hears about," I said.

"Cover-ups don't work, Jackie."

"Sure they do. The proof is that we never know about them."

"Maybe that's true, Jackie. I guess sometimes you have to be flexible."

"What's the worst that can happen if some of those animals are charged with the fire: they beat the rap? They're screwed on all of the other counts. Besides, you know in your heart that those Pangea activists torched the place, that's their M.O."

Trouble exhaled slowly. I hadn't told him anything that he didn't already know. I suppose he had to hear the words—the awful narrative from my lips.

"Be careful, Jackie. If not for yourself, for that little girl you watch over."

"Okay."

Trouble escorted me slowly to Our Lady of Lourdes hospital.

The Crickets

"Fortune slips away."

Sally had lost a lot of blood. The knife had narrowly missed an artery, but the wound was large, while still superficial, slicing mostly through skin and muscle. I joined her in her room. She was wearing a hospital gown and looked like a little bird in the bed. Sally dismissed Count Smartfarkle, and gestured for me to sit down. It was odd to look at her with gray hair.

"You knew Murrin was coming, didn't you, Jackie?" Sally asked.

"I think that way. You know how I am."

"Should I be grateful to you or angry with you?" she asked.

"For saving your life?"

"Yes."

"Should I have let her, uh . . ."

"Kill me? You would have never allowed it, no matter what I said."

"Sounds like you're pissed at me."

"Of course not, Jackie, I am so grateful to you, a quick thanks just cheapens it."

"No, it doesn't."

"Thank you, Jackie . . . oh, Fortune slips away. It's incredible."

"Not really."

"No?"

"Did you ever hear of Bartholomew Roberts?"

"No."

"He was a pirate in the 1700s. He was on the run from British troops after he looted some ships in the South, near Charleston. They caught up with his fleet right here in Delaware Bay. One of the pirate's ships sank. He lost a half-million dollars in gold and silver. Imagine what kind of money that was back then."

"Did they ever find it?"

"No, but it's down there somewhere."

"Did they capture him, Jackie?"

"He got away."

"Without the loot?"

"Without the loot," I echoed.

Sally gazed at the ceiling. There was a part of her that probably preferred death to a life away from Cricket Crest.

"There are a few things I still want to know," I said, breaking the silence.

Sally nodded. "I owe you that."

"Why the big donation to the college when you went public?" They got rid of your files, you know."

"That was part of the deal, Jackie."

"I figured that."

"If people knew that Sally Naturale of Cricket Crest had been crazy Selma Natelman of Ancora State Mental Hospital, what would that say to Wall Street, my customers, everybody?"

"Madonn'," I said.

"'*Madonn'* is right. The college knew my story. With the work I had done"—Sally pointed to her face—"nobody would recognize me. You knew all along I was from Jersey, didn't you?"

"I did."

"How did you know?"

I couldn't believe this question. It wasn't genius on my part; she spoke like me. Would it break her heart to tell her that?

"You speak Phlersey. We have the same accent. *Wudder.* You know." Sally crinkled her nose. She didn't make the connection. I imagine she thought she spoke like Queen Elizabeth. I wouldn't attack her with the truth.

"Tell me, Jackie, why did you go looking? It had nothing to do with our work."

"I didn't know that at first. I had to see if I was being used."

"You weren't."

"As it turned out, that's true."

"Is that the only reason why you went looking?"

"I don't know, maybe not."

"You know, Jackie, I don't think it's crazy to go looking for people that you've lost."

"It feels crazy."

"That's because of this disaster game you play. The guns, the sneaking around in the night. You're allowed to miss parents. I do. You're allowed to see their smallness."

This was hard for me. Sally saw me flinch, and accommodated me when I changed the subject. "The crickets. I know you like them and all, and I know they remind you of when you were younger, but I never understood why you had the chirping noises during the daytime. You're a romantic, Sally, but you're also a businesswoman. Confess to me, what was with the crickets?"

Sally leaned in toward me and whispered: "Have you ever heard the sound that metal wheels make along the train tracks?"

"I guess so."

"What do they sound like, Jackie?"

"They squeak a little."

"So do crickets. Squeak. Chirp. Squeak."

"That's true. The sound of the crickets is like the sound of wheels against tracks."

"Yes. The cricket chirping obscures, has a masking effect, if you will. It masks the sound of madness moving through the pines, Jackie."

"People hear the sound and they just think it's the crickets. How could it be trains? There are no trains in the Pine Barrens. After a while it's white noise. An audio illusion," I said, educating myself.

"Don't be too impressed," Sally said. "I didn't think of it."

"Who did, then?"

"During Prohibition there were little metal hand squeakers. The gangsters used to hire pineys to chirp them in the woods when their railcars came in, and even when they didn't. Blame the squeaking on the crickets. People around here aren't into nature. They don't know nocturnal from diurnal. They assume crickets chirp when they chirp. A tiny little man gave a squeaker to my father years ago. He told me the whole story when I was little."

Son of a bitch. Mickey Price had that squeaker.

I blinked rapidly. I turned away from Sally, thinking, thinking.

"What's wrong?" Sally asked, more confident and far less fragile than I had ever seen her.

"I can't explain it," I said. "My mind's whirling. I'm sorry."

"Don't be sorry, Jackie. You've done well for yourself."

"I hope so."

"You are what you are." Sally closed her eyes and sang, *"Show a little faith, there's magic in the night."*

I had to catch my breath. This was a line from Springsteen's "Thunder Road," a song about breaking free from one's Jersey-based ghosts. When it came out on the *Born to Run* album in 1975, I had sat down next to my mother's eight-track deck and wrote down every single word.

I answered her with the next verse, singing, *"You ain't a beauty, but hey you're all right."*

And we both sang, *"And that's all right with me . . ."*

Sally covered my lips with her hand. "Let's not be deep." Now Sally covered up her own mouth. Then she mumbled, "I know they say I'm crazy. I know. Do you really think I'm crazy?"

"I did think that at first, but I know now."

"What do you know now?"

"I know class when I see it. And *this,*" I said, holding Sally's little shoulders, "is class."

Disqualified

"I always knew this question was coming."

Jonah rented a house on the beach in Margate during the season's final week. It was one of the older houses, a modest wood-frame ranch, mid-block between Atlantic Avenue and the beach. His wife, Edie, was beginning to pack for their haul back to Harper's Ferry. We stood on the beach watching his kids play in the surf—Jonah was obsessively protective that way.

I handed Jonah his final paycheck for the Naturale caper. He thanked me and said, "I can't believe I get paid for this mischief."

"It's great, isn't it?" I said.

"It can be. You know, by way of full-disclosure, I just talked to Trouble. You know we go back to high school, track meets and all?"

"Right."

"There's noise about Philadelphia looking for a new police commissioner."

"Get the hell outta here!" I said.

"Nothing's in the bag, but you know . . ."

"I take it you provide Trouble with political counsel from time to time."

"A little. He's been wanting out of A.C. for a while, but I told him months ago that you need breaks for that kind of thing. And, what do you know, along comes Jackie Disaster with this caper."

"Trouble was pretty flexible. I was worried about that at first."

"Flexibility's important in politics. I told him that, Jackie. I told him you've got to take the long view, you've got to see Willie Penn's hat on top of City Hall."

"You don't get to wear that hat without a break, though."

"Right. I provided the view, you provided the break. A good partnership."

We both watched Edie close the back door of the truck and head back into the house. "You and Edie. Huh?" I said obtusely.

"Yeah, me and Edie."

"How does a nice girl like that deal with all the twisted stuff you've got?"

"As an exercise in damage control."

I laughed sharply and deeply. Jonah's comment struck me as being hugely profound. Maybe it was just the way he said things.

"I think Angela sees me as a defective product, the theme of my career. I guess a good marriage is one where the people in it can live with each other's defects," I said.

"I've never polled it, Jackie, but it sounds right to me."

"So what's Edie's defect?"

"She thinks people are good down deep."

"That no-good . . ."

"Tell me about it," Jonah sighed. "You know, there was one thing I always wondered about you."

"What was that?"

"I hear you were an Olympic contender or something, but got disqualified somehow."

"It was the Olympic trials."

"Can I ask what happened?"

"I got into a fight over something stupid."

"A girl?"

"No, you wouldn't believe it if I told you."

"I have more faith than you realize."

"I was reading a magazine, and some guys gave me shit."

"Porn?"

"Nah."

"Then what?"

"Father Ignacio gave me a copy of *Aspire*, a magazine for . . . priests. I was a senior in high school and, you know."

"You were thinking about becoming a priest?"

"I was just reading and all."

"So what happened?"

"Well, I guess I was getting into it, and these guys I knew walked by. Maybe I didn't wave or something soon enough and they started razzing me. Then they saw the magazine and started laughing."

"What did you do?"

"I sat there like an idiot for a minute, and then they started the trash talk. Things like, 'You'd only give a girl a novena in exchange for a hummer' and 'Hey, a priest that'll break your ribs if you eat meat on Friday.' "

"So, what, you rolled the guy?"

"I rolled two of them. Broke their noses, ribs. There was a third guy, and he ran. The funny thing is that I'm really not religious."

"You must be. At some level."

"Nah, I'm not the deepest guy in the world. Anyhow, there was this boxing council. They've got all kinds of rules, you know, boxers can't use—what did they call it? . . . their 'craft,' that was great—*craft*—out in everyday life. So I was disqualified."

Jonah studied me, and I could tell he admired what I did in his own way. "Do you regret what you did?" he asked.

"A little, yeah. I was a hothead. For a long time I thought all of this what-could-have-been shit, but who the hell am I fooling? I was a good fighter, but the Olympics? I wouldn't have taken home a medal. No way. Tommy could have, though."

"Your brother?"

"Yeah."

"I don't mean to be obnoxious, but was he really that much better than you, or do you just think that because he's gone?"

"He was incredible."

"What was the highest he ever got?"

"He won the welterweight Golden Gloves title for New Jersey. I was just South Jersey."

"Is that really so much better?"

"Not so much, but it's better. But where's a welterweight going anyway?"

"I think you took a better route, Jackie. Your mother would have been proud."

"Ah, she always used to say, 'You'll be what you'll be.' Tommy and I got as far as we could."

"You know what Mickey once told me, Jackie?"

"What?"

"Nothing in life is free unless you steal it."

Emma was back with me full time. I was sitting on the sofa, and she plopped down next to me and leaned her head against me. This was unusual. It was a childlike display, and Emma was usually above childhood. I actually liked seeing this side of her, which I did all too rarely.

"What's with you, Em?" I asked.

"Jackie, I need to ask you something," she said.

"Okay." I was preparing myself to answer questions about Sally, the fire, the midget, the arrests, when it occurred to me that I didn't have an Emma-worthy answer. I abhorred being ill-prepared.

"Who was the fighter with my father when he died?"

"Is there somebody you think it is, Emma?"

"Sometimes I think it was you."

"Why?"

"Because you feel so rotten about my Dad. Because you worry so much about me, like everything's your fault."

"I feel responsible for you, you know that," I said.

"I know that. But I would feel better if I knew."

I always knew this question was coming. I walked through life with a chronic sense of dread. I suspected that my discomfort was tied to a particular secret, but I had been at the scene of so much mischief, I lost a sense of what my particular crime had been. I was waiting to sweat, hyperventilate, or display some medical manifestation of panic, but nothing happened. I brushed Emma's hair aside as she sat up straight, bracing for horror.

"The other fighter was a guy named Chipo Garry," I said. As soon as I said it, Emma collapsed into me and sobbed. I had never seen her do this, not even when she was an infant. I didn't stop talking though. "Chipo was a pretty good fighter, but I didn't think he was in your father's league. Tommy always trusted me to check things out and give him advice about other fighters. I didn't check too hard though. I figured it was just a sparring session and that I didn't have to check out every guy Tommy sparred with. I had fought Chipo and remembered that he had a mean left hook, but for some reason I didn't tell your dad that. I just told him that he was better than Chipo and not to worry about it, it was just sparring. He was doing so well in those days that I really didn't think anyone could beat him.

"I probably should have told him about Chipo's left hook, but I don't know. From what they told me, your dad got in the ring, Chipo threw a left hook and . . . it happened. Maybe that's why I check so much about things, but I don't know about that either. Sometimes my mind goes nutty and I think maybe I knew Chipo would hit him that way, maybe I was jealous of your dad, maybe in some dumb psycho way I let it happen . . ."

"No you didn't," Emma said, kissing me a million times. She wouldn't let go of me, perfectly content to burrow.

I had always expected this to be a cataclysmic moment—the revelation that I felt responsible for what had happened to Tommy. But Emma was right: my little psycho theories about unconsciously wanting it to happen were just the nightmares of a man with a chronically guilty conscience who saw it as his chosen purpose to take the hits for things that he did, things that he didn't do, and things that God did, or had allowed to happen.

Emma dug herself deeper into me and fell asleep. I carried her upstairs and put her to bed.

Epilogue—
Sail on, Silverberg

"The myth of damage control is the unblemished escape."

It was Labor Day and I was pressing slices of steak down on the grill. Angela brought out onions that she had just sautéed. It was going to be an evening of homemade Philly cheese steaks. We had invited over the Imps, Father Ignacio, and a laid-back Blinky Dom.

A lot of people who live down the shore year-round get depressed on Labor Day, because it marks the end of the teeming summer season. I love this weekend for precisely this reason, although I see Labor Day as a beginning. Invariably, the great dredging ships of the Atlantic crank into full throttle and begin to replenish the beach with the sand lost during the summer months. One was just then on the horizon.

A huge white tent was billowing on the beachfront a mile to the south, in Longport, like the ghost of a hundred summers. To the north, Atlantic City slowly began its nightly melt into ice cream, sparkling with jimmies and M&Ms. It made me wonder what Angela brought for dessert. I was hoping it wasn't anything too good because then I'd have to eat it.

A flame-yellow tractor was massaging the sand into a compact and unmarked tablet. It made me feel clean, the same way I felt when the nuns in catechism would erase the chalkboard in pure sweeping arcs, opening the possibility for flawlessly scripted lessons, the same hope that I held at the end of summer when my mother would buy me a fresh white notebook, and I'd vow that everything I'd write that year would fit neatly within the margins. It never happened, but I never stopped thinking brightly of Labor Day—no matter how old I got—as the launch of the "school year."

"Are you happy, Jackie?" Angela asked me, grabbing me from behind.

"About what?"

"About how things worked out with your project? With Sally, with that

Murrin girl? I'm not expecting you to tell me everything, my little choirboy, just how you feel."

"I feel okay about it. Public relations is telling pretty lies. Crisis management is telling ugly truths."

"Do you know why they didn't beat you, Jackie?"

"Why?"

"My dad used to say that the guys you could never duck were the ones who *wanted* to fight."

"Maybe there's something to that. I read in the paper that some chiropractor bought Cricket Crest."

"I know. I saw it. Does that bother you?"

"Who knows, maybe he's got his own noble *lin*-yidge to shove up everybody's ass."

"Maybe he does. Well, what about my question?"

"Are you asking me if I feel guilty about sending Murrin back under the rock she crawled out from?"

"Sure, I am."

I turned and faced Angela, taking note of Blinky Dom over her shoulder.

"Dom's happy today, all vindicated that a doctor told him he had a stroke, his crowning achievement. I've had my fill of victims, Angie. I hate 'em. I hate wickedness when it's all wrapped up as weakness. You know, I'm sorry Murrin's life sucks, but you know, Sally's life sucked, too. Murrin's in Ancora Hospital where she belongs. Look at what Sally was able to do with her life despite it all."

"Yes, but Jackie, look how she did it."

"How she did *some* of it. Sometimes good can grow out of bad. Nobody knows that better than you, Angela. *Capeesh?*"

"Okay," Angela nodded, appreciating her shaky footing. "Okay."

A horn honked on Atlantic Avenue. Angela and I turned around and saw Dirk Romella gliding by in a Mercedes convertible, the real little one. He waved, his gelled hair managing not to blow in the breeze. Angela and I waved back, and I studied her eyes searching for a hint of regret over the path she was taking with me, or appeared to be. I wasn't sure what I saw, but maybe Angela wasn't sure what she felt. Dirk Romella. Oh-*well*-a.

Dirk shrunk as his cute car slid ambitiously toward Longport, where I assumed he was going to nibble paté beneath that billowing white tent. I supposed that Ralph Lauren (formerly named Lifshitz) awaited Dirk, where together they would cross polo mallets or do whatever people whose ancestors were named Moishe and Tuccio did in the toddling millennium. Chill out, Jackie, I told myself, it's America and She's been good to you.

Angela turned away from Atlantic Avenue and snickered in the direction of the gathering Imps. "Looks like the other choirboys are waiting for you," she said in a way that made me feel jazzed to have a girlfriend going into the school year.

Angela removed the steaks from their propane purgatory and set them aside to cool. I headed up toward the beach alone, trying to determine if there was a lesson borne out of my summer job. I was inclined to think that if there were lessons they were the same ones I had learned in every caper.

In determining why people (and companies) do what they do, you cannot separate their seminal nature from what external circumstances call for. Sally had been right about everybody being specialists. At her essence, Sally was an illusionist, a sleight-of-hand thespian. She was an actress playing Sally. Creating feints and diversions was not what she did, inasmuch it was who she was.

Whatever tiny emptiness floated at Selma Natelman's core, that vacuum gave birth to something tangible, however absurd. Sally had the same fertile American talent once attributed only to masculine pioneers, the gift of improvisation. Whether it was called chutzpah, blarney, or moxie, I couldn't help but believe there was something divine in it, some flecks of God that had not fallen anywhere near the empty white protoplasm of Murrin Connolly, who had managed to cloak her barrenness in something holy—a *jihad* against someone very damaged, but infinitely better. Sally Naturale was more full of shit than the Gold Coast Compost she peddled; but being full of shit—the evangelical belief in doing something huge based on nothing but spirit—fueled the emergence of America.

It is unlikely that Sally Naturale will ever return to her former glory, but that's what damage control is all about—preserving the bare essentials, surviving, and nothing more. Sally's new company will either make it or it won't, but this was incidental to the fulfillment of our mission, which had been stopping Murrin's attack and rigging Sally's escape. Sally has become what she was—a Camden-bred stringbean with mousy hair and a bump on her nose.

I suspect that Sally is disappointed in me for not delivering a full resurrection, something that even the most benevolent megalomaniacs think they can contract out for the way they would a cleaning service. The myth of damage control is the unblemished escape. Nevertheless, there is a price for one's way of life, and Sally will surely pay it like a mortgage as she attempts to gentrify Camden. *Sail on, Silverberg, sail on by . . .*

Blinky Dom and I chose not to engage each other over the hospital episode that followed his latest performance. Contrary to what we've been taught by the insipid culture of "breakthroughs" and "closure," he didn't know what to make of my actions, and I had nothing else to say. I had tackled him because I felt like it, not because I thought he would learn anything.

Nor had I gained any definitive insight into why Blinky Dom hated me privately but praised me publicly. I found an article on the Internet by somebody claiming to be a shrink. It said that fathers sometimes hate their sons because the son steals the mother. I don't know. Maybe Blinky Dom blames me for not saving Tommy, for being a better fighter than he was, being a lesser fighter than I should have been, for being richer, for surviving. Or maybe, wacked-out Sally had a rare lucid moment when she said with confidence that people just are what they are.

I approached my father without any delusions of possessing divine gifts that could mastermind peace. I just asked him, "What was the best Jersey shipwreck, would you say?" There were hundreds to choose from, and he knew them all.

Blinky Dom pushed his glasses higher on his nose as Father Ignacio and I awaited the answer. "Probably the *Stolt Dagali* in 1964. Sliced in two up north a little. You were still pissin' your pants. Always liked the modern ones more than the pirate wrecks."

"Yeah, why's that?" I asked.

"Pirates . . . they deserved it. The others? They were just trying to go someplace. Makes you think. Both types get it, good and bad."

"Pirates, huh? Those were some tough guys," I said.

Father Ignacio and Blinky Dom nodded effusively as if I had just issued a revelation, which, of course, I hadn't. I walked toward the beach, as the Holy Cannoli ambled toward the evolving cheese steaks.

Emma approached me, balancing on the seawall. I grabbed her and kissed her nose.

"I know what Angela named the panda," she said.

"So do I, smart ass."

"You said 'ass'."

"So did you."

Emma pouted. She did not like being outwitted by me.

As I walked from Emma along the seawall, a man in his fifties wearing a crisp beige windbreaker began to approach me. It was as if he had risen from the sand. He had a strong corporate captain face, the build of a collegiate gridiron hotshot in his autumn, and chastened, bloodshot eyes—the look of a king who had just had his throne shot out from under him. The look of a client.

"You're Jackie Disaster." He said this as a statement of fact. There was a touch of conspiracy in his manner.

"Yes, sir, I am."

"A mutual friend said I'd find you here."

I nodded neutrally.

The man began, "I've got a problem."

"Most of us do."

"Yes, but our friend said you have answers."

"That's not a promise I make on my web site."

"You don't have a web site," the man said with authority.

"You're right, I don't."

The man identified our mutual friend and we spoke for a couple of minutes. He did indeed have a problem. His public relations chief had diagnosed his situation as "complex," and we knew what that meant. Jackie Time.

"Yes," the man said, "We tried talking to this bastard who's going after us, but . . . we got nowhere."

"With a certain kind of enemy," I said, "It's not about information, it's about how bad you can kick his ass."

The man smirked. "It's the only thing some people respect."

"Right," I said. "Some people."

We parted ways after agreeing to talk again.

The Imps huddled fifty yards down the beach on the concrete steps beside the seawall. They saw the brief encounter and waited for me to approach. I mumbled a short prayer, crossed myself, and headed over. The Lord and I wore lightweight leather jackets, inviting autumn to come a little sooner. I felt my lightweight aluminum knuckles in my jacket pocket. Nate the Great's hair was slicked down following a workout and a shower. Teapot Freddy's hair blew wildly in the breeze—he actually looked kind of tough with a day's beard growth. I felt like Danny Zuko approaching the T-birds in *Grease.* I went with it.

As I approached the Imps, I felt a flash of fear that I'd lose them. When I saw their eyes, which were hungry like puppies, not wolves, I felt better. I quickly figured out why, as soon as that photo Sally had of Leonard Bernstein flickered into my conscious. The Imps, for all of their assets, could not implement. They could perform tricks on cue, but they needed a conductor, someone who could plot out their skills toward an end that served some focused purpose. While I was not without technical skills of my own, what I recognized in a gorgeously clear way for the first time was that my role at Allegation Sciences was to conduct the Imps.

The Lord tugged at his ear. We were in for a revelation. "Hey, Jackie, when we were growing up, who did you think was really cool?"

"To be honest with you, for a while I liked Efrem Zimbalist Jr.," I said. Zimbalist had played Inspector Erskine in *The F.B.I.*

"Awww," the guys said, appalled. I think they wanted somebody lethal like Shaft. Can you dig it? I decided to appease them.

"But I'd have to say Billy Jack," I said.

Nate nodded, "Definitely."

The Lord said, "Oh, yeah."

"That's because he beats people up, boydogs," Teapot Freddy said.

"Actually," Nate the Great said, "I didn't think there was anything cooler than Elton John in those platform shoes in *Tommy*."

"Hee hee," the Lord laughed like a third grader, "Nobody knew he was queerbait in those days."

"Yeah, who knew?" Teapot Freddy said, blowing a strand of gray hair up off of his forehead.

"Who was the dude you were talking to?" the Lord asked.

"Employment," I answered.

"Wooooweeee, boydog!" said Teapot Freddy. "Everybody wants a whack at Jack!" he added, tussling my hair. I felt like a nimrod.

"You up for a new caper?" asked the Lord, hopefully.

"Yeah, what the hell else am I going to do this fall, quarter for the Eagles?" I said.

"Heard you rolled your father at the hospital," Nate the Great said. "You two doing all right?"

"You know, guys," I said, "In forty years I've had only one conversation with that man. Same conversation, a million times. *'I'm dying. I'm broke. And you never help, you selfish prick.'* Not to sound deep, but you know the big irony? He made it come true. For forty years I was the best son I could be, but now I really *am* a selfish prick. The son of a bitch made it come true."

The Imps nodded, but I think only Teapot Freddy understood. They all lurched away in the direction of the barbecue. They always had a knack for sensing when I was distant, although today I was actually feeling quite—well, *here*, especially with the scent of the grill chasing me. I surveyed the

Atlantic, which momentarily choked me up. Underneath it all, I was a bigger candy-ass than Teapot Freddy. When I turned my back on the sea to catch the sun shuttle toward the Pacific, I whipped on my sunglasses and restored the cool I needed for my next gig.

Two children with nets began chasing minnows in a puddle that had formed on the beach. I secretly hoped Emma would feel unburdened enough to join them, but it didn't work that way, so she sat on the Margate seawall painting floral prose in her diary. She was loosely surrounded by a panorama of fugitives who love her fiercely. Blinky Dom swatted in the direction of a distant jet ski, undoubtedly grousing to Father Ignacio of sunken galleons embedded with plunder that would be his, were it not for a godless tide. Angela, the pirate's daughter, was resting in the hammock on my porch. The panda she christened Disaster sat on her shoulder and spied out the receding Jersey shoreline for incoming buccaneers.

Acknowledgments

I found out after my outline of *Jackie Disaster* was accepted that St. Martin's Press would not be providing me with a ghostwriter. Fed the line, "We ask that writers produce their own material," I bitterly set about writing this novel myself. Well, mostly.

My editor at Thomas Dunne Books, Sean Desmond, played a central role in the creation of *Jackie Disaster*'s basic plot and characters. He also admonished me to "please write sentences that make sense." Sean's long-standing investment in me is appreciated more than he will ever know.

My agent, Kristine Dahl at ICM, helped me find a publisher and a market for writing what I know and love. Catherine Brackey at ICM has also been a critical touchstone for me in the entertainment business. Bob Stein, Esquire, keeps me covered, as always.

Meyer and Teddy Lansky's granddaughter, my friend Cynthia Duncan, was always there to remind me of atmospherics from the old days. Cindy and Julio, Havana in 2005!

The silence of my old South Jersey gang (a.k.a. the "Baton Rouge Avenue Mob") that wreaked havoc upon the Jersey Shore in the summer of 1980, including Fred Squires, Jerry Janove, Jeff Klein, Craig Schwartz, and Stu Novek is greatly appreciated. There are things people don't need to know.

My colleagues Maya Shackley, John Weber, Nick Nichols, Jill Horowitz, Ryan Knoll, Steve Schlein, Mike Johnson, Chris Myers, and others at Nichols-Dezenhall supported my endeavor. Ann Matchinsky, Jim McCarthy, and Mark Pankowski provided me with insight into Catholicism, which, being a writer, I distorted shamelessly. The sacrileges in this book are mine alone.

My buddy, "Boss" Ed Becker in Las Vegas, Bugsy Siegel's former (but very handsome) aide is always a reliable teller of memorable tales, which I never hesitate to exploit.

Budd Schulberg pointed me toward boxing literature.

I appreciate the efforts of the organized crime families with interests in the Philadelphia–South Jersey region for making certain that bookstores understood that it was in their best interest to carry *Jackie Disaster.*

I am grateful for the inspiration of my high school English teachers, Mr. and Mrs. Joseph Truitt, and the support of Cherry Hill High School West principal George Munyan.

My late mother, Sondra, quietly encouraged my writing, as has her sister, my Aunt Pat Bronfman. My sister, Susan, and father, Jay, and my friends Marc Wassermann, Gordon Platt, Joe Diamond, Matthew Klam, Frankie Trull, Sharon Saline, Linda Panicola des Groseilliers, and Bruce Ochsman have been great sounding boards, as have organized crime experts, author Gus Russo, Alan Hart of Burlington County Community College, George Anastasia of the *Philadelphia Inquirer,* Gary Klein of the Federal Bureau of Investigation, and the ruthless and super-secretive Hollywood power-broker, Reeva Hunter Mandelbaum. Thanks also to Les Macdonald, and Josh and Jay Pate in L.A. for their interest in damage control.

My media molls, Nina Zucker, Sandi Mendelson and Judi Hilsinger have always put the right spin on my literary adventures. Thanks also to Carol Saline for her maternal instincts.

Finally, and most important, my wife, Donna, and my kids, Stuart and Eliza, to whom this book is dedicated, for making middle age a lot more fun for me than youth ever was.

Eric Dezenhall
Washington, D.C., 2003